SKinKneader

Tammy Seley Elliott

Contents

Acknowledgements.....................1

Prologue....................................3

Part I: Voices............................5

Part II: No Cure.......................105

Part III: Dead to the World...........197

Part IV: Blood Family...................289

Part V: Skin Deep.....................375

Epilogue................................427

Acknowledgements

A great big thanks to my husband, Mike, and son, Sam. Mike, as always, listened patiently as I rambled endlessly during the creative process; the man is either a saint or a clandestine selective listener, but either way, I'm grateful at the completion of each novel that we are still married! Sam has been in on this book with me since its inception; he wrote some of the heavy metal lyrics for the opening sections, inadvertently turning his old mom into a late-in-life metal-head! Thanks, Sam…rock on!

Thank you, as always, to Mary Waddell and Debbye Boe, my editors; their insights help tremendously. An additional thanks to Mary, a licensed therapist, for her consultation on mental health issues as they apply to SkinKneader's colorful characters.

I deeply appreciate the fascinating help from supervising forensic scientist, Amy Geröw. She navigated me through the forensic elements of this story; while I stretched the limits of reality, she assisted with accuracy and invaluable insight. Not to mention, I got major cool points for being in cahoots with a real forensic expert!

Thanks to my cousin, Mike Newby, a martial art professional, for his expertise regarding a critical fight scene; it might be a small part of the book, but the information he provided was vital for accuracy.

I am grateful for my amazing illustrator, Donika Mishineva, for her unbelievable patience as we sorted through images and ideas for the right cover, and for her grace as I kept having to delay publication due to "life" interruptions.

One of my favorite lines in this book originated with a friend during a random conversation years ago, and I told her then it would find its way into one of my books. Readers, when you see the words, "…like Jupiter and oranges," (and the rest of the analogy), they came from Cindie Usevich. Thanks, Cindie!

Finally, thank you to Michelle and Andy Jones for the use of their beautiful summer home with a view of Mt Rainier as a writer's getaway, allowing me to complete the second half of this novel in the course of two weeks!

Prologue

"Where the hell am I?"

The voice was so loud, L.Z. lost control and slammed his bicycle into the curb next to the bike lane.

***"Jesus Christ! Look out,"* the voice cried.**

L.Z. overcompensated by jerking left and came within inches of hitting a passing car. By now, his heart competed with his tonsils for throat space as he swerved right again, trying to stay within the confines of the too-narrow lane.

"The traffic light, you moron, it's red!"

Panicking, L.Z. clamped his brake levers, skidding to a stop as he acknowledged the upcoming light had, indeed, turned red.

He glanced sheepishly at the glaring man behind the wheel of the car next to him, shrugging and raising his trembling hand in truce. The stare suggested the guy certainly considered L.Z. to be a moron, but the closed passenger window made it unlikely he owned the shouting voice; the voice had been too loud to have come from a passing car anyway, he thought.

Checking the still-red light, L.Z. flicked sweat from his eyes and turned toward the sidewalk to identify the source of the yeller. He needed to thank the person who, however brashly, had probably just saved him from becoming a pretzel, although, in truth, their first shouted words had caused the whole scene. Too shaken up to split hairs, he put his foot on the curb and turned, saying,

"Hey, thanks for the shout-out," but he stopped in mid-sentence.

The sidewalk was empty. He twisted around to see if there was, perhaps, another biker; the lane behind him was deserted. He squinted in confusion, facing forward again with a confuzzled headshake.

Maybe glaring-car-dude raised his window after a drive-by screaming? But all that was left of that guy was the back of his head because the car was already across the bustling intersection.

The light had turned green.

"Shit, I *am* a moron," L.Z. muttered as he pushed off, more concerned about the skinny lane and rushing traffic than the origin of the mysterious shouts. But that was all right. Unbeknownst to him, he'd have plenty of opportunities to try to skin that cat.

PART I
Voices

Regarding the Mansons

L.Z. Manson wasn't a complicated guy and, although his life was on the verge of developing complications beyond comprehension, he strove for structure in things he could control. Which was very little.

If he had the imagination to paint his world in the best possible light, he'd say he was a food health inspector, was wildly fit, and was the single heir to a brilliant and worldly woman whose exploits were known by thousands. He would also answer the inevitable question of what "L.Z." stood for, with an eloquent lie, like, maybe Lawrence Zachary, or Lindberg Zane. And would likely point out that he was no relation to the psychopathic cult leader Charles Manson, which he mentioned nearly every time he introduced himself or was introduced by others. If one weren't paying close attention, in fact, they would think his last name was hyphenated: "Manson-No-Relation," a word string he learned as a child from his uncle, whose given name was Charles Alvin Manson. It was a sensitive subject for Uncle Al.

5

But, as it was, L.Z. worked as a mid-level manager for the Red Missile Burgers fast-food franchise, where he was able to live out his dream of meticulously ensuring food safety (mostly because his Uncle Al owned the entire franchise and loved, if not pitied, his nephew). While not exactly "wildly fit," L.Z. was probably in decent shape since he rode his bicycle to the various Red Missile Burgers locations throughout the Boise area. He *could* drive but chose to bike as an escape from life's mundane challenges. Work was an endless trial between demanding customers who'd rather rage at fast-food staff than make their own sandwich at home, and a mostly teenaged team who cared even less about pleasing the customers than they did about food safety.

And home? It was basically a black hole.

It was where L.Z. lived with the heiress; at least on some days, that's what she was.

When she wasn't a spy.

Or a target of the US government as national intellectual property because of her singular genius.

Or a fugitive-in-hiding due to her sketchy connections both inside and outside the law.

Her exploits *were* known by thousands, at least that's what she'd tell you in detail, whether you asked or not, as long as it was a day when she talked at all.

Adding to the Manson domestic intrigue was the fact there were no mirrors in the home since they'd been taken down or intentionally broken, suspected of being two-way or fronts for cameras or, during more disturbing bouts, soul stealers.

Elle Manson, while possibly falling short of being the aforementioned murderous psychopath to whom she was *not* related, was a deeply disturbed woman who had never been diagnosed or medicated because it would have been over her dead body before she'd go to a doctor.

She was, in fact, extremely intelligent, and had led an unorthodox life. On her occasional "good days," she could be engaging and caring. At the end of every day, though, she was L.Z.'s mother and, right, wrong, or indifferent, he was faithful to her care since institutional commitment was an option he couldn't stomach. Not to mention, she'd need to be hog-tied to make it happen.

On the outside, L.Z. bore every sign of being a dork. He owned no jeans, but had several pair of Dockers, mostly black, as those were required for work and typically wore button-down shirts and loafers. Inside, however, he nursed a rebel, a *heavy metal* rebel. Beneath outerwear, he donned his subtle form of insurgence: t-shirts branded with names and emblems of heavy metal bands. When feeling particularly wily, he'd wear his "battle jacket," a lightweight, pressed hoody with sewn-on patches of every band he wished he'd seen live, which was *every* band he loved because he'd never been to a live concert. He couldn't bring himself to sport a traditional battle jacket which would be a faded, unwashed vest of sorts; a bit too untidy for him. Although he secretly knew the scores and lyrics to every Disney movie ever made and harbored a clandestine love for Celine Dion, his music downloads were almost exclusively metal. It was his armor.

Thus were the lives of Led Zeppelin Manson, son of Elizabeth Taylor Manson, hard core hippie in her early days; a 97-pound, chain-smoking, coffee addict in her twilight years.

Oh. And sometimes Elle heard voices. Sometimes she talked back, while other times she took copious notes or hid in her closet till they stopped. And she also knew about things which were happening in places where she *wasn't*, or things that were going to happen before they happened; it clouded the water that the accuracy was hit and miss...so the "hits" often drifted to the bottom of the murky waters into which only she could see.

Due to Elle's gift (or curse), L.Z. was used to the phenomena of voices as an outsider, but he was wholly unprepared to be on the receiving end. If he saw things as his mom did, maybe he could have prevented future events.

But sometimes the choice isn't ours.

L.Z.'s nerves were still raw when he reported to his store-of-the-day, which was only a few blocks from his near-crash. He doffed his backpack in the breakroom and removed his Red Missile Burgers polo, jumping when a voice piped up out of nowhere.

"Wow. Slipknot. Really? You listen to that shit?"

Even before turning around, he recognized *this* voice; its owner was sixteen years old and utterly infallible, as sixteen-year-olds tend to be. She was one of the three Britneys who worked at that store and was, without a doubt, the most annoying. He'd heard *her* playlist and, as he pulled his work jersey over his band shirt, he asked through the red fabric,

"You know what kind of music balloons are afraid of?"

He was gratified by her pause, which insinuated she thought it was a legitimate question. Poking his head through his shirt collar, he saved her from the pain of any further thought by answering his own question.

"*Pop* music."

As limited as L.Z.'s sense of humor could be, he *loved* puns. What he loved almost as much, was tripping up the already questionable wiring of Britney's mind.

He smirked as he brushed past her, hearing her reply,

"Wait. Was that a joke?"

He grabbed an apron embossed with a prominent red missile across the breast and answered,

"Why don't you Google it. If it's not on Wikipedia, then, yeah, it's a joke."

Accepting the challenge, she whipped a phone from her back pocket with the speed and ease of a gunslinger.

"*After* work," L.Z. directed. "Put that thing away."

Britney rolled her eyes, but, shockingly, complied, then yanked on her own apron.

He shook his head as he scanned the kitchen to ensure every wildling (his private title for staff members under twenty-years of age) was present for duty. He loved Game of Thrones about as much as he loved puns and appropriated the wildling term with satisfaction.

L.Z. went to the large refrigerators and meticulously checked dates and labels of every item in sight; *this* was his thing. That he had to fulfill his dream of food inspection in a string of burger joints fell short of his desires, but for now, it scratched the itch.

A decade before, he had completed the first two years of a degree in public health nutrition with a goal of becoming a *real* food inspector. Considering Elle was the reason behind L.Z.'s food safety obsession, it was ironic that he'd had to quit school because of her. It was nothing short of a miracle he'd survived his childhood as it was, bad food notwithstanding. But when your mother intermittently thought electricity was not only dangerous, but optional, perishable food had the habit of perishing.

"Hey! Can I get a hand on the grill?"

Peg's voice jolted L.Z. from his reverie, and he responded to the distress call as he envisioned flattening a palm on the grill just to rack up his second pun of the day; the burns might be worth her reaction. About his age, Peg Warner was older than most of the crew, but seemed nearly as naïve as the wildlings. He was a little more comfortable around her now that she seemed to have gotten over her unexplained obsession with him when she was initially hired. He wasn't well seasoned when it came to women, but her staring had felt more weird than flirty. They had fallen into a rhythm, though, and she kept her distance now.

Another shout distracted his ill-advised plan to palm the grill.

"L.Z., could you get drive-through? Freakin' Britney and Joe disappeared. We got a line."

Grabbing a headset, L.Z. yelled for someone to look out back; the two were probably on an unapproved smoke break. He moved toward the take-out window as he put on the headset, feeling familiar disdain for this part of his job, the part *with people*. Young people, jackass customers, and…

"Where the hell am I?"

11

Annoyed by the question, L.Z. muttered, "Red Lobster, you dumbass," before he pressed the button with a more courteous answer to the customer's absurd question. Then he realized the set wasn't turned on.

He blinked. The question suddenly took on a new meaning. *Wasn't that what the voice on the road asked...*

"Dude! The line is backed up to the parking lot."

Britney and Joe had come back in from the smoking area. Their report might have been helpful if they hadn't been the cause of the back-up in the first place.

L.Z. pulled off his dead headset and tossed it to Britney.

"Turn that thing on before you use it."

She blew a bubble, popping it as she displayed yet another impressive eyeroll.

"Duh, yeah, got it, *Slipknot*."

Her attempt at disrespect served to embolden the normally nonassertive L.Z., as he retorted,

"Funny girl...*knot!* And spit out that gum."

Now that the delinquent Joe morosely manned the grill, L.Z. ducked into the restroom, running his hand over his thinning brillo pad hair.

The unidentified voice he'd heard on his bike was one and the same as the not-a-customer he'd just heard all too clearly on the dead headset. He swallowed, finding his mouth and throat were suddenly dry.

He'd heard voices.

Or to be exact, *a* voice.

Grabbing the edge of the sink before his legs gave out, L.Z. was face to face with his own pale image.

There was only one thing he was more afraid of than bad food, and that was losing his sanity. Being crazy, like his mom.

Barely able to breathe, he decided to face the monster. While L.Z. was hardly a brave man, he was also not one to procrastinate and this wasn't something he would put on hold. Clenching his eyes shut, he gripped the sink's edge until his knuckles turned white. His question echoed in the empty room, as he queried the voice,

"Is there someone there…um…*in* there?"

The response nearly put him to his knees.

"Fuck, dude! Some privacy, please?"

L.Z. gasped, not wanting to believe this was happening. But when it spoke again, relief flooded him.

"Really, L.Z., I could give you a courtesy flush, but it might be best for both of us if you, like, just left?"

It was Keith, the last of the other real adults on day crew.

L.Z. turned toward the exit, offering a wave toward the only closed stall door.

"Right, man. Sorry."

Not waiting for a response, he pushed into the short hallway, exhaling as he plucked at the shirt fabric between the apron and his chest, trying to cool off. Heading back into the trenches, he wondered which was crazier: hearing voices, or talking to the voices?

Then he shook it off; it wasn't something he wanted to know.

Dear Leddy

There's things u should no about your heritage. My father, your granddad, he had DNA from another universe. Here on earth, he acted like a religus man and started different packs of followers as he shared his acultic meter-physical belives. He done healed people in ways that most stupid humans wouldn't even get.

As your mother I should have shared with u that there are millions of xtra-terrestrial creatures all around and they do things here on earth.

Of course, I am in touch with them and supposebly they want me more but I try to ignore it mostly for u. But in case they want to take me back to where Im from, I need to share this with u. I also need to pass this on because obviously me and u have alien DNA so I have to tell u all this.

I know this sucks to here but u need to know that most humans are stupid selfish and hateful and they serve the Raptor god.

In my temple there are two deities in this universe. We have the goddess of life, Sva-Dam-Ling. Her enemy is a dead god, a deity known as Goth-Dla-Phen. He is dead as a doornail. But his attacks against Goddess was so harsh that it created this universe as a scientific construct. I no these r big words but u are a smart boy.

I don't know about u, but I don't chose death. If you except your hertage and your place at my side, we will not have to die here in this dark place. We will rise against it all. We are rightful hairs to the universe. We can have it all.

I need your answer. Oh and we're having hungry man mexcan delux 4 dinner.

15

Your loving mother.

L.Z. already wore his helmet as he straddled his bike in the Red Missile Burgers parking lot, reading the e-mail from his mother. Although it was a short one by her standards, he only read the first paragraph and skimmed the rest, less phased by the mania it displayed than the poor spelling and grammar.

He shoved the phone into his backpack and slung it on before pushing off to pedal home.

He'd thought it had been a long day, but if the e-mail from his mom was any indication, it might prove to be a longer night.

Too bad he couldn't connect the voice in his head with those in hers. While they planned a galactic take-over, he could get some rest.

L.Z.'s coworker, Peg Warner, always had voices in her head, or to be more accurate, like him, it was one voice. Although it berated her, questioned her, and constantly reminded her of every mistake she had ever made, it didn't scare or startle her. It had been there most of her life.

My God, you're stupid! You should have paid closer attention. You were too lax.

She was outside the office of the dilapidated trailer park on the outskirts of Eagle, Idaho, a Boise suburb. She just stood there.

Looking down the dirt path between "units," as the property manager so eloquently called the rusted bucket homes, she saw where she'd lived for the past seven months with David. She couldn't see the locked door from here, couldn't see the only things left were the junk furniture and crap carpet that had been there when David had moved in God knows how long ago. She couldn't see how it looked tossed rather than vacated, or all that was left of her things had been left in a pile on the splintered porch planks. She didn't need to see any of it now, because it was exactly what she saw when she'd come home from work. To a locked door. To no David. To no note from David. To the smartass trailer park manager who figured Peg was the stupid one to not notice *everyone* was moving out because a developer had bought the park to build high end condos which would be much more fitting for the former farm town, now the home of much money.

The manager told Peg that David had given today as their termination date over a month ago.

So, he'd known then.

And she knew now.

She should have known something was up when he hadn't picked her up from work; it had been a long walk, but not the first such walk since she'd moved in with him.

That's what you get for using him in the first place.

She ignored the inner voice; it was after six in the evening, and she had to work the next day. She needed a plan, but she didn't know a soul in this stinking town other than her coworkers from Red Missile Burgers, and most of them were practically children other than Keith and L.Z. She had reasons for not wanting to call either of them.

So, smart girl, what are you going to do now? Call home?

"No, no, no, never," she said to no one at all as she slowly trudged back down to the trailer to gather as many of her sparse belongings as she could. Of course, she didn't have a car; she had always walked, or David had driven her. She pictured him tossing everything she owned onto the porch, mentally cataloging her sparse possessions when she felt a surge of panic.

My journal!

She ran the last twenty feet to the trailer. Rifling through the pile of her belongings, only breathing again when she found the beaten-up composition book which harbored more about herself than any human knew, including her family.

She was hundreds of miles away from her family now and while she'd left them with her eyes wide open to come exactly

18

where she was, the pang of homesickness was almost more than she could bear.

She started to cry as she shoved her things into an old milk crate she pulled from the overgrown grass in the yard. It had lived there longer than she had, maybe longer than David. But it was something.

Once she'd crammed everything into the crate and her oversized handbag, she dropped heavily onto a battered step and absently attempted to chew her nonexistent nails, drawing blood with the first chomp. When she reached into her pocket in search of used tissue, her fingers struck keys. She only had three. One was to her parents' home in Eugene, Oregon, one was to Red Missile Burgers, which she only had tonight because she opened tomorrow.

And one was to the trailer.

She hadn't thought about it when she'd talked to the park manager, and David probably forgot she even had it when he'd bugged out.

He'd had the key made for her when she moved in, when he'd been so enthralled with her from their whirlwind online romance. She knew, and he must have figured out since, that he was only "enthralled" because she'd made herself appear to be exactly what he wanted her to be. She'd studied his profile on the app as well as on Facebook and Instagram until she'd had a picture of what kind of person he was probably

19

looking for. Then she sent the first "wink" on the app. The rest was history, albeit not good history.

And now it was all literal history, and she was dead in the water.

Speaking of water, the power and water should still be on. A floor's better than a park bench. Besides, where else are you going to go, you dumbass?

She glanced around; not that anyone there had ever cared about the goings-on at this or any of the other "units." Standing, she backed up to the door, then quickly turned and unlocked it, dragging the crate in behind her.

Once inside, she slid down the wall till her butt hit the floor.

You've never been any better than this. This is what you get.

She didn't argue with the voice in her head. Why would she? Arguing with your own voice would be crazy.

"Thanks, kid. Let me know when she turns up."

Charles "Al" Manson disconnected the call with his nephew, L.Z., and reached for his cocktail as he took in the mountain view from the deck of his home near Ogden, Utah.

After taking a deep drink, he ran his hands up and down his rubbery face and sighed.

He loved his sister, but that broad was bat-shit crazy. He also loved his nephew and felt strongly that the boy deserved better. The "boy" was thirty years old, but as Al's only nephew, he'd always be the curly-headed waif he'd not seen often enough over the years.

Al's gaze dropped to the deck flooring as his face went still. He'd tried to get custody when it was obvious his sister wasn't a fit mother, but the little boy, while timid, had been fiercely attached to his hippie mom. Later, Al financed L.Z.'s education, thinking it would be his leg up and out. But Elle made the situation problematic with her views of conspiracy between her rich-ass self-entitled brother and her unworldly son, throwing as many wrenches in the works as possible, up to and including sabotaging L.Z.'s schoolwork, showing up at the school, and calling the dean. Despite his academic success, L.Z. had thrown in the towel halfway to getting his degree, favoring peace with his mother over his own future. Again.

Al's stare broke with a stern shake of his head, causing the drooping skin between his chin and his neck to waggle in a turkey-like fashion. He stood to get another drink as he examined the problem that would never be solved. It was a tough pill to swallow for a man like him.

Al was a retired general. He was a big man with big features, and staying in suit, his personality often seemed bigger than life.

21

He had been a leader in the nuclear missile arena and, although he retired from the military before earning his third star, he often still thought and functioned as a senior military leader. He had supreme earning potential as well as significant connections in the nuclear industry, yet surprised everyone, including his wife, when he opted to step away from his life's work and buy a fast-food franchise in the northwest United States.

Of course, he had his reasons. He always had his reasons. He was a cerebral man, brilliant, in fact, with lofty ideas which sometimes misplaced their clarity between his brain and his mouth. He could talk at length about his thoughts with great enthusiasm, but because his thoughts moved faster than his speech (which was not slow) he often lost the listeners' attention before delivering his grand finale.

His conclusion for his career choice had been simple. He was a leader, a provider, and a man who had grown up poor. He wanted to feed the masses while still having an avenue to mentor and shape the youth of America who were, conveniently, the target employees for fast-food chains. He could give a three-hour speech on the virtues of his plan (and had), but all the bankers cared about was the money and the credit; he had both, thus, it was a done deal. He changed the name of the franchise from Red Roof Burgers to Red Missile Burgers as a nod to his former trade. He'd never seen a red missile, of course, but he was frugal at heart, and it would require fewer renovations if the restaurants retained a red theme.

His wife, Abby, was a very patient woman, and she blessed his plan, primarily because she was much happier when he was preoccupied. She was also a very smart woman. She understood that while his goals were honorable, the only "masses" he'd feed were the ones who happened to choose the Red Missile drive-thru over the hundreds of other options. She also knew that he'd be no closer to the "youths of America," i.e., the line-cooks, than he had been to the youngest troops for most of his career. But she knew he was a good man, and that was all she cared about.

She did not, however, have energy left for anything regarding her sister-in-law, or sadly, her nephew, L.Z. Abby admired her husband's loyalty and loved their nephew, but she was pragmatic and knew there was no cure for someone who would never acknowledge their illness, and Elle was mentally ill. L.Z. was thirty years old, and his choices were his own. Abby had their own grown daughters to contend with.

The subject was off the table, indefinitely.

That's why when Abby called Al in for dinner, he gave her a bone-crushing hug, gesticulated over the prepared meal, and didn't mention his sister was missing. Again.

The Red Missile Burgers mogul ate and chatted, while in the back of his mind he continued to work the Rubik's Cube of Elle and L.Z.

23

L.Z. had not told his uncle about the new wrinkle in the family saga. And, although Uncle Al heard voices all the time in the form of non-stop ideas and philosophies, if he knew of that day's goings-on between his nephew's ears, he would have been on the next plane to Boise.

Enough was enough, after all.

When he'd gotten home that evening, after turning off the oven -- relieved it didn't contain charred Hungry Man cuisine remains -- L.Z. jumped into action in the eerily empty house.

He called the police, not to report his mother missing, but to see if they were hosting her for the evening in a cell; it would not be the first time. But she wasn't there. He called the neighbor, Linda, the closest thing Elle had to a friend. He knew very little about Linda, other than she, like Elle, drank a copious amount of coffee and smoked like a chimney. And she nodded a lot. She might have nodded during the phone call; he didn't know, but she did deny that Elle was at her house. He would have called White House security, considering how many e-mails his mother had sent to various national entities there, but one of the only comforts he had at the moment was it was *2379 miles* from the nation's capital. He knew *that* because Elle had told him once as she'd packed her bags to walk there to lunch with the president so she could tune him up on his policies.

Too bad he didn't have a number for the Goddess of Life…what was her name? He pulled up today's e-mail. Sva-Dam-Ling. *Pretty sure she doesn't have a published number*, he thought with tale-tell tension in his stomach. His guilt mixed with impatience.

He was about to phone hospitals from his spreadsheet of "who to call" numbers when Elle was on the lam, when he heard a thump from above, followed by a muffled exclamation,

"Jesus Christ! It's too damn dark!"

L.Z. looked at the ceiling. He didn't feel the earlier panic; he knew *this* voice. What he *didn't* know was how his mother ended up in the crawl space that doubled as an attic.

"Fuck me running! I can't see a *damn thing*. Leddy!! Are you home?" The shouting was followed by a stampede of stomps directly above him. Feeling more frustration than relief, L.Z. headed through the kitchen to the garage.

He flipped on the light and saw the attic hatch hanging open over the ancient VW van, a barely functioning leftover from Elle's prolific hippie days. He also spotted prints from his mom's Dearfoam slippers on top of an old filing cabinet which had been shoved next to the van. *Check that*, he thought with frustration, realizing she had climbed onto the filing cabinet, then onto the top of the van in order to pull herself into the space above. He didn't question why she hadn't used the step ladder hanging on the wall. That would require him to think like Elle and that was just too scary.

A tiny part of him considered closing the hatch and just going away till the noise died down, but the part of him that was L.Z. yelled,

"Stay where you are, Ma, I'm getting a flashlight!"

There was no power in the low space between their ceiling and the house roof. He figured she went up while there was still daylight coming through the vents, but he had no idea why she'd stayed till after dark, or why she'd been so quiet. He had even less of an idea why she went up in the first place.

After lifting the external garage door, he retrieved the van keys from their hidden location under a box of Halloween decorations. Surprised the junker started so quickly, he backed into the driveway so he could use the ladder rather than adopt his mother's risky and far more acrobatic option. As he ascended into the crawl space with a small flashlight gripped in his teeth, it occurred to him that perhaps it was the goddess's temple up there. Anything was possible in the world of Elizabeth Taylor Manson, and he had no doubt he was about to hear all about it.

Honestly, he almost preferred the new and unknown voice in his head to the familiar one ranting in the darkness. At least it was something new.

And he was so tired. He was *always* tired.

He was still tired the next day as he sat at the desk in the manager's office at Red Missile Burgers, disheartened by the text he'd just gotten from Uncle Al. L.Z. had messaged the night before to let him know Elle had been located and that she was okay – which was a relative term, of course – and assumed that would be the end of the subject.

He didn't tell Al where Elle had been. Or why. He was not inclined to share her explanations: she said she'd been cold. And heat rises. She wanted to save the environment by taking a nap in the naturally warmest spot, which of course was the attic – cobwebs, dust, and mouse poop notwithstanding.

There had been no mention of the temple or her goddess. And no reference to the fact that perhaps the alien DNA made her more susceptible to cold. L.Z. certainly hadn't probed her on either issue.

He'd foolishly thought it was one more episode now complete in their personal reality show.

But then he'd received his uncle's unwelcome suggestion that it was time to consider in-home care for Elle. L.Z. knew his uncle meant well, but the idea would be about as welcome to her as a job offer from the NSA, her arch enemy agency, although she would undoubtedly think she could whip those clowns into shape.

Before he could concoct a diplomatic, "thanks, but no," Al, his uncle *and* big boss, had followed up with an additional text,

> In fact, time 4 me 2 C the ID stores. Will fly up soon.
> More 2 come.

L.Z. rolled his eyes as he did every time he read such contradictory language from the retired general who texted like a teenager. He didn't know if his uncle was trying to be hip or if it just helped him try to type at the speed of his brain, which, frankly, would have probably melted his phone.

L.Z. buried his head in his hands but before he could slide into total despair, the door flung open and Keith stuck his head in,

"Peg's late. Britney called in sick. Probably has a hangnail. Oh – I'm talking about Britney C., not Britney F. Britney F. was on the schedule, but Britney C. was supposed to cover for her today. Anyway, boss man, need you out front."

L.Z. felt the heat rise, wishing like hell he lived in a world where he didn't understand the nonsense that had just been spewed at him.

Just another day in paradise, he thought as he left the office, nearly colliding with the delinquent Peg. He stepped back as she trudged toward the breakroom, lugging a bag and a crate full of what looked like clothes. Their eyes met and he wasn't sure if she looked more flustered or apologetic. He didn't get the chance to decide.

"Meg Ryan, right? **No,** *only if she was, like, thirty years younger and didn't own a comb."*

L.Z. froze. He knew the voice by now. And for the first time, he was sure his ears hadn't played a part, but he'd *heard* it, nonetheless. *It was in his head.*

After getting out of Peg's way, he scanned the hallway and backed into the office, closing the door with his elbow.

Eyes clamped shut and hands against his temples, he tried to calm his heart, but was interrupted when it spoke again.

"Wait. Just wait. Where am I? **Am I dead?"**

L.Z. remembered to breathe as he slowly opened his eyes. He was alone. He started to answer, for *whatever reason,* but the voice beat him to it.

"Who AM I?"

Using the wall for support, L.Z. headed for the desk. He hadn't had an answer for the first questions and he sure as hell didn't have one for the last.

He said the only thing that came to mind.

"I was going to ask you the same question."

Just then, Peg poked her head in the door with a hesitant look.

L.Z. held his breath and stared at her. Her bloodshot eyes darted back and forth across the room, then she looked at him with her eyebrows raised; it was a silent request to enter. He bit his lip and exhaled. Silence. *No voice.*

He waved her in with a shaking hand.

"Right. Yeah, sure. Come in."

That's what he said. What he thought was, *she* does *look like Meg Ryan. Only with bigger teeth.*

Blessedly, there was no further comment from within the tangles of his gray matter.

Peg hadn't offered an explanation for being tardy, only an apology. Preoccupied with his own drama, L.Z. didn't notice her nervous body language nor that she looked exhausted. Peg noticed *everything* about L.Z. and wanted to ask if he was okay but lacked the nerve.

As it was, neither had a chance to dwell on their troubles because in addition to the Britney C. no-show, another employee, J.D., decided the job wasn't as important as his self-respect and walked out during the late morning rush. He'd taken exception to being on the receiving end of an enraged drive-thru customer who stormed in, Red Missile

Burgers bag in hand, berating J.D. in a manner that would suggest his food had been poisoned as opposed to the real problem: he had onions on his burger when he had specifically asked for none.

After J.D. pointed out in less than diplomatic terms that while it had, indeed, been an employee error, said customer could have simply removed the onions. But when J.D. suggested where the customer could *put* the erroneous onions, things got a bit out of hand.

In the end, J.D. stomped out, tossing his apron onto the lobby floor, and all L.Z. could do was calm the customer and offer to replace the criminally tainted burger. The exchange was tricky since the voice in his head, *not his own*, called the offensive onion-hater names L.Z. had never heard.

Fortunately, the voice vanished along with the onion-hater, but it was of little consequence to L.Z. since the crew was down two people and the customer flow was non-stop.

Peg was so busy that it was quitting time before she faced her crate of clothes in the breakroom, a painful reminder of her quandary. She chose to leave them shoved in a locker and left with no idea where to go as she followed L.Z. out the door.

When he cycled away and offered an offhand wave to the slow-walking woman, he couldn't know that the next time he saw her, she'd be in a jail cell, and he'd be in a sling.

Apparently, the phenomena of hearing voices didn't include clairvoyance.

It was getting dark out and Peg had no plan...but she still had the key to the trailer. She figured if she'd gone undetected one night, she could pull off one more, if not two or three.

Unfortunately, she was unaware of break-ins into other recently vacated "units," probably by other homeless opportunists. Peg hadn't considered that she actually *was* homeless, until she said the word to the cops. This was after they burst through the door, wild-west style, having been alerted by the irate manager of signs of life in the empty trailer.

Upon their dramatic entrance, Peg dropped to the floor and raised her hands in the air, grateful she'd just been to the bathroom. Otherwise, she'd have added to her humiliation by peeing her pants; she was sure of it.

The policemen almost looked disappointed when they took her in. That she could be considered a danger to society was laughable, almost as laughable as the notion that a slowly dying trailer park was so worthy of the Eagle PD's resources.

But they hauled her in, nonetheless. When offered one call, she immediately rejected the idea of calling family in Oregon.

There was only one other person she could think of. And later, she would wonder if the opportunity had been fate.

L.Z. was so startled by his phone's vibration in his pocket, he thought he might throw up. It didn't help that he was pumped full of pain medication from when they'd set his fractured arm or that his mother had sworn that she'd drive to the hospital to pick him up when he'd used the poor judgment to call her about his accident. She hadn't driven in years and while he was certain she'd never find the keys; he wasn't so certain she didn't know how to hot wire the old VW beast.

These facts alone should have peaked his stress level, but they paled in comparison to the dark dread expanding in his heart and gut. The angst increased each time he relived driving directly in front of a UPS truck which, fortunately, had excellent brakes.

It had been the voice. What it had said, out of the blue, wasn't the crux of his terror. Instead, it was the realization that it was still there. It was in his head, and *he had no control over it.* After a lifetime with Elle, this was his worst nightmare.

That he might be like her.

With no medical staff in his ER cubicle, L.Z. violated the "no cell phone" protocol and answered the call, figuring the night couldn't get any worse. He was mistaken, of course.

"L.Z.?"

"Yeah."

"This is Peg. I'm sorry to call you, but I'm in jail and I guess I need someone to come get me."

When Keith dropped L.Z. off at his house, he offered to come in to make sure he was okay. L.Z. refused because he had a strict policy of never introducing Elle to anyone if he could help it. Too much risk, too many disclaimers, too much of a lot of everything.

He needn't have been concerned, however, because Elle wasn't home. She wasn't in the attic this time, unless she'd beamed herself up, because the hatch was closed.

He was surprised, although not pleasantly so, when he went to the bathroom and found a note from her on the medicine chest mirror in what looked like lipstick. *How very Hollywood,* he thought. He'd lived with her long enough that he didn't wonder why she left the message there or in that manner, but he groaned when he read it.

He collapsed onto the closed toilet seat; she'd taken an Uber to the hospital to rescue him.

He hadn't even known she knew what an Uber was, which wasn't quite as big of a problem as the fact he was unsure if she understood she'd need to pay the driver. He pictured her heroic burst into the hospital emergency room, demanding to see her Leddy. He dropped his head onto the hard sink's edge, feeling no pain with the impact.

Then there was the fact he hadn't told her which hospital he'd called from; there were many emergency rooms in the greater Boise area. *That should keep her busy.*

He abruptly sat up, remembering his promise to Peg. *Shit!* He should have asked Keith to go pick her up, but she'd begged him not to tell anyone else until she could explain. He'd been stoned on an IV with no way home himself at the time of her call, yet he'd agreed.

Jesus, you're a schmuck, he berated himself as he stood in the tiny bathroom, feeling 80 instead of 30, also feeling what must have been the glaring absence of his balls. He should have *not* called Elle and he should have told Peg to suck it up. He should have let Keith handle Peg. He should have told the damn voice to fuck off the first time it invaded his head.

He should have done a lot of things, but instead, he did one more thing he shouldn't have done.

He resurrected the dinosaur VW and, chugging toward Eagle with a trail of dark exhaust, he went to rescue Peg.

His fugitive mother was on her own and worst-case scenario, a second person would have to be picked up from jail that night.

Unbeknownst to him, he'd predicted the worst-case scenarios, but his facts were slightly askew.

"Some knight in shining armor you are!"

"Good morning to you too, Ma."

L.Z. plodded into the kitchen as his mother stood with a coffee cup in one hand and a cigarette in the other. He was surprised to see her because he thought she'd been behind the closed door of the home's sole bathroom. But his head hurt almost as much as his arm, not to mention the various and sundry other body parts which had been slammed into the pavement the evening before, so he just headed for the coffee pot.

"What're the odds you'd finally have your shot with a girl when you were cuffed and stuffed, eh? You're livin' proof a boy don't need a father figure to know how to show a girl a good time!" Her raspy cackle had the same decades-of-smoking tenor as her speaking voice and L.Z. wished, not for the first or hundredth time, she had a volume control. Or better yet, a mute button.

He checked the inside of the cup before he poured his coffee. He was convinced his many bouts of food poisoning as a child had as much to do with unclean dishes as tainted food; June Cleaver, his mother was not.

"She's not 'a girl,' Ma. She's an employee. She needed a ride."

"Right, *from jail.* I know the whole story, Romeo. Seems to me you two are a match made in heaven. You both got arrested for the first time on the same night. It's fate and a mite cheaper than that E-Hormone-y.com!" She laughed loudly at her own joke, smoke billowing from places unknown. She probably had pockets of smoldering soot in her lungs from 1973. Elle hadn't been this animated for months.

L.Z. sat at the kitchen table and covered his eyes. He'd only had one hangover in his whole life, and he'd trade it straight across for how he felt now. He had little faith there was a cure for what he'd experienced in his life this week.

As if to prove his point, a figure appeared in the kitchen doorway.

Stricken speechless, he gulped coffee with his eyes clenched, hoping it would all go away.

"Jesus, Leddy! You act like I taught you no manners. Come on in, Hon! Coffee's on!"

L.Z. didn't know if it was denial or defeat seeping through him as he watched Peg Warner cross the kitchen wearing one of his old band t-shirts and what appeared to be Elle's sweatpants. She kept looking at Elle in the manner of someone who didn't want to appear to be looking at

37

someone; she seemed as uncomfortable as L.Z. felt. She complied with his mom's directions, edging close to the old bird.

L.Z. couldn't believe what was happening on the heels of all that had *happened.*

His mind reeled through the previous night's events like a movie on fast forward.

He'd sprung Peg from jail and hadn't gone two blocks before failing to signal at a turn – actually, the *VW* failed to signal because the bulb had been long burned out – when he was pulled over by a police car. Still under the spell of pain meds, his constricted pupils must have alerted the patrolman. It didn't help that the van's registration had expired years before, or that a headlight was out. Even less helpful was when the cop recognized Peg from the earlier incident.

His most significant infraction, of course, was driving under the influence. He thought he'd be in the clear when he quoted the information from his ER release papers; it was second nature for him to remember verbatim anything he'd laid eyes on. But his perfect recollection of the data on the papers from the emergency room only intensified the cops' interest; that kind of recitation was unnatural. L.Z.'s logic was instantly shot down when the officers pointed out the advisory printed on the same paperwork he quoted: he was not to operate heavy machinery. Apparently, that included the decrepit throw-back van, which was subsequently impounded.

L.Z. winced at the recollection. Not willing to endure any more play-by-play, he skipped ahead to the part when he'd called Keith *again,* humbly requesting a ride for himself and Peg. This time he didn't refuse Keith's help at the house, leaving Peg in the car, and was grateful that Elle was not "out" where he'd have to contend with introductions and God-knows-what. He'd seen flickering light in her bedroom window, so he knew she was home. He'd gone straight to bed without his usual admonishment about her late-night candle use.

Maybe he'd wished they'd just burn down. Maybe he'd wished he'd wake up and the past few days had been a long bad dream.

Peg gingerly sat at the table as Elle sashayed about the kitchen, banging around the stove, possibly under the impression she'd suddenly know how to cook. After glancing at his way-too-perky mother with suspicion, he looked at his coffee and spoke softly to Peg.

"Uh, thought Keith was taking you home?" Then he added more quietly, "Might have been nice if I could have explained it all to her myself, by the way."

Peg looked confused and offended, but before she could answer, Elle swung around with a skillet in her hand, and shouted accusingly,

"The girl's got no home, Sherlock!" Noticing the position of the pan and the terror in Pegs eyes, Elle lowered it, pointing her cigarette at her son.

"If you *knew* your employees, you'd know that."

"I'm sorry, L.Z., I didn't want to stay, but Keith couldn't take me to his house, and I didn't tell her *anything*. I swear!" Peg tried to plead her case, but Elle continued.

"But when Keith-bo brung her in, I come out and fixed shit, *as usual,* since you don't have a fucking…" Peg interrupted Elle, grabbing Leddy's wrist.

"*I'm sorry.* I sort of lost my living situation…that's why I was late yesterday and kinda why I got busted last night."

L.Z. studied Peg silently. Her statement made no sense to him, which was fine because he was very close to not caring about any of it anymore. He studied her as he drained his coffee. Her short curls looked like battered corkscrews shooting at all angles.

"Medusa." He didn't realize his thought had leaked from his mouth before he was admonished from inside his head.

"Oh, fuck no, she's way cuter than Medusa, although I'll bet she could turn certain parts to stone…"

"Shut *up,* for Christ's sake," L.Z. expelled as he slammed his cup onto the table and covered his ears.

Peg blanched and whispered, "That was harsh," while Elle doused her cigarette and reached out to pop her son's head in one smooth move.

Realizing what they both thought, he threw his hands up defensively and shot to one, then the other, "I wasn't talking to you...and I wasn't talking to *her!*"

He was still pointing at a beet-red Peg when it dawned on him that he'd not only spoken back to the voice again, but that now he might have to explain who exactly he had been talking to.

And then L.Z. discovered they had the most guests they'd had at one time *ever,* as a scruffy looking older man appeared in the doorway with bedhead and wearing L.Z.'s robe.

All bones of contention shattered as Elle slinked across the room and slid her arms around the stranger. L.Z.'s eyebrows nearly touched his hairline, receding though it was. He looked at Peg, who hid behind her coffee cup as if she could disappear.

"Son, this here is Maynard. The ooo-ber driver, and ooooo can the boy *drive!*"

L.Z. stifled a gag as he suddenly understood his mother's mood and behavior. He didn't understand how Elle and Peg had connected the night before if Elle was having candlelit

Olympic sex, but just thinking about the latter was enough to make him drop it cold.

"We're going to work. Leaving in fifteen," he said to Peg as if it were their daily routine. She didn't point out that she was off that day or ask how he proposed they'd *get* to work, but, instead, nodded reluctantly as they pushed past the smooching septuagenarians into the next room where L.Z. noticed, for the first time, that the couch had been slept on. He wasn't the only one who noticed. His head boomed.

"Seriously? The old broad's getting more action than you? By the way, where the fuck am I?"

L.Z.'s filters were gone. He was almost out of the living room when he said between gritted teeth,

"Just get out of here! Would you *please* just leave me alone?"

He was talking to the voice, of course, but it was Peg who answered.

"Well, *I will.* I'm freakin' sorry! I'll do it while you're at work, because, for your information, *I'm* off today. Is everyone in this house crazy?"

L.Z. turned to see her yank the blankets from the couch in frustration.

He started to answer, but it caught in his throat.

Was everyone in this house crazy?

It was a valid question for which he had no answer.

"Soon" is a relative term; it's almost as vague as the phrase, "more to come."

Due to the bizarre events, L.Z. had forgotten about Uncle Al's text the day before, but even so, he wouldn't have assumed that the promised visit characterized as "soon" would be within 24-hours or that "more to come" would be a next-day text with his flight information.

Charles Alvin Manson, L.Z.'s uncle and owner of Red Missile Burgers, was touching down at the Boise Airport at 4:15 that afternoon.

L.Z. knew the local district manager would be having kittens about now and he expected a flurry of manic instructions for all stores to be cleaned from top to bottom, all personnel to be within dress code (no small trick when 85% of the staff was teenagers), and to be ready for a "dignitary visit." He could handle that, even as he still licked his wounds. He popped Tylenol like candy and limped around at work where only he knew he violated doctor's orders to stay at home the next couple of days due to a possible concussion.

He could also handle that Maynard-the-Uber guy had transported him to work since he no longer had a bike, although he did have citations for driving a dilapidated van with an expired registration and no insurance…while under the influence. If he ignored *why* Maynard had been at his house, he could be grateful for the ready ride and for a reason to get the stranger away from his lusting mother.

He could even handle that Peg had spent the night, because it hadn't been his decision and she would be gone that night.

He was good at handling stuff, because after a lifetime with Elle, he was a natural at just shutting things out. It was how he'd survived.

Until now he had muted the painful acceptance that his mom wasn't just eccentric, just an aged-out hippie rebel. That she was, in fact, mentally ill.

He'd also shut out the nagging knowledge that mental illness could be hereditary.

But now, with *the voice*, he could no longer ignore those things any more than he could handle them.

He couldn't take feeling like he walked a tightrope on the edge of sanity. He jumped at every new sound because it could be from inside his head instead of outside his ears.

He couldn't wrap his brain around the fact that he'd talked to the voice. Repeatedly.

And he wouldn't be able to handle the look on Uncle Al's face if he knew what was going on with his only nephew.

He was so caught up in the cyclone of anxiety that he had forgotten the real reason for his uncle's visit. It wasn't about him at all, and it wasn't even about Red Missile Burgers. It was about Elle.

For the first time in L.Z.'s life, his mother was the furthest thing from his mind.

"Damn, boy, looks like you got hold of the business end of a lawnmower!"

Uncle Al's essence filled the room as he burst into L.Z.'s office just before his shift was over. Normally for "dignitary visits," the manager would get a call, but General Manson, as he was called, had rented a car without checking in with the district manager before heading to his nephew's location. He'd do the obligatory store visits the next day; today was for family and he wasn't going to waste a minute.

Al Manson's smile was huge and contagious. Pain and stress aside, L.Z. grinned like a six-year-old after he closed the office door to be folded into the closest thing to a fatherly hug he'd ever known.

When his nephew grunted with pain, Al stepped back, and with one hand on L.Z.'s cheek, his elastic face suddenly went still as his blue eyes penetrated the blood-shot brown ones before him.

45

"Led, did she do this?" Even when grave, his deep voice was melodic. L.Z. was stretched so thin the concern might have finally moved him to tears if the idea wasn't so absurd. Elle was off-balance, yes, and had never had a chance in hell of getting "mother of the year," but she had also never laid a hand on her son. Feeling suddenly vulnerable, L.Z. backed away from Al, and looked away in embarrassment.

"No, Uncle Al. A UPS truck beat her to it. I was on my bike. I…" He remembered the obnoxious voice shouting in his head just before the accident and suddenly stammered. "Uh, well, anyway. Bike's gone, UPS truck is fine and, as you can see, I'm still here." He offered a weak smile and gestured to one of the plain plastic chairs for his uncle, mostly because he needed to sit himself.

The reunion had shaken L.Z. out of his paranoia long enough for him to remember the real reason they now shared space.

Elle.

In-home care.

Oh shit.

God he was tired.

"Uncle Al, I…"

Al Manson often seemed to operate from another planet, so busy was his brain. But sometimes, he'd do what he did now. He was so tuned in to his nephew that L.Z. *felt* him as

46

he stopped the conversation with a tip of the head, comedic smile, and outward thrust of the hand.

"Wait! Hold that thought. How about you and I do dinner? Any place you want," he stopped with an exaggerated look of skepticism at their surroundings. "Anyplace else. Whadya say, Pal?"

L.Z. exhaled for what felt like the first time in weeks. Uncle Al gazed with a smile, and his eyes, as they always had, actually twinkled. But then he leaned forward and sounding more like he was delivering a critical United Nations proposal than posing a question in a burger joint, he asked,

"But…what about her? Is she okay for a few hours? Do we need to make arrangements? You know that's why I'm…"

L.Z. recalled Elle all aglow that morning and interrupted with a rare laugh as he stood and removed his work apron.

"Oh no, she's fine. *Fine.*"

Al cocked his head with an amused look. "Do tell."

L.Z. grabbed his backpack and gestured toward the door.

"Dinner first. It's good to see you, Uncle Al." Once out of the office, his jovial uncle glad-handed and chatted up every staff member as well as a few unsuspecting customers. It was twenty minutes before they made it out.

In the meantime, L.Z. leaned against the exit door, resigning himself to the conversation and possible war ahead.

And he offered up a prayer for silence in his head.

"*SKinKneader?* Do I…" Al paused and leaned forward as if the two of them discussed national secrets while sharing chips, salsa, and a pitcher of margaritas. "…do I want to know? Sounds a little scary, y'know what I mean?" He winked and took a slug of his icy drink.

"It's a band," L.Z. answered as he carefully scraped a blob of salsa from his shirtfront bearing the band-in-question's logo. "Heavy metal, Uncle Al. Probably not on your play list."

Al raised his eyebrows with a challenging expression and impish smile.

"*My* playlist, my boy? Let me tell you a thing or two about music." It was more like a hundred and two things.

L.Z. drank more margarita, amused, yet oddly comforted by his uncle's characteristic over-the-top enthusiasm, in this case, for forms of music ranging from classical pieces he'd never heard of, to Disney theme songs he barely remembered. He didn't care what his uncle talked about as long as they could just stay in this bubble that was a booth in a hole-in-the-wall Mexican restaurant. Time stood still as Uncle Al gained momentum, which he tended to do once he was fired up. He'd give L.Z. an occasional strange look as he talked; it was almost apologetic, as if he knew he had gone on too long but just couldn't stop until the subject was consumed.

But it was finally exhausted, as were the chips, the margaritas, and their excellent meals.

There was nothing left to do but get the check and return to reality.

Al's cheeks were flushed with the exhilaration of time well-spent with his nephew, but his expression turned serious after the waiter took his card away with the bill.

They looked at each other, eyes locked. L.Z.'s heart dropped because he knew what was next and he didn't have the strength to argue on his mother's behalf against the idea of having a "babysitter." Al would make a brilliant case and foot the bill for in-home care, but Elle would resist. It was what she did. And L.Z. should defend her; it was what he did.

Before he could decide his course, however, Al nodded and stood, as if the decision was already made.

"Next stop, Dysfunction Junction?"

The laughter spilling from L.Z.'s lips as he stood might have been from the margaritas, but it might have been from the painfully accurate phrase his uncle had just used to describe his mother's world. Check that, *his world*.

Their world.

He laughed more in the car even though he felt like he was being driven to his own execution.

Peg hadn't left the Manson home. After Maynard-the-Uber-guy's abrupt morning departure to transport L.Z. to work, an annoyed Elle had insisted on her staying for more coffee, appealing for sympathy after having been robbed of her lover.

Peg was mesmerized by the gaunt, cigarette-wielding old broad who wove the most rapt and bizarre conversation she'd ever encountered. Elle's rusty voice and eerily bright blue eyes spurred a form of morbid curiosity Peg couldn't resist. The woman's stability was debatable, but there was no question whatsoever as to her intellect and magnetism. Peg tried to hang onto every word so she could journal about it, whenever and wherever that would be with nowhere to go and no transportation.

She became increasingly nervous, however, as the time for L.Z.'s return from work came and went. Elle was so enamored with having a captive audience, she didn't seem to notice it was getting dark out.

It was nearly seven in the evening when they heard a car in the driveway. Elle adopted a cold look as she glanced in the direction of slamming car doors. Peg's anxiety rose so abruptly, she was light-headed.

She didn't have a plan or explanation for her presence as she remembered L.Z.'s last harsh words to her that morning to "get out and leave him alone." Then she was taken off-guard when he walked in looking much like she felt. It was a double whammy when a large, powerful looking man followed him in.

L.Z. looked confused when he saw Peg shrink against the back of the couch, and she wasn't sure whether to be relieved or to panic when the man spoke directly to Elle with a calm but in-control voice.

"Sis."

Elle's color rose, but she didn't. She didn't move her elbow from the table as she took a draw from her cigarette and eyed him coolly.

"Well, if it isn't Charles Manson."

Al's face tightened and L.Z. cringed, reaching for a chair with his good arm, as if for support. Peg's jaw dropped. *L.Z.'s uncle is Charles Manson?*

She leaned forward. This was only going to get more interesting.

Upon her movement, Al noticed the tousle-haired young woman and his face relaxed into his signature smile and in two steps he'd extended a hand.

"Good evening, I'm *Al* Manson-no-relation. And who might you be?"

Peg stood and shyly shook his hand; the man was charming. She was getting so much more than she'd bargained for.

"Peg Warner. Um, I guess no relation, either?"

Al clapped his hands and laughed. The sound was music to her ears, although it might have had a less pleasant effect if she realized he was her big boss, *el jefe*. The Red Missile Burger Enterprise's top banana.

Elle, however, was not subject to his charm and got right to the point without standing.

"What do you want, *Charles?* Too late to pull the old child protective services threat. Leddy, here, is all grown up. 'Course, you wouldn't know that from your lofty pedestal." She lifted her brows in challenge as she lit her next cigarette from the cherry of the almost spent one.

"Ma, please." L.Z. dropped into a chair, seeming to forget Peg was there. With his bruised face, pained expression, and sling, most mothers would have backed off. But Elle wasn't your average mother.

Al continued to stand, folding his hands in front of him. Unlike his sister, he understood diplomacy. His voice was firm, but smooth.

"Elizabeth, I've come to help. It's the least I can do."

She went from zero to sixty as she stood and pointed her Marlboro at him as if it was a weapon.

52

"Give me a fucking break, Mister General Manson. Last time you 'helped,' those goddam Nazi's tried to kidnap me, and you know as well as I do what they wanted. I bet your military cronies don't know who I am, do they? Your idea of help comes with political strings; to you I'm just a pawn, but to them, I'm queen. Checkmate for them, motherfucker!"

Elle continued to point, her arm shaking with a perpetual tremor. Her lank bleached hair hung in clumps and her preternatural eyes shone as a spaghetti strap from her tank top snaked over her bony shoulder.

Peg was less affected by the woman's words than her appearance. She suddenly had a vision of the Crypt Keeper from a terrifying show she'd watched as a child. With conflicting emotions, she eased out of the room for a timeout in the bathroom.

If she'd noticed L.Z. clamping his one good hand over an ear and pressing the other side of his head against the chairback, she'd have assumed he was at the end of his rope in the face of domestic discord, particularly after the night before.

She would have been wrong. It had nothing to do with the conversation *she* could hear.

The margarita buzz was gone and, although his pain was alive and well, L.Z. didn't notice it. It was difficult to notice anything over the noise, both inside his head and out.

"I know exactly what I need and a hired guard in my own home ain't my idea of you 'helping.'"

"Jesus, Elizabeth, this is not a *guard*. Rather, it would be someone, uh, trained to help elderly..." He paused with frustration, then raised his hands. "Look, I'll cover all the costs."

"Dude's got money? Who is this guy, anyway?"

L.Z. squirmed.

"Did you say, 'the elderly,' *older brother?* Forget your Geritol, didja? Let me tell you, Mister, I've been on to you since I got out of diapers. Your 'paid help' sounds like a paid spy to me! If you want to help, how about you pay your nephew's bullshit fine and get my van out from its unlawful confiscation?"

"Ol' girlfriend is a whack job, no offense, but damn!"

L.Z. bit his tongue so hard it started to bleed as Uncle Al played his best card yet.

"I'll do one better, Elizabeth." It seemed the more emotional Elle got, the calmer Al became. Negotiation was his thing. "I'll pay his fines, his medical bills, and get L.Z. a decent car..."

L.Z. heard that part and uncovered his ears to defend himself from such a ridiculous offer.

"Uncle Al, a new bike would be fine…" He hated driving and, frankly, didn't want Elle to have an excuse to go out more.

"What are you, a moron? Take the friggin' car, besides, how are you going to drive with that shit on your arm?"

Good point, L.Z. thought as he looked at his sling.

"…as I was *saying*, Sis, I'll do all of that, although God knows *you* could afford it, and cover the costs of you having a companion…*hup!*" He raised a hand to stop Elle's near protest, and finished, "…a companion of *your* choice as long as L.Z. and I have no objection."

Because of the competing conversations inside and outside his skull, L.Z. didn't catch his uncle's full comment, although his uninvited head-guest didn't miss much.

"Wait, what? You catch that part about she could afford it? Why are you living in this shithole…"

Elle was suddenly quiet, and she began a stare-down with her brother as the ever-present smoke hung between them. Al was hard to turn down for most, but for Elle, it had zero to do with him and, as all else in life, 100% to do with *her*.

Al lifted his brows and hands as he waited; he looked like a gunslinger.

Right then, Peg walked in and, noting the silence, was struck still. Elle drew on her cigarette, her eyes shifting from Al to Peg.

"Fuck. This is like a scene from the Good, Bad, and the Ugly. Check him out...he looks like he's about to draw on her!"

Once again, L.Z. couldn't argue. The voice had nailed it.

I've lost my mind, he thought.

"It's a deal, and I've chosen," Elle said triumphantly, plopping back down and extinguishing her cigarette.

Al's surprise was apparent. He gave his head a quick shake which reverberated down his waggly neck, offering his sister a bewildered but guarded smile. "Excuse me?"

Elle scooped up her Marlboro pack and leaned back, the woman in charge.

"You pay his fines *and* bills, get the van out, buy Leddy a bike, and us a car..."

Before Al could tune Elle up on her embellished terms, she explained her earlier proclamation.

"...and for a companion, I choose her." With unnecessary grandiosity, she swung her stick-like arm toward Peg, whose eyes widened in confusion.

"And she will be a live-in, but you will still pay her. It'll be a far sight better than what you pay her now for working in your sweatshop!"

Elle gave her brother a sugary sweet smile, lit up, and leaned back in satisfaction. She was the only person in the room who wasn't shocked or confused...or both. The only person who could be seen, that is.

For the first time, L.Z. was treated to something besides smartass remarks from the voice. His head filled with raucous laughter.

In the depths of his soul, he wished for one more margarita.

Peg, however, believed she'd hit the jackpot.

Never been 'cused of being normal

Never going to give time to formal

I don't listen to everything I hear

'Cept the voices in my head when they're

clear

I imagine the heads, bloody and falling

The voices are relentless, won't stop calling

L.Z. yanked out the earbuds and stopped the SKinKneader track on his phone. Metal music was normally his best form of escape, but these lyrics hit too close to home. His favorite musician and rhythm guitar player, Aaron Stoss, had written the song and while L.Z. suddenly felt a kinship with the man he'd only seen on the internet, he couldn't bring himself to resume the song.

"I thought you'd never turn that shit off. And why are you using earbuds while you're driving, anyway? Ever heard of Bluetooth? Give a guy a break in here..."

L.Z.'s hands gripped the steering wheel. It had been over two weeks since the night of the showdown between Uncle Al and his mom, and he hadn't heard the voice since. He was almost at a Walmart and pulled in the entrance so he could park. Not wanting to appear to talk to himself, he gritted his teeth and mentally demanded,

Just hold on. Shut up for one second...

"And another thing. A Kia? Your uncle buys you a ride and you choose Kia? Did you know no one who drives a Kia ever gets laid? It's like a known..."

Can you please wait till I park, L.Z. mentally implored his unwanted head-guest as he pulled into a spot on the outer edge of the massive lot, but the voice continued, unfettered by his pleas.

"...fact. But what difference does it make anyway, you got her right under your roof, and you aren't hitting..."

"Would you please just stop!" L.Z. shouted aloud as he slammed the steering wheel with his good hand. The voice stopped. But only for a second.

"I was starting to think you didn't hear me anymore."

L.Z.'s stomach tightened, and he felt bile rise.

This was happening. During the break, he'd almost convinced himself it hadn't been real.

He clamped his eyes shut and thought,

Can you hear me now?

It crossed his mind that he was taking the last turn to Crazyville.

Then he heard,

"L.Z., can you hear me? C'mon. It's L.Z., right? Or Leddy? What kind of names are..."

L.Z. had a sick realization and, after a quick look around the parking lot to ensure no one was close by, he lowered his head and said quietly,

"Can you hear me *now?*"

"Yes! Yes, what are we, in a Verizon commercial?"

The answer came so quick and sure, L.Z. jerked and looked in the back seat, even though he knew it would be empty. He inhaled and felt a little dizzy as he asked,

"You didn't hear me when I was answering you in my head?"

"What? Seriously? I'm not a mind reader...in fact, I don't really know what I..."

Emboldened and impatient, L.Z. interrupted.

"Why can you only hear me when I talk out loud, and I can only hear you inside my head?"

"Uh, maybe because you have a head, and I don't have a mouth? How the fuck do I know?"

L.Z. closed his eyes and rubbed his face.

I'm a lunatic, he thought. He started to speak when a woman and her kids walked in front of the car.

"Did you hear me? I..."

L.Z. smiled at the woman and, wanting to ask rather than answer, he lowered his head. Covering his mouth, he quietly asked,

"Who are you?"

"I don't know."

L.Z. felt a chill and looked up, as he tried to slow his racing heart. Something terrifying occurred to him. He grasped the wheel of the car and, with closed eyes, asked as calmly as he could.

"Are you dead? I mean, were you someone I…"

"No! I mean, I don't think so. Shit…I…"

For the first time, the voice didn't sound so cocksure. L.Z. suddenly felt dizzy as the barriers in his mind between what he knew was real and what he didn't understand or *want* to understand blurred.

His mother. She heard voices too.

"Look, I don't know if you're real." He said it and wanted to throw up.

There was no answer. He remembered the tone of the voice moments before and, crazily, wondered if the – whatever it was – was thinking about an answer.

But if it was, it needed a long time because as quickly as it had popped up, it was gone.

After ten minutes of silence, L.Z. leaned his head against the steering wheel and forced himself to rein in the swirling thoughts and emotions.

Once he felt a semblance of calmness, he reached to restart the car, when he had second thoughts.

If he was going to talk to Elle about what was going on in *her* head and possibly mention his recent mental shenanigans, it would require fortification, lest she question his motives, which was almost a given. He'd have to come home bearing gifts.

Twenty minutes later he was back in the car with a half-gallon of moose tracks ice cream.

Hearing voices was one thing; speaking to them was another. Having a "mother-son" conversation with Elizabeth Taylor Manson about it was another thing entirely.

Peg now occupied the "guest room" which, until the advent of becoming her bedroom, had been Elle's "office," AKA a den of horrors to L.Z. Pictures, charts, spreadsheets, and computer printouts which only made sense to Elle had to be peeled from the walls under her scrutiny. Boxes of unknown but "priceless" items, "evidence," albums, and books were relocated and stacked against the garage wall alongside the reclaimed and defunct van. If L.Z. had thought it out, he could have transferred everything (including the blasted VW) to the landfill, or even had a big bonfire. On the other hand, Elle had a sixth sense for these things, and he was sure she'd miss even a microscopic item under a mountain of trash. It was like the princess and the pea, he'd thought, only the princess was his mother, the mattresses were a mile-high pile of invaluable artifacts, and the "pea" would be something akin to an incriminating memorandum with the power to crumble the entire US government.

Thus, the garage had become the Elizabeth Taylor Manson archives and museum. The brand-new green Kia lived in the driveway and Peg, the new full-time companion on retired General Manson's payroll, resided in a small, but private room.

L.Z. missed her at work, mostly because she was over 18 and dependable, but he was surprised how much peace the arrangement provided during the past two weeks, with the knowledge Elle was not at home left to her own devices. His guilt over not being Elle's primary overseer for the first time in his life was assuaged by the fact he was certain Uncle Al paid Peg *very* well to essentially have a roof over her head, listen to Elle's daily litanies, and ensure she didn't set the house on fire or pack out to join the Peace Corps.

He had also been taken off-guard by how much he liked driving as opposed to biking. Although his arm would heal, he questioned whether he'd go back to his old mode of transportation.

L.Z. hadn't realized how he'd painted himself into a corner, limiting his own choices and taking it at face value. Maybe it had been his way of coping; maybe it had been due to a profound lack of imagination. But regardless, for the first time, he felt an inkling of independence.

Maybe that's why he'd allowed himself to believe the voice had not only gone away but had merely been a manifestation of stress he hadn't acknowledged until it was gone.

And maybe that's why when it came back, he'd foolishly let his guard down enough to consider initiating a conversation with his mother about the subject. A subject with which she was familiar, and he was not. Isn't that what mothers and sons did?

It was. Unless, of course, the mother was Elle Manson.

It hadn't gone well. It had gone horribly, in fact, and Elle had gone to bed, leaving her son and caretaker in her indignant wake.

The sun was setting, but it was still light enough outside for L.Z. and Peg to sit on the patio chairs without the porchlight. The low light made it easier for the still-new housemates to digest the evening's events.

L.Z. stared at his root beer can and said, as if speaking to it instead of Peg, "We should have warned you." He took a drink and glanced nervously to gauge her reaction to the evening's events.

She pulled on a curl and released it, instantly grabbing another after the first had sprung back in. She caught his gaze and said in a surprisingly light tone,

"That wouldn't be right. That's my job. *I'm* the warner."

He looked at her full-on, confused but curious. He also feared his mother might have rubbed off on the already-odd young woman.

"What?"

"Warner. My name…Peg *Warner?* Get it?" She offered a goofy smile which exposed her not-Meg-Ryan's big teeth, but all her Meg-Ryan-like cuteness. "I thought you liked puns."

He responded without thinking,

"That was *pun*-ishingly bad."

It was her turn to look confused.

"You know…PUN-ish…oh, never mind. I suppose 'Peg' has a meaning too?" He wasn't quite ready to discuss the elephant on the patio, the scene she had witnessed earlier which had provided her with a full dose of Elle-ocity in one night.

She watched another extended curl, nearly cross-eyed, as she stretched it as far as it would go, releasing it to rebound to the nest on her head. Then she set to chewing her nails, stopping when she couldn't gain purchase; her fingertips looked like little bald heads, having been chewed into the quick. Then she answered.

"*Peg.* Steely Dan song. My mom loved Steely Dan. You know it?" Before waiting for his response, she sang a quick line so out-of-tune that if L.Z. hadn't, in fact, known the song he wouldn't have recognized it. "*Peg, it'll all come back to you,*

Peg it'll all come back to you..." Her volume rose. "*When the shutter falls, you'll...*"

"Okay, okay!" He raised his hands in surrender and to shut her up. Besides the fact it hurt to listen, he pointed out the most obvious reason to reel in her concert. "We don't want to wake the beast." With a dark expression, he tilted his head toward the house.

She gnawed into her index finger, speaking around it.

"Oh. Right."

She waited. She didn't know how to talk about something that she probably shouldn't have seen or heard in the first place. How to inject herself into something that had been set in place long before she arrived. Although after two weeks of intense conversation and observation of Elle, she probably understood a lot more than he'd guess.

He didn't know how to start either, so he said,

"Funny. The 'Peg' thing. Want to know what L.Z. stands for?" He'd never posed the question to anyone before now, but it was better than talking about what they weren't talking about.

"I thought maybe it was an extension of Elle, like the letter 'L?' You know, *L.Z.*...like, maybe Elle, Jr.?"

L.Z.'s eyes widened. That had never occurred to him. Had his mom actually...? He shook his head to clear the thought that his mother's colossal ego could have gone that far.

"Led Zeppelin."

"Get out!" Peg's giggle was like a brook in a desert. Even at thirty, L.Z.'s social interactions had been so limited he could count on one hand the private personal conversations he'd had with anyone who wasn't his mother, uncle, or a co-worker. He joined her with a snort. She was in her zone now.

"That's kinda cool, you know. You're named after a band, and me and my sibs are named after songs. In fact, one of my sisters is named after another Steely Dan song...*Aja*...you know..." She closed her eyes and raised her face as if to launch into another performance, but he cut her off.

"Yes, I know it. And that is kind of cool, although mom's and my taste run a little harder than Steely Dan." He pointed at his band t-shirt of the day.

"Wow. There's really a band called *Goatwhore*? I thought that shirt was merch from a horror movie." She wrinkled her nose and picked up his empty root beer can and shook it as if she planned to take a drink if there were any left. He stared at her, not quite knowing what to think, other than there must have been some universal plot in action when she ended up being his mother's companion.

Peg Warner was a little off in her own ways, which might have been why she'd fit in so quickly in a home dynamic where nothing ever seemed to fit. She appeared more relaxed than he'd ever seen her, which was remarkable under the circumstances. Pulling her knees to her chest in the deck chair, she asked,

"So, what about your sibs? They have funky names too?"

"No siblings," he responded, squirming a little. This was getting personal, and it was getting dark out.

In the wan light he couldn't see the flicker of confusion in her eyes.

"Oh," she finally said with a shrug. "I have, like, four brothers and two sisters. We're close, but I've always felt like the black sheep, you know? The odd ball. Not nearly as out there as one of my sisters, but different, anyway." She trailed off. He thought she was getting bored with him, while she thought of how much she missed her family, even though she was different from them in every way.

The silence was only broken by the sound of cars passing the front of the house as they both slid into their own thoughts and the night grew.

"L.Z., don't sweat it."

He could barely see her now. He felt as though his life had been split in half and spread open for the world to see.

Until now, his mom's proclivities were his dirty little secret. He cleared his throat and responded.

"It's…well, I'm used to it. I'm just not used to 'it' having an audience." *And I'm not used to seeing it as my future*, he thought, pondering the voice.

He felt exposed and vulnerable. And scared.

"It's cool, Led Zeppelin. I knew she heard voices because she told me. As long as they don't tell her to play Barry Manilow or to chop me up into bite-sized pieces, I just see it as part of her personality. She reminds me of one of those kaleidoscope thingies. If you looked at it while you were already trippin' it would freak you out, but if you're clear on what it is, well, it's kinda cool. Unique."

L.Z. felt like he was being sucked through a straw as he tried to process what this non-Manson said so matter-of-factly about the taboo that was his world. He'd spent his whole life coping, hiding, and doing damage control, and this woman just boiled it down to "kinda cool?"

He saw nothing cool, kinda or otherwise, about Elle's performance that night.

After the three of them had ice cream earlier in the evening, Peg had excused herself to shower and, feeling that his mother was in one of her better frames of mind, L.Z.

conversationally asked her opinion on the validity of "auditory hallucinations." He had mistakenly thought if he appealed to her vast intellect and used objective terms, he could ease past her paranoia into an assessment of her experiences.

He was sadly mistaken.

After she threw her ice cream bowl to the floor, she'd stuck her head in the sink to rinse the residue from her mouth. She went on to systematically jerk curtains closed, unplug appliances, and block the heater vents. She'd ignored his pleas to just forget he'd asked, then ignored his lies that he'd seen a documentary and simply wanted her opinion as she swiped his and Peg's phones from the coffee tables and removed the batteries.

The Mansons were so involved in their decades-long dance of dysfunction, they'd forgotten time and place as well as the fact they weren't alone in the house.

Elle had remained tight lipped as she flew into L.Z.'s room and began to inspect under the bed, ripping the sheets off, removing lampshades, and practically dismantling his desk after jerking the laptop cord from the wall. He pleaded with her to stop, trying everything from swearing he was joking to apologizing for not being a better son.

As quickly as her flurry had started, it ended when she strode into the center of the living room and stopped. Resembling a sweat slicked skeleton, she'd lit a cigarette, even in her breathless state. Her eyes blazed when she asked in a voice that sounded simultaneously stern and sorrowful.

"What did they say to you Leddy?"

Her words struck him stone still.

"They?"

He'd never answered one of her ludicrous questions with a question before. Until now, he had never internalized any of her delusions and what he felt was entirely new. Did she know or was she guessing? Did her question have anything to do with him *at all?*

She rushed and grabbed his arms, ashes flying, suddenly nose-to-nose with her son, speaking through gritted teeth.

Rather than attempting to de-escalate as every time before, this time he was compelled to listen...*just in case.* He was mesmerized by her watery blue eyes.

"Don't listen to them, Leddy. Don't do it!" Her voice had dropped to a whisper.

He thought, *but it's not 'them.' It's one...*

He stopped the thought; the point hardly seemed to matter while he was stuck in her tractor beam.

She let go of one arm and shot a finger outward toward the television.

71

"*They* will tell you it's auditory hallucinations, or schizophrenia…or even fucking alien transmissions. But *they*," with this she jammed her finger into her temple and continued, "*they re* like a virus fixin' to rewire you. They want to siphon your brilliant mind, my Leddy, they know you're *my* son. They know you're a, what do they call it? A precious national resource. Don't. Let. Them. *In*." Her eyes were like lasers, doing far more damage to his brain than the dreaded "them."

And just like that, his disorientation drained away, and he felt like a balloon that had just popped.

He wasn't contending with her villainous "they." His disembodied voice was a single, smartass, non-governmental parasite.

And his mother was crazy.

An overwhelming sense of foolishness for himself and pity for her flooded his eyes with rare tears.

"Oh, my sweet Leddy, I'm so sorry I done cursed you with this shit," she cried as she threw her arms around him.

Not half as sorry as I am, Ma, he thought with a helplessness he'd never felt before.

For just a moment, he'd succumbed to his mother's surprisingly strong hug, crushing his eyes into her neck to banish the tears. His knees grew weak, and he felt five-years-old again.

"Mama," he whispered hoarsely, loving her fiercely despite it all.

When he raised his head and opened his eyes, he saw Peg standing in the hallway, hugging herself, fighting off tears of her own.

L.Z. was onstage in full badass mode. His face was thick with theatric grease paint rendering an image somewhere between Slipknot and KISS; his cheek bore a bloody red missile like a wet pictograph. He was rocking out, body and soul, in his Red Missile Burgers work shirt and black Dockers, with Gene Simmons-worthy platform shoes and one sequined glove, ala Michael Jackson.

Back-to-back with Aaron Stoss from SKinKneader, he played an invisible but gnarly air guitar to Aaron's electric blue Squire, while they jointly screamed the metal version of harmony into a spit splattered microphone.

It's so dark, are you dead?

It's the voice in your head...

I knead your skin, I need your eyes,

If you don't answer, I'll fucking die.

L.Z. was in utter bliss, leaning against his hero as the crowd roared. The stage lights were so hot he was drenched in sweat and didn't care.

73

In perfect sync, L.Z. and Aaron spun to face each other to perform a mind-bending guitar duo, but instead of launching into the next verse, Aaron threw his guitar into the crowd and grabbed L.Z. by the shirt, twisting his head in an unnatural angle as he shouted into his face,

Where are you? Are you dead? Am I dead? It's dark...it's so dark...L.Z....Leddy...WHERE'D YOU GO...

Wait...this isn't our song, L.Z. thought, feeling the terror rise as Aaron jerked him closer until he could feel hot breath on his face. Then it wasn't Aaron, because *the face was gone.* The featureless skull came closer until it melded with his. He felt the invasion as its essence overrode his own with a voice that didn't sing, that didn't belong to Aaron Stoss...and with knowledge that wasn't his own.

The utterances and thoughts merged, becoming searing tentacles squeezing his brain and shooting down his throat. He couldn't breathe. He strained to break away.

L.Z. sat bolt upright in bed, gasping from such a deep place, the guttural sound startled him, accenting his fear with jagged punctuation. He jerked the drenched sheets away and threw his legs over the bed, pressing the heels of his hands into his eyes to calm himself and regroup.

"Jesus, so dramatic! What, were you sleeping?"

L.Z. leapt to his feet, his heart somewhere between his chest cavity and the roof of his skull when he recognized the voice. It was the voice Aaron had used...just before he lost his face...just before...

"I musta woke you...did you hear me? This is a new wrinkle, gotta say..."

L.Z. stood in the middle of his room wearing only his boxer shorts. He closed his eyes and inhaled deeply, making space in his brain before he even tried to respond.

"Hey...you hear me?"

"Yes, you woke me. Just shut up for a minute. Just..."

"Jeez. All right, already."

L.Z. waved off the response and moved stiffly to his desk and sat, running a hand over his short wiry curls.

In that gauzy state between fresh consciousness and a too-real dream, he tried to scrape off the feeling of terror and dread which were somehow worse than the very real voice that had just spoken to him.

"You alri..."

He sharply raised a hand toward his own face, intuitively knowing "it" would see it and get the message. It worked. The sentence remained incomplete.

Lining up his mental Legos, L.Z. tried to grasp what had just happened. Obviously, he'd had a dream, but it felt too real. Too familiar. He squinted in thought as he glanced at his tangled bed.

The dream was a dream. The voice…well, it was as real as it had been all along.

But it was *the overlap* he couldn't shake. A joining that felt like a found puzzle piece.

The voice *belonged* in that dream. And there was violence there.

"Look, I'd go away, but frankly, I don't know where I would go, and I don't exactly run this…"

And yet, when the words passed through his mind, it sounded just as it always had.

"Yeah. Right. I get that," L.Z. answered a bit too naturally.

Did he get it? Was this thing real at all? Was the connection perceived?

Or was this just one more hinge loosening on his sanity?

His choices were limited, but there were still things he could control.

Standing, he said to the empty room, "Hold that thought, or I guess I'll hold it for you. I need coffee and we need to talk. Or whatever it is we do."

"Are you seriously paying for a stranger to live with Elle, paying for L.Z.'s car, who I might add is employed because of you, or should I say *still* employed by you after his recent arrest and DUI...oh, and speaking of which..."

Abby stood in the doorway to Al's study, holding bills in one hand and shaking legal paperwork with her other, while wearing a familiar look of exasperation.

Al looked up from the low light of his mahogany desk with a recognizable expression of his own: guilt. He rubbed his eyes and stood with a clap of his hands and a childish smile. This normally signaled the beginning of an explanation-filled diatribe for which she was not in the mood.

"Stop before you start, Mister," she said as she handed him the papers, then swiped her hands together as if washing them of the whole affair. She handled all their mail and finances, so her discovery was hardly a case of snooping.

He looked at the documents, then up at her like a guilty child in the body of a senior citizen. They both knew he didn't willfully keep secrets from her or mislead her by intent. She knew his mind operated on such a level that keeping track of his mental universe was practically more than he could handle, although it didn't make life with him any less exasperating. And he knew she was forgiving and typically patient, although that didn't assuage his guilt in the least. He'd always said he'd "married up" when he joined with Abby, and for him, it was a sincere assessment.

He sighed and dropped into his chair, messily pushing the bills and legal correspondence across the cluttered blotter.

"Honey, I thought I told you…"

"You told me you were helping them out."

He raised his eyebrows and scratched his head as he slid the documents into some semblance of order. He knew it wasn't the money she was worried about. He also knew it wasn't his sister or nephew that troubled her; she lost no sleep over his distant and only family outside their own. It was her concern over him and his overactive need to fix things; she'd once told him he was compassionate to a fault.

She knew a response was not forthcoming as he stared beyond the papers at the desk's woodgrain, his fingers tapping as they did when he was lost in thought. She pulled her chin inward, and a disquieted look replaced the previous one of annoyance.

He jumped when she touched his arm; he hadn't realized she'd come to his side of the desk, squatting so she was slightly below him.

"Are you really that worried about her this time?" She looked concerned, albeit confused. The issue of Elle had been a constant in their marriage and his next statement summed up an understanding they'd come to years before.

"Nah, Honey, you can't fix crazy." Pleasantly surprised by her soft approach, he swung his chair toward her, leaning to kiss her hand. She never took her eyes from his face as she waited. Staring at her hand in his, he said quietly,

"It's not her I'm worried about, it's L.Z."

"The DUI? Do you think there's more to it?"

Al almost laughed as he answered, "Ah, no…that boy is as strait-laced as they get; it was the ER thing and his greatest flaw that caused his trouble. He drove when he shouldn't have, but he was helping someone in the process. His 'say-no' gear is permanently stuck."

"Not as stuck as I am right now," she said with a grimace. "Help me up, will you?" Al stood with a gentle laugh and pulled the love of his life into a standing position as she grunted then pressed her hands into her back. At their age, that she had risked crouching for more than a few minutes was enough for him to understand her concern for him was legitimate.

She leaned on the desk as she stretched her legs and he continued, scraping the papers together.

"He's…well, something's up with him. And there's something about that Peg character…" He trailed off again as his brain got away from his mouth.

"Well, why'd you hire her then? Did you even do a background check?"

He waved the papers toward her, and she took them; they both knew she never intended to hold him to task on the actual details of the documents to begin with. He continued with his hand in the small of her back as they headed toward the door.

"Well, yes, and she's clean other than the misunderstanding at the trailer…never mind that. She's clean. It's just that the whole thing with her, you know, the timing, was maybe a little too convenient? Maybe she was too willing? I mean she did need a place to live, and she already knew L.Z." He closed the door to the study as Abby turned to face him in the hallway.

"Then what? Think she knows more about Elle than L.Z.?"

Al pressed one finger against another in the form of an "X" and widened his eyes in mock horror.

"Don't go there, my dear, let those sleeping dogs lie."

There was much L.Z. had not figured out about his mother, and that was for the best. Al continued.

"I don't know what I don't know, I just know what I feel. For some reason, she doesn't feel like a stranger, but L.Z. – well – he felt a little strange on that last visit and I don't think it was his banged-up state."

Abby stared at the floor thoughtfully as they walked down a long hallway toward their kitchen. She nearly tripped though, when Al popped her on the rear and threw his hands into a jazz waggle, face contorted with comical helplessness.

"But what do *I* know? I'm just the guy with the big brain. You know, a nuclear engineer with a bad back and a million-dollar burger joint fetish!"

She laughed with him, but her eyes didn't join in. She knew her husband, his shortcomings, and strengths. He didn't get where he was because of faulty instincts.

For the first time in years, she wondered if she should be a little more in tune with his distant and strange relatives.

"You're shitting me. You told her *what?*"

L.Z. and Peg spoke in hushed tones in the kitchen after he'd come home from work to discover Elle smoking on the back patio. Until that day, the old woman had never set foot out there because she felt "exposed." Despite his complaints, she'd spent years applying layers of nicotine to the home's interior walls, yellowing windows, and probably giving her son cancer from second-hand smoke.

Peg, whose general appearance had become increasingly disarrayed over the weeks of her residence due to the absence of mirrors, scraped at a fuzzy curl as she replied.

"I told her smoking indoors was exactly what the cigarette industry wanted because the resulting nicotine residue leaves infrared layers which eventually allows them to survey your every movement with laser-sensitive satellite technology."

L.Z. opened his mouth, then closed it, pacing the small kitchen to control his anger before responding. Peg chewed on the quick of her thumbnail, watching him from the corner of her eye when he wasn't looking at her. This had become the norm and while he'd caught her a couple of times, he was unaware she took in his every move.

He finally stopped by the window, studying Elle who was still frighteningly thin although she'd filled out a bit under Peg's care. He made note of this and the additional value of having the young woman there, softening his comments.

"Don't get me wrong, I don't want her to smoke in the house and it's been a losing battle till now, so *thank you.*" He strained to be so amenable before he got to the point. "But do you realize how dangerous it is to not only feed her delusions, but to create new ones?" He spun to face Peg as she leaned against the counter, arms crossed. She held his gaze and he felt stuck. He had yet to understand her so-natural inclusion into his jacked-up family. They stared each other down.

Her expression wasn't exactly obstinate, but it was confident, which concerned him; it was a departure from her less serious and meeker stance.

"Why do you assume it's that farfetched? I mean, can you prove otherwise?" There was whimsy in her question, but it also held a challenge.

L.Z.'s brows shot up so quickly in conjunction with his gaping mouth that with his fuzzy hair, he looked as though he'd received an electric shock. Peg held up her hands to try to quell the eruption.

"OK, *OK,* I totally made it up! But do you really think pushing against her reality makes it any less real to her? Have you ever once 'reasoned' her out of something she believes? *Have you?"* Once her challenge was out there, she seemed to shrink a little in anticipation of his response but held her shoulders a little straighter as if to validate her position.

"Girlfriend's got a point, you know..." As always, the voice was like a landmine.

"Would you please just..." L.Z. clapped a hand over his mouth to dam the rest of the admonishment from coming out. He thought he'd had an understanding with his unwelcome visitor.

"Oh, yeah, right...you want me to be seen, not heard, but wait! No one can see me!"

L.Z. turned an unnatural shade of red as he glanced at Peg and held a finger up to pause their conversation.

Her shoulders relaxed and her eyes narrowed as the man in front of her seemed, not for the first time, to be struggling with an unseen force.

"Excuse me for a minute?" He spat the words as he left the room.

Peg waited and listened as she peered out the window to check on Elle who was holding a lit smoke while also holding a lively conversation with no one at all. Peg turned when she heard L.Z. reenter with a face of forced composure.

"I'm sorry. Look, I appreciate all you're doing for Mom and for me." He looked up and set his mouth, either choosing his words or having another weird spell. He looked at her again. "I know how convincing she can be, and I'm really glad you guys get along, but you haven't spent a lifetime dealing with this." He stopped and with a defeated look, said, "Peg, she's sick."

The fight had left him, and he dropped his head, reaching for a kitchen chair, sitting as if it were the only other option than just laying down. The man looked sapped.

Peg followed with the smallest of movements, watching him, as she often did, side-eyed. Once in the chair next to his, she quietly said,

"You know it's all real to her…and whether or not you like it, some of what she says could be really real, you know, like *real*." She raised her hands and looked around the kitchen to demonstrate what she meant. And he looked at her in tired disbelief. She'd actually referenced tangible truths in the same sentence as his mother.

He wasn't even sure if he wanted to answer Peg, when the devil herself burst through the patio door, saving him from the challenge.

"It's a lovely day to be alive. I like it out there; outdoor meditation, what a great idea. Leddy, I don't know why you didn't take me out there before. I think I'm in the mood for company. I'm going to invite the Poldats over to visit and we can sit *outside!*" With a knowing look at Peg, she flounced through and out of the room.

L.Z. watched his mother's departure then slowly looked at Peg, who smiled at him, displaying her deep dimples and big teeth. It was an expression of victory.

L.Z. couldn't. *He just couldn't.* He nodded to her with an insincere smile, stood, and exited as he processed his mother's announcement.

Other than Maynard the Uber guy, a handful of other questionable lovers, and her friend Linda, Elle had never invited guests into their home. And the Poldat family? That was a whole different matter. With a much-needed smile, he moved through the dusky living room, considering the upcoming visit from the non-existent family with whom his mother had "worked with while an emissary in Turkey."

As much as he liked Peg, mostly because he couldn't help it, she needed a deeper immersion into the deranged world of Elle Manson. He'd make sure he was home at the appointed time for the Poldat visit when *no one would show.*

He heard his mother "making the call" to invite her friends as he entered his room. Once he closed the door, he stood, hands on hips, and started what would appear to be his own one-way conversation.

Neither Elle nor L.Z. knew Peg stood in the shadows of the hallway between their rooms, taking mental notes. Once the voices quieted, she retired to her own room, pulled out her journal, and began to write. Since moving into this house, the demeaning voice in her head had become strangely quiet. Maybe it was because she had never felt more at home.

It was dark and utterly quiet. He'd learned by now this meant his host was sleeping and although it didn't suit him at all, he felt he should try to accommodate. It didn't go well last time he woke L.Z. up.

It wasn't his nature to wait. It also wasn't his nature to follow or comply. He didn't really know *why* he knew that because he still didn't know who exactly he was or what he was doing "here," and "here" came and went in a manner over which he had no control.

Control.

That was something he knew, without knowing why; he was accustomed to having it in totality. His frustration was extreme, but he controlled it because it was something he understood. Until he had a grip on the bigger thing, he'd shape and tighten his grasp on the smaller things. Smaller things like L.Z.'s will.

He was lucky the head in which he lived part time belonged to a schmuck; a schmuck who was oddly endearing to the basically apathetic entity. There was just something about L.Z. that felt familiar, although the two of them couldn't possibly have been more different.

Again, maddeningly, he didn't know *how* he knew that since he still had no idea who he was, how he'd ended up there, or his origin. The time he wasn't in L.Z.'s head, completely dependent on the man's eyes and ears, he was…well, he *wasn't*. There was nothing until he "woke up" inside of the mind of the poor son-of-a-bitch he'd unwittingly violated.

He'd told L.Z. that he wasn't dead, but he didn't know that for sure. After getting a load of the mom, Elle, who was obviously a nut job, he ascertained that L.Z. must be considering that he had inherited some of the bats from Elle's belfry. But he was not a manifestation of a crazy man's imagination; how could he be, when he had his own will and consciousness, in fact, it was all he had for now. And L.Z.'s fear, he reminded himself; he had that in his proverbial back pocket.

While L.Z. slept, the dweller stayed as long as he could, trying to remember, and when he couldn't remember, he *felt* and reached out for what came to him.

And as he did, L.Z. dreamed, with thrashes and moans.

"You there?" L.Z. asked.

No answer.

"C'mon, cat got your tongue? Not 'feline' well today?"

Nothing. He knew the voice could laugh, because it had filled his head with the discordant sound before. Maybe it wasn't a pun fan?

"I know you're there. What, are you a dog dude? Don't like cats?"

He pulled into the driveway at the house, saying,

"Look, I'm putting the car in *bark*. How's that?" Despite his frustration, he snickered.

Still nothing. No voice, no boo-hiss for the puns. No anything.

Normally the silence would be welcome, but the problem was, L.Z. could feel the presence. And this awareness was almost as common as the voice itself lately, the feeling that it was there, but not saying anything.

Oh Jesus, I'm done for now, he thought, and laughed weakly as he opened the car door. *Add paranoia to hearing voices. All I need now is a few hallucinations to reserve my own spot in the looney...*

His thought stopped along with his breath when he stood from the car, and indeed, "saw something," *Somethings* to be exact.

A car had pulled up to the curb. Not just any car, but one with a prominent sticker on the front bumper. The sticker was red with a stretched crescent moon and star. The bumper sticker looked just like the tiny flag attached to the car's antenna. It was the national flag of *Turkey.*

L.Z. closed the door slowly, almost as if he were in a trance, as he watched an elderly couple get out of their car. They smiled as they spotted him.

"Is this the Manson home?" The man had a thick foreign accent. The woman wore a scarf, despite the heat, and she nodded to L.Z. as she took the man's arm and they walked toward him.

"Are you the Leddy we heard about?" They were in front of L.Z. now, who had been stricken speechless. It had to be a hallucination, this Turkish couple. But he nodded slowly as he mechanically took the man's extended hand, which felt real enough.

"It is lovely to meet you, Leddy. Your mother has told us so much about you. We are the Poldats. I am Ahmet, and this is my wife, Zehnep. We met your mother in Turkey years ago; isn't it funny we would all end up in Boise, yes? We are delighted to finally see her again."

"Well, check that out...the old broad pulled some Turks right out of her ass."

L.Z. grimaced at the suddenly present voice but made no sign of acknowledging the intrusion as he stiffly smiled at the visitors.

"Yes. Very funny," he forced his lead tongue to say.

As he guided the couple to the house, he had three thoughts.

His first thought was Peg had been right that some – or at least one – of Elle's hundreds of outrageous claims was "really real, you know, like *real.*" The implications of this little gem were staggering.

He opened the front door as the second thought snaked its way through his brain: that this entire thing was his own delusion, part and parcel with the freakin' voice.

But he dismissed it immediately because...well, because he *just knew.*

"Ma, your company is here." He shouted words he'd never said in his life, as the third thought came with a conflicting combination of validation and doom. That the voice, or its owner, *had* been there all along in the car on

L.Z.'s way home, even though it hadn't responded to his prodding. *It chose not to respond.*

Was it getting stronger or was he getting weaker?

Elle swept into the room in all her glory, wearing an old peasant dress she'd always sworn she'd purchased during her undercover "duties" in Turkey.

As the Poldats embraced her, L.Z. leaned against the front doorframe and took it in with the same feeling he'd had when the voice first appeared – that merging of reality and something less real.

Then he saw Peg, and their eyes met. He squinted, tipping his head in question, and she shrugged, splaying her hands with a dazzling show of her dimples. Then she touched a finger to her tongue and made an invisible chalk mark in the air.

Touché, L.Z. thought.

He looked at the dingy nicotine caked walls and suddenly wondered if somewhere out there, a laser-sensitive satellite shone a beam on them, documenting the momentous occasion.

There were no unfamiliar cars in front of his house the next day when he came home from work. That, in addition to the fact that no voice outside his own had horned in on his brain or thoughts that day, made L.Z.'s heart uncharacteristically light as he checked the mail and headed for the door. The advent of no mail added to his near delight; living with Elle lent itself to all kinds of surprises in the form of underground publications, unmarked packages, and junk mail she managed to construe as undercover correspondence. When he walked into the house and it was not only absent of smoke, but the television wasn't blaring, he thought he detected a slight leap of the heart.

It was probably a good thing it didn't occur to him how defunct his life had become when the absence of bad stuff constituted a good day. He might have even called it a great day if he hadn't walked onto the patio and found himself in a scene straight from *One Flew Over the Cuckoo's Nest*.

Elle, her friend Linda, and Peg sat in eighty-six-degree heat wearing what looked like crudely made potholders stacked on their heads. Peg was furiously manipulating yarn with long metal needles; multiple balls of fleece in various colors lay at her feet. Before she saw him, she grabbed scissors and snipped off a dangling extension from a square piece identical to the ones atop their heads and tossed it onto a pile on the patio table.

Before he could retreat, Elle saw him and carefully nodded her greeting as to not topple her head-stack. Linda did the same as she sipped her coffee, which is all he'd ever seen her drink regardless of the season, raising her other hand just before flicking her cigarette. She could be Elle Manson,

Part II, if she'd ever had an original thought; however, she mostly just nodded as Elle talked, although that was clearly a less handy task with half a dozen knit whatevers on her head.

He felt the first fissure in his otherwise decent day.

"Hey Linda. Ma. And Peg? Didn't know you could knit," was all he could muster as he wondered if he even wanted to know what was going on.

"You never asked," she said matter-of-factly as she grabbed a ball of yarn and started to pull out a strand. He pondered if he'd just been the target of a snarky remark when she shot him her big-toothed smile which sent a twitch through his chest and, surprised, he touched his heart. Elle's throaty voice invaded the notion before he could assign meaning.

"Ah, Leddy, you sense it too! They can't reach through the walls anymore so they're coming VFR direct to our skulls. Thank God for Peg's handiwork." With a sly smile she tapped her headcovers, triggering a grunt and tiny nod from the ever-expressive Linda.

L.Z. processed his mother's statement with a poker-face before his mouth responded without consent from his brain.

"So, the ol' aluminum foil hats are out of style? Oh wait, or would the sun's reflection be too revealing?" He glanced at the sky with mock suspicion before he even realized what he'd said. In addition to not feeding his mother's fantasies, he also avoided responding with sarcasm…until today, anyway. He closed his eyes, blaming his recent weariness for the slip.

"Don't be so naïve, Leddy. If we sent back the transmissions, it would be just like sticking our heads in the sand. We need to protect ourselves, but also be able to absorb, you know…suck in…the information to figure out the threat. Peg, here, is not only very crafty, but a sheer genius! These protective pads are exactly the ticket."

Peg nodded, bouncing her mass of curls, counting stitches, and wrapping the yarn around a needle as she shot L.Z. a pleading glance. She didn't want him to make a big deal; he wordlessly returned her stare with widening eyes to express his displeasure. She, in turn, pursed her lips with a searing gaze. He just didn't have the energy to continue the mute battle and thus, rendered a salute and turned to leave before he was fitted with his own custom oven-mitt-beanie.

He hadn't even gotten to his room when another crack appeared in his good-day façade.

"Please tell me you're going to tap that."

L.Z. stopped just inside his door, his mood dropping another notch.

"What. Tap what? And oh, welcome back. Missed you," L.Z. said sarcastically to the empty room, scrubbing his face hard as if he could erase the whole day.

"Jesus, you know...tap, shag...hump. How about boink? She's too damn cute to say fuck, but at the end of the day..."

L.Z. clenched his fists.

"How about you have some respect, you leech? What I do or don't do with my body is my business."

"Hey, at least you have a body...and, I might add, that includes a dick which seems very neglected..."

"I'll tell you what you can do with your dick..." L.Z.'s jaw snapped shut when he heard the floor creak. He spun around and ceased to breathe.

Peg stood just outside his doorway; a bag stuffed full of yarny-looking things clasped to her chest. She bit her lip and stared.

He forced air in and out, staring back. He knew she'd heard at least his last outburst. Somehow that was worse than the voice itself.

After a long minute, she reached into her bag and pulled out a rainbow-colored square.

"Maybe you need this more than me?" She offered it with a small smile.

Still wordless, he took it, mainly because he didn't know what else to do.

She turned to leave, saying over her shoulder, "By the way, it's *crochet*, not knitting. I can't knit and this probably does a better job of absorbing those transmissions, anyway."

She disappeared into her room and L.Z. stood silent, staring at the handywork.

"Can you spell booty call? What are you waiting for?!"

L.Z. smashed the crocheted square over his face and slammed his door.

Because he'd spent most of his life minimizing confusing and uncomfortable things, it was completely natural for L.Z. to avoid talking to Peg about what she'd overheard. Besides, he didn't have a grip over what was happening himself; there was no way he would talk to someone else about it. It didn't help that he was confused about his feelings for his new oddball roommate. He didn't necessarily want to "tap" her; but he had feelings he'd never had before. He was woefully inept about women, which his cerebral squatter was only too happy to point out as often as possible.

A week had passed since the Poldats' visit. The potholder standoff had come and gone. Other than the fact that Peg now wore thimbles on all fingers and thumbs, for reasons he dared not ask, it had been an uneventful week in the Manson home. Uneventful, on the surface, that is.

Elle had spent hours drafting e-mails to the FBI, CIA, NSA, the Pentagon, and the owners of Ben and Jerrys (not Ben and Jerry themselves, she insisted, as the company was a cover for Putin sympathizers in the U.S.). Peg tried to navigate daily living with metal fingertips, while scribbling page after page in her journal each night (sans thimbles; she wasn't that dedicated or coordinated).

L.Z. was simply in survival mode. The voice in his head, whom he now called Rex, only because the voice vehemently objected to Gilbert, as in Gilbert Godfrey, owner of the world's most annoying voice. Of course, since Rex couldn't actually read his mind it/he had no idea L.Z. agreed to the name because it was a homophone with "wrecks." It was a one-way compromise, making L.Z. feel he'd gotten over on the presence who felt significantly more intelligent, if not more cunning, than himself. He didn't have tangible reasons to explain this assessment, it was just a feeling among many. There was a clinging awareness superseding their "verbal" interactions and while he couldn't remember his dreams, he felt certain they'd become Rex's domain. Rex denied this, and of course L.Z. couldn't know it was true. But just like Rex could not read L.Z.'s mind, he also could not see his dreams. But he could linger, and he could assess; and he did both at an increasing rate, which L.Z. could sense. He was beyond tired and needed a break before he broke.

His break came from the most unexpected and stupendous source: his hero, his idol…his escape via earbuds, Aaron Stoss, rhythm guitar player for SKinKneader.

It wasn't a direct rescue, but even as roundabout as it was, it was epic in L.Z.'s eyes.

L.Z. had listened to the KBRK 505 rock station every morning for so many years he'd lost track. Besides digging the music, he was a serial entrant in the frequent station contests. So frequent, in fact, he had the station's number on speed dial.

He was on his way to Red Missile Burgers for a morning shift, mentally cataloging the reasons Peg would wear thimbles on all her fingers as he rocked out to SKinKneader's latest release, No Cure. When the song ended, the DJ, Bob "the Beatman" Bennett announced that tickets to the Fracas Fest in Salt Lake City would go to the first caller. In anticipation of such an announcement, L.Z. had his phone in hand, number ready, and had already dialed when Bob finished by saying the tickets would include backstage passes to *SKinKneader*, one of the bands scheduled for the rock fest.

L.Z. almost rear-ended the car in front of him and changed lanes to pull over when Bob answered the line,

"Congratulations, you are the first caller! To whom am I speaking, other than the proud winner of *tickets to the Fracas Fest?*"

L.Z. nearly dropped his phone as he skirted another car to get into a convenience store parking lot.

He heard Bob continue their conversation over the car speakers before he managed to say anything.

"Hello! Caller one, are you there? Going, going..."

"I'm here! This is L.Z. Manson – uh – no relation, that is. You know." He stopped to catch his breath. He couldn't believe this was happening. He'd never won anything in his life, and now, backstage passes to *SKinKneader*?

He heard Bob the Beatman's cheesy chuckle in stereo between the radio speakers and his phone.

"Good to know, there, *EL.Z.ie*, was it? Not sure we could live with ourselves if we hooked up Charles Manson's kin with tickets to *Fracas Fest!*" He gave the last two words the obligatory DJ boost.

"Well, my uncle *is* Charles Alvin Manson, but still no relation. And my name isn't EL.Z.ie. It's *L. Z.*, as in Led Zeppelin." He nearly swallowed his tongue as soon as the words were out of his mouth. He was on the radio, now the whole world would...

"Uh, right, L.Z. as in Led Zeppelin, and Manson, not related! Got it! Well, my friend, congrats and stay on the line for more info on how you can claim your *Fracas Fest tickets with backstage passes to...*"

"SKinKneader. *Aaron Stoss.*" L.Z. whispered as he held the line.

All thoughts of voices, thimbles, and obnoxious fast-food customers fell away as L.Z. realized this was really happening.

He was almost happy, if he could just get the sudden image of Aaron's melting face out of his mind, he'd have been ecstatic.

But that had been a dream.

And this was *real.*

For just a moment, he suspended the other realities in his life, sat in the Kia, and smiled.

It was only about a five-hour drive from Boise to Salt Lake City, but to L.Z., it would be nothing short of an odyssey. Although his mother had dragged him around the country in the VW van as a child, she not only drove, but was driven by various goals, none of which had anything to do with enhancing his childhood. This would be his first real road trip, and thanks to Peg, he could go alone.

Well, quasi-alone, unless Rex dropped away with one of his periodic and unexplained absences. L.Z. wasn't a religious man, but he offered endless silent prayers focused on the exoneration of the voice from his brain, if not forever, at least for the four days of his trip.

One of the world's great mysteries is why radio stations only give tickets away within a stone's throw, timewise, of the event. Maybe the DJs don't have lives, thus planning isn't a factor? L.Z. only had two days to plan his trip, and if the lure was anything short of the chance to see his favorite band and meeting Aaron Stoss, he wouldn't have bothered.

He had so much vacation time accumulated at work, they couldn't justify denying his request for days off. Besides, although L.Z. himself never brought it up, his local bosses were very aware who L.Z.'s uncle was. He could have asked for a month, and it would have been granted, albeit with gritting teeth.

Speaking of Uncle Al, L.Z. had never been so grateful to his only male family member. Because of Al's involvement in the legal challenges after his post-ER DUI, L.Z.'s driving privileges were intact. He guessed he could have taken a bus or flown (over Elle's dead body of course, due to her string of objections to air travel), but this? A road trip alone was so much better. Never in his life had he needed a break as badly as now.

Finally, lodging wasn't an issue because, again, Al came to the rescue. The biggest surprise was when his delighted uncle announced over the phone that it was Aunt Abby's idea for their nephew to stay in their home. *That* was news. L.Z.

didn't know Abby well, and he figured there were reasons for that, most of which were likely boxed away and labelled, "Elizabeth Taylor Manson." In fact, the only reason he'd be in Salt Lake a couple of extra days was at his aunt's insistence. He was so excited and nervous, he didn't assign this advent much thought, although later he'd give it a lot of thought.

Since hearing of her son's trip, Elle had vacillated between having suspicions about his true mission and trumpeting that he had nothing to worry about on the home front, because she and Peg had each other.

As he looked at them on the patio with their coffee the morning of his departure, he questioned her confidence. Peg struggled with her still-armored fingers as she tried to crochet what might have been anything from more transmission jamming devices to the latest thing in the wide world of Elle, butt pads for her emaciated derriere so she could more closely resemble J.Lo. Both women looked unkempt and like people he'd avoid on the street.

Then it occurred to him that they also looked happy. Peg had never seemed content at Red Missile Burgers and his mother had been less of a handful since the younger woman moved in.

L.Z. did something very un-L.Z.-like. He just let it go.

Without a dozen more reminders to Peg that he was only a call away, without asking that they be careful to put leftovers in the fridge, that they not initiate any anti-government phone campaigns, or suggest they stay home in his absence, he just said goodbye with a wave and left.

In the car, he told himself this was not just a new adventure for him, but maybe even the start of a new chapter of his life.

He was right on both accounts, but in ways he never imagined.

PART II
No Cure

But I can't tell them what's going on
Or they'll medicate my head
Because I know I'm not crazy
I choose to live with it instead
And this won't end no matter how you drug my brain
Because there is no cure when you can't prove or explain

-- Aaron Stoss (SKinKneaders)

If L.Z.'s entire getaway had consisted of just the five-hour drive from his home to his uncle's place on the outskirts of Salt Lake City, it would have been enough for him.

On the first leg of the trip, he had to force himself to adjust to the disembodied voice of the GPS unit Keith had loaned him. Although the robotic female voice sounded nothing like Rex, it triggered his nervous response every time it piped up unprompted with tips and directions. He'd never used navigation before but had also not had unbidden voices in his head until recent history. After the first fifty miles or so, he was able to discern that one was definitely more welcome than the other.

Driving on the open road without his mom, without an immediate destination (home or work), and with his very own metal playlist blaring from the car speakers (Keith had also shown him how to use the Bluetooth to connect his phone to the car stereo: amazing!), he knew he was in a new plane of existence. And it was good.

Although the music was loud enough to practically drown Rex out if he had broadcast any of his never-welcome postulations, he remained quiet in L.Z.'s head, but naggingly present. They'd never "discussed" the times Rex would pop in but remain silent. L.Z. refused to let on that he knew Rex was "there." And he had no way of knowing that Rex, with frustratingly meager means to control anything about his spotty existence, held tightly to his few choices as he sought definition to his existence. Perhaps they both grew stronger in the process.

Once headed southeast on I-84 in Utah, L.Z. was taken by the view of rolling hills, then mountains. He switched from his general playlist to the latest SKinKneader album and encountered an almost spiritual moment as he lost himself in lyrics while driving as the mountains rose on the left and the Great Salt Lake took form on the right.

At some point, the lyrics written by Aaron Stoss starkly stood out, weaving their way through his psyche with eerie familiarity.

It's so dark, are you dead?

It's the voice in your head...

Here they come, marching in,

I'm victim to the voices once again.

The cure, what cure...there is no cure

Don't know who's who, who owns the sin

L.Z. had never had an epiphany in his life; he had never even used the word. But as the lyrics reached the emotional center of his brain, he suddenly knew beyond the shadow of a doubt he was connected to Aaron Stoss and that their meeting was predestined. He just *knew it* and with a rush of the closest thing to joy he'd ever felt, he began to smack the steering wheel in time with the pounding bass beats filling every square inch of the car.

He was certain he was right about Aaron, and he knew something profound would happen the following night.

He was half right.

L.Z. was in such high spirits, he hardly seemed himself when he arrived at what the GPS told him was his destination. He had visited his uncle and aunt at previous residences a few times as a kid, and those had mostly been on military bases. This place was so grandiose, he started to double check the address when Abby stepped onto the wrap-around porch through a massive front doorway. He hadn't seen her in years, but there was no mistaking she was one and the same. She was short and stout and although her natural black hair color had given away to gray, she looked healthy and, well, sturdy. She was the perfect offset to his uncle, both in physique and manner. As he recalled, the woman was pleasant but no-nonsense. She couldn't have been more unlike Elle. As a kid, he'd theorized the two women were from different planets.

L.Z. got out of the car, suddenly feeling a little less man-of-the-world when he noted Uncle Al hadn't joined Abby to greet him. He wasn't exactly afraid of the woman; he just didn't know her. Or maybe he was afraid of her. But now wasn't the time for analysis.

As he approached the steps leading to the huge home, his consternation turned to panic as his eyes met hers at the exact moment Rex made his grand entry.

"Damn, what do they call this place, the Manson Mansion? And this must be Al's woman, solid gal. Shit, she's looking so hard, I feel like she can see me..."

L.Z.'s face froze as Rex filled his head. He was within a few feet of his previously smiling aunt, who suddenly studied him with a directness that made him wonder if Rex was onto something because her expression changed as soon as Rex started talking. What L.Z. didn't consider was that his own continence had changed as well.

Abby saved him, however, by relaxing her scrutiny and offering her hands with a smile. L.Z. started breathing again,

108

thinking he'd just been paranoid. When he extended a hand to hers, she pulled him into a surprise hug.

Her smile faded as she hugged the too-thin young man who'd been such a gawky boy. He'd looked well enough when he'd gotten out of the car, but something crossed his face just as they met which was the first hint that her husband might have had valid concerns. There had been an unnatural shift in his expression and disposition. Was it *terror?* No, that was too strong. But she was certain she saw panic, and something told her it had nothing to do with the fact that Al wasn't there with her.

As she led her nephew into the house, although his manners were intact, he seemed to struggle to pay attention.

Something was afoot. It wasn't a ridiculous stretch that she'd intuit such things. She was a psychologist, after all.

The next 24-hours flew by without a fraction of the awkwardness of his first moments at the "Manson Mansion." Although he'd finally seen Uncle Al and been voraciously hugged and welcomed with unmatched enthusiasm, both his aunt and uncle had to work the next day which allowed L.Z. time to roam the absurdly large Manson home and test his city driving with the aid of the GPS navigation. He also managed to find the concert arena where the Fracas Fest would take place starting that afternoon. He even squeezed in a clandestine look at a couple of Red Missile Burger locations in the greater area.

The big moment arrived and before he knew it, L.Z. was being herded into the bowels of the arena with a small gaggle of other fans with backstage passes. He tried to act cool, a behavior completely foreign to him, but it was difficult considering he'd never been to a live concert, let alone gone backstage. His tidy and clean "battle jacket" hoodie, dockers, and loafers sharply contrasted with the others' dark and radical dress, but accustomed to being different, it didn't faze him. He tried to control his pounding heart and rehearse what he'd say when he'd *meet Aaron Stoss.*

The group was herded what seemed like miles through underground walkways led by an SLC rock station rep. As L.Z. looked nervously behind him, hoping they'd be led back *out* again when the time came, a lanky-haired kid in the group grabbed his arm excitedly.

"Dude, this is it...SKinKneader's hang! You 'bout missed it." Feeling like he was in a dream, L.Z. followed the rep, the goth kid, and a few others into a large room and nearly ran into a thin pale man with long jet-black hair.

"Excuse me," he muttered, looking around as his eyes adjusted. He didn't know what he was expecting, but this place was not it. The room looked like it could have been any room, as long as that room doubled for storage and lacked temperature control; it was cold and damp. He reasoned that with multiple other bigger name bands at the festival, SKinKneader took what they could get.

All judgement stopped when photo flashes caught his attention and his eyes settled on a line near the back of the room leading up to two leather clad men.

"No way," L.Z. said.

It was Yuri Anger and Bennie Blade, SKinKneader's lead singer and lead guitar player, posing for selfies with too-cool fans. Nearby were tables stacked with the band's merchandise.

"Way," came a response. Shaking his head in disbelief, L.Z.. glanced to his right at the man he'd narrowly avoided running into upon entry.

"Oh, sorry, guess I didn't know I said it out loud." L.Z. smiled as he glanced nervously around for his target. When he turned back to his right, still looking for Aaron, he saw the necklace hanging around the guy's neck.

It was a red tortoise shell guitar pick. *That was Aaron Stoss's trademark.* Mouth agape, his eyes ran up the man's chest and landed on his face; the guy smiled wryly.

"Yeah, no stage make-up, oh, and the hair," the man glanced down at his own unremarkable shirt, "…and street clothes. Throws 'em every time." He stuck an unlit cigarette behind his ear and casually extended a hand as he looked at the small crowd where Anger and Blade signed autographs on the backs of shirts, programs, and at least one girl's bare chest. L.Z. didn't see the boob display and probably wouldn't have cared if he had because he was less than a foot away from...

"Name's Aaron. Nice to meet you. Most go straight for the big guns." He tipped his head toward the other group.

L.Z.'s mouth was so dry, he wasn't sure he could lube the words enough to come out even if he tried. He managed a croak after Aaron Stoss took his hand back and looked at his biggest fan with vague interest.

"L.Z. Manson. No relation," L.Z. sputtered. Aaron's brows went together as a smile crossed his face.

"Well, then, L.Z., can I just leave it at that? Where'd you come in from?"

The question seemed so normal, so not-super-hero-metal-soulmate-like, L.Z. looked a little confused as he answered.

"Boise."

"Ah, good drive. Well, L.Z., thanks for coming. Hope you enjoy the..."

L.Z. felt his chance slipping. He also knew it was a rare moment when Rex wasn't invading him, and he didn't want Rex anywhere near this conversation. He pulled a paper from his pocket with a letter he'd written earlier in case he was unable to have a direct conversation with Aaron. It detailed his revelations and even had his contact information, just in case.

Just in case he was right about their connection.

"Aaron! Look, I…I didn't come because of them…well actually I came because I won a prize, but what I mean is, I am a band fan," he pulled open his hoodie, revealing his best SKinKneader shirt beneath. "I know all the songs you wrote. The ones you personally wrote anyway, and, well the lyrics, they mean something. Like I know more than I should."

He had Aaron's attention, but from the expression on the performer's face, it wasn't the kind of attention L.Z. had in mind.

"What do you mean? What do you know?" He looked alarmed and a little pissed off.

L.Z. pulled his face back in confusion. This wasn't going as planned. He swallowed and tried again.

"What I mean is…well, three of your songs from the last album, they're about voices, and no cure, and, well…I thought maybe we had something in common. In fact, yesterday, I felt it…*I really felt it*. It was like we have a bond."

Aaron's eyes flickered, and a disturbed expression crossed his face. But then he did the most awesome thing. He put his hand on L.Z.'s shoulder while still holding his gaze!

L.Z. could have died right then and there a happy man. And maybe he should have, because the next thing Aaron

Stoss did was not an awesome thing. It was not so much what he did as what he said.

"L.Z. *Manson*, right? Why does that not surprise me. Here's the thing: *I have no fucking idea what you're talking about.* But thanks for your interest. This for me?"

And with that question, he snatched the letter from LZ's hand, clapped him on the shoulder he had so warmly embraced, and walked away, stuffing the letter into his back pocket.

LZ stood alone for a minute that seemed more like an hour. Then he found the door, no longer worried about having a guide to help him find his way out of the underground maze.

So disoriented from his colossal screw up with Aaron, L.Z. was hopelessly lost among the confusing thoroughfares beneath the stadium. He could hear the beginning of the festival in the form of screaming fans and booming bass but was unsure how to navigate from where he walked to the sounds.

The coliseum doubled as a sports arena, and he ended up in a long hall that looked like an outlet for locker rooms. He suddenly heard a muffled scream that was separate from the concert chaos.

"You hear that?"

Rex's voice was so unexpected, L.Z.'s feet cleared the floor when he jumped in surprise.

"Shit! Yes, I…"

"Quiet! Listen…"

L.Z. was about to point out that he could hardly listen with Rex's high decibel demand between his own ears. Then he heard the sound again, along with the unmistakable din of a scuffle.

"Over there!"

L.Z. ignored the fact that it was impossible to discern to which direction Rex referred, as he timidly rounded a corner into a dark stunted hallway lined with doors which were probably locked tight until hockey season. He stopped dead in his tracks when he saw what they'd heard, and realized it was still in progress.

A man hunkered over a fiercely struggling woman. L.Z. didn't know if the assailant had stuffed something in her mouth or gagged her, but her attempted screams were heartbreaking.

They were almost as heartbreaking as L.Z.'s flush of shame because of his hesitance and uncertainty. He was no hero and, even if the tendency was there, the brawn and skill he'd need to overcome the aggressor in the shadows were not. Besides, his arm, while out of the sling, was still tender from his bike accident weeks before.

But as he struggled to decide whether to act – or run – he suddenly *knew* what he should do and not because of a flash of conscience or uncharacteristic heroic competence, but because a voice told him exactly what to do and how.

Later he would wonder if he really *was* a hero waiting for a cause. Or if his resounding failure with Aaron had left him with a need for validation. Or maybe it was the flash of the victim's Peg-like curly blond hair that gave him superhuman abilities. He'd never know what enabled him to follow through with the swift and effective directions that filled his head in exclusion of all else; he only knew that it worked. In fact, it almost worked too well, and that's what troubled him the most.

After planting a kick squarely between the prone man's spread legs, effectively disabling him, L.Z. jumped with full weight onto the man's closest leg; he didn't even hear the agonized scream. His adrenaline exploded and the ghost pain in his arm disappeared. He went into overdrive as he reacted to Rex's commands, grabbing the man's hair by the roots, and punching hard at a magic spot just behind and below his right ear. In retrospect, L.Z. realized that was probably when he'd knocked the guy out because he was dead weight when L.Z. rolled, more than flipping him, punching his throat in the spot specified by Rex. It wasn't until he had the guy in a headlock with one of his hands on the top of his head and the other

116

gripping his chin per the voice's cold guidance that L.Z. was stunned to his senses. Just before he snapped the man's neck with contrasting force between the two points, his own inner voice became louder than his instructor's.

He was about to kill this man. A man who was probably incapacitated enough with the first move, and most certainly after the second when he was knocked out.

L.Z. jerked his hands away as if the guy's head were on fire and the would-be rapist dropped to the floor with a thwack. Leaning back on his heels, L.Z. felt his sweat turn cold.

"Jesus! Why'd you stop? He's still..."

"Alive?" L.Z. finished Rex's sentence as all the strength left him and he fell onto his butt with his back against the wall.

"There's still her. You might have time..."

"Shut up!" L.Z. screamed as he moved toward the victim. The woman didn't seem to hear his senseless demand, sobbing and muttering profanities as she pushed herself farther from the immobile body and scrambled for her phone. She glanced at L.Z. with a scraped, mascara-stained face.

"Thanks. I mean, if you hadn't come..." Then, after looking at her phone, she slammed her head back against their shared wall. "Shit, there's no signal." She showed the phone to L.Z. so he could see the stagnant "911."

Rex had gone silent, but L.Z. was surprised at how strong his own voice was as he pushed to a standing position, offering a hand to the woman who oddly now looked nothing like Peg at all.

"Come on. Let's find a signal. I don't think he's going anywhere."

The crumpled unconscious figure was breathing, but his right leg extended out at an unfortunate angle.

As he helped the woman out of the passage, L.Z. took one last look at the scene.

I did that, he thought. But he felt no pride, and he also knew he hadn't done it alone.

By the time Derrick James Trumble was revived and arrested for assault and attempted rape in Salt Lake City, back in Boise, Elle took a rare outing to visit Linda, who had gotten a new blender and needed tutelage on margarita making. About the time L.Z. completed his statement to the police and said his goodbyes to Maggie, the attack victim, Peg was alone for the first time in the Manson home.

When L.Z. decided he would now be worthy of Aaron Stoss's friendship after the events since their meeting, he bought a beer and consulted his ticket for his seat location. He would watch and enjoy the Fracas Fest, carrying himself a little straighter than before. He wasn't as proud of what he did as what he didn't do. Only he – and the silent Rex – knew the distinction.

As he threw caution to the wind, doffing the more reserved part of himself, shouting, sometimes screaming, and pumping his fist to the deafening performances, Peg Warner sat in the sweltering attic space of the Boise Manson home with a flashlight propped on a beam. She knew what L.Z. didn't; Elle didn't go to the attic to "get warm" when she'd hidden there, although the 100+ degree temperature would have done the trick. In a dark corner, out of sight from the entry hatch, Peg found the boxes containing a pictorial and written chronology of Elizabeth Taylor Manson's life.

By eleven o'clock Mountain Standard Time, Elle was shitfaced with a shockingly verbose Linda, who was also well into her cups. L.Z. was weary but gratified by the heavy metal escape from all that was his world, singing and shouting until he was hoarse with the last set of the final band. And Peg had been transported, amazed, amused, and at last, overjoyed when she found what she was looking for.

And then she was confused.

Al and Abby were in bed, but that had only happened after they refined their agenda for the next day with their nephew. At the outset, it would appear to be a long overdue

119

family outing. There was no denying, however, the concerned couple's intent; it was to be an intervention.

L.Z. let himself in with the key Al and Abby had loaned him. The sign of trust wasn't lost on him, so he checked the door three times once inside to ensure it was locked. Then he pulled the code from his wallet and carefully set the alarm system. The process was as foreign to him as the GPS navigator had been just a day before, but he managed to get it done without waking the entire house and alerting the police. He'd had enough of police interaction in recent weeks to last a lifetime.

After removing his shoes and creeping up the curved staircase to his room, he took in the inviting space, noting it was bigger than the combined size of the three bedrooms in his home. And he had it for two more days.

He was physically and emotionally spent. Understandably, his arm smarted, but it felt more angry than reinjured. Sitting in the still comfort of the room, he felt as though he were in a cocoon. Almost safe, even.

He found some ibuprofen in his bag and took it before removing his hoodie and rifling through merch from the festival. All in all, he was glad he'd gone. Even with the poorly executed meeting with Aaron, and more strangely yet, after the altercation with Derrick Trumble, he would not regret the evening. As darkness crept into the side of his mind with the terrifying "almost" of the night, he deftly swept it away.

Life with Elle had conditioned him to reframe the abnormal into somehow acceptable perceptions. He'd learned to avoid, deny, and downplay things deemed as strange, to downright deranged, by the average population. So, in the hours since the more questionable elements of his evening, he'd leveled the playing field and felt almost normal, albeit even more tired than his typical exhausted state.

But then, there was the *almost*.

And there was the commanding guidance that had driven him to it.

He'd nearly killed a man. Granted, the man deserved to have his ass kicked, but L.Z. was not inclined to be a vigilante, nor be judge and jury. He was suddenly cold with dread when he let the wall drop to face reality.

He'd never summoned Rex before, but when he was suddenly aware of the presence, he didn't question the timing. He just asked the air, "How do you know that stuff? The things you told me to do tonight?"

The silence of the house felt like a vacuum as he waited. He wasn't going to beg, but he would wait. He deserved an answer. The tone of the answer that finally came was a far cry from the demanding roar that had forced him into action hours before. It sounded almost as perplexed as he felt.

"I don't know. I don't. Maybe I know it the way you know how to inspect food? How to make burgers? Do you even think about that when you do it?"

L.Z. considered the question on the surface, but when he remembered the commands, especially the last one he didn't obey, it forced him to consider it more deeply. He closed his eyes and shook his head with a shudder, no longer able to ignore the fact that he had been a nanosecond away from being an executioner. Sitting on the edge of the bed, he exhaled as he crafted his answer which was more bait than a real response.

"I know those things because they are what I do. What I've done for years."

"Exactly."

And, exactly, L.Z. thought. It took all he had to control his nausea when he asked,

"So, Rex, I make burgers and you kill people? Is that it?"

His voice was calm, but his breath was so constricted he became lightheaded. The silence after his question was palpable, but with every ounce of strength he had, he waited till the answer came.

"Maybe I was a cop? Maybe a soldier. Did you think about that? Maybe I protected people."

In the hush of the big home, L.Z. flipped off the light and stared at nothing while facing an ugly truth. He knew, without knowing how, the voice haunting him and living inside him had never been a hero. He felt the savage energy that had filled his being just hours before and it had nothing to do with *protection.*

In the darkness of L.Z.'s skull, Rex knew it too.

And in the hallway outside L.Z.'s room, Abby leaned her head against the doorframe and bit her lip. Tomorrow's intervention couldn't come soon enough.

The next morning, L.Z. awoke with a start, bathed in sweat. He laid perfectly still, eyes round and darting. For the first time since the sleep disturbance had started, he remembered his dream.

There was no way he could forget the searing image of a man stealthily slipping behind another and slitting his throat in one smooth move.

With a metallic taste in his mouth, he sat up, still dazed, seeing red drops on his pillow. When he wiped his mouth of more blood, he wasn't surprised as much as he was sickened. The blood made sense in a way he didn't want to explore, although he couldn't ignore the sensory memory as it invaded every cavity of his mind.

The killer in the dream had bitten his lip while working to control his own breathing just before he stole his victim's last breath. He'd drawn his own blood and the victim's at exactly the same time, feeling no pain or regret for either.

Of these things, L.Z. was certain. He was as certain as he was familiar with the killer. The killer in the dream was the same person who'd left blood on L.Z.'s pillow.

The killer in the dream was L.Z.

Over breakfast, L.Z. sheepishly explained away his swollen lip with a weak story of mosh pit behavior common to heavy metal concerts. Abby and Al responded with comical expressions of horror, but made light of it all, knowing more serious conversations loomed ahead later in the day.

Although they had plans to visit the local attractions, the Mansons had only walked about Temple Square outside the historic Salt Lake Mormon Temple and lunched at a nearby restaurant when they could see the younger man was less up to the challenge than they were, despite their age differences. It was understandable, considering the rock festival along with the added excitement of the rescue, which he had shared, but stripped the story down to bare bones.

They decided to forgo most of the agenda but agreed to visit Hogle Zoo. It was an easy sell for L.Z. because it was exactly the kind of simple distraction he craved, not to mention, at thirty, he'd never been to a zoo in his life.

That tidbit of information was enough to convince Al who mentally added the fact to the list of motherhood failings on his sister's part. That his nephew had never been to a zoo was as serious in his mind as the young man's mental and emotional health which troubled Abby. Al and Abby were wired very differently, but one reason behind their success as husband and wife was, they invariably ended up in the same place even if they took different routes.

While the stroll through the animal exhibits offered an excellent venue for Abby to gingerly begin a conversation with their nephew, she held back when Al gave her a small shake of his head, his sharp eyes falling on L.Z. as he watched the giraffes with a look of wonder. He'd never really been an animal guy, but seeing the magnificent creatures before him, L.Z. was transfixed. And the haunted look he'd worn since arriving seemed to lift. Abby acquiesced, figuring home might be a better place for their talk anyway.

What they'd ascertained was partly correct; L.Z. was amazed and transported by the animals. All the things he disliked about people were completely absent in the creatures who roamed artificial habitats. They were what they were, and L.Z. felt an ease he hadn't felt for a while. But more than what filled his senses, he found relief in what wasn't there; Rex was not only silent, but the shadow he cast even when quiet was absent. It was one of those days when he just wasn't there. What Al and Abby saw was what L.Z. felt; respite and something very close to joy.

That was until they continued through the African Savanna, beyond the giraffes, and found Lion's Hill. While Abby read about the prides' dynamics and Al, general-turned-mush-ball, cooed over a set of playful cubs, L.Z. wandered a few steps away to take in the adult lions.

Two great tawny males lay together in grass and flowers, so still and innocent, one could forget their prowess. Their lethality. L.Z. studied them with innocent amusement, a smile playing across his lips as he remembered that one of his few toys as a child had been a stuffed lion, Mufasa from the movie Lion King. He'd loved that thing, remembering with a bitter stab that his mother had taken him quickly from the last bed he'd shared with the toy, loading herself and L.Z. in the VW with none of their belongings, never to return.

Pushing away the memory, as he was prone to do, L.Z. tipped his head, still staring at the beasts, imagining how the largest male's fur would feel. Just as he was about to turn away, the lion's eyes shifted slightly and seemed to lock on his own. And just like that, he could see the predator, and the realization cleared his emotional slate like an etch-a-sketch, leaving a newly familiar feeling. Cold, fast, and deadly. It continued to stare, not aggressively, but confidently and with control. L.Z. hadn't even noticed he was no longer alone.

"Look hard, my friend. He has what you lack…and you'd have to safari his ass without my help. I'd…"

The weeks of intrusion, the silent haunting, and the previous night's revelation which L.Z. blamed for the dream, all seemed to explode from the place that was so still just seconds ago.

"What I *lack?* What I'd like to lack is you! Your *help* almost made me kill that guy last night and your help made me do it in my dream. You are nothing but…"

Suddenly L.Z. realized he was shouting at the glass in front of him which bore spit droplets from his outburst. Through the spattered screen, the lion was unimpressed, dropping his gaze to lick his giant paws.

L.Z. closed his eyes tightly as situational awareness and dread crept through him.

"L.Z., son. What is it? Abby was worried…" He heard Al's voice next to him and dropped his forehead against the glass in resignation. Of course, Rex fell silent and was no help at all.

With a sharp inhale, L.Z. lifted his head and turned toward his uncle; Abby was next to him with a grave expression. He could feel other eyes on him and wished, hard, for one of those Utah earthquakes to open the ground wide open right then and just take him.

After being ushered to a bench nearby, the Mansons all sat. No one spoke for what seemed like an eternity. L.Z. evaluated what had just transpired, including his uncle's words and his aunt's face. He remembered Abby's profession. He remembered all the times over the years Al would gently prod, trying to assess the impact Elle had on the boy.

The picture of what today and this entire "open arms" visit was about emerged in his head, and he felt exposed and ashamed. He felt defensive, but there was no power behind it when he leaned forward, elbows on knees, and stared at the pavement.

"It's not like I hear *voices* or anything…" As soon as he said it, he knew he was done for. He glanced at them; Al turned his head with a look of disdain that L.Z. knew wasn't for him — he'd seen Al lay it on Elle too many times before and knew the man was cursing his only sister. Abby, however, searched L.Z.'s eyes with such concern and compassion that he caved instantly.

"Well. A voice. One voice. *Okay, I hear a voice.*" There. He'd said it.

And if he could get past the terror of disclosure welling within him, he could almost discern something else. Relief.

The groan in his head told him his brain-boarder felt something else entirely.

Peg knew Elle was delusional. Even as she'd crocheted the pseudo potholders to be used as transmission jammers, she'd known that. She had also taken advantage of the woman's disorders when she concocted the nicotine-satellite sensor scam to get Elle to smoke outside because she couldn't stand the smoke indoors. She might have felt guilty over the deception if she didn't have a half dozen more significant things to feel guilty about.

Among her other detective work in L.Z.'s absence, Peg clandestinely researched delusional behavior online to try to better understand Elle. She didn't desire hard information, just the basics. She had reasons for her curiosity, besides the fact she lived with the woman 24/7, which was motivation enough.

There were several categories of delusions, but after having lived with Elle for weeks, she settled on "mixed." Elle exhibited every facet of having "grandiose" aspects to her behavior with an over-inflated sense of worth, power, knowledge, or identity. She certainly believed she was sought after, if not stalked, for her supreme intellect and knowledge base. That, along with her complaints of being spied upon, suggested she had the tendency toward persecutory delusions.

Peg would have also thrown in "erotomania," considering some of Elle's grander claims of being sought after and having had affairs with an impressive list of big-name lovers. But after her excavation of the attic boxes, Peg

129

stumbled across indications that the woman had been at least familiar, if not intimate, with men Peg was startled to recognize in the faded Polaroids. And they weren't casual poses, by any means. While she felt fairly certain Elle had not conquered Robert Redford any more than she'd had to get a restraining order against Warren Beatty as claimed, there appeared to be a few legitimate fires to the smoke of the old girl's past.

Just like Peg had told L.Z., there was some *really real* reality buried in the playground of Elle's mind. Hadn't the Poldats' appearance proven something, after all?

So, some delusions, some notoriety, and a lot of mystery made up Elizabeth Taylor Manson. Peg was slowly assembling a mosaic of the woman with pieces of the past and present because she, herself, had vested interest in the family's future. The family, of course, included L.Z., whom she was surprised to find she missed during his absence. And whom she was aware could be more like his mother than he would ever admit. She'd written in her journal,

> *I know that he knows that I know he hears voices,*
> *I mean, he had to be talking to someone those times he*
> *was really talking even though no one else was there.*
> *But just because he knows I know doesn't mean he'll*
> *talk to me about it. I wonder if I should try. I wonder*
> *who it is that he hears. And why don't I think he's*
> *crazy? I wonder if he thinks he's crazy.*

She now knew that some of Elle's potential mental health disorders could be hereditary. Peg had no doubt L.Z. was similarly aware.

She couldn't put her nail-chewed finger on why she didn't believe he had inherited anything other than a dysfunctional way of life and an attic of bizarre artifacts, but she was willing to find out if she was wrong. She looked forward to it.

L.Z. was due back later that day. Elle had survived a monstrous hangover the day before, which made for a quiet day overall, once Peg disposed of Linda's creepy brother. Unlike the Uber driver, Elle wasn't anxious to keep the guy around once the bedroom fireworks sizzled and the tequila's effects faded. Peg wouldn't share that tidbit with L.Z.

As Elle feverishly pounded out e-mails to the CDC about an upcoming pandemic she foresaw, Peg channeled Betty Crocker and puttered around the kitchen to cook her first ever real meal for this family. As far as she could tell, L.Z. was oblivious to her thoughts and feelings, and for now, that was fine.

He didn't need to know that she was cooking up a lot more than a welcome home dinner.

About the time L.Z. pulled into his driveway after an uneventful but overly thoughtful trip home, Al came home from work in Salt Lake City to find Abby in her office on the second floor of their home.

They'd barely had time to process their long heart-to-heart with L.Z. the night before. Abby had taken the lead, partially because the "intervention" was her idea, partly because she was the only one of the two even remotely qualified to deal with the situation, and finally, because Al was out of his league with what they learned.

He was not only conflicted with the feedback his wife had given his nephew, but he was conflicted about what he believed. About what he felt.

Now, Abby turned from her computer and folded her hands on the desk.

"OK, go ahead," was all she said as he dropped his heavy frame into the chair opposite her. They'd been together long enough to dispense with preliminaries, especially if it was time to clear the air.

He leaned back and crossed his legs to try to seem less intense. She saw right through it, of course, and bit back a smile.

"I get the recommendation to see a shrink…I mean, *pardon me*, a counsellor," his elastic face gave way to the smile that could charm the socks off a Gestapo guard. But his eyes held hers and she knew he meant business. "But a medium? And a priest, for God's sake? The only exposure that boy has had to God is the number of times Elle swears in His name, and that number would be infinite, by the way. You're a trained professional, Honey. And he's my...our..."

"Nephew. And he's your godson, without the title. He's the son you wanted. And he's in a world of trouble, Al."

Al leaned forward, putting his elbows on the desk, resting his chin on his laced fingers. They stared at each other, and she marveled, not for the first or tenth time, how a brilliant, accomplished, grown man could also be so idealistic, almost naïve.

"Abs, a medium? Seriously? Have you seen that nutty woman on TV? The boy already lives with Elle, for God's sake, why would you complete the deal by sending him to another fruitcake, just of another brand?"

Abby fingered a FedEx envelope on her desk, pulling out the contents as she eyed her husband.

"Because he must find what works for him. I don't know what he believes, but he's scared. That dream, Al, that's scary to me."

"Exactly," he leapt up, and began pacing, showing the early signs of going full-on-Al as his thoughts ramped up. His gestures were in sync as he argued his case. "It is damn scary, Abs! He's hearing voices. His mom is whack a doodle from the word go and you know as well as I do that stuff can jump from mother to son, even if it's delayed. He's not only hearing a voice, but he's responding to it. He named it, for God's sake! He's filled the checklist. He's your textbook case, Dr. Manson. He's…"

"He's off-the-charts believable and shows absolutely none of the other signs associated with delusional behavior or even schizophrenia. But I will not treat or diagnose our own nephew, thus the referral to a mental health professional. And I will also not be arrogant enough to assume that my chosen field of study has all the answers, thus I recommended he explore other alternatives. *And* even after years of study and even more years of practice, I still give some credence to what my gut tells me." She looked up at Al, who had also stopped, mid-pace, with one finger frozen in the air which had been placed to help accent his last un-made argument.

He dropped his hand and crossed his arms, staring at the floor. When he looked up, she pinned him with her eyes.

"Your gut," he said, quietly.

"Yeah, my gut, which is telling me the same thing as yours. This ain't 'crazy-Elle' simple." The fact that she used one of Al's nicknames for his sister, which she'd condemned, spoke volumes. She had leveled the playing field and hit one low.

He had no more fight because there was nothing to fight. No agreeing to disagree, because, without him having to admit it, they were on the same page, and it was wholly unfamiliar to both.

He exhaled, cocked his head, smiling slyly as he walked around the desk and offered his hand.

"My dear, may I have the honor of escorting you downstairs for fine dining? Mac and cheese, perhaps? With some fine chianti?"

She did not take his hand but stood with a tube she'd withdrawn from the mailer.

"Sounds like a deal, you silver-tongued devil, after you give up some spit. Here. Fill it to the line!"

He stepped back, throwing up his hands, eyebrows raised. "Excuse me?"

She patted the envelope and said, "Find-Your-Family.com. As long as we're doing a deep Manson dig, I say we go all the way. Come on now, swish and spit!"

With a dour expression, he complied, having to work a bit to hit the spill line. Once he finished, she reached for the tube to secure it with the stopper. He yanked it back with an exaggerated look of suspicion, leaning down, closing the near-foot gap in their heights.

"Waaait a minute. You aren't trying to prove a connection to you-know-who, are you?" He held her gaze, keeping the vial out of her reach.

She poked him in his only known tickle-spot, which gave her enough advantage to grab the spit collection from his hand. "Of course not. Manson-*no-relation,* remember?

135

Besides, that Charles couldn't possibly be related to *my* Charles. *That Charles* had women lined up for days. He might have been insane, but man, he had it going on..." She stoppered the tube, stuck it back in the envelope, wiggling her eyebrows at him as she walked out of the room.

He stood dumbstruck as he processed what she'd said. His finger was back in the air as he hustled out of the room.

"Hey, now, Missy, just a dang minute!" He raced after her to defend his honor.

Rex experienced L.Z.'s homecoming exactly the way he experienced everything, through L.Z.'s eyes and ears. From the looks of the dinner on the table, he was glad they didn't share olfactory glands and taste buds as well.

Unlike dinner, Peg was looking good. Better than usual, in fact. He noted she had taken care to tame her hair, wear something that wasn't shapeless and, if L.Z. would look at her long enough, he'd be able to see she was actually wearing make-up. He noticed that kind of shit, but apparently L.Z. was a eunuch and missed every cue that the chick was prime and ready, giving off all the signals. Opportunity was wasted on those with bodies, he thought from his elusive place.

As it was, he was forced to examine some kind of roadkill that might have once been – chicken? Pork, maybe? And the sauce on that unidentified protein-ish product along with noodles was so watery it probably would have done well to float in bowls rather than to slosh within the near flooding conditions of plates. There was a bowl of green stuff one could only hope was supposed to be green. The old broad, Elle, looked as rough around the edges as usual and barely picked at her food. Of course, she looked like she was on a 200 calorie a day diet anyway, so, *whatever.*

While Elle prattled on about some oncoming Asian pandemic that she was trying to warn the government about, L.Z.'s view vacillated among the plates. He occasionally shot glances at Peg who was looking back at him *every time.*

Rex strained to stay quiet. In fact, his latest efforts were to avoid detection at all. He didn't know how L.Z. sensed him, but there was something and as long as there was *something,* he felt sure he could slowly reduce it into an acceptable *nothing* without eliminating himself.

Himself; whomever or whatever he was.

He'd spent nearly the entire way home trying to casually convince L.Z. he was harmless. He'd even made him laugh a couple of times. Between the too-clear-cut fight directions the night of the concert and hearing the idiot tell the Mansons he "heard a voice," damage control was paramount for his survival. If he'd been "present" during L.Z.'s conversation with Al and Abby, he would have gone into overdrive to head off any kind of outside treatment or intervention. Unfortunately, he'd involuntarily checked out during the conversation and didn't resurface until L.Z. was driving out of Salt Lake.

He wasn't sure what was more maddening, what he knew or what he didn't know.

He still didn't know who he was or what was happening, where he went between awakenings, or where he'd come from. He didn't know why he just faded into blackness, only to pop back in with no concept of lost time. These mysteries would probably have pushed him over the edge if he had an edge. But his time was chopped and limited with little opportunity to ponder or solve, although he was getting better at withdrawing from L.Z.'s active goings-on to deliberate with himself.

What he *knew* was that he was made from a much stronger mold than L.Z. He knew he had either once had great capacity or was *intended* to. He knew he had skills he was unable to use and wouldn't know what they were until he was freed, or until opportunities arose such as the beating of the shitbag at the stadium a few nights before. He knew he had a will and was accustomed to exerting it. He had a core sense of superiority, of power. Of brilliance.

But as it was, he had the worst sense of being all dressed up with nowhere to go.

L.Z. coughed, causing Rex to focus on the here and now. To the boy's credit, he could see L.Z.'s plate was almost empty; Rex wondered if the cough had actually been a gag.

138

He got a flash of Elle's empty place; she must have gone away while he was thinking. Wait. *What?*

He was *thinking!* He'd been there, quite possibly unnoticed, and was...

Nothing.

Just like that, he *wasn't.*

He was gone again.

Elle sat back down, cigarette pack in hand for her after-dinner soirée on the patio.

"I'm telling ya, if they don't get ahead of this thing, it'll shut our country down. I'm doing what I can, but I don't think our CDC is ready or funded." The information sounded as though it scraped her throat on its way out. L.Z. looked at his mom with renewed interest. He was used to her abrasive voice, but it was the tone that threw him off. She sounded uncharacteristically grounded.

"Oh, you finally tuned in, Leddy? I done said it five ways since you sat down. I was starting to think you wasn't listening. Like *that's* something new."

What was new to L.Z. was coming home to dinner on the table. His mother was correct with respect to the fact that he'd tuned her out as much as possible up to this point. It had taken all he had to choke down Peg's well-intended attempt

139

to make what he thought was supposed to be chicken cacciatore. He still hadn't identified the pale green stuff in a bowl he hadn't sampled.

It was also new to him to have feelings for a woman. Contrary to Rex's assessment, L.Z. had noticed Peg's effort to jazz up her appearance. And the fact the dinner was on the night of his homecoming wasn't lost on him.

But he also needed to seize the moments when his mom was in a bearable state, so he turned his attention to her, hoping he'd choked down enough dinner to appease Peg.

"Why do you think this thing is going to happen, Mom? You were saying something about a virus?"

Elle looked at her son as if he couldn't see a spider right in front of him.

"Leddy, you know I know things." She looked at Peg, who was looking at L.Z., but jerked her head away when Elle pecked her arm with a finger. "I don't know if I told you, but sometimes I just know things and then they happen."

L.Z. had a familiar sinking feeling as he realized he'd judged his mom's level state prematurely. She was just on another tangent after all. She was, however, eerily in tune with her son's thoughts.

"Did you go and forget I predicted 911?" She asked her son but gave the wide-eyed Peg a knowing nod before adding, "I also warned about that Malaysian Airline Flight 370. And the Haiti earthquake. And then there's Whitney Houston's death. I called that. Not to mention…"

L.Z. raised a hand. "I'll give you those, Ma." Peg was interested now, leaning her elbows on the table with a look of delight as L.Z. continued, "And you also told me they would catch Osama bin Laden, like, the day before it happened."

Elle stood with a look of triumph, snatching her cigarettes, and heading for the door. "So, remember this, young man, when a virus hits the world like a freight train and turns it all upside down."

As soon as Elle was outside, L.Z. looked past Peg and said to the door, "Oh, and she also predicted the world would end in 2006, that the Russians would blow themselves up three years ago, and that Mel Gibson would overcome his scandals and emerge as a last-minute candidate for the 2016 presidential campaign and win the election as a write-in with an overwhelming majority."

His eyes landed on Peg's, and she smiled. She didn't know who Mel Gibson was, wasn't sure what a pandemic was, but was impressed by Elle's accuracy on the predictions she'd nailed. L.Z. could see the girl was on the fence with his mother's potential clairvoyance, so he turned the tables with,

"She's a little less accurate with past events. She still doesn't believe we landed on the moon."

"Which we did *not* do." L.Z. jumped at the sound of his mother's voice, looking around, confused, as it continued, "I'd be delighted to remind you of the facts tonight after I order a case of face masks which will disappear from the market as soon as the virus hits our shores."

Peg smirked as she pointed at the patio-facing window L.Z. hadn't realized was open. He stood and pushed it down with, "You do that, Ma."

Now the window was closed, and he and Peg were alone. She looked at him expectantly.

He suddenly felt uncomfortable and almost wished Rex were there to give him some pointers on how to proceed with Peg. He nearly laughed at the notion; for weeks he would have sold his soul to get rid of the damn voice and the force behind it.

He sat back down at the table and thanked her for the lovely meal. It was the least he could do, not to mention he had no idea what else to say.

"But you didn't try everything!" L.Z.'s heart sank as Peg lifted the bowl of questionable-looking green food. As soon as she offered it, she said,

"I'm carrying around a lot of emotional cabbage."

He stopped, both of them holding the serving dish as he processed her statement. Her huge smile started to falter during the pause. He caught onto her quip just in time and laughed more loudly than the joke merited.

She had not only spruced up and cooked, or at least tried to cook dinner, but had concocted and delivered a pun for dessert.

She glowed as he continued with a forced chuckle, scooping a tiny portion of the purported cabbage onto his plate, with the disclaimer that he liked cabbage, but it didn't like him. He patted his stomach and she nodded understandingly.

With a sudden guilty expression, she burst out, "L.Z., I've been thinking about a lot of things and there is stuff I need to tell you."

He froze; because he thought he knew where she was going with this, he found himself at a sudden decision point. He had been emboldened by his full disclosure to his aunt and uncle, and because he thought he knew what Peg was going to say, in a very un-L.Z. fashion, he made his own proclamation.

"Peg, I've been hearing a voice in my head. For a while now."

She squinted, confused.

He stammered, feeling flustered after his spontaneous confession.

"I, well, I guess I just thought you should know."

She tipped her head and shrugged.

"L.Z., I already knew that. But thanks for telling me."

He blinked wordlessly and she suddenly looked unsure of what she should say next. She bit her lip as she pulled a string of limp cabbage from the bowl in the awkward silence. Putting an end in her mouth, she sucked the rest in like a noodle.

Although she'd stolen his thunder, he was somewhat relieved she already knew his secret. But he was a mile off on what he thought she wanted to disclose, disappointed that she seemed to back off what was on her mind. He knew he'd missed the boat when she crossed her arms, leaned on the table, and said,

"How about your concert thing, anyway? How were the skin guys? And did you meet the guitar dude?"

"SKinKneaders. And Aaron Stoss. Yeah, good. But weren't you going to tell me something?" He nearly strangled on the last words, but he really wanted to get their feelings out in the air.

She reddened, fanning her hand in front of her face and shook her head, "Oh, it's no big deal...just dug up some bones while you were gone. It can wait."

She had no idea of the power of her words. L.Z. dove into the cabbage stuff, as to not reveal his sudden apprehension. His mind filled with the images from his dream the night before. The dream where he'd buried a body, someone he'd watched himself kill.

Dug up some bones?

He shoveled in food he mercifully couldn't taste as he wondered just how much else she knew.

She stared at him, confused as to what had set his hair on fire. She stood, disappointed in herself for losing her nerve, and started clearing the table.

She let him recover and dropped hope of any more conversation.

She didn't really want to know about the stupid concert thing anyway.

L.Z. thought he was dying. His lungs felt as though they were full of holes. His chest felt ablaze, and he had trouble breathing. And his eyes burned, but that was probably because of the salt in the sweat rimming his lashes.

The only thing keeping him going was the pounding bass in his head, compliments of his earbuds…and it also distracted him from the depressing sounds of his sneakers plodding on the pavement at a way-too-slow cadence.

L.Z. Manson was jogging for the first time in his life and with every step, he suspected it would be the last.

145

Since he hadn't replaced his bicycle after the unfortunate tangle with the UPS truck, he'd become quite fond of driving. The downside of the deal was he'd lost conditioning, but more importantly, biking to and from work and about town had been his one and only stress reducer. It was a cruel fate that his singular fitness mode disappeared when his stress level was at an all-time high.

His co-worker Keith was a runner and suggested L.Z. give it a try. L.Z. figured it would require no investment other than time, but now he wondered if it would cost him his life.

It was his day off, however, and the alternative was to stay home and discuss how his and Elle's alien DNA would probably make them immune to the imminent pandemic. Or hang out with Peg who was rapidly becoming an enigma, he just didn't have the energy to unravel. Or worse yet, think about his latest too-real dream. He wasn't sure what bothered him more; the violence by his own hands, or the ease with which the dream-L.Z. stalked and killed victims who were complete strangers to the awake-L.Z. When he could capture the details upon awakening, he was further disturbed if not intrigued by the knowledge level of the dream-L.Z. on weaponry and assault techniques. And those thoughts always led him down one path, and that was directly to Rex and the night he issued such commanding and precise orders nearly leading to a real-life murder.

So, he ran. Or jogged. Or slowly *trotted*. And he kept going, despite his physical distress because on some level he was running from all the alternatives.

He didn't know if Rex was there and didn't want to know. Between the blasting music and what felt like cardiac arrest, he hoped to overwhelm the unwanted presence.

His playlist switched from a too-fast tune by Amaranth to a recent SKinKneader song...one written by Aaron. L.Z. was no longer humiliated when he thought of or heard Aaron. He felt a strengthened bond which he couldn't explain, and the notion was about to become reinforced. The beat of the song, Blind, was of an exact pace which allowed L.Z. to keep going without depriving his brain of needed oxygen. To further his conviction that there was a yet unreconciled connection between himself and Aaron, the lyrics played directly into the resolution of the dilemma he'd faced since returning from Salt Lake City: to seek help, or to proceed blind with his situation.

I'm blind, I'm blind, I'm blind, I'm told

But maybe I choose to keep my eyes closed

If I don't look, don't think, don't try to see,

What's chasing, biting, and shouting, can't get me,

I hear it, feel it, it's even in my dreams,

But if I close my eyes, maybe I won't scream.

But I can't make it go, if I don't come clean,

Only if I face it, can I be redeemed.

L.Z. stopped, gasping as much from exertion as from the mini explosion in his brain.

He paused the music and leaned, hands on knees, as he tried to catch his breath. In bursts, he said aloud to himself,

"I can...only make it go...if I come clean." He stood straight and wiped his face with the back of his hand. He thought of Aaron Stoss and nodded in thanks with his eyes closed. "I have to face it."

"Now that I can think in here, I'm glad to hear it. It's about time you came clean with Peg, or whatever you call it in your little mind, to get it off the ground...or get her on the ground, if you know what I mean... What's up, you dying or what, partner?"

So, Rex had been there. L.Z. didn't answer but instead blasted the music back on and picked up his pace to a quick trudge, motored by the satisfaction of drowning Rex out. And by having decided to take his Aunt Abby's advice along with Aaron's indirect advice.

He was coming around, and Aaron would too. Some day.

Almost 2000 miles from where L.Z. slogged back toward his home, Aaron Stoss sat in a hotel room in downtown

Cincinnati. He had just gotten up, smacking his mouth, tasting stale remnants of the previous night's post show party. Sitting on the edge of the mattress, he reached for water from the bedside table, knocking his wallet to the floor. After taking a long slug from the bottle to soften the sandpaper that had replaced his tongue, he bent to retrieve his billfold. He groaned as he noticed cash and random other items had escaped onto the floor.

He scooped it all up with one hand, holding his pounding head with the other. He stopped halfway to standing when he saw a folded notepaper jutting from the others. It was from that guy backstage in Salt Lake City...Manson. *L.D.? L.Z.?* The one he'd tried to forget.

Aaron was alone in the room, and yet he implored to the air,

"Are you there? Don't fuck with me now! I could really use some help here!"

Nothing. Not that he'd been able to summon the "anything" before, it pretty much just came, and he always kept a small, battered notebook in his back pocket for those moments. It obviously wasn't one of those moments though, and he knew he'd have to handle this; this whatever it was. This *situation*. Unfolding the note, he read the name at the bottom: L.Z. Manson.

The guy with the fucked-up name knew too much.

Elle hunker-walked as to not hit her head on the beams of the attic. She was having a "good day," as L.Z. would call it when he thought she was out of earshot. Her son's rendition of her "good days" were often a little depressing for her. On days like this, she could see her own life more clearly and it caused a rare humble outlook, making her unbearably weary. She knew she was erratic, and that she could be arrogant and unkind. She questioned some of her own theories and recent rants – the ones she could remember. She felt badly for Leddy whom she knew devoted his life to her well-being.

There was a certain invincibility that came with her more typical demeanor, which was accompanied by a high. The opposite was a feeling of intolerable vulnerability, and the inevitable low. *Damn Sir Isaac Newton.*

Leddy was out and Peg was on the patio talking to her family back in Oregon, which was apparently more like a tribe, so Elle knew she had time to get into her private space in the attic and hopefully stay undetected. Today's mission was simple, free of goddesses, alien communication, or desire to hide. She had secreted away her life in a corner of this attic. Many of the things she knew her son disbelieved could be proven by the contents of these boxes and containers and, conversely, many of her more manic assertions could be disproved. She liked to control the balance, so she kept her universe tucked away. Sometimes she came up to check things just because she often didn't know the difference between her best memories and what was not real at all.

Least important to her, but of potential great interest to Leddy and any would-be burglars, were the trunks under all the other things, furthest against the wall. Everyone should have a nest-egg for a rainy day and there was no way Elizabeth Taylor Manson would trust a banking institution with her life's earnings (and the balance which hadn't exactly been earned but had been accumulated).

Damn but it was hot up there. She started to sweat as she moved boxes around looking for one with souvenirs from her European travels, travels Leddy didn't believe she ever took. His face the night the Poldats visited had been priceless! Never striving to prove what was real and what wasn't with her son was one of her few effective leverage points and she intended to keep it that way. She was only digging in today because it was Linda's birthday, and she thought a nice memento from Germany or Italy would be a good gift for her only real friend whom she was sure was of European heritage.

She paused and ran her hand across one of the boxes with her most secret and revealing treasures; it contained photographs and documents. As she glanced at the seams of the closure, her whole body stiffened.

"No," she whispered and pulled out her flashlight to examine the flaps. "No!" she said more loudly as she moved the box and inspected the one beneath it which held similar valuables. This one too! A hand flew to her mouth, and she gasped.

Someone had been in her things. Because she trusted no one, she always employed rudimentary methods of detection control.

She had been violated in her own home.

And just like that, "lucid Elle" spiraled out of center, and the brilliant, hyper-aware Elle ripped the boxes open to discern what had been touched, or worse yet, taken.

She needed to know which of her enemies, person, or agency, had excavated into her life. And why.

"*Fuckers.* You have no idea who you're dealing with," she muttered as she carefully catalogued her greatest treasures in the forms of photos, letters, journals, and documents. Her mind was afire, and she was filled with energy enough to bring them all down.

Meanwhile, the real culprit, not the CIA, NSA, or some other mortal enemy, was on the patio speaking to her sister on the phone. Peg hadn't seen the booby traps on the boxes the night she'd found Elle's photos and letters any more than she could see Elle spinning out of control just thirty feet above her.

She was on a mission of her own.

"I know I'm asking a lot, Aja. I know," Peg hung her head as she rubbed her eyes. She'd been dreading this conversation, but she needed her sister's help. "But it's really important to me. Maybe the most important thing in my life."

"I just don't know if you know what you're asking of me," Aja said with a tone of admonishment.

The conversation was somewhat ironic considering that even with Peg's wayward ways, she was considerably more stable than her sister, yet her sister was an analyst in a DNA lab. Aja was brilliant, but with her fine-tuned brains came liabilities like a slightly loose moral compass and undependable moods. It was the moral compass thing Peg was exploiting with her request and her own conscience was already screaming.

"I know. And I know you could lose your job. But…but you are the smartest person I know, and you've always been my savior. When I can't count on anyone else, I have you." Peg felt her stomach lurch because Aja was the last person in the world to whom she wanted to be beholden. She also felt a twinge of guilt because she was using Aja's own game to get what she wanted; her sister had been a master manipulator her whole life. And she also had the biggest ego of anyone Peg knew; she was banking on this factor with her last statement.

And it worked.

"Well, you're right there, Peglet," Peg felt a leap of hope when Aja used her childhood nickname. Aja continued with her special air of superiority. "There's not much you could ask that I couldn't pull off, it's a matter of being willing to take the risk and…"

Peg joined her sister, finishing the line she'd heard so many times, "…*risk is my middle name.*"

She'd hooked and reeled her sister in. But, like she'd said, it was probably the most important thing in her life right now and she needed to get it right.

Aja told her to get a pencil and paper, then proceeded to tell her exactly what "Peglet" needed to do on her end to fulfill the extraordinary request.

L.Z. turned away from the dry stock after checking dates on bun packages and headed to review produce when Britney C. limped in through the back door. He sighed and waited for her to explain. He really didn't want to know what she had to say, but as she was the reigning drama queen at the Garden City Red Missile Burgers, he knew the story was forthcoming whether he cared or not. It wasn't so much that he didn't care, it was that he didn't trust she was genuinely hurt; he'd watch her closely to see if she kept track of which leg was injured, noting she currently favored the right leg.

She leaned heavily against the fridge as she explained the trauma. She claimed to have fallen on the stairs at home before coming to work.

"My ankle…it 'prolly isn't broke, but it might be strained or sprained or whatever." She raised her eyebrows hopefully at the poker-faced L.Z. He nodded understandingly and walked around her to check how morning prep was coming, stopping next to Keith who watched with amusement. L.Z. glanced back as she hobbled toward him, now favoring her left leg.

He stopped and looked at her gravely and said,

"I'm not at all surprised that happened. I don't trust stairs. Know why?"

With a twinge of impatience, she lifted her right foot with an exaggerated wince. "No, why?"

He snapped his fingers and pointed at her with his reply, "Because they're *always up to something.*"

Keith cracked up, slapping L.Z. on the back.

Britney stared, obviously confused over what was so funny, and hobbled after L.Z. His phone buzzed in his pocket, and he headed for the office; he was expecting a message.

"But L.Z.…think I should maybe go, like, put it on ice or something?"

As he fished his phone out, he said, "Maybe first you should figure out which one of those ankles might, like, need ice or something." He wore an expression of faux concern while glancing at his phone. Britney, her grave injury, and his own awesome joke vanished from his mind as he scanned the incoming texts from his Aunt Abby. She'd wasted no time answering his query from earlier that morning.

Unfortunately, as he read the second message, he felt his mouth twitch even before he heard Rex within the housing of his brain.

"Wait, what? An appointment with a shrink? What for? Dude...that won't help solve anything. That's not the kind of help I, I mean we, need. I'm real."

L.Z. closed the door so he could respond.

"Well, if that's true, then you have nothing to worry about, right? But if it's not, I'm sure they have some pills that will make you just go away..."

There was a notable pause before Rex replied in a calmer voice.

"OK, just thinking of you. Do you know anything about psych meds and what that shit does to you? Side effects? Do you..."

"No, in fact, I don't. So, how do *you* know?" L.Z. did a mental fist pump. He was getting pretty good at Rex management; if only he could erase the pest completely and get his life back.

Silence again. L.Z. shoved the phone in his pocket and waited.

"Don't I get a vote?" was all Rex said.

L.Z. laughed out loud. He was so exhausted from serial nightmares now, things that would have never been funny before were becoming hilarious. Once he calmed down, he cleared his throat and headed back for the door as he answered.

"Why should you? *I* didn't. Apparently, this hearing voices thing isn't a democratic process."

But sometime between when Rex asked the question and L.Z. answered, the discussion was over. L.Z. could feel it — or *not* feel it – he tiredly mused. He paused to make sure he was right before he pulled his phone back out; radio silence in his head and he couldn't sense Rex lurking. Good.

He had the name and appointment time to see a psychiatrist who was an old colleague of Abby's. It was a week out. He groaned at how much time that would give Rex to make his case.

The text Rex didn't see, however, was a more immediate commitment. That very night he was to see a medium who had been recommended to his aunt by a friend who dealt with "such things."

157

He texted a quick thanks to Abby as he left the office.

"Such things," he said to no one. Who knew there could be an expert for "such things?" He still didn't even know what *things* he was dealing with. All he knew was he was on the brink of exhaustion and needed to prepare himself. He'd get Keith to cover and go home early.

And he had to talk to Peg. He wasn't going to do this thing alone.

Even though his key turned in the lock, L.Z. couldn't get the door open. He went around back, and the same thing happened. The windows were curtained, so he pounded on the glass.

He heard scraping on the other side of the back door just before Peg opened it and shooed him in, quickly closing the door behind him, then shoved a chair against it. He did a double take when he realized she held one hand against her chest, a forefinger and thumb extended with her other fingers folded.

He screwed up his face and pointed.

"A gun? Oh wait, a *handgun!*" He snorted and laughed; he was so punchy at this point, anything would have cracked him up. That had been a good one if he said so himself, which he almost did. But Peg cut him off by calling out,

"It's OK, Elle! It's only Leddy! We're still secure! You get ready and I'll cover the doors till security gets here!"

He raised his eyebrows as his life-long inner alarm reared its ugly head and blasted his nerves. It was a trained response when it became apparent that Elle's rollercoaster was shifting for a 360-degree loop. He started to go find his mother when Peg grabbed his hand.

That stopped him short as a thrill ran through him. He felt his face go hot as she whispered,

"It's OK. I have it under control. And don't go in there unarmed...she'll think you're under duress."

L.Z. struggled between just wanting to hold her hand and yanking loose to stop the nonsense scenario before Elle went completely off the deep end with whatever the hell the threat of the day was. And this looked like a doozy.

As if she could read his mind, Peg pulled him into the pantry and whispered, "Look, she thinks we've been invaded. Something about her traps being sprung and someone is after state secrets. She locked the place..."

As much as L.Z. would have loved to stay in the pantry and hold Peg's hand, he'd heard all he needed to hear and dug deep for dwindling resources to deal with his mother's condition. But again, Peg countered him by blocking the exit. With a low and urgent whisper, she said,

"Listen…trust me on this! Telling her it isn't real would be like trying to get her to dance to a broken record. It won't play and she won't dance!"

L.Z. screwed up his face, "What? Peg, what are you…"

She nearly growled as she got in his face. "Your mother *believes* this. It's her reality whether you like it or not. We can't fix that, so what we do is steer her to something normal. She's supposed to go to Linda's tonight to celebrate her birthday and if all goes according to plan, she'll get drunk and stay and…"

"Where are you? You sure it's Leddy?" They heard Elle's voice; she was in the kitchen and closing in. Peg lifted her "gun" again and pointed at L.Z.'s hand, directing him to do the same with eyes that meant business. He found himself doing it and wondered if he shouldn't just go to the funny farm now and forego any preliminaries.

"Work with me on this. *Trust me.*" Peg brushed against him in the narrow space, their eyes inches apart. He had a flash that if she asked him to self-combust right then and there, he'd do it; he felt very close as it was.

So, out they came, wielding their weapons as Peg took on a competent matter-of-fact air.

"He's briefed up, Elle. He did a perimeter check before coming in and so far, all's clear. But when Dark-Cyber security gets here, they want the target gone, do you hear?

That means *you need to leave* and plan on staying the night. It's too risky for you here. Got your bug-out bag?"

Elle had a too-bright-eyed look L.Z. knew well as she hustled into the living room and returned with an old woven backpack, she'd supposedly carried all across India.

He watched in amazement as Peg whispered top secret instructions into Elle's ear, then went to the door to remove the blocks.

"L.Z.?" She commanded and he felt as though he should snap to attention.

"Uh, yeah?"

"You have your instructions. Go down the alley and the back way to Linda's and 'deliver the package.' Linda knows the score. Get right back so we can go over the op orders when Black-Cyber gets here."

L.Z. stared wordlessly as Elle gave Peg a quick hug.

"I don't know what I done without you all this time, Hon. Be careful, yes?" With a quick pat on Peg's cheek, she ducked out the door.

L.Z. mouthed, *Dark-Cyber?* to Peg with a confused look, and she rewarded him with her huge-toothed, dimply smile, winking as she held up her finger gun and shoved him out the door.

His proposal for the evening was an easy sell when L.Z. got back from "delivering the package" and timidly invited her to his scheduled psychic encounter.

Elle was out for the night and Peg was primed for adventure. It was a date.

On the drive to the other side of Boise, Leddy found it easier to bear his soul to Peg than if they'd talked face to face. He spilled his guts about how and when it all started. He told her what happened in Salt Lake City and about Aunt Abby's suggestions. He was debating on whether to share the dreams when he realized she hadn't said a word. Suddenly self-conscious, he glanced to see if she was even listening.

She faced straight ahead, but when he stopped at a red light, she turned to him with the kindest smile; it wiped his brain clean. He'd forgotten where he was in the story and for a second, forgotten that he was driving. Possibly sensing the latter, she pointed ahead for him to watch the light and said,

"I know when it – he – is there."

He jerked his head to see her, but she was staring out her window. He heard her all the same.

"Your mouth, it twitches. I figured you didn't know. You get, like, this tense or angry look, then the right side of your mouth starts twitching. When it relaxes, I figure it's over."

L.Z.'s hand was on his mouth as he zoned out for a minute. The horn of the car behind them jolted him back to the here and now and she laughed lightly.

"Yeah. I didn't think you knew. It's kind of cute."

You'd never know that Led Zeppelin Manson was battling the demons of his life if you could read his mind right then.

All he could think of was Rudolph the Red Nosed Reindeer in the ancient Claymation movie right after the little girl reindeer, Clarice, told him his nose was cute. In L.Z.'s mind, he was soaring through the air, shouting, "I'm cute! She said I'm cuuute!!!!"

Peg, L.Z.'s Clarice, was nowhere near on the same track as him. But she was dead-on with the mouth thing and had unwittingly helped him in ways that were yet to be known.

Barb Westly welcomed the couple into her high-end home with little flourish and ushered them to the dining room table. L.Z. had expected something more shack-like and was surprised when the GPS brought them to one of Boise's finer subdivisions. He was a bit let down as he eyed their hostess and surroundings. He'd expected an oversized, big-haired, heavily bejeweled woman. Maybe with pink hair or a rat's nest bouffant. But Barb was of indeterminate age; although she was surely over 60, she was lovely with all the signs of having been a knockout a decade or two before. She wore a loose sun dress that did little to hide her prominent bosom, along with sandals and a lovely smile. She wore no jewelry and didn't have a mystic air at all. So much for every movie he'd ever watched featuring psychics, L.Z. thought. Peg simply eyed everything around as she offered her very best manners.

"First of all, welcome," Barb said as they sat at a heavy dining room table of polished inlaid wood. Her smile revealed extraordinarily straight and white teeth. Upon close examination, L.Z. considered a good plastic surgeon might be the reason he probably couldn't guess her age with any accuracy.

She's either really good at this or has a rich husband, he thought as he tried to relax.

"I understand your aunt knows a friend of mine in the mental health profession," she stated more than asked.

He nodded nervously, but before he could answer, she continued.

"I want you to know that I know no specifics of your situation, except how a referral brought you to me. I would normally suggest that any client experiencing abnormal amounts of emotional issues still seek professional counseling and guidance. My abilities are natural and fortunately, or unfortunately, have proven relatively accurate, but I don't claim to be a professional. I assume that since my friend is a psychiatrist, you have considered or are receiving counseling?"

She smiled warmly with the last question, but L.Z. was so taken aback by her frank and professional demeanor, it took him a moment to respond. Peg kicked him under the table to prompt him.

"Right. I, uh, do have an appointment scheduled, but you were available first and my aunt suggested I go ahead and give this, uh, a shot." He swallowed, shooting a look at Peg, then back at Barb who still gazed at him cordially. "Honestly, Ma'am, I don't even know what this is. I mean, what is it that you do?"

She smiled. "Don't worry, I don't use a Ouija board or bring out snakes." Peg laughed a little too loudly and L.Z. nearly jumped out of his skin. Barb reached and squeezed his hand to calm him as she continued. "Most of my clients come to me to contact deceased loved ones; sometimes it works, but sometimes no one's there. I'm often able to do readings with my clients, do a little guidance and healing on more psychic matters. Mostly I bridge the gap between the living and dead. Although, really, there's no such thing as alive and dead…it's just a transition for the soul. It's not a science, but I've done all right." She raised her hands and glanced at their surroundings.

That's when L.Z. noticed she wore four rings, none of which was a wedding ring. Yes, she must "do" all right. His comfort level increased.

"I, um…well, I don't know if I need you to contact a dead person. I guess…" He was struggling and looked at Peg for help.

"He might have someone who has *transitioned* hanging around," Peg smiled shyly, proud of her terminology, and continued. "He just needs you to see if there is someone there…and if there is, well…"

"Ask him to go," L.Z. finished without forethought. He just realized that's what he wanted from the meeting.

Barb tilted her head and looked at L.Z., then Peg. She shrugged lightly, then closed her eyes, brows raised. L.Z. and Peg exchanged glances, then looked back at Barb when she loudly sighed.

"I'm sorry, but I've actually been reading you since you arrived. I'm not trying to be invasive, it's just natural…believe me, I wish I could turn it off." She waved a hand in front of her face to accent her point, then continued apologetically, "Sorry, sometimes it gets a bit hectic, but anyway, I don't see, hear, or sense anyone around you. At all, really. Often, we are visited by someone other than who the client's seeking, but in your case, well, you don't have anyone from the other side with or near you." She shrugged again and laid her hands on the table.

L.Z. looked at Peg, unsure whether he was disappointed or not, and hoped she still believed him.

"That means he's not dead." Her statement was so matter of fact that he not only understood that she believed him, but that she didn't think the voice was a result of his being crazy. He continued to look at Peg, lost for a moment again in his growing feelings for her. She smiled nervously because she didn't know what else to say.

That's when they heard a small gasp from across the table.

Barb's entire disposition had changed. She was pale and her hand rested near her neck. She squinted and mumbled,

"*Wrecks?* Or *Rex?* What is..." She shook her head in small jerks, looking as though she was trying to read something not quite legible.

Alarmed, Peg looked from Barb to L.Z., whose mouth had grown tense and the side nearest her started to twitch.

"That's him!" she shouted to Barb, pointed exaggeratedly at L.Z., "I mean, that's L.Z., but Rex is the guy who..."

L.Z. didn't hear her because the voice in his head boomed,

"She sees me! She sees me! What does she know? Am I dead? Tell her I..."

Rex's desperate words drove L.Z. to clamp his eyes closed and cover his ears. He hoped Peg caught on; he'd told her Rex could only see and hear through him and, right now, he needed to shut the energy inward so Barb could do whatever it was she did. Besides, he deeply wanted to deny Rex any input or control.

"Open up, man, I need to hear this…wait, she still sees me! Ask her what she sees…I…No! No! No! I need to stay, I…"

And as fast as he'd arrived, Rex was gone. L.Z. could feel the energy drain and his hands slid from the side of his head. Peg grabbed one up, asking, "Are you all right?"

But his eyes were fixed on Barb, who had covered her face.

He asked Peg, "Is *she* OK?"

Barb dropped her hands and while her face regained color, her expression was grave.

"You saw him? He said you saw him. Does that mean he's dead?" L.Z. wasn't sure he wanted the answer, but also had to know.

Barb slowly shook her head, her expression dark.

"He has not passed over, that I know. He is as confused as you are about his existence…but…" She closed her eyes with short head shakes as if to clear her mind.

"So, he's real?" Peg whispered on behalf of L.Z. who was too overwhelmed to talk.

Barb's eyes popped open, and she fixed them on L.Z., their brightness was unsettling.

"Oh, he's real, all right. But…"

"But what?" L.Z. had found his voice.

"But…" Barb reached across the table and took L.Z.'s free hand before she finished. In that moment, he saw her age. Her response was quiet, but certain.

"But he's got no soul."

Al and Abby were enjoying their newly arrived ancestry results with cocktails when Abby received a phone call. They normally refrained from taking calls during their dinner and/or drink times together, but when she saw who it was, she let him know it was an exception. Al, boosted by the unexpected amount of Irish in his ancestry results, whipped up Irish coffee for the two of them. When Abby came back in, she was clearly troubled.

"That was Jan — you know, my colleague in Boise." She took the coffee from Al, too preoccupied to harass him for the whipped cream mustache he wore from his own.

"Mmm hmm?" he said, closing his eyes as the magical liquid ran down his throat. Of course, he was Irish!

"L.Z. went to Barb Westly." She sipped her coffee as she handed him a napkin.

Getting the gist, he waved away her offering, giving his upper lip a voracious licking. This type of behavior would normally get a rise out of his wife, so when she didn't respond, she had his attention.

"And who is Barb Westly, pray tell?" He pulled out her chair and they sat, pushing the colorful pie charts from Find-your-Family.com out of the way for their cups.

Abby updated her husband on who Barb was, ignoring the look of disapproval on his face. Once she'd related the disturbing results of their nephew's encounter with the medium, he asked, "So, how is it that you are getting the whole scoop second hand? No confidentiality for psychics? Isn't there a privacy issue here?" As if his tone hadn't denoted enough disapproval, he reached for the bottle of Jameson's, topping off what was left of the cream-less coffee in his mug.

"L.Z. gave his full permission for Barb to share with Jan, and Jan made the call because she knows me. It was apparently pretty traumatic. I guess he wanted us to know before he takes the plunge with his psychiatrist appointment. We were just discussing the potential complications if he's misdiagnosed. You know, if Barb is right."

Her words trailed off. What she was suggesting was completely counter to her profession and all her training. But she couldn't ignore the feeling in her gut. Before she regathered her thoughts, she saw Al standing in his full "I'm about to take the floor" stance. She settled back, reaching for the bottle to fortify herself.

Shoulder's squared, eyes sharp, Al cut the air with his free hand as he began.

"Let me get this straight. This Barb character, who sees or at least communicates with dead people, detects no dead people around our nephew. *But* she throws in that there is still someone living, how shall I say, *in* our nephew? Just hanging out, being cool? L.Z. has a soul-less mind-mate? And that is, I suppose, worse than a mindless soulmate?" He huffed at his own joke as Abby started to argue. He held up a finger and launched into the rest of his objection.

"So, is this a new skill of hers? I mean, she's the dead person whisperer, right? Or did she reserve it for this 'friend of the family' session. Did that cost extra, or did he get the 'friend and family' discount package deal?" He was just getting warmed up, bouncing on his toes as he gesticulated, "Oh wait, how about *this?* Did she…"

Abby slammed the table so hard the empty Find-Your-Family packaging drifted to the floor from the force of her movement.

Al's face jerked backward, causing an accordion effect on his plentiful neck-skin.

They stared at each other. Her outbursts were rare, and they typically shut him down either from surprise or respect. But this subject hit him at a primal level, and he struck back.

"This is absurd, Abigale, and you of all people know it." He stepped forward, leaning on the table, looming over her. His voice was low and serious. "Elizabeth is ill. Our father spent half our childhood in institutions. He got shock treatments, for God's sake! You know, you know these disorders are hereditary. Suggesting this could be something – something 'woo-woo' – is like treating a compound fracture with a stomach antacid! It makes no sense when the answer is obvious!" He boomed the last remark and when he heard his own echo, he reddened and stopped.

Abby had leaned back in her chair, arms crossed. Her expression was unmoved; stubborn.

Al licked his lips as he looked at the ceiling, counting to ten. Then he sat next to her and said levelly, "It's about the data, Abs."

She stared at him, and nearly blasted him out of his chair with, "*It's about our nephew!*"

He leaned back, eyebrows up, mouthing, "Wow."

She drank the almost straight whiskey from her cup, banging it on the table, then reaching for the bottle.

Al stroked his chin and, as his eyes fell on the ancestry results, a smile began. She noticed and, taking another sip from her cup, asked,

"What?"

He pointed at her DNA feedback which showed a healthy slice of Italian in her pie chart.

"Seems a bit of your heritage is coming out, my dear." He fingered the whiskey bottle, "as is mine."

They looked at each other as the tension in the room evaporated.

"Abby," he chose his words carefully. "This confuses me because it seems like you've spent our marriage skirting anything to do with Elle or that boy. And now...now, this!" He threw his hands up and wore a sincere look of bafflement.

"That boy is an adult now. And he's nothing like his mother. Nothing. And I do know a few things about human behavior. And, yes, I love him."

The room fell silent, but Al didn't give in as he normally did when his wife took a stand, so he exercised remarkable restraint and held his tongue. By the time she finally spoke, he'd *bitten* his tongue, tasting blood. It was an historic effort on his part, but it paid off.

"Fine, Al," she said, standing as she scooped up the papers that had been the center of their attention not long before. Facing him, she said,

173

"If he goes to that appointment and if he's honest, which he's too damn naïve not to be, if that doctor is worth a damn, he will be diagnosed and medicated."

Al nodded in approval, saying,

"It's about time someone in that house set a proper example, maybe it will rub off on Elle and she'll get some help."

Abby held the papers against her chest.

"And maybe everything she believes about the system will be reinforced when that young man is medicated for disorders he *doesn't* have, and it fucks him up good."

She turned to leave. Al was dumbstruck because in all their marriage, he'd never heard his wife use such language.

She threw an arm behind her, jutting a finger in his direction,

"And that will be on you."

She walked out and Al dropped into the closest chair. He was a victim of his history, and he knew it. Watching his father and sister had chiseled his views and prejudices about mental illness into an immovable thing. He was paralyzed by his own fear for L.Z.

Then, he did the only thing that made sense. He finished the bottle of Jameson's and sought out his wife to ensure he'd still be married the next day.

These Irish-Italian marriages could be challenging.

L.Z. was running again, only this time it was to work. He'd slowly built up his endurance, so now he simply felt like he wanted to die, rather than being sure of it. Besides, he needed to leave the car for Peg so she could go get his new meds. His *antipsychotic* meds.

He plodded along, trying to find his rhythm since he'd misplaced his ear buds and had no music. He found it infinitely harder to stay motivated when all he could hear was his irregular foot clops, interlaced with his huffing and puffing, complete with occasional gasps.

With no audio distractions (which included no Rex, thank God), his mind inevitably ricocheted among the past week's developments. Just the thought of the encounter with Barb the medium made his breathing more like panting, so he quickly switched to his next form of "intervention;" the appointment with Dr. Advika Bhattacharyya, a stunning Indian psychiatrist whom Abby had recommended. Aunt Abby warned him that the doctor was direct and no-nonsense without the "touchy-feely" element sometimes present with therapists and psychologists like herself. She felt if he was going to go through with this, it was best to get as objective an opinion as possible.

He jogged along, losing himself in the humiliating recollection of his first ever psychiatric evaluation. The appointment didn't begin well. He was already a wreck by the time he entered her office, and her unexpected appearance threw him off his shaky game. He had pictured someone more akin to Ruth Bader Ginsberg – direct and no-nonsense, as Abby said – and a few decades older. But she was young, exotically beautiful, and "direct" to the point of coldness.

His opening joke that most of her business must come from people breaking down while trying to pronounce her name fell flat. He was so confuzzled at that point, he unwittingly threw out the pun he'd actually prepared as an icebreaker.

"Did you know the middle east doesn't need any psychiatrists because there are nomad people?"

Nothing.

When she gestured at a chair for him with a neutral expression, he spied family photos where people wore traditional Indian garb. Thinking he'd insensitively blundered, considering her ethnic background, he sat and sputtered his apologies if he had offended her with the middle eastern reference.

"Mr. Manson, India is not a middle eastern country, it's considered south or southeast Asia. Now if you're finished with your comedy routine, I'd like to discuss the reason you're here."

He was trying not to swallow his tongue as she began to ask him questions. He answered everything honestly, including the very specific queries about hearing voices. She was unimpressed when he made it clear it was only one voice, and that it was not always present, and that, in fact, it was coming less and less often of late.

She seemed most concerned about his dreams. He understood that since they were starting to scare the hell out of him. The themes were violent, eerily organized, and well executed. And he was the star of the show in them all. In the nightmares, his clothes were not what he'd wear, and his hair was a little off, but there was no doubt in his mind it was him.

When asked, he told her he'd never had a violent encounter or even urge in his life. And, no, he'd never done harm or thought of doing harm to himself. And, no, he had no waking violent fantasies, unless that included wanting to slap the shit out of half of the wildlings at work. Even when he explained that was his term for the self-indulgent youths he supervised and he, of course, would never lay hands on them, she seemed unmoved as she jotted things down.

Next, she'd whipped out the multiple tests he'd taken in preparation for the appointment. This part of the interview encouraged him, as the results had been quite normal.

He was wholly unprepared for the end of the meeting when she handed him two prescriptions for medications to treat his potential disorders.

"What disorders? You just said my tests came out pretty normal."

"Mr. Manson. You admit to hearing a voice and have been hearing it as well as responding to it for weeks. You also kill people in your dreams. This voice also instructed you on how to attack a man whom you admit you nearly killed. These things are not normal. They are indications of psychosis."

"The dreams didn't start until after the altercation in Salt Lake…" His voice trailed off with his only defense.

"Noted. Do you hear the voice now?"

"Well, no…I never know when he's going to come and go…"

"So, you completely believe it is independent from you?"

"I'm nothing like Rex!"

"So, you've named him." As she made another note, he tried to backpedal but knew he was defenseless. Then she played her final card.

"You understand that many mental disorders can be inherited?" As she tapped on the stack of intake forms he'd submitted, his shoulders fell. Of course, he'd been truthful about his mother and grandfather.

The bottom line, according to Dr. Bhattacharyya, was that with his auditory hallucinations and self-implicating homicidal dreams, he was possibly schizophrenic, bi-polar at a minimum. But he exhibited signs of psychosis which would likely get worse if he went untreated.

"Well, assuming no bodies turn up and the voice doesn't go away, then what? In other words, what if you're wrong?"

For a split-second L.Z. wondered if he had gone nuts; it was completely against his nature to proffer such a direct challenge.

She didn't even blink as she stood and walked to the door, "Then you'll feel like crap for a few weeks because these pills aren't for wimps. And we'll look at alternative meds; it's hardly a cookie cutter situation. Or you can get a second opinion."

She had opened the door and waited for him to leave.

He sighed and turned with a mumbled thank you.

"And Mr. Manson, L.Z., was it?"

He turned to her, already feeling defeated and almost wished Rex had appeared to somehow validate his position.

"Yeah?"

She smiled for the first time and pointed to his chest.

"Do yourself a favor and next time, maybe pull a different shirt from your drawer? It didn't hurt…but it didn't help, either."

At the sound of a blaring horn, the memory bubble popped, and L.Z. was back in his sweaty lurching body, surprised to realize he was only a few blocks from Red Missile Burgers. His brain registered the sign, but all his mind could see was a flash of the shirt he'd worn to see a shrink: black and red with evil eyes and a bloody smile. It had been an off the rack jersey displaying the name of an alternative metal band whose unfortunate name was *Disturbed*.

Jogging in place at a "don't walk" sign, L.Z. pushed the button and panted under his breath,

"Crazy, maybe. Moron, *for sure.*"

Peg decided to take Elle along with her to pick up L.Z.'s medications and make it a girl's day. With Elle's long list of proclivities, Peg didn't line up the typical mani-pedi thing, and shopping was out of the question because the potential for a scene (or five) was high with the elderly lady's outrage over commercialism and the capitalistic machine. To further narrow the options, Elle wasn't down for anything that would involve crowds since she wasn't sure if the imminent pandemic-causing virus had hit US shores. On this matter, she was firm. As it was, she asked Peg to pick up some surgical masks for her while in the drugstore. Better safe than sorry.

So, Peg opted for a quick grocery trip (during which Elle could stay in the car), followed by a visit to Zoo Boise, having been inspired by L.Z.'s stories of Hogle Zoo in Utah. They'd grab lunch outside and if, and it was a big if, Elle could stay in the moment, they might actually have a good day. After all, who didn't love animals, and they had to eat anyway, right?

Peg never got a chance to test her theory because sometime between tossing Elle the bag from the drug store and running into the supermarket to fill a short list, Elle was taken by an upset stomach.

The change in the old lady's disposition was sudden but not unusual. Peg was disappointed only because she had been happy for the opportunity to escape the dark house for a jaunt in the Kia. She was surprised, but gratified, when Elle insisted that she'd lay down for the rest of the day if the younger woman wanted to get out and "blow the stink off" for a while.

Peg weighed whether she should leave or not; staying by Elle's side was her job, and doing so secured her room and board, after all. But if she was only gone for a short while, what harm could come?

She decided to split the difference and run to the closest Wal-Mart and get a walk-in haircut for a short outing. Weeks of living in a home without mirrors had made her already disagreeable locks downright riotous. She'd bought stuff to make dinner for L.Z. at the grocers; she might as well try to look a little less homeless when she served it.

Once at the house, Peg saw Elle into her room to lay down, ensuring she had her bag with the masks, then went to get her haircut after putting away the groceries.

As she pulled away, she couldn't have seen that the curtains parted any more than she'd seen Elle's face as she intently watched her departure.

Once Peg was gone, Elle went straight to her computer with the prescription bottles bearing her son's name. Someone was up to something, and she had to save her callow son from himself. Again.

L.Z. hadn't really thought out his plan to jog to work. Naturally, Red Missile Burgers didn't have shower facilities, so he'd felt a bit rank even after taking a sink bath before changing into his uniform. When his shift wound down, the last thing he wanted to do was suit back up in the same jogging clothes from that morning and drag ass home. He started to text Peg for a ride, but decided against it, calling an Uber instead. He had no idea what Uncle Al paid the girl, but he doubted it was enough to justify her being his personal taxi driver. Paying for a ride was a huge extravagance for him, but worth it when he walked into the house to food that actually smelled good, and a Peg who looked *great*.

After issuing an awkward compliment, he headed for the shower only to run smack into Elle in the hallway. She had one hand on her hip as she thrust the pills into his face with the other. She smelled of cigarettes and "ode de pissed-off."

"Do you know what this shit can do to you? These are antipsychotic drugs, Leddy. Who prescribed this? Any particular reason you didn't mention to your ma you were going to a shrink? And his name is *Bat-cherry-what?* You trust your fate to someone whose name you can't even pronounce? It's obviously a fake. Jesus!"

He hadn't planned for this.

"Pull your head out, man. Tell her you're stressed out from work or some shit and didn't want her to worry."

Taking advice from Rex was the last thing L.Z. wanted to do, but the idea didn't suck, and he needed an out.

Adopting his kindest voice, L.Z., not a natural bullshitter, said,

"Uh…sorry, Ma," he reached for the bottles which she snapped behind her back, arching her fading eyebrows, pushing up a few rows of wrinkles along with them. He dropped his hands and continued, "I've been a little stressed out. You know, from work. And stuff."

"Very convincing…"

L.Z.'s face stiffened, and his mouth twitched.

Elle rolled her eyes, shoving the pill bottles into his chest and pushed past him.

"Jesus, boy, you can do better than that. Did you know your mouth twitches when you lie?" She swung around as his hand flew to his face. He was suddenly wondering about the whole twitching thing when Rex weighed in,

"She's just fucking with you. But she's got a point about the pills..."

Elle stuck her finger in her son's chest.

"Stress? Really? I'll tell you about stress. Try going undercover to China, then having to go illegally mine for the Chinese in Africa. Now that's stress, my boy...and a living hell! Why I..."

L.Z.'s shoulder relaxed as he pocketed the pills. This, he could deal with. Classic, crazy Elle.

She continued to rant as he turned to his room.

"You really going to take that shit?"

Rex sounded...*no, felt*...a bit worried.

So now I can sense his feelings too? L.Z. thought. But he didn't let on.

"Yes, I am. In fact, how about now?" He grabbed a water bottle on his desk after shaking a pill from each bottle. The maroon and tan capsule looked a bit more ominous than the round white pill. He tried to swallow his anxiety along with the medications; his desire to unsettle Rex might have been exactly what he needed to take that first step.

"What are you doing! What if you're not psychotic? Don't you think I'd know if you were? What if I'm, like, real?"

He feels desperate and worried, L.Z. thought as he walked into the bathroom and turned on the shower, but all he said was, "Well, then, I guess you've got nothing to worry about."

As he said it, he noticed a small hand mirror on the sink edge. Glad he found it before Elle stumbled across the evil implement, he snagged it up. Peg must have sneaked into his bathroom to admire her nice new hairdo, violating Elle's no-mirror rule. He lifted it, experiencing something for the first time in years…seeing himself within the confines of his own home.

There was another first, as well. As he looked at himself, Rex also saw him for the first time.

"Dude…"

"What?" L.Z. asked as he wrapped the mirror in his discarded clothes to return to Peg later.

His head was blissfully silent for several seconds before he heard the reply.

"Nothing. Take a fuckin' shower, if you smell anything like you look, your Ma will think you were working in one of those Chinese-African mines."

"Maybe I'd finally get some respect," L.Z. said to no one as he stepped into the shower. Even he wondered what the pills would do, but he'd try anything to rid himself of the voice and the dreams; that's what the prescriptions were for according to the doctor. But according to *him,* it was a shot to rid himself of the demon with no soul.

And a chance to sleep at night and not wake up with the feel of blood on his hands.

Elle skipped dinner, citing her stomach troubles, which left newly medicated L.Z. and the freshly groomed Peg to share dinner. Alone.

L.Z. tried not to stare, but Peg looked so pretty, and she looked like she might feel a little pretty too, which increased the attraction. And the lasagna was such a far cry from the cacciatore disaster, L.Z. overrated and over-complimented. In his mind, this was like their first date.

As she cleared the table, Peg suddenly threw up her hands.

"OK…truth in advertising, I didn't make this. I mean, I heated it and stuff…but it was one of those frozen things, you know."

"Don't care," L.Z. said as he stood to help and stuffed a last bit of garlic bread in his mouth.

She laughed and the sound of it was dance music for his heart. He stopped and watched her at the sink as she said to the dishes,

"I even faked the garlic bread. It was already buttered and garlicked and stuff."

"Well, there's one thing you didn't fake."

Shaking water from her hands, Peg playfully swung around to see what L.Z. was talking about. She stiffened when she nearly ran into him.

He looked nervous enough to throw up, but something very different emitted from his mouth.

"Peg, you are...well. You're beautiful tonight and I just...I just..." his eyes had fallen to her lips and he reached for her face.

"No!" she cried, planting wet hands on his chest, and pushing him away.

L.Z. felt as though he'd been crushed like a grape. He backed away, flushing deeply.

"I'm sorry...I..."

They stared at each other, Peg's eyes wide, and L.Z.'s rimmed with tears of humiliation.

"I have to explain," she said with an edge of desperation in her voice.

"No, please…it's OK…you're…" L.Z. grasped for words.

"I'm your sister," she whispered.

He said nothing.

Worst first date ever.

L.Z. was in such a state of sensory overload that he ceased to communicate with anyone at home, and only when it involved burger production and food safety (of course) while at work. He found himself jogging every morning just to escape and fill his head with the most combustible music possible to blast any budding thoughts away. He still hated running, but he hated facing his current life more. He didn't even question that he ran again as soon as he got home. The extra run wasn't just to kill time and brain activity, but because the pills meant to stop or curb his nightmares weren't working. Thus, he ran to wear himself out just so he could sleep, dreams or no dreams. Both pill bottles indicated they could cause drowsiness, but instead seemed to drive him onto the streets.

He didn't answer texts from his aunt and uncle. The blessing of having Peg at the house was, it was the first time in his life he could effectively ignore his mother without neglecting her or risking her well-being. For all his misgivings about Peg now, for some reason, he trusted her with Elle.

Why wouldn't he? Elle must be Peg's mom, right? He never got a second past that thought before he obliterated it with another subject or very loud music. He just couldn't go there.

So, he got up every day, took his pills, ran, went to work, came home, ran again, ate in his room, and went to bed.

Peg was pitiful and Elle, whose entire universe typically revolved around herself, was caught in orbits of her own. Regardless, she was still L.Z.'s mother and had noted his distance, but concluded it was about time the boy developed some independence. And she had Peg now; the girl was distracted of late, but still attentive enough to feed Elle's ego, but distant enough to keep out of the old woman's very important business.

Such was the state of the Manson home until about two weeks into the stalemate when L.Z. decided to look at his phone after his evening run and shower. It was less with intention than out of boredom.

There were multiple missed calls and texts from Al and Abby, including an alarming message from his uncle that he always had business interests in Boise if he needed to fly up. The message was clear. L.Z. reluctantly responded to his aunt and uncle with a joint text; he still didn't desire to communicate but wanted a physical visit or phone discussion even less. Once he hit send, he continued to scroll, ignoring messages about work – he always answered actual calls about work, but anyone too chickenshit to use the phone didn't deserve a return text.

Unimpressed with the overall contents of his inbox, he started to put the phone down when a new text popped up. It was from Peg. He felt his heart surge, then immediately had a cramp in his gut; it was a one-two punch he'd dealt with over past days whenever she, and more specifically, her announcement, entered his mind. His cheeks filled with air when he resigned himself to opening it. She was probably no more than twenty feet away, thirty tops, if she was on the patio, but this was still safer than face-to-face.

Blowing out a slow breath, he touched the text with her name on it. He felt like he had on the only time he dared to jump from the diving board as a kid; that hadn't gone well – he'd thought he was going to drown.

This one had a similar effect.

> The truth is I THINK I'm your sister. That's all. And you didn't imagine the feelings, really! Please trust me. I'm working on it. I miss you.

If the message was supposed to make L.Z. feel better, it missed the mark. All it did was increase the velocity of his emotional hurricane. He threw the phone across the room and reached for the bottles next to his bed. Maybe an extra night-time bad dream repellant pill would do the trick?

His conservative side slapped that idea into left field and the pill bottle ended up somewhere near the phone on his bedroom floor.

He buried his head under the pillow, confused, exhausted, and overwhelmed.

One out of two was the phrase of the day.

He missed Peg too but didn't miss Rex at all.

One pill was working, and the other was not.

One for two, buckle my shoe…three, four, my phone's on the floor…five, six….

He started the mental song, hoping he'd get to sleep before he got to ten. It didn't work, so he watched Game of Thrones instead and fell asleep before the opening theme song was over.

Again, one out of two wasn't bad.

Abby and Al were in bed reading when Abby's phone vibrated. She set down her Kindle and reached for her cell as her husband continued to read from what looked like a twenty-pound volume of an historic variety; she had yet to get him into the digital age when it came to reading.

Because of his wife's job, Al knew the text could mean a patient crisis, so when she remained quiet, he stuck a finger against the page to mark his place and glanced to see if she was staying in bed.

He watched her swing her legs over the edge, and he stared at her back as she appeared to stare at her phone.

"Everything OK?" he asked anecdotally as he started to read again.

"It's L.Z."

Al lowered his book and removed his readers.

"Well?"

She put her phone down and lifted the blankets to roll back into place. Once she faced him with her hands tucked between her face and pillow, she answered,

"Well, he hasn't heard 'Rex' since he started his meds. Two weeks now."

Al lit up, raising his hands in victory, "Hey, hey, hey!"

His implication was clear, then he bit his lip, waiting for Abby to say the magic words, that he was right, and she was wrong. But when he gauged her look, his smile faded.

"And?"

"And the dreams are just as bad, if not worse and more specific."

Clopping his book onto the bedside table, with a few grunts, Al turned over to face his wife, gasping with relief when his head hit his own pillow.

"That's great news, right? I mean, it means the doc nailed it with the diagnosis for the voice, anyway. Maybe the other pill just takes longer." He strained to keep the smug look at bay, remembering their rare argument over this same subject. Besides, he was gratified enough just thinking of the years Elle had denied treatment and now she had an example right in her face that she was wrong!

Abby had closed her eyes, but the lines in her forehead told Al she was thinking. When her brown eyes opened, she looked directly into those of her mate.

"It could be great news, depending on your perspective." When she stopped talking, but continued the eye lock, Al took the bait. He wanted to hear what she had to say, yes, but also, even after all the years, he could look into this woman's eyes forever. This was a moment he'd grab, no matter what the subject.

"And?" he asked, pulling the covers up to his neck.

"Olanzapine, the antipsychotic Advika prescribed L.Z. for the voices normally takes 4-6 weeks to work, although sometimes patients get results a little sooner. But immediately? I just wonder..."

Al adjusted, and offered, "Maybe he's an exception?"

"It's impossible that it would work the minute he swallowed it and if you look at his text, the voice quit the same day. *Same day*, Al. And the other med? Ironically, Prazosin, the one usually used to treat those with PTSD and nightmares...well it usually works faster, yet it's had no effect." She stopped there. She was clearly troubled, and this troubled Al. He tried humor to diffuse this too-serious conversation for bedtime.

"Well, Honey, you gotta admit, the boy does have other blood running through his veins besides Elle's. Perhaps a more extraordinary strain?" His huge grin as he patted his own chest worked for just a moment as she punched him, then kissed his hand.

They were quiet as the outside light faded from dusk to night. Her uncertainty grew with the darkness and Al could feel it.

She stretched to click off the headboard lamp and they lay in the dark. Al kept his eyes open; he knew they weren't finished. But Abby stayed quiet. He felt around till he found her hand.

"Abs. Tell me, in all your years of training, did you ever see anything that would counter this being something besides, well...the obvious. Seems like Advika is on point, doesn't it?"

Silence. But he knew she was still awake. Then she answered.

"No and yes. Everything you say is nice and 'on point.'"

He waited for the "but," hoping they could wrap this up and get some sleep.

It came after a few long, dark minutes.

"You didn't know it, but L.Z. signed a release permitting Advika to share his information with me. His tests were completely normal, Al. I mean, *average Joe Public normal.* And Barb's never had a reading like the one she had with L.Z.....I mean, what she experienced isn't even in her normal realm, but she's shaken up."

Despite his convictions, the term "no soul" invaded Al's brain and he felt a chill he couldn't calm as Abby continued.

"And even after all these years, I've never underrated the power of intuition, Al. This all feels wrong no matter what my training says. I've always believed that the day we think we know everything is the most dangerous day of our lives. And this just *feels* dangerous."

It was quiet again and somehow their sanctuary of a bedroom had been fused with the feeling of a ghost story session at a child's sleepover. All they were missing were flashlights under their chins and sleeping bags.

Al felt the bed shift as his wife offered her final analysis.

"But what do I know? You're the guy with the big brain, right? Night, Honey."

Her soft snores came soon, but Al's were hours behind.

PART III
Dead to the World

Am I dead or am I alive
Can't be alive if I can't thrive
Still blindly I onward drive
Off the edge, off the edge I go
Into space I've been hurled
Don't talk at me because I know
I'm dead to the world

-- *Aaron Stoss (SKinKneaders)*

On the same day L.Z. started his new medications in Idaho, in the foreign land of New York, a nurse injected a placebo into the IV of Subject N-7, or as his admission paperwork stated, "patient unknown male Alpha 5/16" at a brain trauma institute. This would be the first of a series of placebos after 60 days of the experimental nootropic drugs for the seven patients in the program; previous nootropics were designed for cognitive improvement, while the experimental drug was created to spur brain activity for patients in permanent vegetative states. While all seven comatose patients had received doses during the initial trial period, there were differences among them. The main standout was "unknown male Alpha 5/16" or "N-7," for drug trial purposes. He was the only patient in the study whose identity was a mystery. He was also the only person whom the center did not have consent to treat. And he was the only patient in the ward in whom the police would have a vested interest.

The staff called unknown male Alpha 5/16 "Mitch," because one of the nurses thought he looked like Billy Crystal but couldn't remember the actor's name. She had just seen the old movie *City Slickers* in which Crystal played a character named Mitch Robbins, so it was that simple. None of the staff particularly liked the institutes various alpha-numeric identifiers, and "Mitch" rolled off the tongue much easier than unknown male Alpha 5/16 or N-7, which tagged him as the seventh patient in the study. So, it stuck.

There was nothing simple about the patient's situation, however. He had been admitted about two years before, May 16th, 2017, to be exact, thus the "5/16" in his identifier. He had been the first unknown admission of the day, which is where the "Alpha" came in. That he was a male was without question.

He'd been found unconscious on the side of a road with no identification or car keys; his pockets had been empty. Examination revealed he'd suffered some sort of blunt force trauma to the head which was responsible for his state. He was well groomed and wore quality clothing, so it was unlikely he was homeless. The police had responded since the patient appeared to be a victim of a crime, they'd reported his information, sans name, into the missing person's database, as well as collecting DNA, hoping to find an identity. The reason they would come back later was an entirely different matter.

No one had come forward looking for the man, nor were the authorities able to match him to a missing person's report. It was like he was dead to the world, and for all practical purposes, he kind of was.

After a few months, he was relocated to the brain trauma center where he never regained consciousness but gained his nick name. Mitch's noggin showed no activity while his body was kept alive by complete strangers. In the absence of a living will and without family to decide his fate, he simply took up space. Every day he breathed in and out without giving it a thought.

He didn't mind his situation since his mind didn't function at all.

He also didn't mind that it took over a year for the nearest law enforcement DNA lab to get around to handling his sample. Nor did he mind when he was moved to a long-term ward with like no-minded people.

He might have minded, if he'd had a mind, when he was placed in the center of a ward, half of which had been designated as a testing site for a progressive new drug. The reason he might have minded is that to be part of the test, consent by family or designated guardians was required. Yet there he lay as he was erroneously administered his first dose of NootropiCAN.

Nurse Kerry Albright, a "floater" staff member, not typically part of the research support staff and unfamiliar with "Mitch," didn't realize he was an unapproved, unidentified patient when she compared his chart to the list of six patients whose legal entities had given permission for their loved ones to take part in the study over the previous two years. The chart on the bed belonged to a poor soul named Adrian, or Subject "N-2" (NootropiCAN, subject #2), a patient who had been receiving the drug for the entire course of the study with decent results. By the time techs discovered that Adrian and Mitch's charts had been switched, or that, perhaps the nurse read the wrong chart, it might have been an easy enough thing to fix and justify. They could just document the oversight and not give Mitch any more NootropiCAN.

But there was a slight problem...or, for the doctors, it was the antithesis of a problem. It might have been the beginning of a solution.

Mitch's brain had responded immediately. The monitors had shown consistent activity almost from the moment Nurse Albright had injected the IV with the magic drug. While two of the other six approved patients had had good results thus far, one (Adrian) more than the other, they had not responded so quickly with their initial applications.

Although Nurse Albright was disciplined for the mistake, she was troubled nonetheless; she ensured it was fully documented and was outspoken that procedures be enforced to prevent a similar oversight. She went home with a clear conscience and considered it to be over.

When weeks later, her shift brought her back to the same ward and task, she was shocked to discover that "Mitch," or "patient unknown male Alpha 5/16," was on the list for drug administration, now as "N-7;" she balked. Even if his identity had been discovered since she'd last tended to him, there was no way permission could have been granted so quickly to enter him in the study; besides, the study had started two years before; it broke protocol to start a new subject so late in the game.

She challenged the directives. Yet, before her shift was up, Mitch, or N-7, had gotten his latest dose and Nurse Albright had been told from the top administrators via her supervisor that the bases had been covered to ensure continuation of testing and monitoring of this remarkable patient.

Nurse Albright had a problem with that. She didn't like it two months ago when she'd inadvertently given him a live dose of NootropiCAN, and she didn't like it now.

The fact that the placebo would undoubtedly stop the activity and void out the effect of the drug didn't undo 60 days of unapproved testing on a helpless, unknown man.

She loved and needed her job, but she also documented everything about patient unknown male Alpha 5/16 at home. It was a matter of ethics.

It allowed her to sleep at night.

What she didn't know yet was that she slept even better than Mitch, who seemed to have a very busy mind at night, even after removal from the miracle drug.

Homicide Detectives Doyle and McMurdy had more cases on their docket than they could ever properly tend to, let alone solve. They shared snarky remarks about how nice life would be if it resembled art. The glut of forensic and investigative television shows and podcasts had made every citizen an expert, not to mention created unrealistic expectations. Almost half of America's murders went unsolved, and New York's percentages weren't far behind.

No victims were more important than others to the investigators, although some cases rose to the top. Obviously, serial murders as well as suspected serial crimes were critical. And whether they liked it or not, the detectives were forced to follow any high-profile crimes with vigor. Then there were the very disturbing ones. Particularly violent crimes stuck like adhesive even to an overwhelmed cop. And anything involving kids was a priority, no matter how impossible the case.

But then there were the creepy ones. "Creepy" wasn't exactly a trade identifier, but it nailed it when the details of a case were, well, *creepy.*

One coldish case was on their short list under the creepy category. They had little information outside a small DNA sample from one of the crime scenes which didn't match the victim's sample. The crimes were undoubtedly related though, due to the skill and specificity behind the two murders they knew of. They also knew the crimes weren't isolated because there were multiple similar cases throughout the US; they knew the FBI had a bead on it, but the FBI didn't have DNA on any of the other states' cases and, as far as the New York detectives knew, the tiny sample was still lost in the layers of bureaucracy in the larger organization.

Doyle and McMurdy didn't even know the identity of one of the NY victims and the only reason they knew who the other one was, was because of dental records and a missing person's report.

It was difficult to identify victims who'd had all their skin removed.

"I could see if he exhibited brain activity while the drug was still in his system, but it's completely out according to the tests. And besides, you know the life of this drug is extremely short, the scans show the activity typically ceases in mid-wave when the NootropiCAN wears off. The other two aren't showing the same indications."

"The other two didn't start reacting within minutes of administration either."

The doctors were in a closed-door session with the patient study charts on the conference table. The screen at the end of the room showed electronic images of the file test results.

"He's been in his own class all along. This will require much closer scrutiny." Dr. Afflick flipped through images till the two he wanted were on the split screen. He pushed up his glasses and pointed. "Look at the variations in the nighttime activity and this example of one of his daytime bursts. The indications are different. It was unique to the others even before we switched to placebos. The others were directly related to dosage. N-7 has had nighttime activity with increasing frequency for the last 30-40 days, and now it appears it was unrelated to the drug." He removed his glasses, chewing on an end as he stared at his associate. "It doesn't add up."

Dr. Winston's eyes flickered, and he pulled a file from the stack between them. He flipped through the pages as Afflick stared absently at the images on the screen.

"Here," said Winston, sliding a readout across the table. "N-2 has had intermittent activity almost since the beginning. None of this night stuff, but some random signs since he started the test at the very beginning...sometimes sans NootropiCAN. We probably thought it was an anomaly.

Looks like it started two years ago, May. *Ummm*...May 16, right here. This was the first incident when he responded without the drug, in fact, he was on a placebo at the time."

Afflick looked at the reports, then at Winston. This was outside the parameters of their objective fields of thought. They focused so hard on what they intuitively felt would be elusive that they both overlooked the glaring connections.

It was in black and white on "Mitch's" chart. It was as clear as his identifier, "patient unknown male Alpha 5/16," later added on as N-7.

Mitch was admitted on May 16th, two years before. And that was when Subject N-2's brain said hello. Or the other way around.

But the primary significance to the scientists was a fact known only to them; the two men were the only pair in the study group receiving the exact same composition and dosage of the experimental drug. Every other subject had received variations to maximize end-test results.

These two doctors, alone, knew that N-2 and N-7, or Adrian and "Mitch," represented mirror subjects in the trial and were most responsive. Yet there was much the doctors didn't know.

It was late afternoon when Detective McMurdy slammed the phone down and ran his fingers through his greasy hair.

"Jesus Christ!"

Doyle lifted her head from the pile of papers before her, looking almost as unkempt as her partner. "What?"

"Jesus!" McMurdy repeated, smacking his hands down before jumping up and grabbing his jacket.

Doyle blew away a tuft of fuzzy hair that had dropped in front of her face. She looked to be half McMurdy's towering height but was probably twice as tough. She was a woman of few words. She stared at him with raised brows.

"Unless you just saw the light, I'm guessing this is unrelated to Jesus Christ?"

He tossed a piece of paper on her desk, pointing at his own scribbles as if they were the most offensive thing he'd ever seen.

"Our guy. *Skin Guy*. We got a DNA hit. The shit's been available for months. We gotta go."

She slowly stood, as if the news were about the weather rather than a break in one of their most intriguing and stagnant cases. She pulled a ratty scrunchy band from her bush of a ponytail and recaptured it, reading the note as she tamed the reddish mess.

"Byrde Brain Trauma Institute?" She picked up the note and handed it back to her partner. She bit her lip, lest she make a smartass remark about the name of their destination. If it had been any case other than Skin Guy, she knew McMurdy would have already capitalized on the ridiculous title of the distinguished medical center. She grabbed her weapon and phone, then they headed for the parking garage. She knew more information was forthcoming since her partner was far more in love with his own voice than she with hers. She waited as he throttled through a series of colorful exclamations regarding how long it had taken for the information to get to the lab, the length of time for testing, then for a match to one of their pet cases.

"The wheels of justice fucking stopped on this one." He punctuated the end of his tirade as he folded into the passenger seat of his partner's dented Mini Cooper.

Doyle pulled onto a crammed boulevard. They had plenty of time for conversation in this traffic, with an hour's drive ahead once they were out of the city.

McMurdy laid out the information. Doyle listened. The unidentified DNA from their disturbing Skin Guy case had been matched to a sample only recently entered as a crime victim and potential missing person. The owner of the sample was a patient at Byrde Brain institute.

Doyle, who hadn't said a word, accelerated and shot across lanes, grabbing the only open parking spot for several blocks.

"What the fuck?" McMurdy spewed as Doyle removed her seatbelt and grabbed her wallet.

With a hand on the door pull, she looked at him with the seriousness the case demanded.

"I wish you'd shared this valuable information before we left."

"Well, you know now, and *now* is the part where we go investigate, remember?"

She reached up and patted his hair, grimacing and wiping her hand on her pants before removing the car keys from the ignition.

"No, *now* is the time we get food. Our boy has been asleep for how many months? Pretty sure he can wait till I get a meatball sandwich." She got out and slammed the door. When he opened his mouth in protest, she shouted over her shoulder, her comment nearly lost in the noise of the city. "With those fat fries! I'd die for some of those big ass fries."

He watched her not-big-ass as she sauntered into the diner as if they hadn't finally gotten a lead on one of their most frustrating cases.

He begrudgingly followed her, pondering an equal mystery to the Skin Guy case.

How did that tiny woman eat so damn much?

By the time they'd eaten, crept their way out of the city, and driven to the institute, it was getting dark. Upon arrival, the detectives wrestled with several layers of red tape, tightly represented by self-important information clerks, stern nurses, and low-level administrators until they were awarded visitors' badges. Then they had to wait till one of the doctors affiliated with their unsub's treatment was called in. Finally, they were escorted to the eighth-floor ward which felt more like a morgue, only with a lot of monitors and machinery.

It was well into the evening and Dr. Winston was none too happy with having to return to work within an hour of getting home, but he was alarmed when he'd been notified that homicide detectives were inquiring about his premier subject. The stakes in this study were high; he wanted to be in the loop on any information regarding the unknown man and to be in absolute control of any queries regarding the patient. While the cops couldn't possibly know about the work-around he'd personally approved for patient unknown male Alpha 5/16's inclusion in the study, without proper consent, one couldn't be too careful.

Neither detective showed the keen interest they felt as they studied the pale, emaciated man who lay prone before them. He had tubes attached and more monitors than a sports bar around him.

McMurdy and Doyle already had sparse information regarding what was and wasn't known about this patient whose DNA had rung their doorbell, as it had been a matter of record back when the sample was collected. But the lifeless figure before them was something of a letdown, even for the seasoned professionals. This guy wasn't capable of tying his shoes, let alone skinning someone alive, or even postmortem.

The silence became awkward amongst the hums and beeps of medical equipment.

Doyle unwrapped a stick of gum as she squinted at the man's slack face. She tipped her head as the gum disappeared into her mouth and pointed at him as she said,

"He looks a little familiar." She didn't really care who he looked like; she was just killing time as she mentally compared what they'd been told with what they knew and all they wanted to know.

"Right? He looks a little like Billy Crystal when he was a lot younger. That's why we call him Mitch." The night nurse, Alice Lopez, spoke before she thought. Dr. Winston shot her an annoyed look, but the detectives exchanged puzzled expressions. The woman's statement made no sense, but no stone would go unturned. McMurdy, generally funky looking but inexplicably appealing to the ladies, offered Nurse Lopez a smile as Doyle crossed her arms and watched.

"Come again? What was it? *Alice?*" His eyes had dropped to her identification tag; the question sounded weirdly seductive, and Doyle blinked slowly and deliberately to avoid rolling her eyes. Dr. Winston looked ready to protest as the blushing nurse responded.

"Oh, well, you know. That movie, City Slickers? The guy Billy Crystal played…"

McMurdy snapped his fingers and gratified the nurse by finishing her sentence.

"Oh, right! Mitch – uh – *Robbins*, right? Yeah! And remember Norman, the little cow?" The detective and the nurse shared a hearty laugh while the doctor pinched the bridge of his nose and Doyle gave in to the urge and rolled her eyes.

"Calf, McMurdy," she said with no indication of patience. To his confused expression, she responded flatly, "Little cows are more commonly known as calves…"

Suddenly they were all distracted by a series of beeps on the monitor nearest the subject's head. Flat lines became squiggly lines and Doyle finally spoke.

"So, doctor, what's that? We were told Mitch, here, was brain dead?"

Her insinuation was clear, and the doctor overlooked the crass reference to his patient's condition and spoke carefully. Sharing patient information without a warrant was dicey enough, even when that patient wasn't receiving unauthorized treatment.

"Well, this is something we're trying to figure out now that you mention it. This nighttime activity is unique to him. But ours is a research institute after all. This young man is giving us a run for our money. There's much we need to learn and will strive to do so."

"You and us both, doctor, you and us both" Doyle said as she retrieved one of her cards. The doctor was in such a hurry to get them out of there, he didn't notice McMurdy sliding his card to the blushing nurse.

After the detectives and doctor took their leave, Nurse Alice Lopez glanced at the card with wide eyes. She hugged herself and stared at the only patient with activity on their neuro-monitor.

Those had been homicide detectives.

Was Mitch a murder suspect? She rubbed the goosebumps covering her arms as she glanced at the squiggly lines.

"Are you dreaming or are you remembering?" Her whispered question was lost among the echoing sounds of technology, but the implications of either possibility made her suddenly want to go find other people. Awake people.

She hustled to the nursing station with no idea of the power of her question.

In the dark car, Doyle listened to McMurdy overanalyze the likelihood of the comatose Mitch being their man. The timeline fit; to their knowledge, no victims with the Skin Guy's signature had been found since Mitch had been admitted. He seemed kind of small, though, to be capable of such violent crimes. He also had no known identity whatsoever and in today's day and age, that was no small trick. Their guy had been all over the northeast and no one had even looked for Mitch. How could someone be that invisible?

Doyle tossed a flavorless wad of gum out the window, pulling out a fresh piece as McMurdy's endless back and forth flowed. She was used to it. He processed everything externally and incessantly, while she conserved words but kept the wheels turning inside, just as constantly.

He finally exhausted himself with speculation and what he considered a complete and fair assessment of every possibility. It's what he deemed as objective policework. It was only then he seemed to remember he had a partner, and asked through the grayness,

"So, whatdya think?" He sucked what was left of the melted ice in his cup from dinner, filling the car with the scraping sound that Doyle had also become used to.

She answered with her version of objective police work.

"DNA doesn't lie."

On a nightshift in a DNA lab in Portland, Oregon, Aja Warner waited for the printout of the clandestine test she'd run for her sister Peg. She casually glanced around at the limited crew to ensure she wasn't about to receive undue attention. She could more than lose her job for what she was doing, but the deterrent wasn't as powerful as the adrenaline rush she got anytime she bucked rules. It was her thing, as was a lifetime of being a premier manipulator. It was as natural to her as breathing.

In fact, she had manipulated routine worksheets to hide the samples she'd obtained from Peg, grateful her agency hadn't gone to the upcoming paperless system which would have seriously constrained her unofficial testing. Additionally, she labelled the test as a training sample, giving her a little more camouflage to complete the task.

As the printer rumbled to life, she swatted a fuzzy clump of silvery purple hair between her face and glasses and thought about her little sister Peg. "Little" was a stretch, as they were within months of being the same age. As a childless woman, it would always be a mystery to Aja why their mother had not only taken in a house full of kids, but a few who were so close in age they were infants at the same time. Their mom, Andi, said it just added to the fun and ensured built-in playmates. Sounded like hell to Aja.

She cranked up her "obnoxious music," as one of her co-workers called the endless stream of heavy metal, from her wireless speaker. It was a good way to keep unwanted eyes from her fake processing.

She throat-umphed along with the bass of SKinKneader as she reached for the test results, popping her bubble gum at the exact moment she snapped the paper from the spool.

She looked at the sample comparisons with little interest. There was added data, so she looked again.

The new bubble she'd just blown popped and dropped over her bottom lip as she stared at the results, then ran to the screen which was populated with the source of the information she held in her hand.

"Holy shit," she said with a low thrill.

Aja loved drama, intrigue, and conflict and what she saw before her offered a holy trinity comprised of the three. She cranked the music and logged in to her personnel file to see how much time off she had coming.

"You did what?" L.Z. dropped his head so hard to the table, the thump made their drinking glasses rattle. He just left it there, forehead throbbing as he stared at the creases in his dockers, inches from his nose. "I can't believe this is happening."

Peg eyed the wiry fuzz on his head, knowing he had one hair less than a few weeks before as she chewed on her skin in lieu of fingernails. In the past weeks' tension between her and L.Z., there was nothing left to chew. Tasting blood, she yanked her hand out with a yelp.

L.Z. lifted his head slightly and looked at her.

"Really, I'm the one who just got a concussion, here. Quit chewing your fingers, *please,* and tell me I misunderstood what you just said."

His head was pounding. He rubbed his closed eyes but snapped them back open. The images from his dreams were burned like daguerreotypes on his eyelids. Only, unfortunately they were in color, red being predominant.

Peg nervously gripped the table, looking too much like a deranged Shirley Temple for L.Z. to stay mad. He was just. So. *Tired.* Yes, Rex, his head invader, had been silent for days now, which was a giant relief. But the detail, violence, and frequency of his dreams were so alarming, he didn't want to think of them, let alone discuss them with anyone, including his psychiatrist. And now, even real life was becoming a nightmare. Peg looked away but spoke with the whine of a six-year-old caught with a finger in the Cool Whip tub.

"I took a hair from your brush. And I took your toothbrush…"

"That was you? Do you realize I crawled around on the bathroom floor looking for that? No matter how much you clean a bathroom floor, it's still…" He stopped himself, holding up both hands as if the physical act could create a barrier from further blather. He inhaled calmness, then said to Peg, "And I even questioned Ma...you never know what she's up to."

"I'm sorry! I said that already. But my sister needed items with your specific DNA so she could..."

"What? What did you say?" L.Z. leapt to his feet, arms in the air. It was finally happening. He was losing it. "Please tell me I'm dreaming. Oh wait...can't be that. There's not enough blood. I'm not, you know, peeling the skin from..." He stopped cold and lost his color.

Peg's head jerked away, so she wasn't looking at him as her brain reheard what he'd said. She knew he was having bad dreams, but *peeling skin?*

"L.Z.?" His name was a question on Peg's lips. His back was to her, and the air seemed to have been sucked from the room.

One fuckery at a time, he thought. Without facing her, he said hoarsely,

"Please. You go first. It appears we have a lot to discuss. My DNA, my toothbrush, and your sister. You know. *Normal stuff.* Let's table the Quentin Tarantino dreams for now."

The silence between them was only breached by Judge Judy's voice in mid ass-chewing, drifting in from the living room where Elle watched her daytime heroine rule with a fist.

217

L.Z. turned, eyes down, and slowly sat with Peg.

"My sister Aja is a DNA lab person…you know, like in CSI?"

L.Z.'s expression told her she needed to get to the point. She glanced over her shoulder toward the living room, then grabbed his hand, whispering almost as if in a panic.

"Look. We're all freaking adopted. All of us. My mom, she said she liked to collect strays, you know?" L.Z.'s eyebrows flew up as he finally looked at her. And he'd thought *his* mom was weird.

Then it hit him.

I think I'm your sister.

His throat closed and he shook his head and tried to say something. Anything. Even with the idea volley-balling around for days, this made it a little too real. She was talking again in hushed tones, and he tried to listen past the noise in his head that had nothing to do with Rex.

"…and I was digging through my mom's stuff. She would never tell us where we came from, because she said if those people had wanted us, we'd still be with them. Anyway, I found some stuff including pictures with your mom from…" She could see his slack jaw and squeezed his hand. "L.Z.! Listen to me! When were you born? Just tell me?"

Dazed and unsure what his birthday had to do with it, he said, "January 1990."

She squeezed his hands so hard, a high-pitched snort escaped his nose.

"Me too!" She squealed quietly through her big teeth.

"Wait, what?" He pulled his hands away and stared into her face. His wheels were overrun, but still turning. "You're really losing me here. It almost sounds like you think we're twins." Ready to put up a fight, he grasped for words of reason when she clamped his knee with such force he jerked.

"No, triplets!"

It was too much. L.Z. raised his arms in surrender and stood. Then he froze there when an old and ridiculous claim of his mother's surfaced.

No! It was just one more of her delusions or stories. Or…the list of other claims which had turned out to be true bobbed to the surface of his mind and he swooned, grabbing the table just in time.

"It's OK, L.Z.! I mean, I'd love it if we could be – you know – but now you know why I couldn't kiss you. I mean…yuck!" She blushed and hurried to mitigate her words, "I mean, not yuck *you,* but yuck to the sister and brother thing…"

He looked as if he'd just taken a multi-volt shock to his head. No words came, which was just as well because his mouth felt like it was full of cotton.

Judge Judy's symphonic theme music drifted in, and Peg jumped up and grabbed the zombie-version of L.Z. by the shoulders.

"But my mom, she's a little off, and her papers are a mess, so, I just thought if we could do a DNA test…"

"Triplets?" was all L.Z. could muster.

Knowing Elle could walk in at any time, Peg got nose-to-nose with L.Z. and whispered so fast she sounded like the disclaimer portion of a drug advertisement.

"I know, right? But I found other pictures in your – maybe *our* mom's – anyway, Elle's stuff. Three babies, L.Z. With curly hair! I don't know, but maybe the other one is one of my sibs, but I should hear from Aja any day…"

"Well, aren't you two getting cozy." Elle's throaty voice dragged through the air, and they could smell her smoke aura as she passed through to the patio door. She tossed a prescription bag onto the table. "Once you two are done with the tongue tango, here's your mind-altering refills that are probably reprogramming your gray matter with every pill."

The screen door slammed and the two stared at each other. Their faces were so close, L.Z. could single out Peg's eyelashes and smell red licorice on her breath.

He couldn't, *wouldn't* believe it.

Then he heard it in his head. But it wasn't Rex's voice. It was his mother's from long ago.

220

"And I chose to keep you, Leddy. Three beautiful babies and I chose you."

Physically and emotionally exhausted, L.Z. was in his room to hit the sack by 8 PM that night. The space around his bed looked like the set for a bad horror movie now. He still took the pills to drive out nightmares, although he had no evidence whatsoever that they worked. But he was desperate. That desperation also fueled his additional efforts to either block or prevent the dreams, as well as measures to force sleep when his fear kept his eyes wide open in the dark due to anxiety.

"Sleep-aiding" headphones were draped across the headboard; he wore them nightly and had experimented with every kind of music from classical to Disney tunes to meditative brain wave tracks to redirect his mind and prevent nightmares. His desk chair was near the bed to hold his laptop where he'd tried playing reoccurring peaceful scenes, videos of jumping sheep, and aquarium screen savers with serene tropical fish swimming back and forth.

He'd hit the internet with flourish and purchased "weighted blankets" boasted to wrap you in comfort and battle a number of things that can prevent a good night's sleep. He also purchased a Simba Hybrid duvet made of stuff inspired by spacesuits purported to cool you down if you were too hot; it had done nothing to prevent his awakening in rivulets of sweat after the horrible dreams – but it lay on his bed, still. Various sets of noise cancelling ear apparatus were scattered across and under his pillow. He'd also purchased herbal sleep remedies as evidenced by bottles of pills and drinking glasses with differently colored liquid solutions.

He was standing on his pillow, placing a newly arrived native American dreamcatcher on the wall over his bed when he heard a tap on the door. He sagged, head against the wall hanging; it had to be Peg; nothing about Elle was that gentle. What the hell, how could things get any more discombobulated; besides, if he didn't lay down soon, he'd just pass out anyway and what better place to fall than on the bed.

"Come in."

He heard Peg gasp as she saw the condition of his formerly organized sleeping quarters. She had composed herself, however, by the time he turned around, having struck a too-casual pose against the door jamb.

"May I come in?"

"Well, I guess it's safe since you could be my sister and all." Just saying it caused a stabbing sense of grief followed by a rush of guilt. *What kind of weirdo was in love with his sister?*

He waved off the thought and stepped down.

"Look, I've heard everything you said and once we get rid of Ma tomorrow, we'll look for that stuff you found. But, Peg, I'm the walking dead here. I really need to hit the rack."

"If you think I'm going to turn off the lights tonight or climb up into that dark attic tomorrow before you explain that whole peeling skin…comment…*thing*…you said today, you're…" she stopped and visibly shuddered, hugging herself. But when she looked at L.Z., she saw the same regular guy she was so fond of. He looked pathetic and she was suddenly disgusted with herself.

"I'm sorry, it's just, well maybe if all this junk isn't working, talking about it will?"

He sighed and sank onto the edge of the bed, wondering how he would be able to drive to work the next day, let alone perform in any acceptable way. He looked at her and shrugged.

"Peg, I assure you, if I told you about what I see at night, you'd never turn off your lights again and wouldn't go into that attic even if you thought you'd find Elvis."

"It's that bad?"

"It's worse than Texas Chainsaw Massacre."

She lit up with big-toothed humor. "I love horror movies! I've seen them all, it's OK."

He looked away. She bit her lip as she watched the weight of a decision fall on his face. When his bloodshot eyes circled back to her, he said,

"Yeah, but I wasn't the star of those movies."

It took her a minute, but when she understood, she closed the gap between them, sitting and looping her arm around him.

He really wished she wouldn't do that.

"L.Z., you're in the dreams? And the skin stuff...?" She couldn't finish.

He sighed and tried to feel sibling affection rather than the other things he felt as she squeezed closer.

"Peg, I can see it all, like it's not me...but the guy doing it? It's me. No doubt."

She hugged him and his body hummed; he wasn't sure if it was the extreme fatigue or his perverted sibling passion, but the empathy was as welcome as his need to share.

"But do you, I mean...you don't *like it* in the dreams, do you?" He felt her tense as she asked the question and wasted no time with his honest answer.

"No! I find it revolting...and I see it, but I don't, like, *do* it. It's like watching a movie. With me in it." He felt lame, but relieved. He brightened as he told her, "Lately, though, it's not all blood and guts...it's blood, guts, and money, and hideouts, I think. I guess all it needs is a little sex, right?" As soon as the words left his mouth, he felt himself shrivel with embarrassment. But she was hanging on to his former comment.

"Money? Hideouts? Shit, it sounds like a movie, but what if it means something, L.Z.? I mean, are you writing this down? I keep a journal because I forget stuff, even if it's important."

He gently pulled away so he could think as he answered.

"I don't need to write it down…it's up here. Like burned in there." He stood and stretched as she sat looking up at him with her impossibly round eyes. He felt his heart do that thing and looked away, sweeping his hand toward his desk. "You won't find an address book, phone list, or check register in here anywhere, you know why?"

Her expression not only told him she didn't know why, but that she was confused he was asking in the middle of such a critical conversation. So, he answered his own question.

"Because I have a photographic memory, that's why. Everything I see makes a permanent picture. Whether it's pretty or not. It's here. *Forever.*" He pointed at his temple, nodding at her to affirm his own announcement.

Her nose wrinkled as the impact of his statement sunk in. No wonder he couldn't let it go. It was still there when he was awake.

He wavered a bit as the room fell silent. She stood, knowing she had possibly done more damage than good, and all for selfish reasons. She was still scared by what he'd said earlier, but now it was for him, not for herself.

As she headed for the door, he tried to lighten the mood.

"Don't let me forget the tape and match sticks before we head up there tomorrow." When she turned, he was pointing at the ceiling with an odd smile on his face.

"Um, I was thinking more like a flashlight than matches, and why do we need tape?"

"We don't want Ma going into another paranoid tailspin when she sees a security breach of her innermost secrets."

Peg was now thoroughly confused. She crossed her arms and shook her head.

With a hand on the door, he said,

"A matchstick stuck in the attic hatch. If she goes out to the garage and it's on the floor, she knows someone has been up there." Peg's dropped jaw spurred him on. "And those boxes and stuff up there? She strings a strand of hair across every opening, taping the ends. No way you would have noticed in that light, but as soon as you opened them…"

"…the hair broke…*that's how she knew.*" Peg shook her head in wonder. "Genius."

That's one word for it, L.Z. thought as he followed her into the hall and said, "Well, that's how she knew someone had been up there. We'll cover our tracks tomorrow. I got the tape and matches; you get to provide the hair. You already took all I had to spare, after all. But at least your toothbrush is safe."

She licked her finger and swiped the air.

"Touché," she said.

Fifteen minutes later, L.Z. was crashed, headphones intact, belly full of magical internet herbs. Five minutes after that the mental film reel rolled and his eyelids flitted as his face contorted.

Far away, in the Byrde Brain Trauma institute's eighth floor research ward, one monitor awoke as the rest remained still and silent.

Elle was safely settled at Linda's for an Ancient Alien's marathon on the History Channel. L.Z. still smelled of burgers and fry grease from work when he moved up the step ladder for the deep dig into Elizabeth Taylor Manson's archives. After pointing out a well-placed matchstick, he opened the hatch and Peg scrambled up after him, grateful to have a partner in crime this time.

As she illuminated the cache with an LED light, L.Z. pulled out the first container she pointed to and he added additional light with his phone flashlight along the edges of the lid till he found a hair and tape seal, pointing it out to an intrigued Peg.

When he popped the top off, he offered the inevitable comment, "All's hair in love and war!"

She snorted a laugh, and he got *that feeling,* hoping against hope they'd uncover evidence that they were not, indeed, related.

Two hours later, he still smelled like burgers and fry grease, with the addition of dust-coated sweat. And Peg had several fewer hairs. He secured the attic door, placing the match back in its spot to cover their tracks and they were soon gulping water in the kitchen.

All they'd brought back down was what they'd taken up with them, but their phone camara rolls were filled with discovery of what Peg had already seen and more.

They stood in the kitchen, minds spinning with what they knew and what they needed to know. The sources for the missing information were a block away, a state away, and a phone call away in the form of two mothers and a sister.

"Aja will call when she gets any results." Peg said, relieved to have L.Z. in the know, although she also had mixed feelings about the final verification of her biological roots. L.Z. absently flipped through his phone gallery. He felt like he'd swallowed a bucket of rocks and questioned a legion of long-held beliefs about his mother. And now, about himself.

"We need to talk to Ma first," He looked at Peg with an expression she couldn't read. She nodded, but he could see her doubt.

"We'll wait as long as we need to. You know."

She knew. They had to wait for a "good day" for Elle; one when her feet were on the ground, if they had any chance at getting the truth.

"Yeah," she said, picking cobwebs from her curls. "I just hope it's before Christmas."

She was trying for a joke, but they both knew the truth. Although they hadn't openly discussed it, they'd both felt it. Something bigger than them, uglier than L.Z.'s dreams, and crazier than Elle Manson's mind was at hand. Christmas was months away and they both knew L.Z. could only stretch so far.

Even rubber bands will break eventually.

Aaron Stoss learned about an upcoming short tour break after their last gig in New Hampshire. Since his parents lived in Lake George, New York, he wouldn't have an excuse not to visit. More importantly, he badly wanted to see his brother, so he would take the two-hour trek south while he was in the area. If he was honest with himself, *that* visit trumped his real reasons for considering a stop at his childhood home. If he thought he could pull off being in the state without his parents knowing, he'd have gone straight to his brother. But as the black sheep in the family, it had taken years to mend miles of broken fences with his folks, so he convinced himself they were his priority even as he mentally planned his escape to where he really wanted to be, just north of the big city. Where he *needed* to be.

The other truth was the tour hiatus couldn't have come at a better time. He had to tend to loose ends.

After having an awkward phone conversation with his mom informing her he'd be in town, he sat on the miniscule balcony off his motel room with a folded letter and his cell phone.

He didn't need to read the letter from L.Z. Manson again; he'd read it so often it was tearing at the creases.

It wasn't uncommon for fans to fixate on performers, to contact them, and imagine connections. While Aaron was hardly a rock icon – *yet* – and wasn't even a front man as rhythm guitar player for SKinKneader, he'd provided the idea for the band's name and had written most of their hits.

"I don't just relate to your lyrics, I get them. I believe we have a lot in common even though you don't know who I am. I promise I'm not some kind of stalker. I just get where they come from, your lyrics, I mean. I think I understand the inspiration. Especially *Voices* and *No Cure*. I even had a dream about a song I haven't heard…

It's so dark, are you dead?

It's the voice in your head…

I knead your skin, I need your eyes,

If you don't answer I'll fucking die."

The fucking letter *said that*. Aaron had it memorized and as he thought of it, he crushed the letter.

I just get where they come from, your lyrics, I mean.

The songs Manson referenced during their conversation, then the letter, were the songs that counted. The ones that had put him on the charts, well, had put SKinKneader on the charts anyway.

Yet the most disturbing part of that letter were the "dream" lyrics. They weren't new to Aaron. They were word-for-word a song he had only started but didn't finish because it was too far out there even for him, regardless of his source of inspiration. How did that guy know?

I just get where they come from, your lyrics, I mean.

The innocent enough words were caustic to Aaron and just the thought of them caused him to unfurl the smashed letter so he could get the phone number.

231

Too much was on the line. This guy knew things he couldn't possibly know...but he knew, nonetheless.

As the phone rang, Aaron Stoss strained to dig up a conciliatory voice; he'd been such a dick to the guy in SLC, he might need to suck up a bit to get to the bottom of things.

The phone picked up and his mouth went dry as he heard the vaguely familiar voice say,

"Hello, do you know why you shouldn't have phone sex?"

What?

Aaron didn't even begin to know how to answer, but he soon realized he didn't need to when the voice continued after a slight pause.

"Because you might get hearing AIDS! *Ba-da-bump!*"

The hard-core rocker's face contracted with confusion. He didn't get the pun and was wondering if he'd even gotten the right guy. But the message continued, solving the mystery.

"Yeah, this is L.Z.'s phone. Leave a message."

This guy is whacked, Aaron thought, then he heard the tone.

"Yeah, hi, L.Z. This is Aaron Stoss. You know, SKinKneader? Uh, yeah. I just ran across that letter you gave me back in SLC. Sorry it took so long to read it, life in the fast lane and all. Anyway, sounds cool. Let's, like, hook up and talk about your, uh, *thoughts*. One-on-one would be great

232

but can't remember where you are. Seems like it wasn't Salt Lake." He paused and grabbed his hair. Jesus. He was fucking this up. "So, right, give me a call. Talk soon, I'm out."

He disconnected the call and dropped the phone.

He remembered very little about the guy, other than he'd really come across as a geek.

A geek who possibly held Aaron's cards in a death grip.

All he could hear in his head was that song that never was.

It's so dark, are you dead?

It's the voice in your head...

I knead your skin, I need your eyes,

If you don't answer I'll fucking die.

He hoped L.Z. Manson answered soon.

L.Z.'s phone rang during his evening run. He hadn't gotten any faster, although he felt less like he was going to die with each venture out. But answering his phone, let alone try to carry on a conversation while simultaneously trying to breathe and not trip over his own feet was still out of his league. When he slowed down in front of the house and retrieved his phone to stop his running playlist, he looked at the missed call. It was an unknown number. He assumed it was a robocall and with sweat burning his eyes, he didn't notice the tiny voicemail icon.

When he walked into the living room, he could see Peg crocheting again with a small pile of completed rectangular items on the end table between her and Elle. Elle was cutting out what looked like coffee filters. Of course, the evening news was on the television; God forbid his mother miss out on fodder for her upcoming theory campaigns.

"Craft night, ladies?" he asked as he plopped on the couch. Wiping his face with his t-shirt sleeve, he tried to scrutinize his mother by peering under his arm without being obvious. A small nod from Peg told him it might be worth it.

They had been walking on eggshells around the unpredictable old bird, trying to find the right time to discuss knowledge that increasingly felt like time bombs in their hands. Peg had been unable to get ahold of Aja, which only increased the tension between L.Z and her.

"Right, Leddy. You know I'm no Martha Stewart. I am, however, forward thinking. Mark my words, we can sell these things for bank once the shit hits the fan." She held the cut filter in one hand and one of Peg's creations in the other, shaking them in her son's direction.

He couldn't keep track of her obsessions, and his legs were starting to cramp, so he stood as he tossed a question to humor her, assuming he'd misunderstood the intent of Peg's nod moments earlier. Didn't appear Ma was "level" tonight, after all.

"Uh…let me guess. Signal jammers for the masses? And the filters, what? Increase effectiveness?"

If he'd learned anything from Peg, it had been the value of not persistently challenging his mother's delusions. And in his late constant state of fatigue, it provided welcome peace in the house.

"Don't be daft. These are masks for the pandemic. She's making attractive exteriors, but with pockets for the filters which will block germs. Cheap, nice to look at, but effective. Ideal business model. And unless I'm sadly mistaken, they will soon be in high demand since apparently, I'm the only one who sees this thing coming."

L.Z. exercised extreme control in stopping the reflexive eyeroll as he turned to go shower.

He offered a weary smile and shrug to Peg but stopped when his mother exclaimed, "Eureka!"

He spun to see what could have possibly transpired in the past nanosecond but saw the same scene as before. Except now his mother was pointing at the TV with one hand, grappling for the remote control with the other. His eyes swept to the flat screen just as the volume shot up.

"…multiple cases of an unknown virus in Oregon and parts of Northern California. There seems to be a cluster in the Portland area which leads authorities to speculate it might have originated overseas, considering the international influx in that area. It's highly contagious, by all indications, but without more information, the CDC declines comment at this time."

Elle was standing now, stock still with a chiseled and serious expression.

"If they'd look at their goddamned correspondence, they would not only comment, but have a plan. This is going to be bad, folks."

She didn't sound crazy. She didn't sound triumphant. She sounded incredibly sad and became uncharacteristically silent.

A cold finger traced L.Z.'s spine, and he reached for the couch to steady himself. When he looked at Peg, she looked like he felt.

This was different. This felt like one of Elle's handful of hits in an ocean of misses. And it was a big one.

And it also indicated something else; she was as grounded as she could get, and the gravity of the situation just might keep her there for a while.

The weary-looking old woman wordlessly walked out to have a cigarette.

L.Z. and Peg watched the news without listening for a few minutes before he stood again.

"Guess I'd better shower. Seems like it might be a good night for a talk."

"Yes, she'll need a distraction," Peg agreed, but obviously understood his point.

They needed to catch Elizabeth Taylor Manson while there was a chance she was all there.

Aja wanted to test the samples one more time before she dropped the bombshell on her sister, but to avoid running the risk of being caught, her efforts had been delayed by a shift rotation which had landed her on days.

When a co-worker needed coverage for a night gig, he was shocked when the normally self-possessed Aja volunteered to take his shift.

She proceeded with caution, even though she'd done the last analysis without detection. But as a natural schemer, she understood the danger of complacency. Luck was on her side though, when the handful of other analysts who were teammates gaggled together to discuss the local virus that had just gotten national news attention. Being scientists at heart, a spirited debate commenced among the analysts, and one result was a wide berth for Aja to complete her task with time to spare.

The secondary result was validation that Aja Warner possessed life-changing information. She wondered how much her sister knew when she'd sent hair and toothbrushes via FedEx.

She remembered Peglet's words when she'd nearly begged Aja for the favor. *Maybe the most important thing in my life.*

Aja loved a good plot twist; it was one of the reasons she'd sought this career. Granted, the job wasn't nearly as cool as they made it out to be on CSI or Forensic Files, but to be at the heart of important discovery charged her power-hungry generator.

And this time it was personal. Of course, she loved Peg, but she loved holding all the cards more. She needed to play this hand just right.

She texted Peg, not to share the news, but to get her address so she could send her an ambiguous something or other which, of course, would never make its way to the post office. She needed the address for something else entirely.

Fortunately, she had discovered she had vacation time available, and it was a good time to take it. Some news was better served warm and in person.

By the time Peg responded to Aja's text, it had already become clear that the magic moment to have "the talk" with

Elle wasn't going to happen anytime soon. L.Z. was called in to work to cover for another manager who'd fallen ill on the job.

A grave-faced Elle stuffed one of the coffee-filter fortified crochet masks into her son's hand.

"This thing is going to travel fast, Son. If that sick guy at work has a fever, runny nose, and a headache, you wear this thing and don't you take shit off anyone."

Oh, right. L.Z. controlled his sarcastic facial muscles with the next thought. *Those are only the symptoms for the common cold and flu and every other virus known to man.*

She continued in a hushed voice as she squeezed his arm with a vice grip.

"*We* might be immune," she paused, staring hard into his eyes with unsaid meaning before continuing, "but better safe than sorry. Besides, leading by example is critical in times of crisis."

Among the satellites of stressors orbiting through L.Z.'s mind, a snarky thought of his mother giving advice on "leading by example" whizzed past its cue in conscious thought. Somewhere in there was the question as to why "we might be immune," but since it hadn't collided with her assertion that they had alien DNA in its mental storage craft, that little bit of logic eluded him.

Knowing he'd work till closing, he grabbed his pills.

It was an oxymoron for him to continue taking either medication. Although Rex's voice had ceased practically the moment L.Z. swallowed the first Olanzapine, he couldn't shake the notion that the voice, the essence of Rex, was not a figment of his mind or the result of mental illness. It just didn't compute with what he'd seen with his mother, and it didn't feel right. And, of course, the Prazosin had zero effect on mitigating his night terrors, yet he would stay on track with the dosing. If for no other reason than being able to look Dr. Bhattacharyya in the eye and say he'd taken the pills religiously, but...

He didn't have the "but" worked out yet, although he would before he set foot back in her office again; he'd wear a Disney T-Shirt.

Already on his way to work, he tried to rack and stack his various dreads as he swallowed the capsule and pill with a Monster energy drink (he wouldn't share this particular cocktail with Dr. B.). He dreaded a potential extended delay before he and Peg could have "the conversation" with Elle; he sensed a shift in her centeredness even before he left the house.

He also dreaded getting home that night exhausted, only to drift off into his own version of the most macabre Stephen King movie ever.

Most of all, he dreaded what waited for him at the Red Missile Burgers restaurant in nearby Nampa, where the manager had gotten sick.

He didn't dread symptoms of "runny nose, fever, and headache." He didn't dread the return of Rex, the possibility of which always lingered on the edge of his brain. He didn't even dread the flashes of his nocturnal murderous rampages flashing through his mind at will.

What he dreaded most now was the immediate threat: a whole crew of unfamiliar self-centered teen-aged food service workers with the health of every potential customer in their hands. That was the true definition of horror in L.Z.'s mind.

It was well into the evening as Detective McMurdy leaned over stacks of documents with a slack jaw and face void of expression. His hands gripped oily strands creating the perfect balance to prevent his faceplant onto the pile. If she couldn't hear him breathing, Detective Doyle might have thought he was in a coma.

Staring at her twin stack of paperwork from the Byrde Brain Trauma Center, she felt his pain. Even with the warrant, they'd nearly had to pry "unknown male Alpha 5/16's" file from the dour Dr. Winston's hands.

Now they wondered if it was for naught. Even if they could understand half of the medical jargon in their evidentiary heaps, it would likely shed little light on the case.

In discussion, the detectives referred to the patient as "Mitch" now, following the hospital staff's lead. McMurdy refused to call him "Skin Guy" because even with the DNA match and favorable timeline of no skinless victims appearing since Mitch's hospital admission, his gut wouldn't allow him to take the leap. Something felt weird about it, as if skinned corpses didn't make the whole thing just weird enough.

For Doyle, there was nothing to debate. She followed the science.

When their joint desk phone rang with the opportunity for distraction, the game was on. Although McMurdy's reach was easily twice that of his tiny partner, she had turbo charge between her brain and reflexes; she reacted with lightning speed. While this made her an extremely valuable field partner, it was a constant practical frustration for McMurdy. Just as her hand hit the phone receiver, her perpetually wild ponytail was in his reach. But his slight delay defeated him again as she anticipated his move, ducking and landing in her chair, phone in hand. She glanced at him with a barely detectable smile as she answered.

"Detective Doyle."

McMurdy slammed his hand on his pile of riveting brain charts, then grabbed his cup.

When he returned with his mug o' acid from the towering non-stop cop coffee maker, Doyle was off the phone and looking from her empty cup to her bleary-eyed partner.

He scrambled for a smartass reply for her unspoken request when her next words nearly caused him to drop his Folgers.

"Boss is going to be thrilled the ancestry DNA warrant paid off." She turned her cup upside-down and exaggeratedly watched as nothing poured out.

In an uncharacteristically swift move, McMurdy grabbed her mug and dumped half of his coffee in and roughly handed it back.

"There. Now, tell me."

Offering a rare smile, she took a swig and after wincing from the taste, she said to the vile liquid,

"Looks like Mitch has an uncle. Darla is sending the report."

Her statement was still sinking into McMurdy's mind when her computer dinged with an e-mail notification.

Doyle thunked her mug against his in a toast.

"Here's to Find-your-Family.com."

L.Z. could write a screenplay for a blockbuster slasher movie if only he had the wherewithal, imagination, and mental presence to fill in the gaps between the dozens of detailed scenes in his mental library.

The "mental presence" factor was becoming more prominent as was evidenced by the fact he was at work, but his cell phone was at home. It was a pivotal oversight on what turned out to be a momentous day.

He didn't get Uncle Al's text that he'd be flying in that day and that it was not on Red Missile Burger business. Nor did he get the text from a drunk Aaron Stoss who was fed up with not having heard back from L.Z. who, in his advanced state of fatigue, never realized the multiple calls from an unknown number in New York were not, indeed, robocalls leaving sales messages, messages he'd deleted without listening.

He didn't get the voice mail from the concerned Dr. Bhattacharyya, nor her assistant, because in his new gray world, L.Z. had missed his appointment with her the day before and she wanted to know, point blank if he was still hearing voices and having nightmares.

He could not have gotten a warning text from Peg who would have surely sent him one if she'd had any idea what was going on in Elle's room all day. Of course, even airhead Peg would have realized she couldn't send a text to L.Z. at work when Elle had his phone at home.

At no point during the day did he even miss the damn phone. In fact, not having it was just one less thing to distract him. One less thing to stress him out. One less thing; just one less of anything was a relief.

He rode his new bicycle home; one he'd bought so Peg would have transportation to help her maintain the household or to use in the event of an emergency with Elle.

One could have speculated that Elle's discoveries in one short day constituted an emergency all right, but "emergency" didn't exactly constitute the situation he faced ahead.

When L.Z. walked in the house, all hell broke loose.

"At what point was you planning on telling me?"

Elle's voice was deadly calm. Too calm.

L.Z. reflexively scanned the room and hallway. Elle answered his question.

"I sent her to the store. This is between you and me."

L.Z. closed the door, his tired brain suddenly sharp with adrenaline. He'd seen 50 Shades of Crazy in Ma, but this was different. He'd never known her to be dangerous, but he had also never seen this version of her or sensed this vibe. Choosing silence, he eased forward, biting his lip as he reached for the closest chair, not taking his brown eyes off her neon blue ones.

Even as he sat, he couldn't make sense of it until she slowly waved his phone back and forth, her elbow planted on her chair arm.

His mind went into overdrive with flashes of the pictures cataloguing his mother's history from her most private stash. Her "this is between you and me" comment resurfaced, and he was suddenly grateful for Peg's absence, although "it" was actually among the three of them.

"Mom…we've wanted to talk to you. We…"

"We? What, Leddy? Got a mouse in your pocket?"

He ignored the slight and eased from the chair to the couch to get closer. He was still on unfamiliar ground. She seemed "level," and her anger was justified. Lack of sleep and stress had muddied his senses, but even through the fog, this was new, and he didn't know what to make of it.

He just needed to have better footing and wanted to de-escalate before Peg returned. They had been in on the invasion together, but this, this was his responsibility. Regardless of Peg's speculation, Elle was his mother and he needed to answer for their indiscretion.

She looked at the phone now, sliding her finger across the screen and selecting what he assumed was his photo gallery. A sudden question rose, but she answered, as she had done so many times in his life before he asked. He got a chill.

"You didn't think your *mother'd* figure out your password? And just so's you know, it wasn't my goal in life to steal your precious cellular device and invade your privacy…"

He started to speak up with a disclaimer on his and Peg's behalf again, but she cut him off by slicing through the air with his phone.

"…and discover just how much *you don't trust me*." Her eyes suddenly softened, and he thought he saw tears. The sight confused him more than the Gestapo stance just seconds before. Yet, he still didn't sense Crazy Elle. All he saw was his mother, and as the previous weeks crashed around him, he started to crumble.

"I'm so sorry, Ma! We had no right. We should have never gone up there without talking to you first."

The limited energy and wherewithal he had ran out with his first tears. He was on his last leg physically and mentally, and he had to get this right.

He stopped, pressing his thumbs into his eyes as if to quash the tears. When he opened them and the blurriness cleared, Elle was looking at him, only this time she looked confused. In a panic, he realized he'd incriminated Peg, and sliding from the couch, he dropped to his knees and grabbed Elle's free hand.

"Don't be mad at Peg, Ma. Don't. She means well and it's on me…it's…"

"What in the hell are you talking about, Leddy?"

He closed his eyes, shaking his head in short bursts. His confusion was obvious.

He heard the words fall from his mouth.

"The pictures. Of your stuff."

He heard her huff of a laugh, and his eyes sprang open.

In a second, she grabbed his head and pulled it against hers.

"Not the damn pictures, Leddy. I could handle them things." He was slightly panicked as her strong grip held their foreheads so close, he couldn't see her eyes. But her next words were through gritted teeth and laden with sorrow.

"Boy…why didn't you tell me about the voices? And how's about the skin needer business? Son…no wonder you look like you're dying a day at a time. This didn't just start and it's not just going to end. Come here."

The need to remind her of the night he tried to tell her evaporated as her skinny arms encompassed him and his phone fell to the floor. Their sweat mingled and for the first time since he was a very small boy, L.Z. Manson truly felt the comfort of a mother and allowed himself to cry like a son.

Al Manson accepted his credit card back from the pimply faced kid at the McDonald's drive-through, every line on his face indicating he had much more on his mind than the chatty exchange between himself and the awkward young man. He hated to be disloyal to Missile Burgers, but McDonald's was located between his home and the airport, and he would hate even more to pay four times the price for coffee and a sandwich at the airport.

He sighed heavily as he grabbed his bag and headed back to the interstate toward the Salt Lake City International Airport.

Although the flight between Salt Lake and Boise would be relatively short, he was on standby for the first available flight as well as having a reservation for a much later departure. But it wouldn't have mattered if it had been a twelve-hour journey. No amount of time would prepare him for the conversation ahead of him with his nephew and, inevitably, his sister.

Abby had wanted to come with him after he'd shared the information from the conference call with the New York detectives, but he declined.

This was family business...blood family, not married family. The terminology sent a wave of nausea through him as he recalled the specifics from the monotone voice of Detective Doyle.

Abby had reluctantly acquiesced, and Al had called the airline, then packed.

After parking in the long-term lot, he retrieved his phone to text L.Z. to ensure the boy had received his earlier message and to give him an update. His notable eyebrows flicked when he saw the response to his original correspondence to his nephew.

Fuck you and the horse you ride in on, Pilgrim.

He looked up at the headliner of the car, then his eyes sharpened with memory. The most welcome and needed thing happened; he laughed long and loud.

He loved and hated his sister, and suspected she felt the same way as him. But they both loved John Wayne.

How Elle got her hands on L.Z.'s phone was beyond him, but at least now he knew his visit wouldn't be a surprise.

The news he'd bear, however, would be shocking.

Peg burst in with grocery bags of items she still didn't understand the need for, feeling guilty that L.Z. had beaten her there. She stopped short at the scene before her.

L.Z. was on the floor at Elle's feet, wearing her ever-present Snug Band around his own neck and had his head on Elle's boney knees. Peg was baffled. She had never seen Elle without the ratty sweatband fitted with internal ear buds either on her head or around her neck. Whenever the old lady whipped the thing over her ears, all conversations were instantly over as she retuned her mind into music, or podcasts, or God only knew what else.

"Um..." Peg looked back at the door, possibly calculating her escape from this untimely interruption, when L.Z. jumped up and seemed to come to his senses as he started to remove the worn-out band.

"Leave it on," Elle said sternly, smacking his head, then waved Peg in as she creakily stood, grabbing her scrunched cigarette pack. "Peg, girl, I hope you kept the receipt for that shit. We probably won't use any of it anyway."

With that, Elle headed toward the kitchen, shouting over her shoulder, "Come out whenever you're ready to talk about the attic."

Peg stood as though turned to stone, and L.Z. rushed over and relieved her of the useless purchases, moving her with his elbow so he could close the door.

Eyes brimming with tears, she followed him into the kitchen, "L.Z...I'm so sorry! I never would have left if I'd known she knew...and that you were coming home...and that she was going to..."

He set the bags down, and turned, covering her mouth gently to stop the pathetic spillage.

"It's OK, Peg. And I don't know any more than you do, but she has had my phone all day and found the…"

"Ouh cheet…" was her muffled proclamation from behind his hand, eyes wide with terror.

"Shhhh…" he said, removing his hand once he became unnerved by their proximity, and backed away, palms facing her to get her to calm down. "She's not mad, don't know why, but she said she'd answer all our questions tonight and…" he stopped when he saw her staring quizzically at the Snug Band. "That's a part of a different conversation."

Weariness seemed to wash back over him as Peg bit her lip and glanced toward the patio door.

"So, um, what about dinner?" She gestured weakly at the bags, "She gave me the weirdest list of everything we won't eat and sent me about the time I should have been fixing something. Should I…"

"Just order a pizza and order me another Snug Band while you're at it. Purple, this time," they heard Elle yell through the window from outside.

"I swear, that woman has the hearing of a bat," L.Z. mumbled as he went to find his phone.

Peg, feeling like an unneeded table leg, followed him rather than face Elle alone knowing what she knew now.

Before L.Z. could access the Domino's app, he scanned his messages, eyes narrowing then widening in surprise. Then he did something Peg hadn't seen in a while. He laughed.

"What?" Peg asked with a half-smile. L.Z. glanced up and with a shrug, replied, "Because things aren't hairy enough around here, it looks like Uncle Al is coming with some kind of can't-wait news. Fortunately, he can't make it till tomorrow sometime." Peg squinted at him, still waiting for the joke as L.Z. ordered their dinner.

She never saw the message a la John Wayne Elle had sent her brother from L.Z.'s phone, so she didn't get L.Z.'s comment after completing the order and shooing her toward the kitchen.

"God help him *and* the horse he rides in on. It's going to get real interesting around here real fast."

Truer words were never spoken.

Detectives McMurdy and Doyle had a heavy enough workload to stay occupied while awaiting approval to travel to Idaho, or to receive further word from Retired General Manson. But they didn't have to like it. They also weren't happy with Manson's insistence that he speak to his sister about the matter before they could speak to her, and also assured them that she would not cooperate with them if they called or arrived without his prior intervention.

253

He had been vague regarding his knowledge of their suspect, who had to be his only sibling's son, but was otherwise forthright and cooperative. Out of respect for his military rank and his cooperation, they didn't try to stop him from telling his family himself, not to mention, they had no authority to do so anyway. It was sensitive, he'd said; his sister "had issues," he said. It was complicated, he said. He had shared that there was at least one other child, a brother, and wouldn't expand on the "at least part."

The fact that the family name was Manson certainly wasn't lost on the detectives, although Doyle found it amusing while McMurdy was certain it was a harbinger. He couldn't let any of it go, and it was getting old.

"What the fuck?" McMurdy loudly exclaimed out of the blue, and not for the first time. Doyle was driving and although they were working on a separate case, she knew the source of her partner's spontaneous outcry. Keeping her eyes on the road, she worked her chewing gum over as he continued.

"*Complicated?* Yeah, pretty damn complicated. Maybe like having a nephew on life support, strapped to brain probing machines…oh, and a nephew who might be one of the most prolific serial killers in the country because he likes to skin his victims ain't complicated? Jesus!" He smacked his head against the side window and groaned.

Doyle continued to stare ahead, slowing along with the heavy city traffic when her phone pinged. The mass congestion came to a standstill, so she fished her phone out, eyebrows raised as she read the text.

McMurdy was too lost in his emotional stew to inquire about the message and, as always, Doyle took her time with it.

Once they began to inch forward, she said,

"I'll tell you what's complicated. That's how we're going to get eye-to-eye with the Manson regime under the wire before the Feds get word of the DNA match, which it's a miracle that no do-gooders on staff have passed it on to them, by the way."

McMurdy grunted, not finding words to express how badly that would suck.

Doyle played her last card as traffic picked up.

"I mean, that might not be an issue if they don't find out in the next, I don't know, *day or so*, right?"

McMurdy's face registered what she'd said, and he looked at her as she wagged her phone with her free hand.

"Just got approval. Ever been to Idaho?"

The pizza was picked over, and although there was plenty left, it was obvious the three weren't going to eat any more. Even in his advanced stage of depletion, L.Z. wasn't about to go to bed when Elle was prime for revelation. Peg squirmed like a child on Christmas morning surrounded by unopened gifts.

Elle was either in no hurry or relished their discomfort; probably both. Impatient, L.Z. cleared his throat and Elle took a deep drag and as the smoke drifted from her mouth and nostrils, she said,

"I flipped a coin."

In the confused silence, L.Z. squinted as he stared at her, as if trying to discern her meaning through the haze of smoke. Peg's eyes were rounder than usual as they darted from one Manson to the other.

"Uh…" L.Z. started, then wasn't sure where to go with it when Elle interrupted,

"Flipped a coin to see who to keep." At this point her audience simultaneously slumped in disappointed resignation, both assuming Elle had switched channels on them again and they were back to the waiting game. They were mistaken.

"Look, Hardy Boy and Nancy Drew, I seen what you dug up on Leddy's phone pictures, so I know you seen me with three babies," and with a dark glance at her son, she added,

256

"not like I didn't tell this one years ago that I had triplets, but did he believe me? His beloved mother?"

Still confused, but slowly gaining on his mother's train of thought, L.Z. felt himself flush as he stammered, "Well, Ma, I..."

Elle waved him off with her Marlboro as she continued,

"Hush, I get it, I do. But anyway, I knew I couldn't keep all three of you, so I lined you up; flipped a coin for boy or girl, and when it came out boy, I flipped to see which of you boys I'd keep. And there you go."

Peg clapped her hand over her mouth either to stifle a gasp or a laugh, but L.Z. just stared. Even though the tender moment he and Elle had shared earlier was indeed unusual, this degree of maternal detachment, even from Elizabeth Manson, seemed extreme. In the back of his mind, he remembered what she'd told him as a child to make him feel special. Nearly sputtering, he pointed a shaky finger at her and said,

"But you said you *chose* me...you..."

"And *I did*, with a little help from George Washington – you were heads, by the way. Aw, come on, Leddy, you don't..."

"One was a girl?" Peg's voice was barely audible, but Elle not only heard, but, more importantly, noted the younger woman's high color.

Before answering, Elle took another slow drag and blew it toward the sky, eyes following the wispy trail with razor sharp intensity. Then she shot a look at L.Z. who was still in shock over how he'd "won" a coin toss, resulting in his circus of a life. Normally quick, even if her assumptions were wrong, Elle was stumped because she discerned Peg's emotional state, but didn't understand why this kid cared. Maybe it was because she, herself, was adopted?

"Look, Hon, I'm sure your mother had her reasons…"

Suddenly Peg kicked L.Z., who came back from his stupor with a yipe, and Peg threw him an exasperated look as she stood and ran into the house.

Before L.Z. could gather himself enough to choose whether to go after her or answer his mom's demanding questions, Peg was back, and with tears rolling down her face, gingerly handed Elle an old polaroid which was similar but not identical to those the old woman had secreted away in the attic. Elle looked, but thinking it had come from her own stash, just shoved it back.

"Oh, so besides taking pictures of pictures, you steal pictures? I never would have expected this of…"

"Of who, *your own daughter?*" Peg demanded before she could check herself, then for the second time that night, slapped her own mouth closed.

Elle's lips set in concentration as she stared at the appalled young woman in front of her. For just a moment, she lost her focus as if caught in a memory, then jabbed her waning cigarette toward the picture Peg had dropped onto the patio. Elle continued to point while jutting out her chin in the universal "give it to me" motion.

Suddenly regaining free will, L.Z. scooped up the picture of two tiny babies with a woman who was not Elle. The red-faced Peg tearfully nodded her consent for him to hand it over to his mom.

Elle stared at the photo, her eyes narrowing when she seemed to recognize the woman.

She looked up at Peg who was openly crying now, hands wringing.

"That's my mom...my mom now anyway...and...and..."

"And that's my other boy and my girl," Elle said flatly. "This is not rocket science. This broad – I mean your mom," she clinched her eyes closed to refocus and attempt to be more sensitive, "your mom? Well, she wanted to adopt a kid, but just one, so I took her these two...not you..." she shot a conciliatory look at L.Z., "because I *chose* to keep you." She rolled her eyes and sighed at the unnecessary need for sensitivity with these two nitwits. Handing the photo back to Peg, she said, "She said she'd take the girl because she had a line on another girl baby and maybe they'd grow up together...so." She shrugged and leaned back as if it were all a done deal. She seemed impervious to the obvious question hanging in the air.

Peg deflated and sat hard in her chair, hugging herself. L.Z. knew he was in trouble when his pain for her superseded his own self-pity, and he breached the subject himself, although it terrified him.

"Ma." Elle was picking a bit of tobacco from her teeth and didn't seem to hear her son. "Ma!"

"What, for God's sake?" she crossly fumbled for her lighter; she was already weary of the subject line.

"Ma...she thinks the baby is her. She thinks she's..."

"...your daughter. Yours." Peg squeaked the final word, not sure if she was more nervous about confirming her suspicions or accepting that she'd been given up based on the toss of a coin.

Elle blinked, looked away, then blinked again. She looked Peg up and down, then answered the million-dollar question with a downward twitch of her mouth, and one word,

"Nah."

After a short silence, Peg and L.Z. erupted with questions, L.Z.'s clearly supporting his mother's belief, while Peg challenged the quick dismissal.

Elle threw up her hands, shouting, "Woah, woah, woah!!"

In the stunned quiet, she began to count the reasons for her statement on her thin, knobby fingers. Her smoke-dried voice filled with sharp conviction,

"First of all, your hair…too curly. My hair is like a mouse's and the only curly-haired men I slept with were of a slightly different shade, if you catch my drift." As Peg pointed accusingly at L.Z.'s hair, Elle shook her head and laughed. "That, my girl, is fuzz, not curl. And besides, there's the matter of your teeth…nothing personal, I think you're a doll, but those teeth? Not from me or any of my, well, friends…"

Embarrassed, Peg sucked in her lips, and L.Z. was trying not to shout for joy or think about how much he loved those very big teeth.

"Also, my dear thing," Elle said, leaning forward with uncharacteristic kindness as her bright eyes took Peg in, "you're much, much too good of a soul to have come from the likes of me."

L.Z. almost fist-pumped in triumph because he wanted Elle to be correct, when he suddenly remembered *he* had come from Elle; memories of all his sacrifices flashed through his mind and he jumped up on the offense, ready to defend his own "good soul" when the doorbell rang.

261

Peg seized the opportunity to escape the discomfort and ran into the house to get the door.

In his mentally slack state, L.Z. had finally gathered enough words to inform his mom of the goodness of his own soul when they heard Peg squeal and shout before she reappeared, all teeth and dimples, with a young woman with sharp heavily lined eyes, cat-eye glasses, and bushy purple hair. Peg spouted as her joyful tears replaced the earlier waterfall,

"I can't believe it! What a surprise! This is my sister, Aja..."

But Elle's voice cut straight through the introduction as she pointed a crooked finger at Aja, saying,

"No...*that's* Molly Hatchet Manson. I'd know her anywhere. *She's* my girl."

Even after a very late night with the added element of long-term exhaustion, L.Z. lay in bed, his mind a galaxy of out-of-control thoughts. Fortunately, Rex was still absent and for that, L.Z. was grateful. He didn't need his parasite's unwelcome input, although Aja's (Molly's?) snide remarks about Peg and L.Z. having separate rooms were hauntingly Rex-like. In fact, even though the girl was technically *his* sister, not Peg's (outside of adoption), he didn't like her vibe one bit. But, he thought, as he rolled onto his side and punched his pillow, if those DNA results were correct, that also meant that Aja (Molly?) was also Elle's spawn, which left a lot of room for behavioral disruption.

Staring into the dark, he catalogued the information overload of the evening.

Peg had come to Boise specifically to find the Mansons, based upon the pictures and paperwork she'd found among her own mother's rat's nest of adoption archives for her oversized patchwork brood. When she saw the dates for the babies, and photos, she couldn't have known her mom mismarked the pictures; easy enough to do considering how close she and Aja were in age. But even after weaseling her way into the Manson's lives and fitting in so well, one could assume she was related; but she'd felt the need to verify – and what better way when you have a maverick sister working in a DNA lab? One would have thought the results backfired, but for L.Z., it constituted the first good news he'd had in a very long time. Not the news that he had a sister – and a brother – somewhere; those were things he still needed to process.

But the validation that he and Peg were not, indeed, blood related. They weren't what Uncle Al would call "blood family." And that might have been worth it all…worth Elle's gloating that, once again, she'd been proven truthful, and worth inclusion of the still-questionable character, Aja-Molly, into their broadening family circle. Worth all the harassment he'd gotten from Rex for not being bolder with Peg.

263

And that very idea is what had a stronger draw than the need for sleep.

Almost as if he'd summoned her, he heard Peg's loud whisper, followed by a tap on his door, "L.Z.? Are you awake?"

His mouth went instantly dry, and his heart launched into turbo mode as he clumsily extricated himself from his covers, "Uh, yeah. Yes. Come in."

He was standing, hair disheveled, in his skull and crossbones pajama pants and Megadeath t-shirt as she eased into the room, wearing flannel pajamas covered in wooly sheep. Romeo and Juliet, they were not, but the air was charged with the tension and nervous expectation of Shakespeare's young lovers.

Peg quietly closed the door, then leaned against it, seemingly embarrassed.

"I'm sorry...I know you need your rest, but Aja, she...well," she covered her face, shaking her head, "She wouldn't leave me alone about you. And me...and, well, you know..."

L.Z. smiled wearily, hugging himself because he didn't know what else to do, "Yeah, I know someone like that...well, kind of know him."

Peg looked at him and gingerly stepped forward.

264

"Well. I guess the bad news is, I'm not your sister. Or, um, maybe that's good news?" She couldn't hold his gaze and nervously pulled an errant curl and shoved it behind her ear.

He drew his shoulders back and scraped up the nerve to walk closer to her as he said, "That's very good news."

Jesus – his voice cracked! He felt like he was fourteen again and wondered if he was breaking out in pimples as they spoke. But Peg hardly seemed to notice as she visibly relaxed and smiled.

"Yeah, but maybe not as good as the other news…"

As always, her dimples did him in and he stepped closer, "What other news? That you win with the 'good soul?'"

Peg blushed and stepped up, taking L.Z.'s hands.

"Right…a good soul, but very un-Mansonly big teeth! No! I mean the other news. You know…that you are in a family of rock stars." She inadvertently drew him closer with a fit of giggles, as she still grasped his hands in hers. With tears of mirth, she looked into his eyes,

"Can you believe she named her triplets after metal bands? Lynyrd Skynyrd, Molly Hatchet and…and…" she wheezed with laughter and couldn't finish, so L.Z. finished for her as they collapsed into each other, weak from their giggles,

"Yours truly, Led Zeppelin!"

"Wait, wait, wait…" Peg gasped, fishing around in her pocket, pulling out a quarter. She straightened her face and held it up.

"I hear you do pretty well in a coin toss." Her mouth twitched, but she handed a grinning L.Z. the coin as he asked,

"Heads or tails?"

"Heads, of course!"

L.Z. flipped the coin into the air, but before it hit the floor, the two were too busy with their first, but not last kiss.

L.Z. would have done Rex proud that night, but as fortune had it, Rex was not there.

When Peg didn't come back out, and Aja moved into Peg's room for the night, Elle drifted down the hallway in her tie-dyed nightgown.

Aja looked up and saw the woman who was her mother glance at her, alone in Peg's room. She nodded, and heard Elle utter, "About damn time."

She assumed the woman referred to her daughter coming home.

She assumed wrong, however, and couldn't have known that as Elle looked at her son's closed door, hearing the faintest laughter and movement, she smiled and offered the old rocker "shaka" hang loose hand gesture to the door with a wry smile.

There was hope for that boy after all. She wondered absently if triplets would run in the family.

L.Z. awoke with a start. The hot breath on his neck terrified him because he was just awake enough to discern its realness, but asleep enough to linger in the dark dream where he should have been alone, alone with the numbers, alone with the correspondence. Alarmed, he leaped out of bed, knocking the blankets off Peg, who moaned, pulling the pillow over her face.

"Oh." He looked down at her in the tangle of sheets, memories of how the bedwear got that way filling his mind; he saw her sheep pajamas were in disarray on the floor and a goofy smile spread across his face. She snorted loudly and flipped, more than turned over, now facing away from him. As much as he would have loved to stare at what showed of her body, his sense of propriety won out and he gently covered her up and, after pulling on his pants and shirt, he crept out of the room to let her sleep.

Grateful he wasn't scheduled for work until the next day, he noted Peg's bedroom door was closed, hoping it meant Aja was still sleeping. He couldn't handle "Molly" just yet, so he just shook it off and headed in to find coffee and his mother. What he found, however, was his mother and Uncle Al in a heated whisper-conversation at the kitchen table, coffee was nowhere to be found.

Uncle Al. In all the excitement, L.Z. had forgotten he was coming in. Whatever his uncle's "news that couldn't wait" was, L.Z. comforted himself that it couldn't trump the bombshells from the night before. If he'd only known, he probably would have done an about face and rejoined Peg in the land of Nod.

Upon spotting his nephew, Al jumped up, spreading his arms, "Kid! I guess you didn't get my message this morning that I was on my way? Got in so late, I shacked up at the Holiday Inn Express, but no worries."

Eyes on his mother, who looked particularly predatory this morning, L.Z. gave Al a perfunctory hug and set to work making coffee, his efforts were the only sound in the room and it was unnerving.

After flipping on the coffeemaker, L.Z. turned and, doing his best Uncle Al imitation, clapped his hands together and said in a toned-down voice, "So! To what do we owe the pleasure, my good uncle?"

Elle shot him a look, then chortled. "Boy finally gets laid and now he thinks he's a goddamned general!" It was only then that L.Z. realized she had broken her weeks-long trend of no in-house smoking as she lit a cigarette from the pack near a clearly used ashtray. This couldn't be a good sign.

Al was accustomed to tuning out Elle's comments and didn't seem to catch on to her report of her son's new sexual prowess and gestured for his nephew to sit.

"Well, son, I came bearing news of a grave nature, so I'm glad you're here. However, it appears the first part of my news was a great topic right here last night…"

"Jesus Christ on a pony! I told you *all* I had not one, but three babies, 29 years ago. Three!" She accented her point by thrusting her cigarette so close to Al's substantial nose, that he jerked back in alarm.

"Yeah, yeah. And I wonder why we didn't believe you." He gave a wide-eyed, brow waggling glance to his nephew, topped off with an exaggerated wink. Before Elle could counter, he raised his hands in surrender, continuing, "But, alas, even a broken clock is right twice a day, and I guess this hit the magic hour."

Elle settled back, satisfied enough, and glanced at the coffee pot as she fingered her empty mug.

Al's voice lost its sarcasm as he looked at his tired, but oddly content nephew, and said,

"So. Interesting news, eh? You're one of three, and one of the others is here?" Elle stared at her brother with contempt, and he glanced from her to L.Z. with such a look of gravity that her expression softened to one of query.

"What is it?" She tapped her ashes as she tipped her head toward the now-ready coffee and L.Z., accustomed to the move, rose and filled their cups.

Al swallowed and rubbed his elastic face before expelling what sounded to be a lungful of air. Dropping his hands to either side of his mug, he stared at the coffee as he said,

"Well, it appears your brother has been located as well."

"What?" L.Z.'s mouth stayed open with his exclamation, and he leaned forward attentively. After a glance at his silent mother, he said, "Wait. You're kidding, right? You…"

"I wish I was. I am not kidding. And I'm afraid to say it doesn't look good."

L.Z. was confused and looked to his mother who sat stone-faced. It was as if she knew something.

"Ma? Did you know…"

"Let him talk, Leddy."

The fact that his mother wanted to hear what his uncle had to say was almost as disconcerting as her demeanor. She seemed rigid. Not quite scared but…on guard.

"OK." Al said and stood. He did his best talking while pacing, and with his first steps he laid it out.

"I heard from the police in New York; it appears there is an unconscious patient, long in a coma, whose DNA matched mine as a nephew."

L.Z. jumped up, "Police? Why police? A coma? How did they connect him to you? Are they sure?"

He was so excited he didn't notice the darkness which had crossed Elle's face and was further thrown off by Al's grave expression. Even if he was in a coma, wasn't this good news that they'd located him?

Al put a hand on each of L.Z.'s shoulders and the weight of the subject showed in his eyes. L.Z. could almost feel the baritone of his uncle's voice as he told him he should probably sit down. So, L.Z. sat, Elle listened and processed in uncharacteristic silence, and Al paced, gesticulated, and talked. And talked. And when the girls came in, even knowing one was a relative he hadn't met, he still talked.

When he was finished, so was the coffee. Peg hurried to make more as the others sat in silence, but their reactions couldn't have varied more.

L.Z. stood, staring into the backyard, so tired but wired, excited, yet somewhat apprehensive as he tried to catch the end of a thread that was teasing his brain about the news he'd just received. Elle stared at the table, tight lipped, breaching the stance only to insert the cigarette filters. Strangely, however, Aja was bright-eyed and seemingly energized by the news. This was the coolest shit she'd heard in a long time, and it was in direct relation to her favorite thing…*herself!*

Detective Doyle had almost fallen asleep on the airplane, which was no small trick considering she was smashed between her lanky partner, who had the window seat, and Andre the Giant in woman form to her left. She felt like ET stuffed in the closet with the thousand other stuffed animals, and it could have been the memories of her favorite childhood movie which lulled her into a drowsy state. Or maybe she was suffering from asphyxia in her squished state, but McMurdy's elbow landing on her right boob broke the spell.

"Jeez, dude, it's not even like it's such a big target. *Damn.*" She grabbed her injured chest with a grimace, delivering a withering stare to her oblivious partner. A deep, but womanly voice to her left made her release her breast in surprise.

"Men. They are on another planet. No…another *existence.* Not even Venus and Mars, you know, but more like Jupiter and oranges. Yes." The woman looked down at her from what seemed another stratosphere, with a satisfied smile. "Yes. Definitely Jupiter and oranges."

Leaning as far away from the she-behemoth as possible, Doyle side-eyed her with a similar gaze she'd offer any unidentifiable species, something between being perplexed and terrified. Suddenly McMurdy didn't seem so bad. She leaned into him, and for the sake of conversation, asked,

"So, whaddya think?" Her hair had contracted enough static to power a small village, and she eyed him as she rubbed her assaulted chest.

He looked down at her with surprise, noting neither the hair, nor her area of massage. He was just surprised she'd asked him anything; the woman rarely instigated chatty conversation.

"About what."

Turning as far away from the Jupiter-Orange creature, she said the first thing she could think of.

"Well, why do you think the general doesn't even know his nephew's name. Why do you think he's racing us to his crazy sis. I don't know. Why hasn't anyone even looked for skin-guy?" She grunted as she reached down to scratch her leg, which made the distance to McMurdy's even greater when she twisted to see his face.

She really didn't wonder about any of that stuff, but it took almost nothing to push her partner's talk button, and for the first time in their acquaintance, she'd met someone she wanted to talk to even *less* than McMurdy, Jupiter and oranges notwithstanding.

It worked. McMurdy launched into his entire list of theories from A-Z on the subject, none of which had anything to do with evidence, which was her sole directional compass. However, none of that mattered. He put her into a genuine sleep, and never missed a beat.

When the pilot announced their descent into Chicago, their first layover, Doyle wiped the drool from her face and stretched (as well as she could), and patted him on his knee with an approving, "Huh. Great perspective."

Jupiter and oranges. Sometimes it worked.

Having declared an unprecedented truce, the elder Mansons managed to avoid conflict when they surprised the younger members and Peg by suggesting a rare family outing for a late lunch. Even with the bizarre information exchange, Aja seemed mildly bored with the company in general, so she was the first to jump at the idea just to get out of the cramped old house if nothing else.

Peg and L.Z., still in the throes of their new status, gingerly held hands as the party of five loaded into Al's rental SUV. L.Z. still had a nagging feeling of an overlooked detail as they rode to the only restaurant Elle would agree to.

"Seriously, 'Chuck-A-Rama?'" Aja muttered, as she gazed at the mountains surrounding the Boise valley through which they moved. "I hope the founder's name is, like Charles, and goes by Chuck, instead of that name being what we can expect to encounter after eating *buffet* food…"

Peg giggled, picturing the whole group upchucking their dinners, and Elle harumphed at her long-lost Molly's idea of a joke. She never wanted a daughter anyway and now she had to accept the irony that this smartass, gum popping woman was her offspring rather than Peg, although by the minute, the resemblance to herself was more and more undeniable. Damn the luck.

The elephant in the room, then car, then restaurant, with the group was the fact that Al shared their missing family member was wanted for crimes, yet unknown to them. Also, that by dinnertime, they would likely get the whole story from the New York detectives – homicide detectives – who were flying across the country to speak with the only known family.

They were just pulling into the parking lot of the restaurant when something about Aja suddenly reminded L.Z. of Rex, which added to the unnamed nagging feeling which grew inside him. It made his stomach flip with distaste, but also made him grateful, again, that the voice remained silent. He didn't know if it was the drugs or just good luck, but as he squeezed Peg's hand, he sent a "thank you" to the God he was typically unsure of, just the same.

His mom was a nut. Even though Peg was enamored with Aja, L.Z. found his "sister" about as welcome as a mosquito in a bedroom at night. But he figured he loved his mother despite her unpleasant qualities, and maybe he could learn to if not love, but tolerate, Aja. And he loved Al; that was a given.

As they piled out of the vehicle, it occurred to him that this was the largest "family outing" he'd ever experienced, and wanted badly to believe that maybe, finally, family could become a good thing.

He wanted to believe it. But…but there was that feeling.

It's not a bad idea to pay attention to "that feeling," as he would soon learn in a most intimate way.

The New York detectives arrived late in the day and having gotten the address and go-ahead from the general, they showed as promised.

They got the full dose of Manson crazy.

The first of many revelations was clear as soon as they walked into the home. Even if it hadn't been for the DNA results, it was obvious they were in the right place. Although their Skin Guy had been in an unconscious state for over two years, which undoubtedly altered his appearance to a point, there was no doubt whatsoever that L.Z. Manson was related, in fact, their immediate assumption was that the men were identical twins; this was before they got the rest of the story.

After introductions and the cursory questions, personalities began to emerge, and before the investigators could get to the information-giving stage as a precursor to their most critical questions, they found themselves in the throes of an information *receiving* stage. And information continued to flow directly and indirectly amid debates and restating facts from different points of view.

Because there were some gems of information buried in the constant interruptions, points, and counterpoints, the pair humored the five — apparently, they were all Mansons but one, although the one was related by adoption? Or was it baby marketing gone wrong?

Even for seasoned investigators, the lines were blurring, when suddenly Doyle, the smallest and quietest person in the room called a time-out for a smoke break, she grabbed a surprised McMurdy and headed out the front door.

"You don't smoke," he said to her once they were on the dark front porch.

"I do now," she said pulling the overworked band from her hair and wildly rubbed her head as if to remove the information overload. She stopped and looked through the dim light at McMurdy's amused face. "Well, if I had one."

She patted down her pockets, finding one of her many packs of gum, and shoved two pieces into her mouth.

McMurdy leaned on the porch rail and kneaded his hands as he processed.

"So. What are the odds that our suspect is one of triplets, two of whom happen to have just discovered one another and met *last night?*"

With an incredulous expression, the typically unruffled Doyle added, "Mommy Dearest should have been committed and stripped of her parental rights just for naming her kids those, those…*names!* Oh, and let's not forget…the newest and arguably least likable of the bunch, if you don't count ol' Ma Barker in there, is a DNA analyst? And are we to pretend she didn't run those samples illegally in a state forensic lab?"

"And even though she's a chick, I guess there must be some egg-splitting thing that stole her ticket to the 'identical' part. How's that work with triplets, anyway?"

McMurdy shuddered with trivia overload as he took the gum his partner offered. He shrugged, then continued.

"Whatever; we have bigger fish to fry right now, like we need to tell them the ugly stuff next. If nothing else, maybe it'll shake some information out, or scare something loose…anything that might help. Maybe the old bat will come clean about who adopted Skin Guy, although I'm hard pressed to believe any of these 'adoptions' were legitimate."

Doyle sighed and scraped her hair back and with its last gasp of life, the hair band snapped, leaving her locks hanging in wavy clumps around her aggravated face.

"Fuck it," she grumbled, impressing McMurdy as she somehow tied her own hair into a knot on top of her head.

"Wow," he said, eyebrows raised appraisingly as he touched the bun with a tentative finger to see if the hair would stay.

She headed for the door, saying over her shoulder,

"And wait till you see my next act. Let's go introduce the Mansons to the one member of their family who just might live up to the name."

The detectives had played their cards well and the remainder of their time with the Mansons that evening had been surprisingly productive, although much remained to be seen.

During the graphic explanation of the known crimes of which their son/nephew/brother, or "Skin Guy," was suspected, Al, typically verbose, crossed himself and remained sullenly silent. The two with arguably the most at stake in the situation, L.Z. and his mother, were stone still and quiet, both with waxen masks for expressions so it was impossible to read their thoughts, although L.Z.'s facial color ran from flushed to almost ghostly pale through the course of the conversation. Peg stayed close to L.Z., gripping his hand until he pulled away and sat as if he had no choice. Of interest, but probably little consequence to the detectives, was the reaction of Aja Warner, or Molly Manson, as would be simply a sidenote in their report; she was riveted and was the only one of the group who asked questions. She all but frothed at the mouth as they recounted what they knew of the known victims and the conditions in which they were found, and how they were linked to her long-lost brother. Pride in his actions might have been an unreasonable assessment of her behavior, but it was close. But then, she had chosen forensic science as a career, and she was the newest arrival to this family unit, therefore her detached reactions could be justified. Maybe.

The biggest and most surprising break of the evening was when Doyle had paved the way to ask Elle about any knowledge she might have had regarding the suspects adoptive parents. Assuming it would be a sensitive subject, Doyle had put on her best facsimile of compassion as she broached the subject, surprised at Elle's fast response to the question before it was fully posed.

She flatly told Detective Doyle that they could have whatever information she had in her "files" available to them by the next morning. That would have been quite sufficient to further the investigation, but then she added the bombshell.

"But you should know, they're dead, the people who took him, I mean. Just like *he* should be."

That even got a response from L.Z., who had only stared but not participated.

Letting the second part of her comment rest for the time being, McMurdy asked as he jotted notes. "Oh, was it an open adoption?"

Elle scoffed as she side-eyed the detective, "Ain't you adorable," she rolled her eyes with a shake of the head. "You sit there and act like this was done through legal channels. And, no, there was nothing open about it."

The investigators quickly exchanged glances, McMurdy offering a quick wink to claim his "call" about the adoption legalities. They also came to an unspoken agreement that this wasn't in their job jar, and with a nod from Doyle, McMurdy asked the next obvious question.

But when asked how she knew the people were dead, Elle simply replied that sometimes she just "knows things," to which Al started to roll *his* eyes, then checked himself with a more inquiring look at his sister as if to see if there was a chance that maybe she *did* know things all along, and he had perhaps misjudged her. Under the circumstances, it was starting to seem that anything was possible.

An awkward silence followed, during which Elle uncharacteristically failed to elaborate on her occasional clairvoyance. Seeing the detectives' inability to drag more out of her, Peg, in her conciliatory manner, reinforced Elle's claim saying that as weird as it seemed, sometimes the woman appeared to know things she shouldn't and had had a marginal success rate with her predictions.

When they left, Doyle and McMurdy shook hands with everyone in the room, ensuring each person had their respective cards and making sure Elle, and L.Z., as a backup, committed to e-mailing the adoptive parent information by the next day. When Doyle firmly took L.Z.'s limp hand, she seemed fixated for an added moment; her bloodshot eyes lingered on his t-shirt while giving him a slow nod, eyebrows raised, before moving on.

Once they'd gotten into their rental car, McMurdy exhaled as he pulled his seatbelt across his expansive torso.

"So," he said, turning to Doyle who stared at her hands on the wheel of the still car, "I'm swinging between the Munsters and the Addams Family, although I'm leaning toward…"

"You see Led Zeppelin's shirt." Doyle presented the question more as a statement when she interrupted her partner's banter.

He looked at her small profile, a mere silhouette in the darkness, then lit up with his answer.

"Yeah! SKinKneader. Great band. One of my favorites. Pretty amazing for a fairly new group, too."

Without looking at McMurdy, Doyle started the car with a brief silence, then said as she pulled out onto the dark neighborhood street,

"Yeah, well. There's your questionable taste in music on one hand. But on the other hand, you don't have a brother suspected of *skinning people alive*. There's that. Might be an important distinction."

McMurdy sat in dazed silence as they moved through the Boise night to their motel.

282

As soon as the New Yorkers left, everyone moved to the patio and sat; it was unspoken that they all needed some air, although for Aja, it seemed more because she was excited than emotionally moved in any way.

"Anyone else think it's weird that a homicide investigator has a name like McMurdy?" Aja had a vape pen in one hand and waived the detective's card with the other. No one answered, so she continued, "C'mon? McMURDy! Seriously!" When no one took her bait, she stood and inhaled deeply from her device and continued to chuckle as she paced with unnatural energy.

Peg clutched L.Z.'s hand, and he slowly looked at her, then at his uncle, and finally his mother. Standing and drifting to the edge of the patio, he said in a weary, flat voice.

"I know who the voice is."

Peg was the first to react, slapping her own cheeks as she remembered his dreams.

"Rex…" she whispered and lowered her face onto her lap, suddenly feeling lightheaded.

Al cocked his head and stared thoughtfully at his nephew, processing many thoughts at once, as was his way, trying to grasp L.Z.'s meaning.

Elle simply shoved a cigarette between her dry lips and closed her eyes in resignation.

"Voice? What voice? Who's Rex?" Aja demanded, looking at L.Z., then the others.

Peg lifted her head and looked at L.Z., who was staring at her as if she were a lifeline. Aja stepped between them, wanting details, and Peg stood and pushed her away, saying gruffly,

"He hears voices, I mean a voice, OK? And other stuff and, well you need to back the hell off!"

Aja's eyes grew round as she covered her smile which rapidly grew between delight at her wishy-washy sister growing some balls and standing up to her, and the fact that her *actual* brother heard actual *voices!*

But before she could say something which might have earned her a punch in the face, Al stood with an expression of dawning understanding.

"But wait, son," he stepped closer to his crestfallen nephew, and without the slightest note of condescension, he asked, "what about the drugs, you know, the ones you took…and didn't the voice go away when you took them?"

A confused look crossed L.Z.'s face because his uncle had a point, but before he could respond, Aja couldn't contain herself, doubling over, hands fisted in delight, shouting,

"This just keeps getting better! I knew the fucking Warners were way too boring for me. Now *this* is a family…"

With a force which probably shocked Peg as much as Aja, Peg grabbed her obnoxious sister and dragged her into the house, saying, "*This* is not your family…"

Aja's protests faded behind the closed door as L.Z. stared at his uncle, seriously questioning his own logic. But it made too much sense…the timing, the things Rex said and knew about hurting people…the dreams. The dreams were specific. He covered his face and sat in the nearest chair.

"It's too convenient…makes too much sense. But you're right. Even though the dreams, well they didn't stop, the voice did, and it was when I started the pills."

Even with L.Z.'s concession, Al couldn't overlook the obvious connections when Elle finally spoke up.

"He didn't take the pills."

Both men looked at her, confused.

"Ma, I did. I *am* taking them, I have since…"

"No, not those pills, Leddy. Not *the* pills. You haven't taken a single prescribed pill." She exhaled heavily and leaned back looking at the sky with something resembling regret.

"What's this?" Al turned to his sister, and L.Z. suddenly remembered who exactly had handed him the bags from the first prescription as well as the refills. He turned to his mother, incredulous.

"You..."

"I swapped them, Leddy. You been taking an herbal stress reliever and acid reducers. Best I could come up with that would look like the others, but not hurt you," she said with a shrug. Then gaining her old gumption back, she savagely smashed her already dead cigarette into the ashtray as she speared a finger from her son to her brother, "That shit they wanted to give him was poison, it was dangerous... it was..."

"Wait, wait, wait!" Al held up a hand toward his sister and she clamped her mouth as he continued, turning back to L.Z. "But you said the voice stopped the day you took that first pill."

L.Z. nodded his head but wore a look of resignation.

"It did. But something else must have stopped it." He turned away and stared at the moon as they all pondered the mystery. When he turned back, his expression was set, sad, and certain.

"But it's him. It's him who has been in my head. And it's him who killed those people. I know because I saw it all."

Elle had retreated again into her solitary, but angry place, and Al studied his nephew, and raised his hands with a silent question.

"In my dreams. I saw it all…and… and…" tears started falling down his face, "I thought it was *me*. It looked exactly like me, but I was never inside, just watching. But now I know. It was him."

His knees buckled and Al caught him, holding the too-thin young man, murmuring, "Oh, my boy. My dear boy…"

Elle sat in semi-darkness, but inside all she could see was real darkness. It was something she recognized if not understood; she was vexed over something known only to her.

2500 miles east of Boise, Lynyrd Skynyrd Manson, AKA "Mitch," AKA "Skin Guy," and most recently, Rex, lay oblivious to it all as an attendant gave him another placebo rather than the NootropiCAN. Glancing at the chart showing the next week's schedule, she patted his limp shoulder saying,

"Don't worry, Mitch. Looks like in a few more days you can start getting the good stuff again. Just in time for the weekend."

PART IV
Blood Family

I'm not yours I'm not theirs
They got nothing but cold stares
They say we're family but not true
Without blood
Blood makes it real
Blood makes it stick
Family without blood
Ain't family but a trick
Blood or nothing?
I'll make you nothing

-- Aaron Stoss (SKinKneaders)

Self-Fulfilling Prophesy

Back in the New York office, Doyle and McMurdy had a too-small group of notes and photos tacked to an ancient cork board as they attempted to organize what they knew, as well as identify what they didn't know. So far, their efforts to locate Skin Guy's adoptive parents had fallen flat. And without the parents, they were getting nowhere on his real name. Their searches for "Lynyrd Skynyrd Manson" as well as variations were used along with the last known names of the couple to whom Elle had handed over her baby: nothing.

McMurdy's tie was tossed across his desk, probably somewhere near his patience, which he had obviously lost.

"Why was the Warner adoption legal, well, eventually anyway, but the other kid's was not? If old Elle-aroo knew our guy's parents were dead, but wasn't involved, how come they have been missing for years and we aren't putting the screws to her? And wait..." he dropped the papers he'd been holding, grabbing three photos, "and why do Led Zeppelin and Lynyrd Skynyrd look exactly alike, but ol' Molly Hatchet looks like, well like she's been hatched from another litter or whatever? Not to mention, what are the odds that a guy whose birth name had 'Skynyrd' in it end up skinning people...even though he probably never knew that was his birth name. Jesus!" He threw the photos down and looked at his poker-faced partner and threw his hands up in the air.

"Is this a murder investigation or the X-Files?"

Doyle quickly poked the steaming Hot Pocket on her desk, and deciding it would likely incinerate her mouth, she leaned on her elbows and looked at her manic partner.

"Well, if we're playing X-Files, *Agent Mulder*, let's see. First of all, I'm pretty sure Ms. Elle isn't going anywhere, so let's just put that mystery on the back burner for now; might not even be our jurisdiction considering the MIA parents were from..." she grabbed her legal pad, "New Jersey."

She shrugged as she added, "or *were* from New Jersey. At least according to our very reliable witness, Elizabeth Taylor Manson." After a healthy eyeroll, she checked her lunch again, then looked at her notes, continuing, "Also, it doesn't appear she gave a rat's ass about legalities, she just needed two families to take two kids. Maybe the Warners took it upon themselves to make it legal, and the other pair didn't care? More to come on that when we get some feedback on their names. And guess what? It is possible for two triplets to be identical, and one to still be fraternal, so don't blow a fuse over that one. Besides, she's a girl, and girls tend to take control of their appearance, you know."

From his towering stance, McMurdy gazed down at his unkempt partner as his eyebrows popped up; as always, her hair looked like it would love to meet a comb, her clothes had no idea what an iron was, and he wondered if she had ever even stood in a cosmetics aisle of a drug store, let alone ever used the products. "Control" didn't seem to factor anywhere in her appearance. But she ignored him as she stuffed the first quarter of her cool-enough meaty turnover in her mouth, then to his chagrin, continued to talk around the food.

"Also, have you ever heard of a self-fulfilling prophesy? Maybe our boy did know what his birth name was. That's a big maybe, but you make a good point. The skyn-skin thing, you know." She had swallowed and pointed a saucy finger at her partner as his face contorted in disgust, grateful he wasn't within flinging distance, "And let's not forget that band you and L.Z. Manson are all in love with…um…" she rolled her eyes as she licked her fingers, trying to snap them when she remembered, "Need Skin…what was it?"

McMurdy shook his head as he wrote something in block print on a piece of paper, then tacked it onto the board. He couldn't believe he didn't think of that; and it did nothing to take away from the X-Files vibe which took over his gut. He stood back and Doyle looked up.

"SKinKneader," she read, pursing her greasy lips. Then she shrugged, clearly not sharing her partner's sentiments as she located the note with the number for the vital records department in New Jersey and grabbed her phone. "Well, let's see what we can squeeze out of the adoption Nazis without a warrant."

Like the wheels of justice, those driving the machine of discovery are never fast moving. Nothing would be divulged without a court order regarding a perspective adoption around 1990 involving Pat Knemoy and Denise Rogers, and a baby named Lynyrd Skynyrd Manson.

L.Z. had never seen anyone, let alone a woman, eat as much meat in his life. He and Aja were having a solo lunch before she had to return home. Just based on her general wonky appearance and attitudes, he would have pegged her as a vegetarian or even vegan. He couldn't have been more mistaken.

After their second round of grilled offerings by the colorfully dressed waiter, he told her as much.

"Seriously?" she asked as she stuffed a chunk of garlic coated beef in her mouth, "Nothing I love more than to meet with meat. I love all things blood, meat, and skin. All of it, except, you know, maybe fur. Hey, even though I don't look like you other two, maybe there is something I have in common with our brother, huh?"

L.Z. stopped chewing and it was all he could do to swallow the grilled lamb which suddenly reminded him of the grisly matter from his dreams.

Pushing his plate away, he took in the woman he now knew, beyond the shadow of a doubt, was his birth sister. She had shown and explained the clandestine lab results, revealing how she knew that she, not Peg, was the sister of the triplets in their mother's old picture stash. When she had compared DNA between L.Z. and Peg's samples, she had thrown her own in as a control sample. When L.Z. looked confused, she threw out a few terms she knew he wouldn't understand, then added, "It's OK if you don't get it…it's science stuff."

The truth was, for what she'd done, she hadn't needed a control sample. She did it on a whim, due to a feeling that there was more to this whole story. Perhaps she had inherited an unseen trait from Elle; that uncanny ability to "know things" sometimes. Often, she didn't know what it was she was following, but she always noticed the leads – a thing in her gut, or an unexplainable thought or vision.

Having lost his appetite for meat, which was the predominant fare in Aja's chosen restaurant, L.Z. stared at the pale, overly made-up woman, whose fashion choices didn't seem to follow any trend he knew. She'd walked out that morning with some turquoise added to her already purple hair. She wore her share of black, and even leather, but she also seemed impervious to the concept of clashing colors; she had no problem sporting baggy skirts, leggings, or other deeply colored accessories with little regard to color coordination. It was difficult to look at, let alone understand, for her brother. It upset his sense of order.

"Hey," he said, "speaking of science talk, do you mind talking shop for a minute?" This lunch was orchestrated by Peg, wanting the two to get to know each other better before Aja – or Molly, depending on who spoke to her – had to fly home. But L.Z., with quite enough on his mind and psyche, felt little interest in becoming buds with someone he not only would normally be repulsed by, but would possibly cross a street to avoid. But she might still be of use because he had a new fear sprouting in his stomach, and he was already near his breaking point with things to worry about.

"Sure," Aja said, pushing away an empty tapas plate and reaching for L.Z.'s. "You finished with that? That server is a little slow with refills."

Yeah, or the server, like most humans, had never seen a woman eat her body weight in grilled carnage, L.Z. thought. But he said,

"Oh. Yeah, totally finished. So, I was wondering about the thing with triplet DNA. I remember seeing somewhere that identical twins have identical DNA. Even though you already said that it's normal to have two identical and one fraternal...you know, baby...in the set, or whatever," he rubbed his face and unconsciously touched Elle's old Snug Band which was now a permanent fixture around his neck. He stretched his eyes as if it would push the fatigue away and continued while Aja ate as if her life depended on it, making noises that were a little too much like stuff one shouldn't be thinking about regarding his sister. "So, could our triplet, or at least two of us, have identical..."

"Myth, not true, Led Zeppelin." Aja had immediately started using L.Z.'s real name, and had even stated her intent to legally change hers, because, why the hell wouldn't she? "And I know what you're thinking."

It wouldn't take a clairvoyant to follow the worried young man's line of thought; if a DNA hit had connected their long-lost triplet to grisly murders, what would stop the two of them, especially the identical one, L.Z., from being a potential suspect? L.Z. looked at her with such hope, she actually patted his arm, nearly stabbing him with her fork in the process. Gentleness was not her strong suit.

"Not to worry, bro, monozygotic – that means identical – like, you know, like you and Lenny, have *similar* general DNA characteristics, but me, the lone ranger here, my stuff is unique even to you two." She leaned back, arms in the air with a big smile, "No big surprise there, eh?"

With her raised hand, she swooped down and stabbed a chunk of parmesan pork loin, continuing the motion until it was in her mouth, her eyes closing in near sensual delight.

Watching her as if she were a National Geographic feature, L.Z. leaned back, thinking, *no surprise at all*, while thanking God for small and large favors.

His distinctness from the new-found sibling was a smallish blessing compared to the continued absence of Rex – or as he now knew, Lynyrd – *Lenny?* – from his head. That Peg was not his sister was the biggest blessing of all.

Two of those blessings were unchangeable, the other, not so much.

Al also planned to return to his home soon, but due to the recent extraordinary circumstances, stuck around to monitor his nephew's disposition and his sister's general situation.

Not surprising was that Elle's mood had become more unpredictable than usual as she vacillated between sullen silence and flurries of mysterious phone calls during which arguing could be overheard with her demanding tones. She made it impossible for him to determine her motives, of course, which didn't particularly surprise him, as paranoia was one of her most predominant personality traits anyway.

He conversed several times with Abby, partly to get her take on the entire situation, but also to get her professional input on both Elle and L.Z.'s behavior. Now that they were aware of L.Z.'s inadvertent avoidance of the psych-meds, they agreed that Al should recover the original prescription pills (if Elle had not destroyed them) and have their nephew take the ones to help with his nightmares only. Although they initially talked around the notion that L.Z.'s "head voice" could have been his comatose brother, they also saw no reason for him to start a medication for a symptom he did not currently exhibit.

"Besides," Abby finally told her skeptical husband during their last conversation before he went home, "I've had an eerie feeling about this all along, and I don't think we should eliminate any possibility."

"Abs," Al sighed. This entire thing was stretching his sensibilities and challenged a life-long belief system. "I know you're the queen of the head business, but there's no evidence that anyone can communicate from a coma, especially with someone he's never met or didn't know existed. I mean, I can see L.Z.'s reasoning, but this one is tough to swallow."

His wife was quiet for several seconds before she responded resolutely,

"And there's no evidence that it *can't* happen either. I say we keep an open mind. This rodeo ain't over yet, cowboy."

The rodeo was far from over as, at the Byrde Brain Institute, Dr. Winston, himself, prepared the first in the next scheduled rounds of NootropiCAN to patient N-7, otherwise known by the staff as Mitch. He had been notified by the police that potential family members had been located, although an exact patient identity was still forthcoming. Family members meant not only new legal considerations, but resurfacing of old ones; this, their prize subject, was undergoing test drugs without familial permission. The doctor was putting science before ethics, driven by the need for more data.

After injecting the full dose, ensuring the amount and composition matched that of patient N-2 to be consistent, Dr. Winston jotted notes in his private book and looked into the slack, pale face of his patient, knowing he wouldn't see a visual result here, but waited for the audio verification.

He wasn't disappointed as the screens came to life with the squiggles and beeps indicating brain activity.

He smiled and patted the emaciated arm of N-7, and glancing around to ensure no staff would hear him using the unprofessional nick name, said,

"Good morning, Mitch."

Behind the opaque, veined lids, a mind's eye popped open. The first thing Lynyrd Skynyrd Manson saw in his consciousness was the last thing he'd seen through L.Z.'s eyes, in a mirror. It was a face. A face he knew very well, although he didn't quite know why.

He was instantaneously in L.Z.'s head but stayed quiet; he had to think before saying a word.

Goodbyes having been said to her new uncle and wary mother before they went to the drug store at Al's insistence, Aja wanted to put her number in L.Z.'s phone to ensure he didn't ditch her as soon as she left town. People had a habit of putting space between themselves and her, and normally it didn't faze her at all, but this was different. She finally had actual real family and knew there had to be a benefit to her somewhere down the road. She looked at him as if he were the weird one when he said he honestly had no idea where his phone was.

Uncle Al had insisted that L.Z. use his mountain of paid time off with the unexpected and unsavory news about the extra Manson on the east coast. That was also about the time L.Z. simply forgot to care about the device; everyone with whom he associated outside work had been in his company, and since he was on extended leave, work just didn't matter for the first time ever. As it was, L.Z. had looked distant and troubled all morning, so he cared even less about his phone.

Aja stared at her him as if, perhaps, he was psychotic after all, as Peg ran out of the room, returning with L.Z.'s phone, handing it to him to punch in the access code, then to Aja, to input her details.

L.Z. allowed Peg to take his hand as she gave him her best dimply grin, "Girlfriends have to be good for something."

He came out of his day-long funk with the comment, looking at her as if he were seeing her for the first time all day. Her eyes shone and her hair was wilder than usual, making him want to touch it. But mostly, his ears rang with the word, "girlfriend."

Aja took advantage of the pair's starry-eyed moment, quickly flicking through the various apps on L.Z.'s phone, not because she had an agenda, but because she was impervious to boundaries.

"Are. You. Fucking. Kidding. ME?!" Her mouth was in a perfect "o," further accented by her green lipstick. "What?!!?" She held the phone closer to her smudged glasses, flicking through screens and screeching, "No fucking way!"

L.Z. and Peg looked at her in confusion, Peg's expressions showed more amusement while L.Z. just looked mildly curious and very annoyed.

"Please, please, tell me *you actually know Aaron Stoss*, I mean I've seen your shirts and stuff, but *please*," by now she had L.Z.'s arm clenched in one hand as she thrust his phone in his face with the other, "tell me this isn't an elaborate scam, and you actually are getting texts from *him himself?*"

L.Z.'s jaw dropped as he shook her off and reached for the phone. At the last second, Aja jumped away and jerked the phone behind her back, continuing, "No…no, no. Delete what I just said and just lie if it's a scam. From this minute on, I just need to know that my brother is buddies with the *guitar player from SKinKneader.* Got that?" She held the phone from L.Z. as she pointed a finger at him.

"Well," L.Z. said as he held out his hand impatiently; with a tinge of uncertainty, "I have met him and he did have my number, so…"

Tossing him the phone, Aja jumped, high fiving herself, "I knew it! Knew it, knew it! What are you waiting for? Call him! I think you've got voice mail too from the same number…"

Peg, seeing L.Z.'s sensory overload, grabbed her sister and said they needed to get to the airport, and to say her goodbyes. She could tell something was up with L.Z. all day and hated to leave him alone, but he looked close to the end of his rope, and alone time of late, was hard to find. She saw this as a rare opportunity and asked if she could use the Kia, if he wanted to stay back for a bit. He didn't hesitate because it would give him time to kill two birds with one stone.

First, of course he was dying to see if it was Aaron finally reaching out to him, but secondly, he needed to verify what he'd felt since early morning.

As soon as the door closed behind the women, the silence was quickly broken.

"Girlfriend, eh? It's about damn time. Miracles never cease."

His mouth twitching, miracles were the farthest thing from L.Z.'s mind; he had felt the presence all day, but the sound of the voice, so long absent, and now connected to unspeakable things, made his blood run cold. He quickly sat in the nearest chair and closed his eyes as he yanked the Snug Band up over his ears, hitting the music play button near his forehead, realizing too late that for the device to work, he'd need to connect it to music. And that would require him to uncover his eyes, as well as make himself vulnerable to anything the voice…Lynyrd…said.

"What happened? Lights are out! How long was I gone anyway…"

L.Z. pulled the band over his head and fumbled for his phone to connect the devices and started singing badly at the top of his lungs to shut out the voice until he could play real music.

Weirdly, the only song he could remember was the one from his nightmare, the one he'd only shared with Aaron in the note; this was his misfortune, but something else for the confused consciousness in his head.

It's so dark, are you dead?

It's the voice in your head...

I knead your skin, I need your eyes,

If you don't answer I'll fucking die.

Having removed the band from his eyes as he was shouting the semi-vile lyrics, L.Z. also gave eyes to the nemesis in his head; but the sights did not faze the presence once he comprehended the screaming verse that blasted through L.Z.'s head and his own consciousness.

He knew those words and he was intimate with the sensations they brought to his quasi nothingness.

Those words and the thought of L.Z.'s image from the mirror combined into something he'd craved during his random bouts of awareness.

They felt like memories.

Suddenly it all went black again, not because the presence was gone, but because L.Z. had connected his phone's downloaded music to the contraption and had yanked the Snug Band over his eyes and ears, flooding his head with loud beats and words, drowning out any opportunity for communication.

So, they coexisted as one waited for the unwelcome mental resident to go away, and the other slid into yet another place of recognition amid blasting music.

L.Z., of course, had chosen SKinKneader, and the former Lynyrd Skynyrd Manson, who was, indeed, "the voice" in Led Zeppilen Manson's head, marveled at the familiarity of the lyrics, or at least the sickening motivation for them.

He should know. They had to have come from him. His thoughts embraced them like old friends, friends whose names he couldn't quite remember, but whose faces were as familiar as his own, which he now also knew.

As for L.Z., his legs bounced nervously as he tried to breathe, silently thanking his mother for this trick she had long used to block out voices. It obviously wouldn't be a great long-term solution, but it worked for now.

Until he had a plan, now was all he had.

At the brain trauma institute, Dr. Winston nodded as, like clockwork, Mitch, or N-7's brain activity stopped as suddenly as it had started nearly eight hours before. He'd only just returned to the bedside, to see for himself what the weeks of testing had already indicated with this patient, and to a lesser extent, N-2, the young man named Adrian.

He flipped through his notes and glanced at the clock. Unsure how much longer he'd have the honor of testing NootropiCAN on this delightfully responsive subject now, every detail was of the essence. If the past weeks' patterns continued, within a few hours, Mitch's activity would start again, but with entirely different patterns, as seemed to happen every night, with or without the drug.

"Curious," said the doctor, as he looked down into the lax face, possibly one of a murderer, a possibility which held little interest for the scientist. His eyes narrowed and his lips pursed as he thought. It was ludicrous to think the night activity could be dreams, any more than he could dare to assign meaning to the livelier drug-related activity. But it meant something. He just hoped he had time to find out what it was.

L.Z. knew exactly when he was "alone" again and yanked the sweaty band down his face to his neck, relieved to be free from the loud isolation and what felt like a perverse chess battle.

Once his eyes adjusted, he saw he wasn't alone after all, as all his loved ones shared the room, watching the evening news. Peg, who sat most closely to him, was the first to notice he was free from his self-imposed isolation.

"Hey there," she said softly as she scooted closer to him from her place on the couch.

As long as Elle was present, no one was going to disturb her son from practicing her failproof method of blocking brain invasion, thus, once everyone was home, she'd been ever present. But this had also given them time for a heated debate about what to do with L.Z.'s prescription refills they'd just gotten to replace the ones Elle had flushed down the toilet.

Al adamantly insisted that L.Z. at least take the nighttime pills to block the nightmares, and felt that if, indeed, the voice was back, L.Z. should take the others as well. His logic was that even if…and it was a big if, that voice was inexplicably related to the comatose brother in New York, that same person was a potential serial killer and nothing good could come from him anyway. Elle, however, made it clear that for such a smart man, her brother was certainly acting like an ignoramus, i.e., one wouldn't take a cancer med for a skinned knee, so you shouldn't take a psych med for things which were clearly not related to a psychological condition.

Peg had gnawed her scabby fingertips and listened as she kept her eye on L.Z., whom she was grateful appeared to have fallen asleep for at least part of the time he was glued to his chair with the band activated. She, if anyone, knew how poorly he slept, and she was too familiar with the dreams to believe his night sleep was in any way peaceful. Musing, she'd wondered if he could sleep, even with loud music being pumped into his head, if the sound would also block his dreams; she was working this out as he looked around the room, rapidly blinking his eyes.

"I, uh…" he fingered the head band as he looked from Al to Peg. Elle stood, anxious to smoke now that her vigil was over, and interrupted her son.

"I told them. So, you don't owe anyone an explanation, not that you would anyway," she arched her waning eyebrows at her brother, more skin arching than actual brows, pushing a series of wrinkles toward her receding hairline. Clearly, the unprecedented truce between the elderly siblings was coming to an end.

Al leaned forward as his sister left the room, eager to plead his case with his nephew regarding the medications, but Elle's gravelly voice floated in,

"And don't you dare hand over those fucking pills, Charles Alvin Manson!"

The backdoor slammed and Uncle Al winced as he looked longingly at the two bottles on the coffee table.

As tempting as it was to just toss one of each pill back, to hopefully silence Rex – or Lynyrd – and to sleep like the dead, L.Z. had plenty of time to think on this in his bass pounding sight-deprivation chamber for the past few hours. He knew the real prescriptions would be an option but had made his decision.

307

"I'm sorry, Uncle Al, but I'm not taking them."

Peg's face melted with sympathy as Al looked as though he'd just bitten into a lemon, but quickly regained his composure.

"Son," he said, his voice reverberating intensely, the waves of which struck the exhausted young man right in his emotional center. In truth, there was nothing he'd love more than escape. To be taken care of by the powerful man sitting opposite him. To just rest. Pulling the band from his neck, and reaching for the charge cord, he exhaled and with his own words, resigned himself to a fate which terrified him.

"No, Uncle Al. No pills…" He held his hand, palm out to Peg, lest she try to convince him otherwise; she was his Kryptonite, after all, and he would have difficulty denying her any request. But she sat, silent, looking at him as she bit her lower lip. She knew what he was going to say before he said it.

"I know who this is. I also know that if someone doesn't help the police, he'll never be held accountable."

"But son…Leddy, they have the DNA linking him to at least one case…and besides, how can he pay for what he's done? He's a vegetable, for God's sake."

"Uncle Al, there are so many more…" L.Z.'s voice cracked as he clenched his eyes, then finished, "…bodies.

They don't know the half of it and there are families out there."

Al and Peg stared at L.Z. in stunned silence and did not notice that Elle had appeared in the doorway. She listened but did not share their perplexed expressions; her's was hard and angry.

Al spoke first, "How do you..." but he was unable to finish as Peg gasped and Elle simply closed her eyes, shaking her head.

"The dreams!" Peg ran to L.Z. and wrapped her arms around him from behind his chair. L.Z. put his hands over hers and looked at his uncle with tears in his eyes. The fatigue on his faced etched the features of a much older man.

"They're just dreams, Son." Al's voice was almost a plea, and his gaze was so intense, L.Z. had trouble holding it, but he did as he said,

"Uncle Al, those aren't my dreams; they're his memories."

It was late evening and Detective McMurdy tapped a pen on his desk, staring at the ceiling, while his partner followed up in vain on the status of a court order to obtain any adoption records involving their Skin Guy's parents, two people whom they had still been unable to track down. The

name Denise Rogers had produced too many hits in too many databases, but the search for "Pat Knemoy" had led to a big fat dead end in a nation-wide search in every database they could access. So now, the adoption record access appeared to be their best chance at not only learning their suspect's adoptive name, but maybe some useful information regarding the parents. Most useful would be their whereabouts, of course.

McMurdy didn't look down when Doyle slammed the phone into the cradle, impressed the thing hadn't shattered with years of abuse via cop frustration. She noticed her usually over-active, verbose colleague and leaned on her hand.

Feeling her stare, McMurdy said as he dropped his eyes and pointed the pen at her,

"Where'd he put the skin?"

Doyle's eyebrows scrunched for just a moment, and considering the question could only have one meaning, she shrugged. "A mason jar under a porch somewhere? Sewn together to make prom dresses? Shit, McMurdy, while I hope we can answer that and, I don't know, about a million other questions one day, it hardly seems relevant right now."

McMurdy leapt up and shook his head.

"Skin. That's our ticket, and I still think there's something entirely too hinky about L.Z. Manson, the mirror image of our perp, you know, pretty much his twin, being obsessed with SKinKneader. And then there's the Lynyrd *Skyny*rd..."

Doyle had approximately one hundred and twelve things on her ever-growing task list, and this conversation was pointless.

"Yeah, yeah. Skyn, skin. SKinKneader. *Skin...twin?* I mean how Dr. Seussy are we going to get here anyway?"

Unruffled by his partner's sarcasm, McMurdy turned to his computer to look up SKinKneader lyrics, which was fine with Doyle because it shut him up.

But only for a minute.

"First, I only noticed just now that the word, 'kink' is right in the middle of this band's name..."

Doyle buried her head in her hands. This didn't exactly seem like a news flash considering it was, after all, a heavy metal band.

"And hear me out. *One guy* wrote all the lyrics for the biggest hits, many involve pretty graphic stuff, you know, blood, death..." McMurdy jotted these things down before he began printing lyrics.

"Wow, imagine that. And unless his name is Lynyrd Skynyrd Manson, McMurdy, I don't give a shit." She stood to run down some paperwork on another case while her partner continued the investigative equivalent of chasing his tale.

In reality, he had about as much confidence as Doyle that this line of reasoning would go anywhere, but he needed to do something, anything, to feel movement on this case.

"Aaron Stoss," McMurdy scribbled on his note pad, pounding a period at the end of the name with exaggerated finesse.

He had no way of knowing that in that name, he had one of their biggest leads yet.

L.Z.'s phone pinged with a text and before he even looked, he knew who it was and what they wanted. Peg giggled and grabbed his phone so she could send a smartass response to Aja. Satisfied with her message, she handed the phone back to L.Z.

"So, wouldn't it be cool to distract yourself from all this and actually call your hero back? I mean, during all the junk going on here, it looks more like he's your fan."

L.Z. had been in such a fog, he hadn't considered the thing which would have been the biggest deal in his life only weeks ago, and now it was so far on the back burner, it had figuratively fallen off the stove.

He looked at his call and text log to see it was true. Aja had conveniently added the unknown number he'd so often avoided to his contacts as Hot Stoss.

"Well, first, I need to change the name," and he quickly did so, as Peg leaned in, happy for a lighter moment after all the drama in recent days.

Finished, he looked up at her, pausing for a minute to let the fact that he not only had a girlfriend, but an amazing companion, sink in. He smiled at her, rewarded by a big-toothed flash, before he continued.

"You're right. It's crazy...but I guess that's par for the course these days." He looked away in thought, then after leaning back to see if Elle was within earshot in the kitchen, he turned to finish.

"Look. I don't want to do or say anything personal if there's a chance he'll catch it...I mean, so far, I'm pretty sure I know when he's there and when he isn't, and thanks to this," he lightly touched the brand new, fully charged Snug Band around his neck, compliments of Amazon, the old one was returned to Elle, "I can block him when I want to. But," he looked into Peg's eyes and reached for her hand, "I might need your help, you know, figuring out where to go from here."

If Peg's smile were any bigger, her face might have cracked. She darted out of the room, returning with one of her trusty composition books. A prolific notetaker, she already had pen in hand and was all business when she sat next to him.

"Thanks, Peg," he stammered for a minute because he almost called her, "Honey," which was a foreign word to his mouth, but had felt so right. He wiped his lips, and continued, "So, even though he's been gone for a few weeks, it seems like there might have been a pattern…you know, for when he shows up and then just disappears. And when he disappears, I mean, he just goes. Poof." He had gathered his fingertips, then let them go with his last word to accent how completely the voice and unwelcome presence would go.

Peg was already scribbling when she stopped and looked intently at him. "I think we need to quit calling him 'him' and, really, Rex doesn't make sense either. So…Lynyrd?" Even as she asked, she wrinkled her nose. The name didn't exactly roll off the tongue. L.Z. looked at her, and without hesitation, he said, "No. Lenny." It felt right, and he nodded with finality, "Yeah. Lenny."

They continued to make their plan to capture as many details as possible, short of writing down any specifics about the dreams. L.Z. remained firm that he would never record anything he saw, besides, he still felt suspicion could be upon him and he wasn't in a hurry to document specifics about crimes, especially with graphic details that only the killer – or an accomplice – could possibly know. He obviously already knew light years more than the investigators, but he had to proceed with extreme caution until he, or they, could figure out how to safely close the gap between what he knew and would learn, and what the police needed to know.

His thinking was spot-on, more so than even he or Peg realized.

Elle, however, knew exactly how close her son was getting as she eavesdropped from the hallway.

She knew that her one bad seed, the errant child who had once been represented by "tails" in a coin toss, had become known as Lenny. Lenny Patrick Rogers.

And she had foreseen his evil early on; she'd been the first to look into his eyes.

Over the next several days, L.Z. spent many waking hours with his eyes covered, listening to music, every podcast known to man, and even meditation tracks, to block the now frequent visitations by Lenny.

Lenny's vantage point was no larger than L.Z.'s mind. Without the benefit of conversation or L.Z.'s sight other than the quick glimpses of whatever was in the viewfinder when he popped in from nothingness, he stewed for hours in darkness, fine-tuning his ability to block the noise of the day, so he could think. And at some point, perhaps due to the available time, or maybe even the tweaked dose of NootropiCAN, of which he was wholly unaware, he was able to develop depth to his own mind, independent of L.Z.'s life.

Initially infuriated at being shut out, he seethed with a focus on his recollection of the only time he'd seen L.Z.'s reflection. Then he'd shift his energy when this reminded him that this constituted a memory. *Memory!*

Although he had instant-recall each time he "awoke," it was only of his host's frustratingly small world and their conversations. But this was different. He knew that face he'd seen. Without knowing why, he knew it was like his own, but not quite right. Like there were the smallest things that should be different. Maybe the hairstyle? The expression? The...

And then he knew.

If L.Z. hadn't had the volume on its highest setting, he would have heard the laugh, or more like a howl; there was something inhuman about it.

Lenny, from his very dark place filled with sounds being pumped into L.Z. Manson's ears, applauded his host. The plan, the darkness, and the noise had met their obvious intent to block him out. But what L.Z. hadn't counted on were the unintended consequences. A mind left to wander...to think. To remember.

It was a good plan, of course. Lenny would expect nothing less from *his brother.*

At the Byrde Brain Institute, Dr. Winston stared intently at the monitors over patient N-7. He had, indeed, increased the dosage for both N-2 and N-7, and he felt his pulse quicken at the notable change in activity. Rushing over to N-2's side, he saw similar increases, still not as significant as N-7, but notable, nonetheless.

From the SKinKneader's tour bus, Aaron Stoss pondered over whether to call that L.Z. character one more time. But then with an abrupt awareness of an impulse which hadn't hit in too long, he leapt up to grab his notebook, and snatched the first pen he could find. He had to write and, knowing the notion could pass as quickly as it had started, he scribbled furiously, picking up where he'd left off on his last song. *The* song. The start of which he'd seen in the letter in his back pocket.

Bennie and Yuri, looking more like college coeds than lead members of a hard rock band, paused from watching the satellite football game to glance at their preoccupied cohort.

"You go, boy genius," Yuri said, stretching to grab a bag of chips. He tossed Bennie a Coke, rather than a beer, saying, "Better perk up. If there's a God, you'll be making some new music by tonight. Just in time, man."

SKinKneader had done well, very well, for a relatively new act, but they also knew how fickle fans could be. To stay on top, you had to keep climbing.

Two hours later, Aaron dropped his pen and paper, clearly spent, and lay back across his bench seat. The game had just ended, and they quibbled over what to watch next, not unlike a family on a Sunday afternoon, when Aaron's phone rang.

He lazily reached to where it had been tossed on the closest chair, casually checking the screen, then sat bolt upright as he stared at the name on the screen.

L.Z. Manson.

He glanced at his notebook then back at the screen with a quick head shake, berating himself for the fear flashing through him. But still, what were the odds. How did that guy know he was working on that song?

This was real life, not the Twilight Zone, and he needed to answer.

It was a coincidence, that was all.

Almost.

Aja was accustomed to dealing with DNA samples, but not at home, and not her own DNA. After filling the commercial Find-Your-Family tube with spit, she wiped lipstick residue off the edge as she shook her head. She didn't know what their techniques were, but she also knew they sure as hell didn't need half a person's bodily fluids to do DNA tests.

As she capped the tube and dug out the return envelope, she mused that there had to be some validity to the overpriced system since those New York wankers found her new Uncle Al strictly from her brain-dead brother's sample and Al's on-file sample with Find-Your-Family.

After sealing the package, she stared at the label and mused aloud,

"I did find my family and now I want to find more. What's a family without a dad?"

Although she badgered Elle, a woman Aja would be hard pressed to ever call "Mom," on the identity of her brothers' and her father, she got nowhere. It wasn't a stretch to think the old bird really didn't know who their father was, considering even the little bit Aja had learned and observed about her birth mother.

She had no ill feelings for her adoptive parents, but the last couple of weeks had been such a rush, especially with the whole people-skinning serial killer brother thing, she wasn't sure she was done.

Her father might be dead, might be some loser wash-out somewhere, or even worse, might be some ordinary Joe selling insurance or encyclopedias...*but* what if he was someone? Or what if he was as prolific or even more so than dead-to-the-world Lynyrd Skynyrd? Ol' Lenny had to get his bad blood from someone, and the things she was interested in and thought about in the darkest recesses of her mind sure didn't come from the Pope or, even as weird as Elle was, not from her.

Grinning, as she made a peanut butter and potato chip sandwich, squirting some ketchup on for good measure because all that red worked for her and she needed something along that vein in the absence of meat, she still marveled over the irony that her birth name was Manson. *Manson!*

Damn, it would be the bomb if *the* Manson turned up as her real father…it was conceivable, but she needed to be realistic. She certainly didn't bring it up while she was in Boise, just like she didn't inform her brother that she had the same dreams he did…but his were recent. Hers were habitual and hardly nightmares.

She spun through playlists on her phone while eating, considering the irony of it all.

Some shrinks became shrinks because they were a little mental themselves. Some cops become cops because they were victims. She had become a forensic lab technician because she figured it was as close to violent crime as she dared to get, knowing her darker proclivities. Besides, jail would suck.

It was all about access and imagination.

Feeling froggy, she picked a 70's playlist and enjoyed a delightful chill that felt a lot like premonition when the Sledge Sister's "We are Family" blasted from her Bluetooth speaker.

She had a large adoptive family, and now her real family was growing. And she did, indeed, want more.

The concept of "enough" wasn't useful to Aja Warner, soon to be legally known as Molly Hatchet Manson.

"I hadn't exactly planned on dropping everything and flying across the country, but it seems like a little more than coincidence that Aaron Stoss would be going to New York about the time I was wishing I could go there too. He said he's from there, going home for a visit or something," L.Z. explained.

Peg sat on her hands to keep from chewing on the skin which used to house her fingernails; the area had gotten too sensitive to wear her "finger helmets" as L.Z. had eventually learned she'd dubbed the thimbles she often wore on all fingers. He'd been grateful hers was such a pragmatic explanation for wearing them, considering all the options he would have had to consider if Elle had adopted a similar process.

"I can see why you'd want to go see that Stoss guy, although I still think it's weird that he's so anxious to be your friend all of a sudden...no offense, but you know." She grimaced at her own words but was relieved when L.Z. didn't appear offended. If there was anyone in the world who understood the unlikelihood of any cool person, let alone Aaron Stoss, wanting to hang out with him, it was L.Z.

Unconsciously touching the stretchy band around his neck as he'd been prone to do, L.Z. glanced at Peg, knowing the next part might be a tough sale.

"Well, I honestly don't get it either, but I think I have enough information collected now that I could really help the cops..." he cringed before he finished, knowing this would go over with his girlfriend like a launch of lead balloons.

"L.Z.!" She grabbed his hands, her round eyes confused and panicked. "They'll never believe how you got all that information...you...you..." she'd released his hands, immediately shoving hers back under her thighs as the need to gnaw became overpowering, "You'll be in jail and, and, well that's what will happen."

Tears started spilling down her face as she stared at him imploringly.

"Honey..." he'd said it before he caught himself, and her reaction to the new name was instant. She smiled through the tears, but she didn't budge because she needed to hear what he had to say and needed just as much not to liberate her hands. He touched her arm with an acknowledgement of his own that his calling her "Honey" had about the same effect on him as her proclamation that she was his girlfriend had on him. But his face became serious as he continued. "First, I have to take a chance because this thing needs resolution.

322

There are families who need to know where...well, where their loved ones are. There's money that maybe they can get as restitution." His fatigue was still overwhelming, and he rubbed his face before looking at her imploringly, "And honestly, I can't keep living like this."

Suddenly, ashamed of her selfishness, Peg's tears resumed as she slid onto L.Z.'s lap and put her arms around him.

After they sat quietly for a while, both acutely aware of the time — it looked as though he was going to have to disappear into no man's land soon, hiding in the protection of his band. He had grown weary of this, but it seemed the best alternative to exposure to his obnoxious and perverted brother's assault on his senses, especially now that he knew so much about what the man had done before he'd met his fate in a terminal — or at least partial — comatose state.

As Peg got up to fetch tissues for her running nose, L.Z. delivered the good news.

"On the upside, Uncle Al is not only going to pay for the trip, but he's going too. Something about being my advocate." He shrugged, as he added, "And even weirder, my Aunt Abby is going along."

Peg turned and looked at him as she processed this update which instantly made her feel better. She hadn't known Al long, but he had a presence to be reckoned with, not to mention years of leadership experience. He might not be a lawyer, but he was a brilliant man, of that she had no doubt. If anyone could protect L.Z., it was him. She had not met Abby, but had learned of her profession, and that couldn't hurt.

She surprised L.Z. with a smile and nod. "Uncle Al to handle the tough guy stuff, and Aunt Abby on standby to field voice-in-the-head and brain stuff. Sounds like the A-team to me." She didn't even ask to go along; she had her job here, which would likely become really interesting; each day Elle had become more morose, agitated, and withdrawn.

Peg's phone alarm went off, and L.Z. grabbed his own device and activated Bluetooth. He moved to the recliner in the living room, blowing Peg a kiss just as he started a full-volume podcast dedicated to the history of manhole covers.

Within seconds, he smiled as arguably the most boring broadcast in history blasted into his head, choking out the imploring voice of his frustrated and increasingly desperate brother.

From his place in the word-filled darkness, Lenny seethed. Something had triggered *something* in his mind; he knew who he was now, and what he'd done. And why.

What he needed to know is what L.Z. knew and what he planned to do about it. Just as critical was, he had finally found his real family, *an actual family;* this was critical in the life of Lenny Rogers. In his mind, the absence of this family, however dysfunctional it seemed, was how he got where he was.

He couldn't help but think that now that he knew this man had to be his brother, *actual blood*, he could reason with him. He could try to establish the one thing he had never encountered: a meaningful bond. Or not. At his core, that was less important than getting answers and control.

All he obtained, however, was vital information that manhole covers started with the Romans, who were obsessed with sewage.

He might as well have been trapped in a manhole himself.

"Bada bing, bada boom!" McMurdy dropped his phone, mimicking a mic drop.

Doyle had just returned from an information run. She looked at her partner with a typical expression of mild disinterest as she removed her jacket and dug out a new pack of gum. She didn't ask to what he referred, and he didn't wait as he held up an index finger, with a self-satisfied expression.

"One, that favor I called in to get the court order to access the adoption records paid off and we should have it by tomorrow. *And,*" he continued as held up the index finger on his other hand, "Just got a call from Charles Alvin Manson-no-relation." In addition to rewarding her partner with a rare smirk – they had both been amused by the old guy's way of introducing himself, as was mimicked by his nephew – Doyle's eyebrows raised, indicating she was actually interested in what he had to say next.

With both fingers poised in the air, he finished, "And he and young Led Zeppelin Manson-no-relation are coming to town! It seems L.Z. wants to 'help' with the case and, of course, supposedly to go see our bed-ridden boy."

McMurdy then did a quick drum solo with his extended fingers and was gratified with a slight increased ratchet-up of Doyle's eyebrows, as they held each other's gaze. Each knew what the other was thinking; it was quite common for perpetrators of crimes, or those complicit in crimes, to try to involve themselves in investigations. This could get very interesting very quickly, although Doyle had no serious beliefs that the brother from Idaho was involved in the skin crimes. But she'd give McMurdy his moment as she threw her own bit of fuel onto their slowly warming cold case.

"Well, their timing couldn't be better, because I just found out that the honorable Byrde Brain Institute is probably doing those drug tests on Skin Guy illegally, or at least outside of ethical boundaries, because they have to have permission from family to do that, as well as to pull the plug, so to speak." She stared at her partner as she drummed her fingers near the phone.

They both knew this wasn't their area of the law, but they did have a vested interest in the test subject, and having the family here soon could be advantageous to the investigators if they were able to manipulate things in their favor with the shady medical goings on. These things, along with their joint dislike for those doctors at the institute remained unspoken as Doyle moved her hand to the phone with a smile.

"I do believe I'll give the good doctors a call now. When did you say the Mansons will arrive?"

While none of the updates constituted anything close to evidence or smoking guns, they were updates. They were movement on a case that had been long stagnant. And the timing was hard to ignore.

Both detectives had been around too long to overlook coincidence, even if the information at hand didn't seem related or even relevant.

They had smoke, and now they just needed to follow it and, with skill and a lot of luck, maybe they'd find some fire.

Since concluding their recent tour and in anticipation for upcoming studio time, SKinKneader's Bennie, Yuri and Aaron had hammered out the instrumental and vocal pieces to Aaron's latest song.

Bennie set his guitar down, and while he wiped sweat from his forehead, he looked at Aaron.

"You, my friend, are one sick motherfucker." Aaron looked at his bandmate with a shrug. He was very happy with the song's outcome, but less happy with discussing the lyrics for the time being, though.

"Yeah, well, sick sells, right?"

"Sure does," piped in Yuri, after chugging water. This piece required more than his usual number of guttural vocals, and not just a little of his signature screamo. "I think we could make some passive income if we started a side gig, you know..." he finished off the bottle and smashed it, "maybe use it as a music-based tutorial for online classes. Maybe, I don't know, 'Even you can be a serial killer.'"

Bennie joined in. "Right? Start a new movement 'Psychopaths Anonymous, no longer anonymous!'" He reached a hand high in Aaron's direction, "You did it again, my man! I don't even want to know where these ideas come from, I mean, *damn!*"

Aaron halfheartedly returned the high-five and made excuses that he needed to book his flights home to New York, as he hurriedly left the room.

The last thing he wanted to discuss was where the ideas came from. He had no problem taking credit for the lyrics as long as the world thought he was the sole source. But now that idea was at risk, although even he couldn't articulate how or why, but only that L.Z. Manson was the key.

The fear in his heart reigned second only to his determination to get to the bottom of what that guy knew and what he meant to do about it. Naïve or not, he hoped that Manson was as unthreatening as he seemed, and maybe that by some miracle the guy could give him a clue as to how the lyrics which they both knew had ended up in Aaron's head had gotten there. After all, they had apparently entered L.Z.'s mind too. But what was the source?

He had his suspicions, but now that fame and money were on the line, not to mention his reputation, he needed to find out what he didn't know at all costs.

Sadly, he didn't know much; he just believed the only thing that made sense.

Doctors Winston and Afflick were not happy after the call from the New York City Detective Doyle regarding her inquiries into the proper permissions and protocols for conducting drug tests such as theirs on an unaware patient without family permission.

The call had taken place on speaker phone and the two men listened on as the detective worked her best unassuming Detective Colombo impersonation. She assured them it certainly wasn't part of her investigation of their patient to make such a call, but just in case the doctors might have their own concerns that the patient's birth family was flying in soon. It looked as though it was only a matter of days before they'd have the missing information on the adoptive family and might possibly locate them.

In the emotionally charged silence, Doyle, with McMurdy listening on, wrapped up the call,

"I just figured as a professional courtesy, I'd let you fellas know, just in case you're tweaking, or I don't know, outright breaking rules or ethics codes, that people who might be interested in that are on their way. And, of course, as a courtesy, we'll come along. You know, in case something crucial for our investigation comes to light."

In Dr. Winston's office at the Byrde Brain Institute, the doctors stared at the phone after Doyle rang off.

As detectives Doyle and McMurdy left their station to head to New Jersey with a court order to access adoption records regarding parents Denise Rogers and Pat Knemoy for an unnamed boy, the doctors Winston and Afflick vented their frustrations, attempting to justify their actions, and made threats they knew were undeliverable to the smartass little cop.

After regretfully agreeing to suspend N-7's NootropiCAN doses and notifying the staff of such, they sat down to plan their own defense with which to face any family members, or worse yet, regulating agencies, regarding their actions. And more importantly, justifying their offense by selling the criticality of their tests and N-7's value to said tests, to the family or families.

The former would cover their asses, a priority to Dr. Afflick, and the latter would pave the way to complete their study, which was Dr. Winston's only priority.

And time was of the essence.

Because Peg had done such an excellent job of figuring out the most likely times for Lenny to pop in on L.Z., Uncle Al booked the flights to New York around those times, and it was no small trick. To avoid overlaps, he ended up reserving flights from SLC to Boise where he and Abby would stay overnight and gather up L.Z., then on to Chicago, where they'd get a hotel during the day (prime brain invasion time), then continue to New York city the next evening, during the time frame L.Z. should be able to proceed without risk of overlap.

While he certainly didn't have to go into sensory deprivation mode when his brother came calling, he was not ready to encounter the voice knowing what he knew now. Besides, if his eyes weren't covered, it would take very little time with all the airport and flight cues, for it to be obvious to Lenny he was travelling. While he still had no real plan of attack once he arrived at their destination, L.Z. knew for sure that he wanted the element of surprise on his side.

Al, while still navigating unsure waters on exactly what he believed about the whole mess, only knew one thing. He was the force between his nephew and people or things that might not have his best interests in mind. He had switched back from restaurant owner to full "general mode," and his confidence was further boosted by the fact that he had his best lieutenant on his side; and the lieutenant looked a lot like Abby.

Having completed the first leg of their trip, Abby and Al had driven their rental car to pick up L.Z.

After meeting Peg, Abby went and waited in the car, correctly assuming that no contact between herself and Elle was best.

Al waited by the front door while Elle paced, arms crossed, in the living room as L.Z. and Peg said their good-byes in the worst possible manner. It was a moment they had both clearly studied up for, each delighted when it was obvious they were on the same wavelength; one of love, and unfortunately for Al and Elle, expressed via puns.

"Just so you know, Honey, when it comes to you, my heart has already taken off!" L.Z. blushed, but delivered his line perfectly as Peg rewarded him with a smack, and a good one of her own.

"Well, that might be, Led Zeppelin, but just so *you* know," and she lowered her voice to a too-loud whisper, "I could TSA-pre-*check you out*, any day of the week!" She burst into giggles as L.Z. gave her an appraising albeit tired look, bouncing back with,

"Well, I'd say that's first-class…just like you." He planted a kiss on each of her hands.

"I got another one…" Peg said excitedly as Al checked his watch, and Elle stopped pacing, looking as though she meant to do harm any minute, then bursting,

"Oh, for fuck's sake! Either say your goodbyes or get a room before I puke. Besides, the boy has a flight to catch."

With sudden inspiration and more life than he'd shown for some time, L.Z. spouted,

"Ooooh, Ma! No need to *fly* off the handle!" And with that, Peg and he guffawed, shared a last hug, and the Mansons, sans Elle, were off to the airport for their late afternoon flight.

Elle pulled her snagged Snug Band over her ears, heading to the patio with a pack and a spare of cigarettes.

Peg watched as she felt around in her pocket for her thimbles. It was going to be a long day. And an even longer week.

In a hotel bed in Chicago, L.Z.'s eyes fluttered open and scanned his surroundings, slow to remember where he was. He did not awaken gasping or terrorized as usual, but deeply fogged and distant. He felt he was coming out of a tunnel. Slowly pushing the covers aside, he let his legs drop to the floor as he rubbed his face, realizing he had slept more deeply than he had in a long while, although his brain had hardly been dormant.

Closing his eyes, willing his dreams forward, he was initially confused.

He was certain he'd been dropped back into Lenny's memory bank, but at an earlier time; puzzle pieces flew into place. He stood, suddenly awake, and paced as his eyes darted around unseeing.

His mental databank unpacked the weeks of scenes which had played out during many a dreadful night, fast forwarding to last night.

And that's when he realized he hadn't really been in fast forward mode at all; it was rewind. He had just witnessed Lenny as a child, with his parents – which for reasons which he would later understand, confused L.Z. – but it had undoubtedly been Lenny in his youth and home setting.

Allowing his mind to drift as he made coffee in the room's Keurig machine, he inadvertently reversed the script to remember the first dream he'd had.

Suddenly feeling like he'd been physically stricken, he dropped the coffee pod and grabbed the counter with one hand and his head with the other as the realization hit him.

The first violent encounter he'd witnessed, and by far not the worst, hadn't been Lenny as a perpetrator. It had been Lenny as a victim.

He'd witnessed the unsuccessful attempt on his brother's life which had, instead of killing him, left him in a coma.

Swallowing as his equilibrium returned, L.Z. swung down to pick up his coffee container and realized, without reservation, that maybe a small part of him was like his brother, and even resembled his blood-obsessed sister.

He found himself wishing that the unknown – and unsuccessful assailant – had been as accomplished a killer as Lenny.

Life would be so much simpler now.

These thoughts kept him from dwelling on what should have been his biggest question; why had the man who'd tried to kill Lenny been familiar, and why did it appear that Lenny didn't fight back? He'd seen what his brother could do, and in this case, he'd done none of it. He'd hesitated, and because of that, he was permanently in a hospital bed.

"Wait, what?" Peg exclaimed as she glanced at the clock, then back at her phone which rang with a picture of the Led Zeppelin band on her phone screen. She had L.Z.'s schedule memorized, and he should be in a Chicago hotel room right now blocking out Lenny. Maybe it was a butt call? But knowing his Snug Band was directly connected to his phone, she figured the worst thing that could happen is her voice would sound off in L.Z.'s – and Lenny's – heads. This was her chance to let that sick SOB know a thing or two...

Violently sliding her finger across the green button, she shouted, "Hello, you butthole! Now that I have your undivided attention..."

Her tirade was interrupted by a laughing L.Z., "Geez! Leave a girl for a day, and..."

"L.Z.?" Peg puffed out air and dropped back in her chair, flushing furiously. "I'm sorry! I thought, well forget what I thought. I know there's a time difference, but my clock tells me that if we're doing this now, we're not alone." She said the last three words loudly, as if she could sneakily let him know that she knew Lenny was listening in.

"No worries, he's not here, unless he's gotten really good at hiding in some corner of my brain. I mean, I can't feel him and sure can't hear him. I mean," during the pause, Peg could picture L.Z. shrugging, "I don't know why, but he's not here. I don't think."

Still suspicious, she had an inspiration, "Hey there, wanna do a nude call…you know, switch to video chat?"

"Um. What?" was all L.Z. said in surprise; she could tell he was understandably confused. But if she persisted, he'd get it, she was sure.

"I mean," she conjured up her best faux husky tenor, "Like, so you can see me all *neked* and stuff. Just me and my hubba hubba birthday suit!"

In the silence, she could almost picture L.Z. looking at his phone to make sure it was really her. *He could be so slow!* He reinforced that notion when he said,

"Uh."

His was the only voice she heard, and he was obviously speechless. She felt confident her experiment had worked, or if it failed, they'd never know. Done with the charade, she came clean.

"OK. Well, then, I guess he's not there after all. I mean, if *that* didn't bring him out, you know, since he'd be able to see through your eyes and stuff, then nothing would. He might be in a coma, but he's still a dude, you know? Sorry if I shocked you, Honey Bunny."

Honey Bunny?

L.Z. couldn't help but smile; it was very Peg-like, although he was pretty sure she'd have picked another pet name if she'd ever seen the shoot-em-up couple who shared the term of endearment in the film, Pulp Fiction.

"What do you think happened?" Peg asked.

L.Z. admitted that he had no idea, although he haltingly told her about his night, his actual almost restful sleep…and his dream. Although he explained he felt the dreams had regressed in time from the start, he fell short of telling her what he'd come to believe about the first dream; of the assault and apparent attempted murder that had led to Lenny's brain trauma.

It wasn't that he didn't trust her. It was that he didn't trust the safety of that knowledge, as he finally accepted the notion that had nagged him all morning.

The guy in the dream who had wielded the devastating blow to his brother's head had been visible. Visible enough, anyway, for L.Z. to realize there was definitely something familiar about him.

Although it was too early, Aja checked her mail religiously to see if any results had come from Find-Your-Family. She also researched how to legally change her name, although the process seemed redundant considering she wanted to actually go back to her original name.

Having coughed up a filing fee at the local courthouse, she had obtained the stack of forms. Once again, she grumbled at the fee, hoping she wouldn't have to hire an attorney, which she'd been advised was sometimes necessary. Considering this was more of a reinstatement than a motion to change, she was annoyed by the entire process already. As she scanned the requirements, she was grateful that she would need to "retain proof of her old name" once the change was in effect rather than having a need to *obtain* proof of the one she desired to reclaim. She'd seen her mom's disorganized records, and she could only imagine what old Elle had going on in the recesses of her attic lair Peg had described.

Noticing the tips of her nail polish were chipped, she went to work chopping her fingernails off to even them out rather than deal with reapplication. She thought about all the possible outcomes of her daddy search. She was OK with her adoptive father, other than he was about as interesting as a butter knife. But she wanted her real dad to be a Bowie knife, in comparison. Brushing her clipped and chipped nails off her lap onto the floor – she'd vacuum eventually if the cat didn't get to them first – as she had a sudden thrill at the prospect of her dad, her real father, being a criminal, and snorted at the irony of them being more or less on the opposite side of the law. Not that she was a cop or anything, real life wasn't like TV's CSI, and she couldn't begin to imagine those tight asses she worked for ever issuing her a gun, although she'd love that shit. But still, if her dad was a criminal, like in jail or something, he'd probably see her as someone from the other side of the fence.

Then it hit her. What if he *was* a criminal or had at least been in the system?

She sat straight up as her blue lips spread into a grin. She had access to that system and, looking at blood on her fingertip where she'd cut her nail too closely, she nodded; she also had access to matching DNA.

As she considered her options, she remembered the hundred bucks she'd paid Find-Your-Family to meet the same end. What she had access to at work was free — at least to her, although not so much to taxpayers — but shrugged it off.

As the mom who raised her always said, the more shit you fling, the more will stick. And all she needed was one good hit.

"You think she might have mentioned that she handed her son over to two women. You know, like that the couple was not a dad and a mom."

"Why? Because old Elizabeth Manson was so forthcoming about everything else?" McMurdy asked his partner sarcastically. "Besides, it's not like there weren't gay couples in 1990." He rubbed the stubble on his chin as he stared at the names on the paperwork. The parents were Patricia Michelle Kneemoi and Denise (NMI) Rogers.

"Yeah, well, that being said, if she 'handed him over' in 1990, then why didn't they adopt the kid till 1994? Not to mention, it seems like ol' Ma Elle would have at least gotten their names, or at least Kneemoi, spelled right, even if she wasn't worried about silly little details like adoption."

As soon as she said it, Doyle got a faraway look as her hand slid over to her keyboard.

"What?" McMurdy asked as he went around to watch what she was doing. He'd seen this look before and knew better than to expect an actual verbal answer.

She ran a general check on Patricia Michelle Kneemoi. Now that they had a different and clearly unique spelling, they might have better results. She assumed it would be pointless to look for any more hits in the glut of Denise Rogers out there. She was right. And she was wrong.

Her fingers flew across the keys and McMurdy's eyes darted from screen to screen, as she switched databases.

"Bam," Doyle said, hitting the print prompt, changing screens and printing again, then leaning back and reaching for her Yoohoo, she downed the dredges from the bottom of the bottle while McMurdy folded nearly in half to read the screen, as the same information came to life on the office printer.

"Patricia Kneemoi Rogers, missing person along with spouse Denise Rogers…ummm…2004?" He read aloud.

"Annnd…" Doyle spoke through teeth partially clamped by the caramel from her Snickers Bar, "there." She pointed with her free hand as she jammed the rest of the candy in her mouth with the other, then went to retrieve the paper from the printer. McMurdy read, then stood with a distant expression.

Doyle stated, still somewhat muffled, "Both declared dead in 2011."

"Well, I guess that orphaned our boy and…"

Doyle shot to her chair as if her hair were on fire, mercilessly pounding the keys and navigating her mouse with such speed McMurdy simply picked up the printouts and waited for a revelation.

"And there you go." She slammed her hands down and pushed her chair away for McMurdy to read the blasé public notice regarding the estate of the Rogers. 100% of their substantial worth went to their sole son, Lynyrd Patrick Rogers.

McMurdy placed his finger on the date of the posting, then looked up at their notes on the same Lynyrd Patrick Rogers, data they had found on their suspect after gaining access to the adoption records.

"He was pretty young. And probably alone."

"And he had a lot of money." Doyle finished.

"Which probably made it easy for him to drop off the radar not long after."

Miles away and an entire world west of them, Elle sat and stewed, wondering how long it would take for the powers that be, including her unwitting family, to put the bent, weathered pieces together.

Of course, she'd given the kid to those broads. First, she wouldn't trust the creepy little creature to a man. He was obviously fucked up as it was, and she hadn't met a reliable man yet. But still, she thought and struggled with how she could have messed this thing up so much, leaving her sweet Leddy holding the bag.

He had believed her when she gave him that asinine story about the coin flip; such a naïve, but sweet boy – always had been. But she'd known from the time those critters opened their eyes that in the triplets, she had the good, the bad, and the *evil* on her hands. It was the only time in her life she could be sure that she'd chosen good over far more colorful, and in this case, darker choices.

The ridiculousness of the name of the facility which housed his brother was not lost on L.Z. and he had immediately texted Peg, gratified by her string of laughing emoji's. The girl had become quite the pun aficionado.

As he, Uncle Al, and Aunt Abby were headed to the Byrde Brain Institute behind the poker-faced detectives, he sat in the back of the rental car as Al closely tailed their escorts – no small trick since Detective Doyle drove ahead in her weathered Mini Cooper.

It appeared that Lenny, for whatever reason, was still on "radio silence," although L.Z. kept his only defense mechanism tucked safely away in his trusty battle jacket pocket rather than around his neck. He still hadn't been bold enough to tell the police that he had the means to not only help them on their "Skin Guy" investigation, but also the means to crack the case. Their disposition toward him was civil, but not friendly. In fact, the tall and imposing Detective McMurdy had seemed borderline suspicious of him when they'd met that morning, which weakened L.Z.'s resolve, remembering Peg's concerns of his being thrown in jail as a suspect.

Needing to get his mind off the conflicting feelings which neared panic, he pulled out his phone and texted Aaron Stoss, who should be in the general area by now; he was still amazed by the irony that Stoss was from near here and had come to visit at this precise time and had suggested the two of them meet. L.Z., with a surreal feeling, messaged Aaron that he'd likely be around all week in the NYC locale and could hook up if his hero still so chose.

After sending the message, he gazed sightlessly at the foreign surroundings, not hearing, or caring to hear the low conversation which took place in the front seat.

He had dreamed again the night before, but also slept well as he had been pulled more deeply into his brother's childhood.

He shook his head at all he'd learned.

Just a few months earlier, he never would have believed how lucky he was to have his bizarre childhood with Elle.

Aaron Stoss answered L.Z.'s text and agreed to meet outside the city at a bar that evening. Shoving his phone back into his pocket and getting out of his parents' car, he tried to downplay the attack of nerves on his already unsettled psyche.

Hand on car, he closed his eyes and breathed in and out until he felt himself calm down. He needed to be on his best game right now; there was too much at stake for distractions.

With one more deep breath, he walked across a parking lot, destined to see his brother. It had been a long time. Way too long.

CODIS, or the Combined DNA Index System, is a computer-based tool containing profiles from convicted offenders and missing persons, along with data from unsolved crime scene evidence. Law enforcement from all levels uses the database to find links to locate persons and hopefully to solve crimes.

With her knowledge of the system, Aja strongly suspected her wayward brother's DNA had been entered into CODIS, since a sample from at least one crime scene was available. But she also knew that it wasn't necessarily automatic protocol for law enforcement to seek a familial link via CODIS. They will first seek an exact match, and apparently Lenny had never been apprehended or provided a sample until he became a missing person. She was guessing but surmised the match with Uncle Al had been the result of an independent search through ancestry companies based on the fact he was a missing person, and that match had somehow been linked back to the NYC murder case. If this were correct, even if their father was floating around out there and had a CODIS profile due to scrapes with the law, it hadn't been discovered by the cops. It would take a specific entry into CODIS seeking a pedigree tree, which is to identify relatives of the person in question.

How convenient that Aja not only had the know-how to make such a query, but also had reasonably unfettered access to CODIS. Despite her age and questionable maturity, Aja was excellent at her job and had established a good enough track record to have been appointed the lab's alternate CODIS administrator. The average technician would likely be unable or unwilling to do something as brazen as entering their own DNA into the system to find a familial link, but there was nothing average about Aja Warner, soon to be Molly Hatchet Manson, and she had the magic key: access.

On the same day her brothers would share a room for the first time since infancy, she worked up a faux profile using her own DNA and entered it into CODIS in a pedigree tree. She knew it was far easier to identify a male-to-male association, so she created a second profile using the leftover samples Peg had so conveniently provided from L.Z. Double whammy, double the likelihood of a hit. What her brother didn't know wouldn't hurt him, and what she was hoping to find out could change her life.

And as in all things, this was all about her.

Standing in the spot where Aaron had stood just a short time before, L.Z. had a similar reaction when looking at Lynyrd Patrick Rogers' face. Al and Abby flanked him, lest he fall, as he stared at a less robust version of the man in his dreams, of the man in the mirror. He gripped the bar across the end of the bed and worked his way around the raised frame until his face was above his brother's. His reaction was far from what most siblings separated at birth would feel, especially if they were an identical pair from a set of triplets. L.Z. did not feel a rush of kinship, love, or longing for what could have been. What he felt was disdain, bordering on revulsion.

I know who you are and what you did, he thought. But, of course, there was no answer. Lenny, formerly Rex, never heard his thoughts, and besides, he had been dead quiet for the past two days in every sense.

Behind the family, near the nervous doctors, Detectives Doyle and McMurdy closely watched L.Z., then exchanged glances. It was hard to get a read on what the young man felt, but even if there had been complicity of any sort regarding the earlier crimes, the conscious brother would hardly blurt out anything meaningful to deaf ears. Before they could decide their next step, Dr. Winston, in his schmooziest voice, asked if the family might want to retire to a private conference room to gather themselves and discuss their loved one's treatment. This was, of course, code for it was time to convince them to continue the test program.

As the investigators trailed the others, Doyle said under her breath,

"This ought to be good."

About the time the Mansons sat down with the doctors, Peg crocheted as Elle sat quietly nearby. The silence was unnerving to Peg who had always preferred talk, even useless chatter, to quiet. It was also such a departure from the early

348

days of their time together when the older woman would talk nonstop because she typically loved to share her thoughts, especially to a captive audience.

Peg glanced over, thinking she'd pay an awful lot to know what was going on in that head behind the bright, too busy, eyes.

Elizabeth Taylor Manson was either confident enough or delusional enough to regret very little in a life which could be, if viewed by others, filled with regrettable choices. However, her current mood and withdrawal were steeped in deep regret as well as entanglement in rare "whys" and "what if's," regarding past and future actions.

Why did she rehome that child, knowing he was so laden with evil? His aura was even evident to the midwife who couldn't hand him over fast enough to his exhausted mother, both still wet with afterbirth. And why hadn't she been more forthcoming to that couple, his new moms, when they'd reached out at wits end years later querying about family history so they could better manage their different and distant child. They had eliminated autism, dyslexia — they offered examples of how he seemed to spell things in his own way — as it turned out, by choice. They had gotten counseling for him, but while he behaved in a charming and appropriate manner for the therapists, he continued to show a different face to his mothers, one which was pleasant as long as he got his way, but inexplicably terrifying when he did not. *Why* didn't she tell them what she felt, what she knew while he was

349

still inside her with the others, one who was innocent, the other, the girl, only fractionally tainted by whatever had possessed that boy.

Possessed. What a perfect word, she thought as she lit another cigarette, not caring that she was inside the house. Maybe she should have suggested they try exorcism? She laughed darkly as she exhaled, drawing a curious look from Peg.

What if she'd taken him back and did then what she'd tried to do not that long ago…what should have been done as soon as he'd taken his first breath; something to ensure it was his last. Naturally, no mother should consider snuffing the life she labored so hard to bring into the world, but then, there was nothing natural about that child.

If she'd done what she should have done while it was still in her hands, so many others would still be alive. With a rare tone of compunction and sadness, Elle said,

"I was too late."

Peg stopped working and looked at Elle with surprise.

"Excuse me?"

Without looking back, Elle took a slow drag from her Camel, and replied,

"I didn't kill him when I should have, when he was small," she unconsciously held her hands about a foot apart; "…and it would have been easy. Then when I tried later, I didn't try hard enough. And it was too late anyway." Jamming the spent butt into the ashtray, she shot a disgusted look at the confused young woman,

"You just can't get good help these days."

"May I see his dosing schedule?" It was the first thing L.Z. had said after the doctor's compelling explanation as to how patient N-7, or Lenny Rogers as they now knew, had inadvertently ended up in the NootropiCAN trial, followed by remarkable results. And they, of course, had pleaded their case on the vital importance of the test itself, as well as long-term implications.

His request took everyone, including the detectives, by surprise. Typically, the elite scientists wouldn't openly share such details, but the stakes were high regarding the outcome of this conversation, so Dr. Winston dug through a file to find a simple document which would be easy to understand, showing the dosing schedule for the short time N-7 had been on the trial.

While Al and Abby had asked a few questions, they now deferred to their nephew and only Abby thought she knew why L.Z. was asking.

The room was quiet as L.Z. reviewed the schedule with the expression of a dawning understanding taking over his face. Suddenly nodding, he shoved the paperwork across the desk and said,

"I presume I am his closest next of kin; if it would be my mother, I have a general power of attorney for all of her matters, which should revert back to me, right?" He glanced at his uncle for reassurance, and the unusually quiet Al nodded encouragingly. Before the perplexed doctors could answer, L.Z. continued, "And I assume this would also apply to a decision about life support?"

That got a reaction as Dr. Afflick pushed away from the table with a look of alarm, and Winston, unable to contain himself, stood and leaned across the table.

"Mr. Manson, you are treading on very concerning ground here, and I must say, since you've chosen to go there, I have to remind you that although you are correct regarding next of kin, you overlook the fact that your brother was adopted, and your family no longer has legal standing."

L.Z. expected this is where his formidable uncle would jump in, but instead, heard the voice of an equally formidable force, although from a much smaller package.

Detective Doyle spoke calmly, almost aloofly.

"Rogers's parents were declared dead some time ago and he has no other known kin from that family. I'm no expert in this area, but I could make a quick call to verify that these good people should be the next in line for decisions regarding your patient." She stood as she waved her phone. "I could call my expert now, but of course that would also bring light to your questionable practices."

She had barely finished when Al Manson's baritone comment added unwavering punctuation to her suggestion.

"Yes. Yes, detective, that sounds like an excellent idea." Then directing a piercing gaze at Winston, he said, "It's difficult to override the power of *blood family*, in any case."

"Okay, okay, let's get down to brass tacks here," Dr. Afflick, the calmer of the doctors and the one most concerned about the implications of their actions, said. He had raised his hands in a conciliatory manner, as he turned to L.Z.

"Why do you ask, Mr. Manson? We've spoken our piece," he swung a hand toward Winston who, red faced, started to interject, "what was it you had in mind?"

L.Z. had been staring at the table. He knew, beyond the shadow of a doubt now that he was not crazy. And that his brother had been communicating with him; the time of the medication injections had, to the best of his memory, exactly matched the timing of the voice of his near-dead brother in his head. He didn't know why this phenomenon had happened, but it was most certainly due to the drug, at least in part. He also knew that Lynyrd Patrick Rogers was a killer. But, for now, anyway, he wasn't inclined to share this with the doctors, one of whom would be entirely too interested in the fact that his star patient not only had brain activity, but that the activity involved direct communication.

"Mr. Manson?" Dr Afflick prodded, not only to keep peace, but to keep his colleague from saying things they would both undoubtedly regret.

L.Z. looked up and with certainty his aunt and uncle had never seen, said, "For now, you do not have permission to continue the testing. But keep him on life support."

Dr. Winston bit his lip, and raised a hand, clearly about to launch another plea, but L.Z. interrupted. "Keep your pants on doctor, I said for now."

If it was possible for a human to turn purple, Dr Winston demonstrated the feat as L.Z. spun his chair toward the detectives.

"Thank you for all you've done. Now, I think I can do something for you. Can we meet, maybe tomorrow? I will need to confer with my family and maybe my lawyer in the meantime."

All McMurdy heard was "lawyer" and gave himself an internal high five, thinking this could only mean he had been right. Doyle, however, looked at the young man in the eyes, and nodded with a smile.

Abby and Al, or L.Z.'s "lawyer," simply leaned back with expressions of unmistakable respect. Neither really had a full grasp on what was going on in their nephew's mind, but what they did know for certain for the first time was that the boy was nothing like his mother, that he might have finally located his spine. And they knew they had never been prouder.

Back in the ward, flanked by his family and the detectives, L.Z. stared at Lenny again, his mind filled with a myriad of possibilities, things only he could connect or make possible. He was wholly unprepared when Uncle Al elbowed him and gestured toward a guy several feet away near another patient's bed. The man was staring at him, agape. L.Z. turned and when the recognition was clear, the two engaged in a stare down of gunfighter intensity as they both dealt with the blows of disbelief transforming into countless questions and possibilities, not all good.

L.Z. was completely focused on the man, but when the man stepped forward, he caught sight of the immobile Lenny; other than the obvious difference between a healthy man and one emaciated with inactivity, L.Z. Manson and the patient were mirror images. His face paled as his eyes shot from L.Z. to the invalid.

The detectives watched, intrigued, as Uncle Al stepped forward, eyes alert. He was unsure what was going on but was also ready for anything under the circumstances. "Can we help you with something?"

"It's OK, Uncle Al." L.Z. had found his voice, although everything else in his psyche felt as if he'd just encountered an internal earthquake. "Um," sounding like the old L.Z. again, he tried to act casually as he made introductions. "This is Aaron Stoss, he's in a band…well, he's the guy I told you I was meeting tonight? A, um, friend." There was no conviction or even a hint of hero worship when he used the word, but it was the best he could muster as he tried to get a grasp on what the hell was happening.

The elder Mansons looked from L.Z. to Aaron, then the patient a few beds down where Aaron had previously stood.

Al said with a tinge of suspicion, "Aaron. It's a pleasure."

Abby, however, eyed both young men and simply said, "Yes. And quite a coincidence. Now that we've met, how about you just come to our hotel lounge for your meeting."

Everyone was as quiet as the patients as L.Z. finally seemed to gather himself, placing his hand on his aunt's arm with a reassuring squeeze.

"It's okay, Aunt Abby. I got this. I think neutral ground is a good idea. See you tonight, Aaron."

He abruptly turned and left before he lost his nerve. He had no idea what was going on, but nothing could get any more bizarre than the past months and he felt he had an edge.

He might feel confused, but Aaron Stoss had looked terrified.

The detectives had witnessed the encounter with the other visitor on the ward, and while Doyle simply filed the event away in her mental catalogue of things which may or may not matter in their investigation, McMurdy was bursting at the seams by the time he folded into the Mini Cooper.

Doyle fired up the car in thoughtful silence as McMurdy stared at her, waiting for something – *anything* – to indicate she understood the significance of what they'd just witnessed.

As she was about to put the car in reverse, McMurdy couldn't stand it anymore.

"Well?" he burst.

Doyle, with much on her mind, including dinner, stilled her hand on the gear shift and closed her eyes. *Might as well get it over with*, she thought. When she considered the past two hours' events, there were too many possibilities to guess what had McMurdy's hair on fire, so she turned toward his incredulous expression with much less animation.

"Yes?"

"Do you know who that guy was up there?" He sounded as if she'd just missed a Jimmy Hoffa sighting. She looked upward before taking a stab at an answer that might not be too denigrating to her excited partner.

"Well, since we both already knew who all the *other guys* were, I assume you mean the gothy guy, um…Aaron, was it?"

Her words had the effect of the starting gun at a horse race.

As she stared at the windshield, the day's light waning, Doyle listened as her partner reminded her of his recent observations regarding SKinKneader's lyrics, band name, and potential connection to both L.Z. due to his T-Shirt and band choice, and his brother, who was suspected of skinning people; not to mention the weird, although now even more riveting fact that the suspect's middle name was in part, "skyn."

Doyle listened, biting her lip, trying to control her sarcasm button as McMurdy talked himself out.

"Okay," she said tentatively, sensing they were not finished as she continued to stare forward. McMurdy slapped his forehead and expelled,

"That was Aaron Stoss…from none other than *SKinKneader*. The *band*. The guy who wrote the lyrics, some of which sound like they are straight from our guy's playbook."

Doyle finally looked at her partner, lips pursed.

"Right?" McMurdy asked, mistaking her response for serious consideration. "I mean, it's hardly a smoking gun, but it is smoke. This can't be coincidence…and why else would this guy be here if there's not something? I know, I know, not scientific, not evidence. But it's something, right?"

Doyle looked away in thought, licking her perpetually chapped lips. She finally said,

"Did you catch the vibe between those two? It wasn't exactly old home week…" she held up a hand to stop McMurdy who was clearly winding up for a second round of dot connecting. "But, and it's a big but, I do see what you're saying. But Ray, before you get ahead of yourself, how about we focus on the few strong threads we have with this family and any chance we can to nail down the missing pieces of our suspect's life…not to mention, oh I don't know, *a little hard evidence* outside a small speck of blood from a comatose guy found on just one of many victims?"

She stopped as suddenly as she had started, having made a considerably longer speech than usual, her hand eagerly toying with the shifter.

McMurdy was still hung up on the fact that she had used his first name; it was a first. It had derailed his rant and train of thought, and he turned forward, dropping back against the seat, not exactly deflated, but wound down.

"Well, you have to admit it's weird," he said, then reached for his seatbelt which was her green light to get moving.

Once in motion, she said,

"Not evidence, unless this is, after all, X-Files," she was throwing him a bone with her reference to his comment days before. "It wouldn't hurt to find out exactly what this Aaron guy was doing there; I'm sure the good doctors would overlook confidentiality concerns all things considered. But I'll give you that it is weird, for sure."

Weird, it was. But they had no way of knowing this version of "weird" paled in comparison to what was to come in the next few days.

Peg barely breathed. Elle had said so little in recent days, yet what she'd just said might have been a bombshell. Of course, considering who said it, it could also be a dud. L.Z.'s mother had just said she tried to kill someone, someone she could have killed before, *when he was small*. Lenny? Lynyrd Skynyrd? Who else?

Of course, Elle had made countless outrageous claims in the past, but those had come out during her "up" times, when she seemed prone to create a sphere of crazy energy about her which, in and of itself, made her declarations less believable. This was different. And considering the only focus of their lives of late, it fit in a way that sickened Peg.

She felt as if she were in a minefield; she needed to know more, to step forward, but doing so could result in a devastating blow. How could she move forward?

She carefully continued to work her crochet hook, biting her lip. Then she reminded herself that whatever she was dealing with, it was nothing compared to what L.Z. had endured, and probably didn't hold a candle to what he currently faced in New York. And what if Elle's spontaneous statements could help? If they meant what Peg thought they meant, she needed to learn more.

As conversationally as she could manage, Peg lifted her foot over a figurative mine. Considering her focus, this could just as easily blow her up.

"You're too hard on yourself, Elle." Peg gulped a breath as she nearly snapped her hook in half with the tension in her hands. "He's, um, *your son,* after all." She felt so much pressure in her head as the words left her mouth, she felt faint; if she'd had to wait for a reply, she likely would have passed out. But there was no wait.

"I might have carried him and pushed him out, but I assure you, that child was the spawn of evil. You can call me a lot of things, and I wish now one was a murderer, but I am *not* ignoble or wicked. He's no child of mine."

Peg's mind was whirling as she tried to keep her cool. She was all too aware of how Elle could be when pushed; they were conversing now, and she needed to maintain the tone. She almost wanted one of those cigarettes, although she'd never smoked in her life. Once she forced a calm through herself, Peg went into drama mode and pretended they were just a couple of girls talking about a soap opera. It worked, as she expelled a breezy breath and said, offering a casual gesture with a quickly freed hand,

"Well, it takes two, you know! Maybe he got it from his dad?" Elle had repeatedly avoided the topic of the triplets' father, or implied she didn't know who he was, but apparently the flow of conversation and her intense degree of thought pushed all that aside. Elle removed the last cigarette from the pack, pointing it at Peg as she let out a humorless laugh.

"Are you kidding? That idiot couldn't find his way out of a paper bag…and couldn't even accomplish the only thing I ever asked of him since he donated his sperm." She stopped to light the slightly bent cigarette, her next point made in a mixture of smoke and disdain, "Like I said, you can't find good help these days."

A confused expression passed Peg's face before her eyes went wide. She resumed her project, furiously yanking yarn and wishing like hell L.Z. were there with her.

Or maybe not. If she'd understood what she thought she understood…*no*. No way.

Had Elle tried to get L.Z.'s father to kill his brother?

Although the detectives found out in short order the reason for Aaron Stoss's presence at the institute, the Mansons, all, found it quite suspicious, including L.Z. While the senior pair

were more concerned about this man's intentions toward their nephew who they felt was still vulnerable, they also considered an unlikely but possible connection to Lenny – a probable killer. After all, why else would this nomadic entertainer happen to be in New York at the same time as L.Z., and then show up at the very ward where Lenny lay?

L.Z. shared his aunt and uncle's suspicions, and more. Via his distinctive familiarity with Stoss's lyrics, along with knowledge that Stoss named the band, he was unknowingly aligned with Detective McMurdy's opinion; there had to be more to this, and it was beyond coincidence.

Still, as much as Stoss was in the public eye, L.Z. couldn't see him as a psychopath, hiding in plain sight. However, he yielded to Al and Abby's insistence that he change venues for the meeting to the lounge in their high-end hotel for security purposes and, because with or without his consent, they planned to be inconspicuously present. L.Z. was relieved that Stoss agreed so readily; little did he know that Aaron had even greater concerns about the situation than L.Z. and his were less about safety than sanity. He was confounded to the point of terror.

Peg had given up on any attempt to crochet and now leaned toward Elle from her chair. Whatever had kept the old woman sullen and silent seems to have vanished. Perhaps it was the absence of the rest of the family, or maybe she was just ready to talk. And talk, she had. Peg's head was spinning, as were her emotions, but she also wanted to seize the moment lest Elle clam up again.

"If you knew enough about Lenny to want him, uh, dead…" Peg struggled with her words, but continued, "then why didn't you just call the police? I mean…"

Elle laughed, but without mirth. Then she stood and slowly moved toward the kitchen, each movement strained; she seemed to have been reduced to mere bones, sinew, and skin. The woman had quickly wasted away in recent days. Peg panicked, thinking she'd gone too far and there was still so much she needed to find out. But Elle reappeared with a fresh pack of Camels, pounding one end into the heel of her hand as she headed back to her chair.

As she sat, she stared vacantly ahead, sighing deeply. Then she turned, locking Peg in such a potent gaze she felt paralyzed, almost trapped by its intensity.

"Me? The police? I know how I come 'cross. I know what I am. I hope you never hafta know what it's like to have a mind that *has its own mind.* One that will betray you in a split second. A mind that cuts, and sometimes I'm the only one bleeding." She stopped, as her too-bright eyes bore into Pegs with something between sorrow and a plea. A plea to be understood, just once. And Peg wanted to understand with all her soul, but she knew she'd fallen short either in her expression or lack of response, and Elle broke the stare with a sad smile as she opened the cigarette package.

As tears formed in Pegs eyes, she was relieved when the older woman continued in a less emotional tone, a more Elle-like tone.

"And what would I say, girl? I wasn't an eyewitness, I wasn't there. I hadn't seen him in person since the day I cast him off on those poor women. But I knew. I knew where he was and what he'd done. I knew it all. And before you ask why I didn't bring it up or do something sooner, it's pretty simple." She laughed again, that despondent husky noise, turning back to Peg.

"Because I didn't know if it was real. I know, I know…how I sound. And if you hear me say shit, I believe it. But even *I* know that just believing doesn't make it real and if I learned anything about being noticed in this fucked up world, it was that you gotta have proof. What goes on here and here don't mean jack shit." She had touched her head and chest, smoke trailing behind. "And I guess sometimes it really don't, when you have a traitor for a mind."

Peg thought she followed and took a chance with her next question. "So, so…how did you know? I mean before you got proof or whatever." She cursed herself for not being sharper, she had so many questions.

Elle stared at the floor, rage and even sadness shadowing her face.

"I saw it. I felt it. I dreamed it." She continued without looking at Peg. "Just because you never experienced something don't make it untrue, Hon. I was born with this thing, and if it was the only thing I was born with, I guess I could trust it. But even when you have other issues, I guess they like to call it, it don't make the telepathy or clairvoyance less real. It's as real as them thimbles on your fingers."

Peg glanced down at her "finger helmets" she'd jammed on as the conversation had intensified, to keep from drawing blood. As Elle's words sunk in, she looked at Elle in confusion and even a bit of accusation.

"If you know this stuff, why didn't you know what L.Z. was suffering through? I mean he was suffering with that freak in his head, and we were…we were making potholders for God's sake!" She gestured at the growing pile on the coffee table and realized her face had gone hot. When she turned on Elle, the woman suddenly looked so small, she was flooded with shame. "I…I'm so sorry. I forget myself…"

"No, Hon. You didn't and if you were right, I'd deserve a skinning myself." The reference was in poor taste, but Elle was so sincere, Peg didn't react, but just stared, waiting to hear the rest. "This thing…it's not by choice, it ain't even always reliable. And it's not like you can summon it. I didn't know. I swear to you, I didn't know until he told me and then it was too late. That's when I knew the bad seed wasn't dead. All that time, I hadn't been 'getting' anything, no more nasty visions, no more hate, no more probing…well, I just assumed

366

he was dead. And of course, Dinglefritz, who was supposed to do the job, didn't bother to see if he'd done it right. Don't know why that's a surprise…like I said…"

Peg leaned back again and finished Elle's sentence, suddenly as exhausted as she was enlightened, "You can't find good help these days."

"Damn skippy," Elle said, with a disgusted pucker.

When L.Z. entered the lounge, it took no time to see Aaron at a corner table, and he could also sense that he was a different man than the one he'd met in Salt Lake City. Gone was the aloof cockiness, the star status, the confidence. But none of those things lessened his trepidation after their unexpected run-in at the institute. With concerted effort not to bely his own fears, he held his head high and took the upper hand as soon as he sat down.

"I just want you to know that I have people in this room. Also, those other people with me today…not my aunt and uncle, but the other two? They are detectives. They are checking you out right now. If I could, I'd pat you down."

Aaron's look of apprehension quickly changed to incredulity.

"What? What the hell are you talking about? You're the one who knows shit he shouldn't know, shows up out of nowhere, along with your what? Fucking clone? I saw that guy in the bed...in fact," he hit his forehead, then snapped his fingers, pointing at L.Z., "I thought there was something familiar about you even when we met..."

L.Z. leaned forward, accusingly, "So you do know Lenny. I knew it." He leaned back with an air of certainty which was less comforting than validating.

Aaron returned the stare in confusion. "Who the hell is Lenny?"

L.Z. stared back, suddenly feeling as though they were in a chess game. He sucked at chess. So, he changed tacks.

"I was visiting my brother."

L.Z., taken off guard, registered shock, then suspicion as his eyes narrowed. Then he closed those eyes remembering that Aaron had not been at Lenny's side but had been standing a few beds down.

They sat in silence, each wordlessly lost in a myriad of possibilities.

Neither held all the cards, yet their games were related. Just not in the ways either would have guessed.

Aaron's brother Adrian had been in a coma since around 2013, after he was in a boating accident. The loss of his brother's conscious presence had devastated the defiant young Aaron, but it was likely worsened by the fact they were fraternal twins. Although they hadn't been joined at the hip and had not shared the unique closeness so well touted by identical twins, they had still been a constant presence in each other's worlds, and even through frequent falling outs, had remained close.

Aaron's parents still had not recovered from Adrian's condition and eagerly agreed to his entry into a drug trial at the Byrde Brain Institute, willing to try anything in hopes of restoring Adrian's consciousness and, hopefully, functionality. They never considered removing him from life support. They also failed to note how their full attention had gone to their comatose son and paid little notice to how seriously the situation had impacted the one still able to function, and able to hurt. And grieve.

Aaron had put his grief and angst into music, and experienced marginal success after his brother's accident. But it was around 2016 when he suddenly found himself in what he could only classify as "receive mode" for inspirations which, while grim and somewhat disturbing, were ideal threads with which to not only create hard core heavy metal lyrics, but also to inspire the name of the band he was now in. He had always been into the metal genre but hadn't had particularly morbid fascinations which would lead to a name like SKinKneader, or to lyrics as mentally disturbing and sometimes violent as the ones he penned, almost as if in automation.

He couldn't explain it to anyone, and honestly didn't try because the results had brought him so much success, not to mention he really didn't know what was happening. But he did know two things; his brother Adrian had been an adamant fan of horror and had been the first to venture into alternative music, ultimately dragging his brother into the realms of death and thrash metal music. And he had longed for communication, any communication, with Adrian since his accident.

He'd suddenly considered that the dark ideas which seemed to come from somewhere – or someone – could be his brother. Time had only strengthened his conviction, and it had also been gratifying to believe his brother was communicating with him. Other than the fact that Adrian was in a coma, the situation had been beyond beneficial to Aaron, and it had become his life's greatest secret. That is, until he met L.Z. Manson. Manson, who claimed to "understand." Claimed to "know."

Aaron had too much riding on his secret and as he had planned his meeting with L.Z., he'd remembered a quote that said something like three people can keep a secret if two of them are dead. He huffed as he turned it over in his mind; his brother was as good as dead while he, himself, was clearly not. And as for L.Z. Manson…

Elle had become suddenly tired and, giving Peg a squeeze on the arm, excused herself to go to bed. Peg, also worn thin from the revelations, was still too wired to sleep as she roamed the house holding her phone. She badly wanted to call or text L.Z., but knew he'd been at the hospital that day, then seeing Aaron Stoss for whatever reason that night. She knew the guy was his hero, but she didn't understand how meeting him at a time like this could raise to the level of importance to interrupt what had to be a very personal set of events.

She, of course, didn't know what he knew now, but neither did he have her latest knowledge. While the evening's disclosures pinballed around her mind, she kept returning to the biggest surprise of all.

She had believed everything Elle said. Right down to the telepathy or clairvoyance or whatever it was; she didn't know the difference, but she was sure Elle possessed both. She knew the woman could be compelling, even with her wildest tales. But this had nothing to do with the notorious Elizabeth Taylor Manson, and everything to do with Peg Warner and her gut. It told her this was important and true. And it was never wrong.

After hearing Aaron's story, L.Z. was overwhelmed by the stark reality of it compared to where his imagination had taken him. He dropped his head into his hands as he processed. Aaron, spent, sat in silence, and nursed his drink.

Al, no longer able to stand it, appeared out of nowhere, having insisted Abby stay at their secluded table, and placed his large hand on L.Z.'s shoulder.

"Everything all right, son," he asked L.Z., but stared hard at Aaron who avoided his gaze, a bit overcome by his first-ever sharing of his deepest secret. He still hadn't heard L.Z.'s side, but judging by his demeanor, Aaron somehow felt it wasn't as sinister as he'd thought. But he didn't know that "sinister" had yet to rest its case in their connection.

"Oh! Yes, Uncle Al. It's fine, in fact, really, if you guys want to go, I'll be OK." He looked at Aaron, instead of his uncle, at once realizing he was going to tell all as well before the evening was over. His mind was on fire with new implications, and he knew now that he needed someone who was not related to Lenny and himself, or not a doctor whose career was riding on the situation. And who was not law enforcement.

Al straightened and nodded, giving L.Z. a firm pat. With a searing look at Aaron, he faded into the dim light, with no intention of going anywhere. He already had the detectives on speed-dial.

L.Z. laughed nervously and shrugged at Aaron. He wasn't about to apologize for his uncle's behavior but needed Aaron to stay put so they could finish. Although he wasn't much of a drinker, he took a long draw from his beer, then after a sigh, asked,

"So. Your only concern is that I'm going to tell the world that there's a chance you didn't write the lyrics? Because I can assure you that never entered my mind. Really." He held the man's gaze until Aaron's shoulder's slumped with what appeared to be relief. But then he said,

"But you did say we had something in common. You implied you knew where the lyrics were coming from...you..."

L.Z. held up his hands to stop the stammering and waved for the waitress. He no longer felt threatened, but he also knew there was a connection. Too many points of reference, too many coincidences.

As he started to order another round of beer, he paused, looking at Aaron.

"You want to stick with beer? You might want something stronger when you hear what I have to tell you."

Aaron took his word for it. And in short order, he ordered a cocktail. A double.

Peg had fallen asleep waiting to hear from L.Z. Elle lay in bed, sleep eluding her. She not only felt the deep consequences of her failure to manage her worst demon, who

was also of her own blood, but her failure to protect the best part of her life, also of her own blood. She had no idea how someone as good as L.Z. had sprung from her loins, but she questioned now if she deserved the irrevocable tie to his vile brother.

Interestingly, she gave no thought at all to the third of the set. She had no love or disdain for Molly Hatchet, Aja, or whatever the girl went by. Hers was simply a collateral existence to the good and evil with whom she had shared a womb.

Elle probably should have heeded her own words to Peg. That sometimes she simply didn't know things like she knew other things. That her gifts – or curses – of clairvoyance and telepathy were fickle, and often seemed to cherry pick the things Elle should or shouldn't want to know. Or maybe the signs weren't clear or loud enough yet. She would have done well to give more thought to her only birth daughter; Molly Hatchet's day could yet come.

As for Molly, formerly Aja, she lay in bed too. Sleeping and dreaming dreams which would have terrified most. Yet she had the look of a cherub; her cheeks were rosy with joy, her mouth curved into the sweetest smile.

And L.Z. and Aaron talked. They listened. They troubleshot and accepted the unacceptable. They had both lost brothers, but before the night was over, they each had found a new one.

PART V
Skin Deep

Gotta cut through
Gotta find you
Gotta find love
Slicing down to bone
But nobody's home
Only if its real will it reap
Real love is only skin deep

-- Aaron Stoss (SKinKneaders)

L.Z. sat on the balcony outside his hotel room, trying to transform Peg's words into something that made sense.

Her call had awoken him, having gone to voicemail before he came to his senses. Assuming she'd want an update on his previous day, and knowing it would be a doozy, he dragged himself out of bed with little thought to the dreams, made coffee, and called her back. He didn't have a chance to say hello, let alone share his own in-depth report.

As she stopped to catch her breath, his brain finally caught up with what she'd said. He took a draw of coffee, and an image came into focus in his mind, causing him to nearly choke.

"Are you OK?" Peg asked through the line, sounding apologetic.

After a deliberate additional swallow, L.Z. replied, mind still on the information more than the messenger. "Now, that makes sense."

"Makes sense that your mother tried to have your father murder your brother? Seriously, Led Zeppelin? Are we on different planets?"

Just months ago, if anyone had called him by his given name, he would have been quick to correct them, but by now, from Peg anyway, it had become background noise. But her tone brough him back from his reverie.

"Oh, no. I mean, remember the dream, where I saw it? Saw what happened to Lenny? I don't know if I mentioned that the guy, what I saw of him, looked familiar. Now I know. Jesus! That was my father?"

It was hard to imagine that anything could still surprise or trouble him, but apparently the sensation could be infinite. Then he heard Peg say with a sigh,

"Well, that does make sense."

"Right." He just needed a minute, and took another slug of coffee, realizing he was going to need a lot more for this conversation. Then Peg qualified her previous statement.

"Elle said you guys were dead ringers for your biological father."

The reality of it all hit L.Z. in a wave. She likely hadn't left a single thing out of her blast of words which had

376

constituted all she learned from Elle the night before and, somehow, he was less surprised than just weary. The telepathy thing made more sense now that he knew all he knew, and the history regarding Lenny and his moms fit into what he had learned as well. Then he asked,

"Did he, my father I mean," he paused at the sound of that word from his own lips, then after a sudden vision of Luke Skywalker and Darth Vader, he shook his head and continued, "did he know about us? That she split the three of us up?"

Elle laughed.

"Heck no. He didn't even know you guys were alive! She didn't even know for sure who the dad was until you, you know, started growing up a little and you didn't look anything like her, but a lot like a lo..." she stopped for a moment, "like someone she'd, you know, been with."

L.Z. couldn't know Peg stopped herself from using Elle's own words about the unfortunate encounter when she'd only slept with the *loser* because she was loaded and thought he was someone else; Roger Daltrey, in fact. Of course, he hadn't been Roger Daltrey, and once she'd learned she was knocked up, she'd had to play amateur detective to find out who the guy really was; just in case. She'd had no inkling of the nature of the "just in case" which materialized over twenty years later.

A voice came out of nowhere, and L.Z. was grateful he had no coffee left to spill.

"Morning, Bro. Mind if I get some of that coffee in there?"

L.Z. handed Aaron his cup, and nodded as he heard Peg ask,

"Who's that? I thought you were in your room."

"Oh! I am. Believe it or not, that was Aaron…you know, Stoss? I have, well, a lot to tell you, but basically, we were up so late last night, he crashed on my couch. Can you believe I have a bed and a couch? Anyway, I'll tell you everything…"

"Oh. My. God!" Peg interrupted, finally sounding like her less serious self, "Aja…or Molly, *whatever*, is going to have kittens when she hears this!" She even rewarded him with a giggle, and he could almost see her dimples and substantial teeth. Then he thought of something.

"Hey Peg? I think it would be great if you could not tell her, you know, everything you just told me, you know, about our killer-for-hire dad? I mean, I'm pretty sure paying a person to kill someone is, like a federal offense." Elle was a handful, and what she'd done was questionable even knowing the extenuating circumstances, and it was something she could never truly explain that she knew about. And, she was his mom, after all. Peg burst out laughing,

"Are you kidding me? Even though Elle was ready to pay someone big bucks, if necessary, she didn't lay out a cent. All she did was threaten the guy with 18 years of back child support and he was eating out of her hand!" She laughed as he thought.

"Right. And how was she going to come up with big bucks, if necessary, anyway?" It was more of a rhetorical question as he took the coffee from Aaron, who looked more like a disheveled bum than a rock star.

"Oh, yeah. Well, you know those trunks in the farthest corner of the attic? Well, I guess they're stuffed with the cash Lenny's moms forked over for the fake-o adoption. She would have used that. I guess that's why she saved it all these years, just in case."

For the second time in as many cups of coffee, L.Z. choked.

And he hadn't even told her the big stuff yet.

"Will you excuse us for a few? We obviously need to discuss this and look into some things."

Detectives Doyle and McMurdy stepped out of the cramped interview room, leaving the Mansons in their wake.

In the room, L.Z. closed his eyes and tried to regulate his breathing. Abby took Al's hand and stared at his stony face.

While they were anything but sure L.Z.'s actions were in his own best interest, they had vowed to support him in every way possible as he strove to use his gifts and curse to assist in the "Skin Guy" investigation. He was moving forward no matter what and relied on his far more worldly family members to have his back. It had already proven that Uncle Al's demeanor and uncompromising advocacy for his nephew had gotten the detectives' attention.

Down the hall, Doyle and McMurdy ducked into an additional interview room, one without surveillance or mirrors.

"What the actual fuck?" McMurdy said as he closed the door behind him.

Doyle was less demonstrative, but her deportment showed the family had gotten her attention in a big way. She leaned against the wall, arms crossed, then shook her head as she answered, "You're the one who first suggested X-Files, my friend." McMurdy's eyes widened in acknowledgement of his own unknowing characterization of what was becoming of this case. Doyle looked at the ceiling as she recounted their situation.

"So, he's got inside information regarding the multiple murders at the hands of his brother, whom he just met, who is in a coma, and he has come by this information since the brother has been comatose…"

"But only since that brother has been part of this test program..." McMurdy added, hand over eyes. "Or so he says."

"But the general wants something in writing, giving L.Z. immunity from prosecution in this case before he'll talk." Doyle added, examining her too-short nails.

"We'll never fucking get that, or even if we could, it would take a hell of a lot of time to get it, and only if we come up with enough evidence that L.Z. couldn't have been involved. What? Months or years from now?" He wanted to move forward on this case so badly, he could taste it, but he also wanted to temper that with something like reality. What they'd heard this morning was nothing short of lunacy.

Yet it had been riveting, so plainly laid out by a very ordinary man who was clearly not in love with the idea of voluntarily throwing himself into the spotlight. And damn if he wasn't believable.

Playing the devil's advocate, Doyle said,

"Uncle General says L.Z. has not been out of Idaho for most of his life, other than a quick trip to Utah recently which is where he met that Stoss guy. That's easy enough to research and prove...but again, time consuming..."

"...and doable later," McMurdy said, snapping his fingers. "What if we only agreed to no arrest until which time we determine he was completely uninvolved; no guarantees, nothing in writing, no dicking around with the ADA – they'd laugh their asses off if we approached them on this anyway."

"And why would he talk now if we won't guarantee he's off the hook as a suspect or an accessory?" Doyle shot back. She had a point. That would be crazy, especially if he knew specifics of crimes, potential locations, and even money flow; these things would all lead to suspicion of involvement, deep involvement.

She and McMurdy stared at each other for a minute before he answered,

"Because maybe he's an idiot, or my gut tells me, maybe he's a simple guy who never asked for any of this and just wants to do the right thing and to get on with his life. There's that." His opinion of L.Z. Manson had changed.

They fell silent again. It was all ridiculous.

But like McMurdy, the far more discerning Doyle had gotten the same feeling. She normally gave little credence to "gut feelings," but this case was less than normal. And without more information, it was highly likely it would run cold.

They could no more put in a report that their evidence source was a guy's dream, much less if the guy was the suspect's brother, than they could cite the tooth fairy as a witness for dental DNA. As they stared into each other's eyes, multiple wheels were turning. They needed a work around;

they just needed information, any information that could budge the case forward. Surprisingly, it was Doyle, the by-the-book-give-me-evidence partner, who offered a way ahead.

"What if we just…just investigate? Even if he looks guilty as hell, we don't have anything on him to cuff him. We get the information, see if it pans out, and if it does, check out L.Z. and if he is implicated – by evidence – in any way, well, he's done. If the old general is right, we can eliminate him circumstantially and there would be zero hard connection. Granted, we have to get around the general to get the kid to talk. And I guess we need to decide if he's even remotely credible to make this worth our time. I mean, dreams? A comatose source?"

"A comatose source whose DNA was found at a crime scene." McMurdy countered.

"Which could have been planted easily enough…" Doyle said, then they were back to the likelihood of L.Z. having access or not due to distance and supposedly being unaware he even had a brother until recently.

She sighed and said, "How about this. He supposedly remembers such detail from these dreams because he has a…"

"Photographic…" McMurdy said, suddenly getting her point.

"Eidetic, I think is the term, memory." Doyle said, pushing from the wall and stretching.

With no one else the wiser of the turn their investigation had taken, the two headed back down the hallway to do a little testing of their own. If L.Z. Manson could demonstrate impressive sight-only based memory in their non-scientific "tests," they'd take the time to hear his dreams to either get leads and let it all play out…or to dismiss a misguided young man and try to get on with their stand-still investigation.

It took less than an hour and they were ready to listen to what he had to say. Either the man had remarkable parlor tricks up his sleeve, or he could genuinely recall minute and multiple details of pictures and documents or random YouTube videos after a short perusal.

Al wasn't happy when they'd give nothing in writing exonerating L.Z. of any crimes, and even less happy when his nephew later made an additional offer which they'd not discussed.

In the coming hours, L.Z. made an exhaustive and detailed statement of all he had borne witness to over the past weeks while sleeping; even the things which made no sense to him. It was clear how upsetting the information was to him; he took breaks, perspired, and appeared disgusted in increments. He even became nauseated as he answered detailed questions from the detectives regarding specific aspects of the murders and skin removal. His aunt and uncle blanched, but stayed put, refusing to leave except when everyone took a break together.

Even though the amount of information was overwhelming in volume and detail, there were still glaring gaps, as well as things the detectives would like to know. The location of Lynyrd Patrick Rogers' adoptive parents was vital and, more importantly and disturbingly, the location of the skin which had been removed from some, but not all victims, who already appeared greater in number than they'd surmised. Interestingly, they had no questions at all regarding the assault on Lynyrd himself, and L.Z. omitted his dream as well as Peg's revelations about the assailant. At least for now, that would stay off the table. But there were still the other unknown factors.

Then L.Z. offered a solution.

"Let me interview him, you just tell me what to ask."

The air left the room. Al reached for Abby's arm as she focused only on their nephew. McMurdy's brows drew so closely together that they joined in the middle, while Doyle simply asked,

"And how would you do that?"

L.Z. shrugged, as if it were obvious, "Just have those witch doctors give him a shot of the magic juice, and if I'm right, he'll be right there. Loud and clear." He touched a finger to his temple, unable to hide the cringe. No one knew more than him what a sacrifice it would be, but then, no one else knew that he had a plan which would make it worth it all.

Helping law enforcement and grieving families was one thing. True justice was another.

Peg had just gotten off the phone with Aja; her adoptive sister had given her permission not to call her Molly – only because she had been calling her Aja her whole life and it would be a constant rub between them as Peg would undoubtedly slip up due to habit.

It troubled Peg to withhold information from her sister about her biological father; Aja had made it especially difficult as she'd explained to Peg about her Find-Your-Family.com submission in effort to locate her and L.Z. – and Lynyrd's – father. Peg, who had the world's most ineffective poker face, was grateful they weren't on a video call as Aja discussed that while their dad wouldn't have shown up on Uncle Al's family tree, Uncle Al would most certainly pop up on hers now. But what she really wanted was the pay dirt of her father's identity. Of course, she hadn't divulged her underhanded entry of hers and L.Z.'s samples into CODIS, but what Peg didn't know wouldn't hurt her, in Aja's mind. And in Peg's mind, what *she* knew could hurt Aja. She didn't realize how thrilled Aja would have been to hear of the twist that her own father had made an attempt on the life of her brother.

Their secrets were kept for reasons as different as the two women were different in nature. The good heart of one contrasted greatly with the dark heart of the other, but their bond was real.

Grateful that Elle had gone to visit for the first time in weeks with Linda, Peg journalled the load of information L.Z. had passed on to her that morning, still allowing it to sink in, still trying to wrap her curly head around it all. As with her conversation with Aja, L.Z. had omitted some facts as a token of love when he failed to tell her his plans with the police. But Peg omitted nothing in her journal entry. It was her way of coping, understanding, and making sense of her life, and making decisions such as, in this case, how much of L.Z.'s information to share with Elle, assuming the old broad didn't pick facts from her mind.

Her worries were for naught, however, as Elle had made Peg's journal part of her daily reading. Just in case.

Al Manson felt he'd failed his nephew miserably as he sat by helplessly listening to the damning suggestions L.Z. made to the cops. Abby, who was in a mindset Al had never witnessed, seemed riveted by the absurd notion of the brothers' ability to communicate through and past medical impossibilities. All he heard was fodder for L.Z.'s murder trial. That he would call a lawyer with or without L.Z.'s consent was the only sure thing he knew.

"How exactly would this go down?" McMurdy asked L.Z.

"You tell me what to ask. They wake his brain up and, I promise you, he'll be in mine. I start talking to him, and unless I'm wrong, his ego won't be able to stop him. I can't vouch for his truthfulness, but I do know he loves to talk and, well, maybe he'll give me something useful."

L.Z. tried to sound casual, but his pounding heart and ramped up perspiration told a different tale. Abby, who watched closely, interrupted.

"L.Z. You don't have to do this." She secretly wanted badly to see this play out because in her heart of hearts, she not only believed her nephew, but also, as a student of the mind, the possibilities of it all were beyond intriguing. Groundbreaking. But she'd seen the toll the ordeal had taken on L.Z. in the past months and realized this could be the last straw. His well-being was paramount.

Al, thrilled to hear Abby's voice of reason, piled on, "Listen to your aunt, L.Z., she's the pro. This might not be what's best for you." He had lost his battle with L.Z. about the legal implications if he kept talking about events related to multiple murders where, without more evidence, all roads would lead back to him. Abby's argument, regardless of her motives, were all they had before they watched the young man bury himself.

L.Z. slowly turned toward the only people in his life who he felt had come to bat for him, and offered a tired, grateful smile.

"I know. I know I don't have to do anything, but I also know this has to end. Now." He gestured toward the deadpan cops, "They need all they can get to solve these, well, crimes, and I'm sure this is the only way to get it. Even though Rex, I mean Lenny, is a real pain, I know…I can tell…he's scary smart. And he's bad. Evil, even." He paused, lost in thought, images from his dreams drifting unwelcome in his mind. Still staring into space, he suddenly remembered the words of the psychic, "He's got no soul."

His words drove past practicalities and were felt at the core of everyone in the room. He suddenly seemed to remember himself, and shook his head, reaching for Abby's hand. It was an awkward gesture, but it touched her deeply, then he continued. "Besides, even if I end up in jail, at least I can rest. I'm just so tired. I…"

"I know. *I know.*" Abby said with tears in her eyes as she closed her hand over his. Al's heart nearly burst when L.Z. uttered the word "jail," but he held his tongue, almost biting it in half.

Taking a deep breath, L.Z. turned to the detectives, and raised his hands, indicating it the ball was in their court.

"We'd like to be in the room…"

"Won't work." L.Z. interrupted, and seeing their instantly skeptical expressions, he shook his head knowing how ridiculous it would sound, "He sees what I see. So, he'll see you if I look at you…and you won't be able to hear him anyway, obviously."

The detectives raised their eyebrows in sync, staring at the so-plain man. He gave no vibe of manipulation and didn't appear to have the energy to really cook up a decent amount of deception. Still…

Doyle said, just for the sake of argument, "If that's the case and if you don't want him to know what you're up to, how will you keep track of our questions, and how can you write down his answers without him 'seeing'?"

L.Z. smiled, tapping his hair with one finger. "Just show me your questions. And I assure you, I'll remember his answers."

After his astonishing demonstration of memory on sight, the cops leaned back, realizing that if this whole crazy thing had any credibility, the young man was right. And everything they were doing right now was based on the premise that he was being truthful and at the end of the day, all they really cared about was information. Evidence. They could worry about the rest later.

"Yeah. Right. Good point," McMurdy said, then continued. "So, how about if we're in the room, or even nearby. I mean, if you don't look at us, then he can't see us, do I have this right?" Doyle glanced at her partner, impressed. He was, by far, the one with the greatest imagination, and while she was struggling to follow their real direction with this, he was obviously all in which he continued to demonstrate.. "And how much do we tell the doctors, I mean, if I follow you, you don't even physically have to be at the hospital, right?"

L.Z., gratified that the guy was at least paying some attention to how it worked, thought about it. These were valid questions, and he really wanted to nail it the first, and what he hoped, would be the only time.

"I guess, well, would it be useful for them to know what is possible with this drug? I mean, all they know is that there is activity in his brain, but that's obviously…"

"Not even close to the level of discovery they would want for the possibilities of its use," Abby interjected, thinking like a professional, rather than an aunt. "I mean, I don't know what the long-term implications would be or even if they could prove it was legitimately happening, unless…" She stared at her nephew; her eyes narrowed.

"Unless they hook me up to gizmos like he's got, maybe they can tell?" He was way out of his league, and while he really didn't give a crap about the testing, if he was going to risk going to prison, there might as well be a benefit to mankind.

Doyle suddenly spoke up; this was up her alley – evidence-based science. "And maybe, L.Z., if they could discern anything by doing that, maybe it could back up your claims…"

"And give you a defense!" Al slammed his hand on a table with a triumphant expression, everyone in the room jumped and looked at him as he finished, "If they can tell, maybe show that there is something interactive going on, it gives you a toehold L.Z. I say we at least give them a shot."

L.Z. imagined the conversation he'd have with his brother with electrodes in his head. And then he remembered. A smile spread across his weary face.

"What?" Abby asked, noticing L.Z.'s expression.

"It's been a while, but I just realized, he sees out of my eyes…but he can't see me. Unless there's a mirror."

"So! There won't be a mirror." Al stood, clapping his hands, and behaving more like his gregarious self than he had all day. Looking at Doyle and McMurdy, he asked, "Are you calling the good doctors, or shall I?"

"I think we should talk to them together," Doyle responded. "We need guidelines and to make this airtight. We'll set up an appointment, hopefully later today or in the morning to get this going." She closed her eyes, remembering the overly enthusiastic Winston and his sidekick. She hoped for morning, because this would take some finesse to get what they needed out of this without becoming too entangled with the medical side. She also wondered if they were walking off a gangplank, she and McMurdy, with this investigation. She leaned into him, and he lowered, sensing her intent. She whispered,

"None of this goes in writing. Not now anyway. *Nada.*" She looked him in the eye with her last word. There was more than an investigation on the line here now, it could be their careers if what they were doing got out.

He held her gaze, understanding. A part of him really wanted it to be legit, but even he knew their unorthodox methods would more than raise eyebrows. They could send someone whom he increasingly felt was innocent, to jail.

"Keep our eyes on the prize, right?" Doyle nodded.

They'd never see Lynyrd Patrick Rogers behind bars, but what they really wanted to see was families notified, and a case closed.

What they couldn't see was the plan formulating in L.Z.'s head. If he played it right, everyone would get what they wanted, all but one, who would get what he deserved.

Between Elle reading Peg's journal and ensuring she was within earshot next time her son called, she knew more than anyone wanted her to know.

Fools. She might have screwed up mightily with her management of Lynyrd up to this point, but she was on all cylinders now to right a colossal wrong.

Peg was so distraught when she learned L.Z. had not only told the cops everything he knew but planned to intentionally throw himself in front of Lynyrd's scope to further aid the investigation, she gave up all pretense of keeping the latest news from Elle, saving the old lady from having to glean what she could from her journal.

In a role reversal, Elle found herself listening to the younger woman lament openly, not only about L.Z. in his absence, but his uncle who was supposed to be saving L.Z. from himself.

"Some help he is," she wailed into a wad of soaked Kleenex, "I hope he's going to pay for L.Z.'s defense because he's going to need a miracle to get out of this now." She dissolved into tears once more as Elle shoved the tissue box to her, tut-tutting the girl's most recent diatribe.

"That was your first mistake, Peg," she said less gently than she planned, "trusting that buffoon, if you want results, that is."

Peg honked her nose and eyed Elle through renewed tears. "I hardly see how it could be a mistake to trust a guy who was a general to know what he's doing, I mean…" Peg had only started defending herself when Elle shut her down.

She stood and firmly jammed her knobby knuckles into her jutting hipbones.

"Ever heard the term, 'good enough for government work?' Well, there you go. He's as worthless as the tits on a boar outside that uniform. He owns hamburger joints for God's sake! Ronald McDonald, anyone?" She was ranting now, as she dug around in a small drawer of her side table.

Peg sniffled, watching Elle swear until she finally unearthed a tiny key inside a breath mint tin.

"What's that for," she asked, glancing at her phone as if she could will L.Z. to call back, saying he'd come to his senses.

Elle stood, one eyebrow up, seemingly cranking up the ethereal brightness in her eyes.

"Only one way to save men from themselves."

She held Peg's gaze as if she expected the length and intensity of her stare to drive her meaning home; it was one of her most unnerving habits.

Peg's face melted into an expression of surrender as she shrugged with one shoulder, not even committing to a full shrug under the laser-like glare.

Elle snorted and explained her solution to it all.

"Inject a woman."

She lumbered toward the kitchen and when Peg heard the garage door open, she leapt up in pursuit. She might be part of the family and was a hot mess at the moment, but she still had a job.

Unfortunately, she felt as though she was no longer the one in care of the other. She had the distinct impression that Elizabeth Taylor Manson had taken over, and she ran to keep up.

The doctors at the institute, Winston in particular, were enthralled by L.Z.'s claims, but understandably skeptical. However, when L.Z. asked for a piece of paper and quickly jotted down exact dates and rough times for his "encounters" with their patient and slid it across the table suggesting they compare it to N-7, or Lenny's, NootropiCAN schedule, they did so more to humor him than anything else. Their goal was to cooperate as much as possible so they could gain permission to continue the trial with their star patient. They were unable to conceal their shock when the dates of the "mental rendezvous" matched the dates of dosage – perfectly.

McMurdy and Doyle distracted themselves as to not look at each other, giving away their joint thoughts; this kid could have memorized the schedule at one glance and regurgitated it back to the doctors. While the investigators recalled L.Z. asking for the schedule on the first visit, the doctors did not.

And even if they had, they wouldn't have expected any normal person to have such perfect recall. But there was that "normal" thing again. It had become a mutually exclusive concept when it came to this family or this case.

"You're saying that N-7 has communicated directly with you each time he has been dosed with NootropiCAN; directly communicated. Telepathically." Winston looked like he had more than swallowed the canary; he had inhaled a flock and was, himself, soaring. Dr. Afflick, the more practical of the two, held up a hand to further clarify what he thought he understood.

"And this voice, supposing it was N-7..."

"Lynyrd...Lenny." L.Z. interjected.

"Yes, supposing it was our patient, did not know who you were, or who he himself was – or is? But each, uh, appearance or meeting, built on those previous?"

"Yeah," L.Z. answered, matter-of-factly, but not appearing to care if they believed him or not. As far as he was concerned, they were just instruments for his end goal, and he couldn't care less about their study or its implications. They stared at him; Afflick was clearly thinking it out, but Winston looked like he might shoot through the ceiling with excitement.

"This is extraordinary." Dr. Afflick spoke first to try to keep some modicum of professionalism on behalf of them both. "And while we will obviously have to discuss the implications and how this information can best serve the study…"

Sensing the jargon indicated time-consuming measures on the institute's part, Doyle jumped in.

"Look, what we would really love is some off-the-record support enabling a potential, well, 'conversation,' for lack of better words, between our witness here, and the suspect, your patient."

The doctors looked at her as if she were a different species from those they studied, so she continued with a more direct tone.

"All things considered; I think 'off the record' would benefit you due to your questionable practices with this particular patient."

She didn't state it like a threat, her tone was far from threatening, and her demeanor was much like it always was: relaxed, yet no nonsense. But they got the gist.

Once again, Afflick responded.

"What do you propose, Detective Doyle?"

"I propose you give us access to the ward, and you dose, what do you call him, N-7? Anyway, dose our suspect, then let his brother interact however they do. We will be out of sight, but present. And before you ask what's in it for you, we have no problem with you monitoring his activity or whatever you call it, as long as you stay out of sight. Also, if you feel it would benefit your study or help back up L.Z.'s claims, is there a way you can wire him up, or whatever you call it, so you can monitor him too, but so no wires or tubes or anything from his own vantage point..."

L.Z. saw the doctors' joint confusion at the last part and piped in, "When he's in there, he can see through my eyes, but I have to talk out loud for him to hear. So maybe he uses my ears?"

The doctors' eyes rounded almost in unison, and they were speechless. Doyle took the advantage to finish her pitch.

"Anyway, right. You can monitor them both, and if you see anything that supports an actual interaction, we would surely appreciate something in writing to document that." She looked at Al as she said this, and he gave her a nod, gratitude emanating from his sharp eyes.

"Yes. Yes, we can do that." Dr. Winston jumped up, no longer able to contain himself, and needed to leave this meeting to do a few cartwheels before conferring with his colleague as to the magnitude of it all.

Afflick shot his associate an impatient look and, before standing, looked at the others.

"We'll need some time to examine all of this, as well as to plan." He felt it was reasonable.

399

"You have till Friday," Doyle said with no hesitation. It was Wednesday. Afflick balked, but Winston took the lead. He understood their liabilities here for their – his – unorthodox actions, as well as what they had to lose if there was any credence whatsoever to what they'd been told. "We'll do it. But I have one request."

Dr. Afflick covered his face before rolling his eyes. Winston was such a pain in the ass.

"All of our other patients, with the exception of one, have been on varied doses of NootropiCAN. We have one other, however, whom we've kept on mirror doses for…for control purposes." Of course, he wasn't going to tell them that other patient was the one who was supposed to get their suspect's first dose, and they'd just kept them on the same track since. Not to mention, these were the only two patients who'd had any promising results. "We'd like to keep him in the room, and dose them simultaneously. It shouldn't impact your activities whatsoever."

Doyle and McMurdy looked at each other, sharing a "what difference does it make" expression, mostly because it couldn't possibly make any difference to them what the docs did with any other patients, or even if all the patients stayed in the ward since they were unconscious anyway. But before they could answer, L.Z. leaned forward.

"That other patient is in the same ward?"

The doctors turned their attention to him, puzzled. Winston answered,

"Why, yes, of course. We keep all subjects together when they are cohorts in a study, it keeps it…" L.Z. interrupted.

"Would this guy be a few beds down from Lenny? What's his name?"

"Well, for our purposes, his nomenclature is N-2. Of course, we can't give you his name. Privacy issue."

"Adrian Stoss?" L.Z. said, more than asked, and the doctors' near whiplash as they looked at each other then back at him was all he needed to see.

Standing, L.Z. took over for the cops as he said, "Sure, you can do your thing with him. Might as well. His brother will be there too."

Now the entire room of people looked at L.Z. quizzically. He just shrugged as he helped Abby from her chair, having watched his uncle in action, trying a bit of gentlemanly behavior.

"Let's just call him my wingman. See you Friday."

But his thoughts were far less casual than his demeanor; he had to call Aaron immediately.

With a day to kill, Al and Abby suggested a little sightseeing in the big city. In the not-too-distant past, L.Z. would have loved to see all the places and things he'd only heard about or seen on TV in New York City. But all he really wanted was some untaxing rest. He wasn't in a hurry to sleep because he never knew what sleep would bring, but a day of zoned out streaming sounded like exactly what he needed. He had a general plan for the next day, but he also knew that the time with Lenny was going to be partially guided by the information he needed to gather, largely herded by his overbearing psychopathic brother's need to control or whatever it was he strove to do when occupying L.Z.'s brain, and that he would have to think on his feet for the rest. He recalled Elle's old saying, "Men plan, and God laughs." He knew it didn't originate with her, but just hearing her grating yet familiar voice say it in his head not only made him actually miss her, but also settled deeply within him the truth behind the words. He wasn't going to go in cold tomorrow, but he was going to go in with a plan, an open mind, and a goal; a goal to end it.

He was surprised that he even missed work. He teared up, longing for the simplicity of life before Lenny. But he didn't miss life before Peg. He glanced at his phone, hoping for a text from her.

When he'd called the night before, she'd sounded unusually distracted and almost evasive. She was loving enough, but didn't have much to say which, in and of itself, was very uncharacteristic. She'd also told him that she might not be available much today because she was going to get Elle out of the house for a change. He didn't want to admit it, but it almost felt like she was lying, but not quite. He couldn't put his finger on it, and just didn't have the energy to try. So, he'd decided to let it go, humor his aunt and uncle, and hit the Empire State Building and the Statue of Liberty before parting ways so he could "rest" the remainder of the day.

"Resting" equated to binge watching rubbish on Netflix, eating room service, and periodically checking his phone for messages from Peg. He'd already arranged for Aaron to meet them at the hospital the next day, so when it was time for dinner, he opted to eat in, watch more mindless drivel, and go to sleep whenever it came to him.

He did get one text from Peg, although it didn't make much sense. But then, it was Peg.

Hey, Led Zeppelin. I hope you meant it when you told me you love me no matter what. Sweet dreams... really.

He was already dozing when he read it through blurry eyes. He smiled. She was so goofy.

But he might have been gratified – or not – if he'd known she had been telling the truth about getting Elle out of the house.

Lenny saw what appeared to be a hospital room; he had no idea how much time had passed but assumed based upon the surroundings that L.Z. was receiving treatment. He also realized that this was the first time in what he could qualify as "recent memory" that he could see anything but darkness and that there was no music or loud voices in the form of pod casts blocking his own communication.

While one could assume he had no sense of time passing between his awakenings, that wasn't exactly true. Just as comatose patients often later report some awareness of people or activities around them while unconscious, Lenny could sense an extra layer of existence between his aware moments, the ones where he was awake and inside L.Z., whom he now remembered had to be his brother…his twin, in fact, and when he was elsewhere – which was *nowhere*, as far as he could discern. In a rush, the realizations returned of what he had recalled about himself, and about this person whom, for whatever reason, had provided him the only outlet outside his own mind and body. As L.Z.'s eyes moved across screens which appeared to report vital signs such as heart rate and blood pressure, Lenny finally spoke, measuring his words and intensity.

"So, Bro, on the losing end with a big truck again? Maybe you should give up on the bike. Hazardous to your health."

He stopped, waiting to see if he'd been heard, although if he hadn't, it would be a first as far as he knew. From his only vantage point, L.Z.'s eyes, Lenny waited to see if L.Z. caught his use of "Bro." L.Z. said nothing but looked at a new monitor which was unfamiliar to Lenny. It had squiggly lines, which were quite active, but he had no clue or care what it meant. He suddenly wondered if L.Z. had been in a more serious accident this time and was looking at his own monitors but was unable to talk. That would suck, since this was Lenny's only means of return communication. But as soon as he had the thought, it was gone. It was replaced by what he saw and what he finally heard outside of the beeps and whines of hospital equipment. What he heard was,

"No, *Bro*. No bikes, no boo-boos for me. Just the dead weight of you. Take a good look. I'd like to introduce you to yourself. Lynyrd Skynyrd Manson, otherwise known as Lynyrd Patrick Rogers."

Lenny went silent as he stared at an emaciated version of a man whom he instantly knew as himself; it was not like when he saw L.Z. in the mirror and knew the man favored him, not like in the memories of his old life he'd conjured while lingering in the loud noise of L.Z.'s head his last few times awake but ignored. It was like nothing else he had conceived or experienced.

It was an out of body experience, for sure. But he was in L.Z.'s mind, looking at his own useless body. And suddenly he understood, at least in part, where he'd been.

And L.Z., his movement restricted by the lines leading from the probes attached to his partially shaven head, was sweating, but playing his role to perfection. He held his gaze on the motionless patient who looked so like himself, and he realized by the utter silence in his mind, he had hit his mark. And he also knew he needed to kick into gear before his oh-so-clever brother had time to recover.

"Detectives, you probably want to see this." Dr. Afflick quietly gathered Doyle and McMurdy from their spot inside the ward where they could observe, unseen. He also waved for the Mansons to follow, and they did, glancing at one another quizzically.

He took them to a nearby room with a two-way mirror, monitors, and speakers set up to oversee the Manson brothers' interactions. Dr Winston sat, slack jawed. The high-level activity they'd seen in the past during N-7's NootropiCAN doses had returned, mirrored not only in L.Z. Manson's indicators as they "spoke" to one another, but there was also a spike in Adrian Stoss, or N-2's activity. Winston nudged Afflick and pointed through the mirror at Aaron Stoss, who was out of sight of L.Z., but present. He had suddenly sat up straighter with a confused but controlled expression.

In hushed tones, Afflick quickly explained the set-up to the investigators.

"This is extraordinary…" Winston blurted but was quickly hushed by his colleague and the detectives as the one-way conversation in the ward continued.

"You remembered correctly. Someone tried to kill you, but here you are." L.Z. said, and as N-7's waves jerked higher, moving more quickly, they saw L.Z.'s eyebrows raise as he appeared to listen. After a minute, he scratched his forehead as he looked up, apparently tapping his rote memory.

"Seems like they've had you since spring 2016."

Silence, but the lines on N-7's screen danced.

"It's 2020."

N-7's indicators lit up, then slowly settled. L.Z., who was clearly concentrating on limiting his field of vision, thus not glancing at the mirrored window or Aaron, quickly explained the drug trial testing, which, appeared to be at least partially responsible for their unique mental collision and ability to communicate.

Silence again, and N-7's brain activity as well as L.Z.'s annoyed expression suggested Lenny was responding.

Abby, familiar with the screens they viewed, was riveted, while Al looked from the monitors to the window, then back, with an expression of bafflement.

Doyle, however, had unwittingly grabbed McMurdy's arm, hard, and stared wide-eyed at the show, while he juggled his amazement between his partner's out-of-character behavior and the remarkable display which had spellbound the others.

All eyes were on L.Z. as he played his first card; the patient could not see his brother's death grip on the bed rail, but it tightened as he said,

"You know, Lenny, or Rex, or shall I call you 'Skin Guy?'"

Silence, mad spikes from N-7 as well as N-2,'s monitors, and unsettled movement from Aaron, then L.Z. likely interrupted his brother.

"Right. That's what they call you, you know. Because you killed and skinned your victims."

There was a repeat of the last break, including the Stoss's response. But L.Z. was not taking prisoners, and plowed forward with emotion which could win him an academy award.

"How about for just once, you just shut the fuck up and listen? You might be sentenced to lay on your back for the rest of your pitiful days, but now I'm on the hook to spend mine behind bars. I know what you did because you shared shit with me even when you weren't yamming my brains out. Thanks for that. Thanks for dreams that rotor-rootered my soul. Detailed, vile dreams. Before you became a zucchini here, did you have a photographic memory like I do? Yeah, nothing that goes in ever leaves. So, thanks for that. But mostly, thanks for being stupid enough to leave your – no, *our,* DNA at the scenes. Did you know that identical twins have identical DNA?"

He stopped, closing his eyes only briefly, to regain his equilibrium; he had planted his seeds with that last lie, banking on Lenny not knowing there were differences in their DNA, along with his earlier suggestions that these new drugs could also help Lenny gain full consciousness, and possibly his previous capacity.

As part of the plan, L.Z., not having to act out his need to sit for a minute and drink some water, plopped down, closing his eyes long enough to rest, and, more importantly, to give Lenny time to think. He shook his head and smiled exhaustedly at the irony of what had just happened.

L.Z. Manson, a man who had always been honest to a fault, had lied to his brother like his life depended on it. In a way, he felt that it did.

In the space of his mind, Lenny was reeling, as was evident by what resembled fireworks on his monitor. So, they'd found him because his DNA had been entered as a missing person and the dumb luck of that Uncle Al guy having submitted DNA for an ancestry site. He couldn't believe his luck that he had a twin brother for all intents and purposes, apparently the third triplet was not identical and for his desires, offered no interest whatsoever. The impact of the situation hit him.

Much of what had driven his specific psychotic actions over the years were based on his sense of abandonment by his biological family; before now, he just wanted blood family. It was all about blood.

But now that he had that, he had to pit it against something a lot more important – and that, as always, was himself.

His presumably latent brain was on fire with possibilities; he needed to nail this one, and fast.

He had a chance for full recovery, which would only matter if it were paired with freedom. Freedom that was on a thread right now…he could not believe he'd left DNA on multiple scenes as L.Z. had said, but even so, that DNA could save him because now he had a patsy. He wanted a brother, but he wanted his life back more.

How convenient that L.Z. shared his DNA. L.Z. had a freakishly accurate memory and already knew intimate things about the crimes. L.Z., who was too stupid to see that this knowledge was his death sentence, or at least a life sentence. L.Z., who would assume that because he was innocent, he could share information that he couldn't possibly know unless he'd been there.

By the time L.Z. opened his eyes again and Lenny could see himself still as a corpse, the killer knew he was going to tell his brother everything. Everything he wanted to know, and then some.

For the first time in his fucked-up life, he believed the phrase, the truth will set you free.

All the others heard was L.Z. rephrasing his brother's question,

"How much time do we have? How much do you need?"

Although the doctors were feverishly recording every critical element of this exchange, the detectives were there for another reason entirely. Without discussion, they knew they were "in" now, and with L.Z.'s last statement, they gave each other a high five. They'd worry about what their report would say later, but for now, they not only felt a break in the case coming, but a shatter.

In for a penny, in for a pound.

Lenny and Adrian had received larger than usual doses of NootropiCAN, which suited everyone's purposes; the doctors hoped for an extended time and possibly heightened activity, while giving the police and brother ample time to complete the experiment. The doctors had no idea if the family would allow the study to continue once they'd served their own needs, and that was a realistic expectation, all things

411

considered. Their goals were not mutual, thus they wanted to squeeze as much out of the testing as possible.

It was three hours in and while L.Z. had been largely quiet, asking very few questions, he looked utterly spent and Al and Abby were about ready to insist the session be terminated for his own good. The detectives were satisfied from the one side they could hear that L.Z. would deliver answers to fill their gaps, regardless of whether the answers came from his own mind or that of his brother, although neither had their doubts now as to the validity of L.Z.'s outrageous claims.

What few witnesses noticed was that during certain periods of the "interview," Aaron seemed moved to write in the notebook he'd brought along as he sat near his brother's bed but out of L.Z.'s perimeter of sight for Lenny's viewing.

L.Z. suddenly stood, and within the distance allowed by the lens from his head to the mobile machine he clandestinely rolled along next to him, he turned to face Aaron, so Lenny would be able to have a full view.

"This is Aaron, Lenny. You know him?"

Silence.

"Can't say I've had the pleasure."

L.Z. heard the response; hesitant, confused. It was a stark contrast to the disgusting accounts given almost in a bragging tone, over the past hours.

412

Aaron nodded to L.Z., then gestured to the very still man laying nearby, "This is Adrian, my brother. He's been here even longer than you."

Lenny saw the unfamiliar death mask on the patient L.Z. had turned to view. He was unsure what was going on, so he said, as if Adrian could hear.

"Well, that's too bad. Uh…sorry?"

"You know him? This guy?" L.Z. asked, already sensing the answer.

"Oh, sure, right! When the doctors are out, we just play some poker during night shift. Of course, I don't fucking know this guy. He's vegetable soup."

L.Z. just closed his eyes, grateful Aaron hadn't heard the coldly hypocritical comment, then opened his eyes to meet those of his friend. He just nodded and smiled.

This part of the plan was strictly between L.Z. and Aaron, and they'd figure it out on their own, but L.Z. thought he understood the connection now.

He was just about to give the signal to the doctors to wrap it all up, when he heard such a commotion from the hall that he turned, forgetting the protocol not to show Lenny any more of the room than necessary.

"Sorry, Dr. Winston, we told 'em they couldn't come up. Don't know how they knew how to get up here, but short of physically subduing them…" The winded security guard

413

gestured toward the scrawny fiery eyed older lady, closely tailed by a younger red-faced woman. "She's faster than she looks."

Everyone had emerged from the viewing room, and as Al saw his sister, he stepped forward,

"Elizabeth."

She shot him a beady-eyed look, then pushed him aside, stepping into the ward, directly in L.Z.'s line of sight. She took in the probes on his scalp, then glanced at his wasted clone laying in the bed.

Two more security guards thumped up the hall, only to be waved aside by the doctors; there seemed to be a silent agreement among the critical parties to let this play out.

Elle walked right up to L.Z. and stared hard into his eyes, not looking at him, exactly, but more through him. He held his tongue.

"Well, well. Look at what the cat drug in."

L.Z. heard the words delivered with a laugh not typically reserved for the sight of one's mother.

"Hello, Lynyrd," Elle said, her voice dragging something ominous through its smoky passages; of course, she hadn't heard Lenny's greeting, but she knew he was there. Now she knew it all.

Standing on her toes, she was nearly nose-to-nose with L.Z. "I'm your mother, Elizabeth Taylor Manson. I brought you into this world, and now I'm here to take you back out."

L.Z., exhausted to the point of punchiness, cracked a laugh while he heard his brother do the same, only in a different tone.

Unfettered, Elle continued to stare into the eyes of her sons, as she waved a hand toward a nervous Peg who handed a typed, signed, and notarized document to the guys who looked most like doctors.

L.Z. glanced over and saw Dr. Winston go white as he read the paper.

"But, Ma'am, remove life support? Please, we need to discuss the legalities and implications of…"

Elle, never taking her eyes from L.Z.'s face said, "I am his birth mother. In the absence of his adoptive mothers, who he killed, I have first rights to squash his involvement in these tests and for removing all of them lines keeping him alive, the life support. I am here to exercise those choices. It's all there. It's legal."

"Wait, what?" Lenny *spouted for only L.Z. to hear.* **"You said these tests were approved and I was probably going to have a full recovery…you…**

L.Z. smiled as he stared into his mother's eyes.

Then he said the last thing he ever said to his brother,

"I lied."

Regarding the Rogers

Pat Kneemoi and Denise Rogers were gay before it was cool. They were hidden minorities in a time when it was not a celebration to "come out," but when the opposite was a means to peace and survival. They were professionals, one a successful real estate agent and the other an anesthesiologist, who "stayed in" for the sakes of their careers and family relationships. Each were without siblings, and their parents died before they were able to find a child to call their own. It was a mixed bag to lose loved ones before the blessed event because, of course, there was grief, but there was also relief that they would not have to explain the advent of a child, not their own, between two "best friends."

By the time they were ready to have a baby, the laws were not. Same sex couples could not adopt in the late 80's, thus they had to blaze a path through the baby black market, literally stumbling upon the information about a mother of triplets unable to support three children who had a son available for the right price. Any price was right for Pat and Denise, so they flew to California where they met the foul-mouthed bohemian mother who asked few questions. She was seemingly attached enough to the child she kept but was eager to get down to business and hand over the oddly quiet baby boy.

Although it was not to be an "open" faux adoption, they kept in contact with the strange woman (almost completely one way; she rarely responded), a fact which gave them false hope in years to come when they had reason to reach out.

Because of their resources, it was easy enough to arrange paperwork for Denise to appear to be the child's parent once they got him back to New Jersey. It wasn't until Lenny, now Lynyrd Patrick (a nod to Patricia) Rogers, was seven years old that same-sex adoption was legalized in their state (although, ironically, marriage was not,), and they made it official. They were already seeing signs of trouble with the strange child, but naively blamed his poor adjustment to their inability to present as a "normal family."

By the time Lenny was 13 they were able to legally marry, hoping that might give the child the legitimacy he must have craved.

They had always been honest with Lenny about the fact he was "chosen" by them, not borne by either, that he was their kin no matter what. They couldn't have known that any hope of normalcy was lacking from the minute he entered the world, possibly before, and their efforts were moot. Nor could they have known his abnormal spirit became tightly woven with his obsession with having a real family. *Blood family.* That somehow, he became convinced that love was only skin deep, and he knew all too well just how deep skin was, as he explored and learned.

As he grew, Lenny discerned how to say what was desired to be heard with charm and humor, and it only wore thin when he was at home and his guard was down. Thus, while the teachers, doctors, and counselors saw a very bright boy whose humor was often too mature for his age and sometimes didn't acknowledge normal boundaries, they also failed to see any real developmental or social problems. The parents saw, or to be more accurate, *felt* something behind the veil. He exhibited an extreme sense of entitlement which they seemed unable to curb regardless of varied parental methods. He was who he was, and when they reached out to his birth mother, while she didn't say the words, the implication was clear that she knew she'd sold them a faulty product. But return was no option, not that the devoted mothers wanted that; they just wanted insight to guide them through the growing concerns.

There was the track record of pets which never seemed to last, some just disappearing, others flatly avoiding Lenny. The boy showed thinly disguised disdain for the "mothers," who were his lot as opposed to *real* parents; the fact was that he was not only *not* kin, but had never been under either of their skin, they had not created him and were not worthy. If love was skin deep and he had never even resided inside of either of them, he was convinced love for them was an impossibility.

Pat and Denise discovered, much to their disdain, that as a tween the boy had amassed an inordinate amount of information regarding the serial killer, Jeffrey Dahmer, then later found a tattered copy of Silence of the Lambs. They might have thought less of it if he were normal in other ways or might have even felt better if they'd found Playboy magazines instead of the harbingers of a dangerously troubled mind.

But for all they saw, there was much they missed.

Once his crimes were fully vetted out and studied, if the experts had found out about his apparent obsession with not only Dahmer and the fictional Hannibal Lector, but his research on other killers such as Ed Gein, Katherine Mary Knight, Michael Wayne Ryan, and Mona Fandey, they would have thought they'd hit pay dirt regarding his psyche. All of these killers had one thing in common; they skinned their victims.

The experts would have also assumed there had been a sexual element, and there simply was not. Despite his unwelcome off-color comments to L.Z., Lenny was not a sexual person and never attached that to his manic journey.

The bottom line was no amount of study or application of precedents in the serial killer arena would have revealed the true motivation behind Lenny's heinous acts. The profilers would never know about his large stockpile of reading and viewing which focused on love: familial love, romantic love, and maternal love. They never knew he'd concluded if he couldn't see it, he couldn't understand it. Or

419

that he had further ascertained this was why he couldn't feel it. They never knew why his mothers were his first victims. He'd started with them because his studies indicated all emotional development began at home; it stood to reason that his mothers, his fake parents, had to be key elements.

In the end, the one thing he couldn't get past was what was planted in his too-eager childhood brain: "love is skin deep." He couldn't even remember where he'd heard or read it, but it was his magic card, and his mothers missed it completely. Later, those who wanted to publish papers about the Skin Guy would not know.

They would not understand his life-long sensitivity to phrases like, "they get under your skin," "grow a thicker skin," "no skin off my nose," or "they jumped out of their skin."

So disrespectful.

His feelings for skin were reverent. He never saw, nor would he have found satire in the fact that eventual exposure to his proclivities would make skin crawl.

He came to believe that the "insides" were nothing but filler for everyone he laid eyes upon, but if he could only feel, keep, even collect skin, maybe he'd find love and experience it. Maybe he could figure out what the big deal was, what he had to be missing with this counterfeit family which he discerned to be his block to that elusive thing, actual love.

That's when he'd resolved he'd have to start with them. Of course, they'd have to die in the process, but that was simply collateral damage. As a very young man ready to go out into the world, it wasn't lost on him the potential financial gain of his actions.

It was a mild surprise when he'd done the deed and collected the skin, he felt nothing; this just validated that they didn't love him after all. He began to focus on people, strangers, really, who seemed to be likable, even loveable by most standards.

Still no go.

What the experts would never know was he didn't get any thrill in the kill. He was just talented in general, naturally agile, and efficient. He'd considered killing for a living, seemingly a win-win; he could offer a service, have his way with the victims, and get paid. But in the end, he had enough money from his mothers' estate to sustain his off-the-grid lifestyle, and he could pick his own targets which would enhance his likelihood of success.

He never found love, however, although he'd attempted to extract it from the skins of his victims in various manners, things he'd shared with L.Z. in their last conversation.

Although his brain knew better, it was his deep-rooted belief he'd been denied love because he was denied family. As intelligent as he was, as good a reader of people as he became, the one person he couldn't see clearly was himself. He only wanted love because he couldn't have it; Lenny Rogers wanted what he wanted and deserved what he wanted. That was the bottom line.

The even greater irony was, he was incapable of love. He was born without that gene.

Although the detectives knew it was a risk to let L.Z. Manson leave the state until they had thoroughly vetted out the information gathered during their recent unprecedented investigative actions, they sent him on his way with the family. They had brokered a deal with the Ada County police in Boise to have their "person of interest" check in weekly, as if on probation or parole, more to cover their asses than because they expected any trouble from him.

In the weeks and months to come, Doyle and McMurdy followed all their "anonymous tipster's" leads like breadcrumbs, locating Lenny's bank accounts, domiciles, and killing trail, all under false names. Unearthing the bodies, sometimes literally, sometimes figuratively, presented a challenge as they were all disposed of differently; the one exception was the skin. It was all in one place.

The bodies of Pat and Denise Rogers, Lenny's "fake" mothers, were the last and most difficult to find, which was ironic because it was a site well visited.

At the New York Center for Abused and Neglected Children, in the middle of a colossal playground was a prolific sandbox for children who were brought for therapy, treatment, and shelter. The sand was used for creative play, a safe place for outdoor therapy, and an escape for less fortunate kids. The inception of this sandbox was presented by a young male philanthropist who was identified as one of Lenny Rogers's many alias names, and who matched his description. This man not only funded the project, but paid for maintenance of the site, which included annual re-excavation to replace the sand for sanitation and health purposes.

The philanthropist stated he wanted to create a place for children, like his former self, who were unloved and unwanted, and he refused public accolades or documentation for tax breaks. He insisted on remaining anonymous, although he personally visited the site during construction and each excavation. All he asked for was time alone behind the protective privacy construction fence, to meditate and heal himself.

Doyle and McMurdy finally located the site and the story of the "philanthropist" based on tips from L.Z., and the discovery of the place was much easier to reconcile than what they found when the crime scene digging commenced.

Deep beneath the huge sandbox was a grave with two skinless bodies in a lewd position suggesting "doggie style sex;" one could speculate a reference to two "bitches," or, if

423

they'd known his view of his "mothers," it could have also inferred a position more likely for a heterosexual couple, the couple Lenny felt his moms fraudulently represented. More disturbing for the forensic diggers, however, was what they'd unearthed before finding Pat and Denise's remains. Scattered in layers throughout the sandbox were what had clearly been wrapped presents, although the paper and ribbons had largely disintegrated. Inside the various gift boxes were figures of hearts, flowers, and similar sentimental shapes.

Without more knowledge, it would be reasonable to believe the gifts were symbolic offerings to the troubled children who played above the surface. McMurdy and Doyle knew differently, however.

The figures were crafted strips and chunks of skin, skin which ultimately matched the DNA of known and additional unknown victims of Skin Guy. More disturbingly, the ribbon cutting for the immense play spot and the annual excavation sand renewals were all on the same day each year, as insisted upon by the philanthropist: Mother's Day.

The forensic psychologists went wild with conjecture since their real perpetrator would never be able to tell them about the motivation behind his actions. They thought the gifts were for the children, with whom he felt connected. They thought the presents were sick offerings of remorse to the mothers the misguided killer had brutally killed and desecrated in death. They philosophized that Lynyrd Patrick Rogers had digressed so deeply into psychosis that he created his own version of child and mother love when it was too late to have the real thing.

They were wrong.

Lenny's actions were deliberate and clear. Each gift was one more stab into the backs of his mothers, symbolically mirroring the thrusts which had killed them by his own hands. All the skin which he'd harvested in the coming years, hoping to find that "skin deep" love, each dripping piece which brought him nothing but the flatness he'd felt his whole life, were gifted to the two who were responsible for his heartless condition as punishment for their failure.

The tragedy of it all, as McMurdy and Doyle found out once they'd tracked down Pat and Denise's friends from years past was, the women loved their loveless son to a fault. They went above and beyond in every way imaginable to help the self-entitled, unlovable boy; to see in his eyes what they felt for him.

It was like pouring water into a bottomless well, hoping to draw just one bucket back out. But that well, originally Lynyrd Skynyrd Manson, was born dry.

Epilogue

After painstakingly tracking L.Z.'s whereabouts during the estimated dates of the killings, all of which predated Lenny Rogers's hospitalization, coupled with the matching DNA from one scene, L.Z. was ultimately cleared as a suspect. Months had passed since the epic trip to New York, and much had happened.

Lenny Rogers remained the sole suspect in the case, unprosecuted because he remained in a vegetative state. He defied expectations, not to mention caused the deep disappointment of his mother by staying alive even with removal of life support. He continued to be an enigma to the institute's doctors; he was permanently out of the drug study due to the family's demands yet exhibited random signs of brain activity. Their hands were tied, but they continued to monitor him. For Dr. Winston, he became an obsession.

L.Z. and Peg, although not married, were engaged with no hurry to make the actual commitment. Peg was still on Uncle Al's payroll as Elle's caregiver, although it was as good as stealing money since she would be living with L.Z. now anyway. She'd told her future uncle as much. He just waved away this concern and continued the deposits. He had no idea what the future Manson couple's long-term plans were, but in his heart, he hoped they'd stay with Elle, otherwise the war would be on. There was no way, even with their differences, he would leave that woman unsupervised.

His worries were for naught. Peg loved Elle as much as L.Z. did, and never gave a thought to moving out of the humble home. Elle didn't weigh in one way or the other; although she enjoyed Peg's presence, she was busy with her various world saving efforts, trysts with the likes of Uber drivers when she could get away with it, and preoccupation with a deep concern she didn't share. This would continue as long as Lynyrd Skynyrd Manson breathed; this was a factor she badly wished to remedy, but she knew she couldn't do it alone. It was a work in progress.

Aaron Stoss left SKinKneader in the wake of all he learned about L.Z.'s brother, and the mysterious, but undeniable connection between his own brother and the psychotic, albeit comatose Lenny. While there was no objective explanation as to how the thoughts and notions of the serial killer made it from one experimental patient to the other, the NootropiCAN could have explained how the idea for "SKinKneader," and the too graphic ideas-come-lyrics made it from Adrian to Aaron. The good doctors at the institute had field days with the stacks of findings from these two patients, but Aaron knew all he needed to know. He and L.Z., now close friends, agreed on it and that was enough.

He'd gained enough acclaim to go solo, staying with the same genre, but steering clear of death metal. While his brother remained in the drug study, he did his best to only work with his own ideas for lyrics, unsure if Adrian still had unwitting mental access, but discarding anything drifting into his mind which could have been remotely affiliated with the skin game played by Lenny Rogers.

Peg insisted on introducing Aaron to Aja-Molly (a nickname allowed only for her, the Peglet), but it didn't go well. While Aaron had backed away from his darker nature, Molly had fully embraced hers in full dark goth mode. Aaron told her he had to focus on his new career and had had bad luck with long-distance relationships anyway. On a side, he simply told L.Z. (out of Peg's earshot), "That chick is fucking weird, man." Considering this was the guy whose claim to fame spawned from a band named, essentially, from the mind of a serial killer, L.Z. was quietly amused. Molly was his biological sister, but he wasn't offended by Aaron's assessment and was secretly elated that the girl lived hundreds of miles away from his life, which was as close to perfect as he'd ever known. Elle, Peg, and all.

As for Molly, the failed hook-up with Aaron was nothing but a speed bump. She knew who she was and what was in her blood now, a thought which drove her daily. She still worked; the forensic fascination was still there. Besides, it paid the bills till she figured out what came next.

And it came all right. Literally out of nowhere.

She was applying jet black lipstick one morning, SKinKneader blaring from her speakers in the front room, when an unrelated voice echoed loudly, silkily, and clearly in her mind.

Hello, little sister.

Her inky lips slowly spread into a delighted smile.

The world was about to get a lot more interesting.

Thank you for reading, SKinKneader! *It would be magnificent if you would kindly take a few minutes to rate and share your thoughts about this novel on your purchase site; ratings and reviews help with my craft, help market the book, and assist others in choosing a good read.*

To contact me (the author!), or if you'd like to be notified when the next novel is available, please go to <u>tammyseleyelliott.com</u> *or e-mail at ts.seley.elliott@gmail.com. Thank you. TSSE*